# Hannah Sunderland

# Very Nearly Normal

avon.

Published by AVON
A division of HarperCollins*Publishers* Ltd
1 London Bridge Street
London SE1 9GF

www.harpercollins.co.uk

A Paperback Original 2020

First published in Great Britain by HarperCollins*Publishers* 2020

A catalogue copy of this book is available from the British Library.

ISBN: 978-0-00836570-7

This novel is entirely a work of fiction.
The names, characters and incidents portrayed in it are the work
of the author's imagination. Any resemblance to actual persons, living or dead,
events or localities is entirely coincidental.

Typeset in Minion by Palimpsest Book Production Limited, Falkirk, Stirlingshire

Printed and bound in UK by CPI Group (UK) Ltd, Croydon CR0 4YY

MIX
Paper from
responsible sources
FSC™ C007454

This book is produced from independently certified FSC™ paper
to ensure responsible forest management.

For more information visit: www.harpercollins.co.uk/green

*For Mom, Dad and for anyone who has ever felt like a failure.*

# Chapter One

The bevy of children and teens, freshly released from the shackles of school, moved against me and as usual I was swimming against the current. Not too long ago, I had been just like them; full of entitlement, the idea of failure ridiculous, the thought of ageing impossible, and death was just a fictitious destination. But now – after years of unadulterated disappointment – entitlement had transformed into self-pity, failure was inescapable, ageing was in full swing and death seemed like a quiet holiday.

The question I had asked myself over and over since graduating from one of those carefree young creatures to a bitter, twisted, ne'er-do-well, was *How could such big dreams amount to so little?* I'd wanted to write and be read. I'd wanted to see someone reading my book on the train and feel pride swell in my chest. I'd wanted one of those little recommendation cards that sit on the shelves in Waterstones. I still wanted all of those things. I had a finished manuscript sitting beneath my bed, the words obscured by dust. I'd sent it out into the world in an attempt to achieve that dream, but life hadn't quite played out the way I'd planned.

By all accounts, I was a failure.

I failed at everything I touched.

You could gift me the rarest, most beautiful flower in the whole galaxy and it would be compost in my hands within ten minutes.

Failure had always been what I was best at, but funnily enough, my first failure hadn't even been my own. It had been my parents' when they had chosen to burden me with the world's most ridiculous name. My full name is Matilda Effie Heaton, but I'd refused to be called by my first name since I was eight, after years of people telling me to showcase my telekinetic powers and asking me why Miss Honey wasn't picking me up from school. But the actual name wasn't the failure, no, the real failure was the initials and what they spelled when put together. That's right; my name literally spells the word *meh*.

**Meh:** *The universal, millennial term for anything uninspired and unexceptional.*

I'd thought about changing it a couple of years ago, and foregoing the 'Matilda' part altogether, but the process had seemed complicated and, in the end, I simply couldn't be bothered. No one ever used that name anyway unless it was for something official or if I'd angered my mother – which happened to be quite often – and in those cases she would be certain to use my full name, just to piss me off.

As I approached Bobby's corner shop, I reached into my pocket and withdrew my purse. I glanced down at my bank card and saw my full name printed across it in blocky silver letters. I stabbed my PIN into the buttons with my flaking dark green painted nails and pressed the button for twenty quid. The machine almost laughed at me as it rejected my withdrawal and offered me ten instead.

'Fine!' I spat through gritted teeth and snatched the ten-pound note from the slot.

That was another thing I'd failed at, building any kind of savings in either of my pitiful accounts.

But, don't worry, it doesn't stop there. These are by no means my only failures.

I'd failed to do anything other than coast through three uneventful years of university and at the ripe old age of twenty-eight I had failed to move out and begin my own life. I'd simply returned like a homing pigeon to the town I'd been born in, a suburb on the outskirts of Birmingham, famous for producing Emma Willis, having a very large park, and less famous for being within two miles of what may or may not be the oldest traffic roundabout in the UK.

My failures wouldn't have been so pronounced, however, had it not been for the ocean of people around me who seemed to effortlessly succeed to sickening levels. I saw them, with their smug faces plastered all over the internet. I'd stay up into the early hours, slowly torturing myself by browsing through the endless photos of my successful 'friends' posing on their London apartment balconies. They'd always be holding sparkling glasses of Cristal as they toasted their promotion, all whilst draped over the arm of their fiancé, who had cool ice-blue eyes and the torso of Khal Drogo. One of those loathsome people just happened to be my 'best friend', Kate, who at this very moment was on her way to the same café that I was, probably with a sexy new haircut and some exciting news to tell me about all the things that she was most recently excelling in.

What did these people know that I didn't? Had I been sick from school when they'd taught the *How Not to Suck at Life* portion of the syllabus? Or did I just innately lack the talons that everyone else seemed to use to claw their way to the top?

Everything in my life had fallen short of expectation. Every endeavour doomed from the outset.

Failure was and always had been my default setting. In fact, the only thing I'd excelled at in any way, was staying alive long enough to witness every single crushing disappointment; which I hoarded like the greedy giant atop the beanstalk.

A young girl sauntered in my direction, her long chestnut hair flowing lustrously over one shoulder. She flirted easily with the sliver of a boy beside her who listened intently to her every word. Her skin was flawless, as mine had been at her age, before those little lines had appeared in my forehead after years of frowning. The girl's skirt was strategically rolled at the top to achieve the optimum amount of peeping thigh, the rolled-up fabric making her stomach look rounded and floppy.

In a few years she'd need no help getting herself a muffin top, I thought pessimistically. As I passed the two young lovers, the boy's shoulder knocked into mine. His eyes barely lingered on me for a second, before his mouth curled back into a smirk and he returned his attention to a more interesting subject matter.

If she was lucky, the romance would end before the summer holidays came. Short and sweet was the way to handle an adolescent romance. Otherwise, ten years from now, that happy teen would find herself with two squalling brats and a council flat that her partner never spent any time in because he was forever off working nights at the depot and having an on-the-side fling with Kathy from despatch.

I'd always thought that the idea of falling in love at fifteen and staying that way for your entire life would be one of the most depressing things ever. Sure, the idea was romantic, but it left no time for making mistakes and sometimes mistakes were the most interesting part of life.

At least love was one thing I was happy to have failed at, especially when I look back at the saddening array of boys I've attempted to love in the past. I don't know if it's because I'm too picky or if I'm simply never destined for the music-swelling, grand-gesture kind of love that Richard Curtis had fooled me into believing existed. Maybe life is different for you if you look like Keira Knightley, but I'd never had someone turn up on my doorstep with placards, declaring their undying love for me.

I turned away from the lovers and headed towards the high street; the sound of thumping incessant grime music from a passing car masking the calming sounds of the indie-folk playlist that I had stuffed into my ears.

Now, I hope you don't think I was one of those insufferable children who were told that they could *be* anything, *do* anything, that the world was theirs for the taking. I mean I was, but I never have and never will have any grandiose ideas about who I am or what I'm capable of. In all seriousness, if I get through a day without severely injuring someone, breaking something or accidentally insulting someone, then I take that day as a win. I have found, from years of personal experience, that once you accept that you are a loser, a failure, a flop, a piece of white dog turd adhered to the side of a shoe, you will be altogether more prepared for what your loser life throws at you.

Not every person is meant to change the world, despite what everyone told us as we grew up. If we were, then the world would be in an even greater mess than it already is. Maybe being a failure was a blessing in disguise. Maybe my inability to change the world in any way was my gift to humanity.

Being a failure wouldn't even be so hard, had I managed to perfect the art of giving zero shits about anything. But the point was that I gave *far* too many shits, and therein lay my downfall. I gave a shit about my mother and the way she ate with a cacophony of *smacks* and *slurps*. I gave a shit about my 'friend' Kate and her fancy-schmancy job and her penthouse apartment (that I had never set foot in, purely on principle). And I gave a shit about my own shittiness, which was reflected and magnified by the shits that no one else seemed to give. I didn't know how they did it, breezing through life like it was a path already laid out for them and all they had to do was walk forward and the path would find their feet. I had never seen my path. It was hidden beneath the failures that lay at my feet like long-dead leaves.

There was something about seeing the café that made me feel like a dog being dragged to the vets to be neutered. I could see Kate inside through the window, playing with a silky strand of her hair as the sun fell over her face. My stomach tightened with regret before I'd even stepped through the fingerprint-smeared glass door. I moved inside, the aggressive heat from the overhead fan hitting me square in the face. I'd never been in this café before, mostly because it intimidated me with its repurposed furniture and copious choice of coffee beans.

6

I saw Kate up ahead, sitting at what looked like two lidded school desks that had been pushed together to form a table. She sat casually with her long dark hair pulled up into an effortlessly neat high ponytail and her nose inches away from the screen of her phone. She sipped glutinously at the foam of her cappuccino, her face glowing blue in the light that emanated from the screen.

So, here's what you need to know about Kate.

We'd been best friends since we were four years old. When we met, we were both weird and otherwise friendless, so we latched on to each other and it suited us both well for a while. But as time wore on Kate began to acclimatise to the rest of the world, finding a best friend in the most popular girl in school, Eloise 'Fucking' Kempshore (not her given middle name, obviously, but it was what I'd called her since the day in year seven when the teacher had left the room and she'd stood up in class and picked on me about my red hair).

To be fair, Kate hadn't climbed the social ladder without trying to carry me along with her, but I had proven to be a less than willing passenger and after struggling for a year or so, Kate all but cut the line and dropped me back into the social abyss that I should have never left in the first place. Kate had always known the right clothes to wear and the right way to do her hair. She never clammed up in conversation or thought of the most inappropriate thing to say and then accidentally said it instead of keeping it to herself.

Eloise had stolen Kate away about eleven years ago now and since then we had started to feel obligated to remain in contact, just so long as I remained separate from her other friends, her other life. We became interested in wildly different things, Kate with her popular clique and her Ken doll

7

boyfriend, and me with my writing, introversion and hating the world. It wasn't uncommon for friends to grow apart, I knew that, but unlike most people Kate and I simply didn't have the balls to admit that it was over.

I walked over to the table and pulled out the chair while Kate's eyes remained fixed to the screen that glowed in her palm. Kate has always had this annoying habit of becoming so engrossed in her phone that she often forgets she has company and rousing her from it is like trying to wake Sleeping Beauty without giving her a quick snog first.

I managed to take off my coat, sit down, cross my legs and heave a sigh before Kate even noticed I was there.

'Effie! You're here!' she gushed, placing down her phone, the screen still open and showing the other conversations she was having on the side – it was like being blatantly cheated on. She grinned widely at me, her eyes darting to her phone, then back to my face. I wished she'd stop pretending to be excited to see me; we both knew she wasn't. 'I didn't know what you drank these days, so I just got something for myself.'

I desperately tried not to grimace and roll my eyes.

I'd only been drinking lattes for ten years, but then how would someone who still insisted on calling me her 'best friend' know that?

'No worries,' I said through gritted teeth. 'I'll go and get it myself.'

She didn't notice my passive aggression and happily went back to phoneland while I got up and joined the queue.

The guy at the counter was pretty, in a grubby hipster kind of way. He had a thick black beard, which I instantly deemed unhygienic to have dangling that low over the tray of exposed pastries beneath, and wore braces that held up his burgundy drainpipe jeans.

8

He greeted me with an overly enthusiastic 'Hi there!' and waited for my order. I ordered my latte and looked longingly at a cinnamon bun that sat close enough for me to catch a whiff of its sickly sweet goodness. I thought about ordering one, then looked over my shoulder at the slim and beautiful Kate and decided to forgo the calories.

I looked down at the barista's name tag; it read *Bernard*.

I couldn't help but wonder if Bernard was his actual name or if, like Catholics, you got a new name when confirmed into the fold of Hipster.

'Which of our coffees would you like today?' Bernard asked.

I looked up confused.

He took this as an invitation to elaborate. 'You could have our house coffee, which is a dark roasted bean with a bitter finish and hints of raspberry and chocolate or our guest coffee, which is a medium roast with a velvet finish and caramel undertones.'

I looked at him with confusion, wondering when ordering a coffee became like the general knowledge round of *Mastermind*.

'Which would you recommend?' I asked, trying to hide that I was out of my depth.

'It depends entirely on your palate, madam,' he replied, unhelpfully.

I flinched at his use of the word *madam*. It made me feel like an old biddy or the proprietor of a whorehouse.

'Erm, the cheapest one.' The rising intonation at the end of my sentence made me sound like I was asking a question.

He gave me a pitiful smile, as if he thought me a complete philistine, and took my money.

When I returned, Kate had a smile plastered over her sickeningly made-up face. I found it difficult to do the most basic of tasks, like draw matching eyeliner flicks for both eyes without making my entire face look lopsided, but somehow Kate had managed to become the Rembrandt of cosmetics.

'So.' Kate grinned and splayed her manicured hands out on the table. 'I have massive news.'

'Really? Do tell,' I replied, as eager to hear her news as I was to have an unnecessary root canal.

'I've been asked to go to Toronto for three months and broker a deal between my company and some fancy Canadian firm. If they approve the deal, then I can pretty much retire at thirty.'

'Wow,' I said, jealousy building inside me like Vesuvius, 'are you taking it?'

'*Am I taking it?*' she scoffed. 'What kind of question is that? They're practically begging me to go. I mean, the flight, the hotel and every ounce of food and wine will be paid for. It's basically a free holiday with a tiny bit of work thrown in.'

The green monster inside my brain began to scream and tie a noose for itself.

'There's just a lot to think about isn't there?' I tried in vain to talk her out of it, just so I could cease to be friends with someone so perfect and accomplished. 'What about Callum and your parents?'

Kate scoffed. 'My parents? Honey, I'm late twenties.' I felt the blow of Kate's words hit me directly in the gut. She may well have escaped the purgatory of living in the family home, but I was very much still there. 'And as for Callum . . .' Kate paused and I instantly knew what was coming. If the intonation of her voice hadn't given it away, then the sickeningly self-gratified grin had.

I knew what she wanted me to do, but I refused to do it. I would not look at her hand.

It was my one small act of defiance.

When I didn't look down, Kate brought her left hand up into the air and that's when I saw it, the oval-cut diamond that sat on her perfectly polished ring finger. '. . . he proposed.' The diamond reflected the neon green light of the exit sign behind me and all I wanted to do was turn around and use it.

'I'm so happy for you,' I lied. What else could I have said?

'I knew you would be. Of course, you will have to be part of the day,' Kate cooed. The idea of being stuffed into a powder blue bridesmaid's dress and forced to pretend to be happy for an entire day made my toes curl. And if spending an entire day with Kate wasn't bad enough, I knew that Eloise 'Fucking' Kempshore would be there too. 'Eloise has already agreed to be my maid of honour—' boom, there it is '—and I already have eight bridesmaids, but we'll find a place for you somewhere.'

*A place for me somewhere.*

I replayed the words in my head. If that sentence didn't sum me up completely, then no sentence ever would. She would shoehorn me into her special day like that time I tried on a pair of size eight jeans and had to ask the attendant to hold the ankles while I lay on the floor and tried to wriggle free of them.

How stupid I'd been to think that I even warranted the nightmare task of being one of Kate's bridesmaids, when there were already so many volunteers.

'That would be amazing, thank you.' The words fell from my mouth like dry turds during a bout of constipation.

'Enough about me,' Kate said, picking up her phone and staring back down at the screen. 'What's new with you?'

'New with me?' I repeated as I tried desperately to think

11

of something that had happened in the two months since our last unbearable coffee date. Kate's French-tipped nails click-clacked across the screen furiously as she typed out a text and frowned with concentration. I tried desperately to think of something to say, but nothing came to mind. Kate wasn't listening anyway so, in the end, I just said, 'Mum got a new kettle last week.' That wasn't even true.

Kate didn't reply, react or even listen as she continued to tap away at the screen, her nails sounding like tiny hooves as my words hit her solitary bubble and bounced away into the atmosphere.

I felt my nostrils flare as I took a sip of my latte. I guessed that the barista had given me the bitter option because it tasted like battery acid.

I *had* planned on telling Kate that I had a date tonight with some guy I'd met on Tinder; but Kate wasn't listening.

Kate never listened.

Almost two full minutes of silence passed as I continued to force down the coffee I'd wasted four quid on and Kate giggled at a group chat message that I wasn't allowed to join in with.

The argument was brewing inside my mind. It had marinated itself in years of bitterness and subtle betrayals and by the end of those two minutes my words were fully oiled and ready to hit the scalding frying pan. I waited for myself to do it, to slam my mug down hard on the lid of the 'table' and say everything I'd always wanted to tell her, but the truth was that I would never say the words that filled my mouth like bile. I'd never been able to do it before, what made me think I could do it now?

I looked down at the illuminated phone in Kate's hand and noted the time. We'd spent the grand total of twenty-seven minutes 'catching up' – that was record time, even for us.

'It was great to see you again, Eff,' Kate said as she pulled me into a hug that felt both unnecessary and intrusive.

Fuck, she even smelled amazing.

'It was great to see you too,' I lied, almost hearing the thud of more heavy, dry word turds as they hit the frosted pavement.

'I'll be in touch before I leave for Toronto. Love ya, bye.' She blew a kiss over her shoulder and walked away, her ponytail swaying behind her like a silken pendulum.

I stood for a moment and watched as Kate walked away. The memory of our school prom photo leapt into my mind and brought slight warmth to my chest. Our mums had paid in advance and forced us to have it done because, just like us, they'd still refused to let our friendship die the quick death it so truly deserved. The image in my brain was of two sixteen-year-old girls, hugging each other like the years of history would prevent us from ever truly drifting apart. Of two beaming smiles that held years of secrets, shared joys and shared pains; of love.

I *had* loved her once, there was no denying that, but that time and that love was now nothing more than an image in my brain; a memory.

# Chapter Two

I'd never found it easy to make friends and so replacing what I'd lost with Kate had been a struggle. Everyone said that the friendships you make at school and university are the ones that will last a lifetime.

Well, I'm officially calling bullshit on that over-sentimental statement.

I'd made absolutely no friends at university.

Zero. Nil. Nada.

The people on my course had all seemed so childish, annoying or utterly humourless, content only with getting shitfaced and bragging about who they'd slept with the night before.

I'd spent what should have been my carefree years of drunken frolics, nights of regret and getting into awkward situations – stories of which would appear at every dinner party for the rest of my life – studying and working hard. I wouldn't even have felt so pissed off about that, had I not barely scraped by with a third and managed to come out of that failure with a crippling debt, the likes of which I could never hope to repay. All of my friendly ties from school had ended with the final bell and uni had been nothing more than three bloated years of persistent carb consumption and bitter disappointment.

I'd spent a year after that on Jobseeker's Allowance, which had all but stuck the final rusty nail into the coffin lid of my own self-worth. But one good thing that had come from the hours of sitting in itchy corporate chairs under harsh fluorescent lighting was Arthur.

Arthur Dale, owner of Dog Ears Bookshop, had come in to the job centre to talk to me and twenty other hapless, joyless, jobless fuck-ups about owning our own businesses.

Truth be told, I was the only person who got anything from Arthur's talk and when he'd finished rambling on about tax returns and marketing, I'd gone up to speak with him. He was mid-forties with a shaggy wilderness of untamed black curls and a pair of extremely well-worn Birkenstocks that looked as if the leather was hanging on to the sole for dear life. After that, I latched on to Arthur like a parasite and we swiftly became, what I liked to think of as, unlikely friends; whether Arthur liked it or not.

My mother, Joy – ironically named as she rarely found joy in anything – had worried about Arthur's intentions towards her lost and insecure daughter, but I'd soon put her mind to rest when I'd informed her that Arthur had eyes for only one person and that was his accountant, Toby.

Arthur was the opposite of me in every way. He was successful, with an established business that continued to win the battle between book and Kindle, a nice flat above the shop and an unwavering sense of sarcasm that I could only ever dream of reaching. He wasn't self-conscious and was persistent when it came to getting what he wanted, a trait best illustrated by the epic pursuit of Toby that had been going on for at least six years.

He wasn't afraid to put his mind to something and nine times out of ten he ended up achieving what he'd set out to.

I made my way to the bookshop, the anger from the coffee date still swilling around with my stomach acid. I pushed the cold brass handle of the door with a little more force than necessary, catching the bell by surprise. The loud clanging caused everyone in the shop to turn and stare at me with startled expressions on their faces. Everyone, that is, except Arthur who was used to me by now and remained undisturbed. He stood at the top of a stepladder, rearranging travel guides into the order of the countries he wanted to visit next.

'Afternoon, oh ray of golden sunshine,' he droned as I threw my bag over the counter, its contents spilling out and clattering across the floor. 'Don't be shy, come in and destroy the tranquillity by all means.'

'Sorry. I had a shitty morning,' I said as I hoisted myself onto the counter, pulling my feet up and crossing my legs.

'Which by default means that *I* am going to have a shitty afternoon,' he replied, clutching the ladder with one hand and swinging around to face me. 'So, what happened?'

'Kate.' I sighed.

'Ah, I see,' he replied, his lanky frame looming over me from above.

'She's been promoted *and* she's engaged.'

'Ouch.' He winced. 'I bet that stung.'

'I wouldn't say stung. It was more like a creeping flesh disease, leprosy maybe?' I picked up a complimentary mint imperial from the wooden bowl beside the till and placed it in my mouth.

'Those aren't for you!' Arthur snapped with annoyance, quickly descending the ladder and placing the bowl out of reach.

I still wasn't one hundred per cent sure that Arthur liked me, but he tolerated me and that was why he quickly became one of my favourite people. I'd pushed my way into his life with as much subtlety as a baby pushing itself from its mother's womb – desperately attaching myself to him and refusing to let go. In the weeks following his talk at the job centre, I would sit and read at his shop and eventually I began to serve customers when Arthur was busy. After a while he decided that he'd better start paying me and so not only had I forced my way into his life, but into his business as well. In all fairness it was the best job I'd ever had, with no official shift times, no dress code and basically no rules; except to keep my hands off the complimentary mint imperials.

There were a few people milling around the shelves, their eyes searching the spines for their next bedside read. I turned away from them, not caring if they overheard, and looked to Arthur, my very own agony aunt.

'I just don't get it,' I began as Arthur leaned against the counter, making himself comfortable for what he knew would be a long one. 'I try so hard and achieve nothing, yet Kate puts in the bare minimum and people just seem to fling opportunities at her. Should I stop trying so hard to sort my life out? If I just give up completely, will someone come to me with a sexy new boyfriend and a six-figure salary? Tell me, Arthur, tell me to give up.'

'What? You mean you haven't totally given up already?' He smirked.

'Can you be serious for just one minute? I need your wisdom right now.'

'All right, listen, some people just get all the luck and others don't. That's just the shitty way that life works. You are one of the latter, whereas Kate is part of the former. She may get everything she ever wanted, and she'll never have to work for it, but when you finally get where you're going, it will mean all the more because of how hard you worked to get there.'

I frowned. 'So, you're saying I'll try twice as hard to fail at something as everyone else?' I asked.

'Precisely!' He grinned, his tone upbeat.

'Wow, thanks.' I sighed as a customer approached the till. He looked at us sheepishly and held a book out in front of him.

'Can I buy this?' he asked, as if he was worried he'd interrupted our counselling session.

I sighed and pasted on my 'of course I don't hate the customers' face. I took the book from him, glanced at the front cover and felt the familiar jealousy. Each and every book that I sold was clouded with the thought that that could have been my name on the cover with my words inside, but alas, the countless agents and publishers I'd sent my manuscript to had deemed me unworthy of such a feat and so, I had stashed that ninety-thousand-word dream in a box beneath my bed and resigned myself to forever being a bookseller rather than a writer.

I charged the man and he left with the book cradled under his arm.

'You'll get there one day,' Arthur said with a sympathetic smile curling his lips.

'Will I?' I asked, almost to myself.

Seven thirty hit and I found myself crammed into a sticky vinyl booth at the mock-American diner in the centre of town. I'd never liked this place but, Daz – my Tinder date – had suggested it and so I'd decided to give it another shot. The Fifties doo-wop music blared angrily from crackling speakers and the smell of sickly-sweet milkshakes and chip fat filled the air. The place was basically empty except for me, a family of four in the far corner and a lone diner behind me, who munched noisily on his fries.

I wasn't kidding myself, I didn't anticipate much from this date with a guy whose name sounded like a cleaning product, but what did I have to lose?

If all went well, then it would be an evening of flirting, followed by a kiss or two and then we would probably part forever. It was sad really, but all I really wanted was to feel desired for one evening.

I took my phone from my bag while I waited and opened Facebook to complete my allotted self-torture time. The phone was old and battered and the edges of the screen were a spiderweb of cracks from the various abuses it had suffered at my hands.

The first post that made my stomach acid boil in my gut was an overly sentimental inspirational quote about being kind to others. Ironically this was posted by a girl I had once witnessed kicking the shit out of another girl in the park before school started because said girl had *looked at her funny*. Next was a post about someone's dad who'd died fourteen years ago. It was a long, arduous text, almost an essay, which was generous in its use of clichés. I wondered why people posted these. Was it a well-known fact that the afterlife had nothing better to do than monitor Facebook for remembrance statuses? I scoffed and scrolled further.

A woman I'd met once at a job centre workshop had posted a picture. It was a shot of her legs, crossed at the ankles, a cocktail in her hand and a pool glinting in the distance. The caption read: *'So, how's your day?'*

Pretty shitty so far, Karen, thanks for asking.

I hazarded a glance at Kate's page. The latest post was a photo of her and her fiancé, Callum, their eyes squinting into the flash of the camera as they embraced and grinned like maniacs. I wish I'd someone I could grin about like that. Maybe, after this date, I would. Who knew, Daz could be The One.

The more I thought about the date, the more I began to talk myself around to the idea. Life hadn't found me my romcom leading man yet, but maybe Tinder would prevail where life had failed. But those hopes were dashed the moment he stepped through the door. He wore expensive-looking trainers, low-slung jeans and a T-shirt with a V-neck so deep it was basically a cardigan. He was laughable, with a pathetic attempt at a goatee sitting on his receding chin, and yet I knew that I would have to sit through a date with him out of pure politeness. I lifted my hand and waved to him. He lowered his Primani shades and cast me a disappointed glance.

'You Effie?' he barked.

'Yes. You must be Daz.' The lone diner behind me made a loud choking noise and then regained his composure.

'Yeah, dat's me.' He slid into the booth and placed his phone face up on the table. He surveyed me for a second before saying, 'You don't look like your Tinder photo.'

'Really?' I asked. 'Well, it's definitely me in the picture.'

He tapped around on his phone before pulling up the image and holding it out to me. I caught a whiff of his aftershave, which was trying to be *Boss for Men*.

'Who's the other girl then?' he asked.

I leaned forward and looked at the picture, my heart sinking when I understood the confusion. I'd never been one to take selfies. I'd tried it a couple of times but I just ended up feeling like a knob, standing there pouting at the camera. Who was I taking them for? I certainly didn't want them, so all of my photos were in groups, snapshots of nights out where I'd tried to breathe in and stand taller beside Kate. With an encroaching sense of nausea, I realised Daz had thought he was meeting her, instead of the disappointment sitting opposite him.

'Oh, that's my friend,' I said quietly, the word *friend* feeling uncomfortable in my mouth.

'She single?' he asked without irony.

I paused for a moment and wondered if he was being serious.

'No. She's engaged actually. Sorry to disappoint,' I spat angrily.

He tutted. 'All the hot ones are.'

His shoulders sagged and he pushed his shades back onto his nose. The awkward silence hung in the air like a stagnant fart until he finally stood and excused himself to go to the bathroom. My eyes stung as I felt the tears, but I'd be damned if I'd let him see me cry. Maybe I could just leave, slip out while he was gone and make a run for it? No. Effie Heaton would not run from a man-child who thought that an Ali G beard was still an acceptable form of facial hair.

I ordered a Coke – full-fat not diet – and chugged on the straw hungrily as I waited for my disappointed date to return. I could feel the grease in the air, settling on my skin and laying foundations for the bulging spot that no doubt would begin to sprout before the end of the day.

I looked around at the rest of the diner, trying to ignore

the audible masticating of the person behind me. Why did some people have to make such a song and dance about eating? Surely he'd had enough practice.

There were twenty or more rusted metal signs nailed to the wall above the serving hatch, through which grimaced a sour-faced old man with a weak chin and bushy eyebrows. One of the signs depicted the face of a smiling 1950s woman giving a thumbs up. Above her head it read, *Today could be the start of the rest of your life.*

I couldn't help but feel that the message wasn't for me. Daz was not a life changer and I'd be lucky if he even came back rather than trying to squeeze his inflated ego through the skinny awning window in the bathroom.

I saw him walking back over and surmised that the window had been too small. He made his way to the table but didn't bother sitting down.

'Hey, listen, I don't mean to sound like a dick but you're not what I signed up for and I don't really wanna waste my money on someone who I'd have swiped left.'

I recoiled and tried to form a retort but the words collected in my throat and remained there like a cork. He lifted a finger to his forehead and saluted me before sauntering out the door and letting a draught in as he left.

I turned, my jeans squeaking against the pleather, and fixed my eyes on a poster of Elvis that sat on the wall opposite. I tried not to cry, but I could feel the sob building in my throat.

'Excuse me.' I heard a voice in my right ear and turned around to see the face of the noisy eater from the booth behind. 'Hi, my name's Theo and I couldn't help but notice that your date was a complete wanker.' He smiled at me, his blue eyes hidden beneath scruffy blond hair. He held out his hand and waited for me to shake it. 'You can come join me if you want – I'll never eat all of this.' He gestured to the half-eaten burger and grease-sodden fries that remained on his ketchup-smeared plate.

'You were listening?' I asked, embarrassed.

'I'm sorry, but as soon as a douchebag walks in dressed like that, it's pretty much impossible not to pay attention.' He grinned.

'Well, I'm glad there was an audience to my humiliation.'

I pulled out my purse and slammed the money for my Coke down onto the table.

Then, with anger fuelling me, I pulled my bag strap over my shoulder and slid out of the booth.

'Why are *you* the one who's embarrassed? He was the one being a dick,' he said as I walked quickly past.

I spun around, a frown fixed on my face, and said, 'You should try and eat more quietly. You sound like a cement mixer.' I turned on my heel and headed for the door.

'Now who's the eavesdropper?' I heard him mumble but I ignored him and as soon as the cool October air hit my burning cheeks, I let the tears fall and cried all the way home.

# Chapter Three

I woke with a pounding head and a blockage of dried snot in my beetroot-coloured nose. The night before had been filled with a lot of red wine – the evidence of which could be seen in the magenta stain that tinted most of my lower lip – and what can only be described as a 'mama hug meltdown'. For those people not sure what one of those is, a 'mama hug meltdown' can be defined by three invariable characteristics.

1. It is generally conducted on some kind of floor and whilst being called the 'mama hug meltdown' it doesn't necessarily involve a mother and can be conducted in or around the arms of a parent, guardian or trusted figure to whom you look for emotional comfort.

2. There must always be copious amounts of snot, tears and/or saliva, which are periodically smeared onto said parent or trusted figure as you spew forth lines of self-hatred and woe about your life and situation.

3. These events are usually, but not always, followed by wine or some other kind of numbing alcoholic liquid – this can be interchanged for tea if necessary – and the meltdown will eventually come to a close when you end up in bed with a thumping head, a blocked nose and a feeling that tomorrow cannot possibly be as bad as the day you are putting behind you.

I'd opted for the bathroom floor for my meltdown, my tears pooling in the grooves of the colonial-style tiles as my mother tried to soothe me with Cabernet Sauvignon and promises of karma coming back around to give me everything I wanted. Joy and I rarely saw eye to eye. We had the rare talent of being able to make an argument out of anything, and I mean *anything*. We once didn't speak for two days because I insulted the blouse of a local newsreader who happened to be her favourite. But despite how little we got on, I knew that she was always great in a crisis. I had listened and cried and drunk and thought of all the hundreds of thousands of things that I could have (but hadn't) said to Daz in retaliation for his rudeness, before ending up falling asleep at around five o'clock in the morning; my drunken, stained lips still mumbling retorts into the darkness as I drifted off.

Daz had been the final straw in a month that I had hoped would be better than the last, but which had actually turned out to be worse. In the last thirty days, I had received three rejection letters for my novel, been thrust back into my overdraft whilst paying off the charges for being overdrawn the month before, been on two failed dates, had one screaming argument with my parents and broken my little toe. The month had been a shit show of dramatic proportions, but

25

Daz was the rancid glacé cherry atop the shit sundae that had been October.

I showered and washed the scent of Daz's knockoff Boss for Men out of my hair, but somehow, I couldn't get rid of the red wine stain on my swollen lip. I found the sienna-brown lipstick from the bottom of my bag and dragged it across my mouth, covering the stain and making it look like I cared enough about my appearance to have put on make-up.

I always had an image of what I looked like in my mind – an image that had passed through the Photoshop of my brain and which I'd fooled myself into thinking was true, yet the mirror never showed it to me. I'd always straddled the line between curvy and slim, with rounded hips, a small waist and a little pooch of stomach that sometimes made me look ever so slightly pregnant. I stared into the toothpaste-spattered mirror and took in the puffy skin that sat around my large green eyes and the tip of my ski-slope nose that refused to stop blazing red, no matter how much foundation I dabbed on to it. My hair lay in a tangle of russet curls, which should probably have been washed yesterday, reaching down to the small of my back. My hair had always been my defining feature but it seemed to be forever getting caught in display units and car doors.

I applied a third layer of concealer to my puffy purple eyes and pulled the collar of my cardigan tightly around my neck. I tugged tighter and tighter. At first trying to keep warm but somehow, for just a moment, I entertained the idea of pulling it so tightly that I strangled myself, thus ending the sad short life of Effie 'Meh' Heaton.

I let go of my collar and left for work, abandoning the fleeting idea of suicide on the bathroom floor.

\* \* \*

The shop had the good sense to know when to keep quiet. It was almost as if my force field of ennui ran to just outside the door, not permitting anyone through. I knelt beside the bestseller shelves, pulling out the ones that people hadn't been able to get enough of last month and placing them into the bargain bin beside me. Arthur sat at the counter staring, almost manically, at his phone.

'What exactly are you waiting for it to do?' I asked without turning away from what I was doing.

'Nothing,' he replied too quickly.

'You sure? 'Cause you've been staring at it like that for twenty minutes now.'

'I'm just waiting for a call?'

'From who?'

'No one!' he snapped.

A moment later the screen blazed into life and the theme from *Doctor Who* played from the tinny speakers. Arthur leapt back like he'd just seen a viper; his mouth drawn open, a look of terror in his eyes.

'Well,' I prompted after hearing it ring for a full five seconds. 'Answer it then.'

He accepted the call and raised it to his ear. He took a deep breath before pulling his mouth into a smile and donning a laid-back tone. 'Hi, Toby. How's things?'

I couldn't help but smile as well as I finally understood Arthur's strange behaviour.

'I was just wondering,' he continued, clearing his throat a few more times than necessary, 'if you wouldn't mind popping by. I've buggered up on my tax return again and I need someone who knows what they're doing to take a look at it.' His fake smile turned into a real one when Toby accepted his invitation and when he hung up, his face was bright red with excitement.

27

'Tax returns?' I asked whilst trying to keep a straight face.

Arthur's smile dissipated as he tried to shrug his way out of the conversation. 'Oh, shut up. I need him to check it for me.'

'And this has nothing to do with the fact that you're completely in love with him?'

Arthur's face drew into an expression of outrage. 'I am not in love with him, Effie. He is my accountant!'

'Yes, and you're in love with him.'

'I most certainly am not.' His face turned from pink to puce. 'It would be completely inappropriate.'

I made my way over to the counter. 'He's an accountant, not a Montague. If you want to ask him out, then do it, Juliet. It's been almost six years and this will-they-won't-they thing that you've got going on is getting kinda old.'

Arthur sighed and placed his forehead on the counter. 'But what if he says no?'

'Oh please,' I replied as the bell above the door jingled. 'That awkward, specky man is just as much a fool for you as you are for him. Just shag and get it over with already.'

Arthur pressed his finger to his lips and shot me a warning glance before turning to the customer behind and asking if they needed any help.

'Hi, I'm here to see Matilda.' Something about his voice made me feel like I'd heard it before and when I turned, I saw that I had.

'You!' I exclaimed, stepping closer to the man who'd borne witness to my date from hell the night before. 'The Eavesdropper.'

'That *is* my formal title, yes. But I prefer to go by Theo.' He smiled and it was one of those one-sided, dangerously alluring smiles that can lead a girl to make bad decisions.

'Well, Theo, what are you doing here and how do you know my name?' I crossed my arms and shot him a questioning scowl. The anger, born from my utter embarrassment, still burned brightly in my chest.

'The waitress handed me this after you left. I guess she saw us talking and assumed we'd come in together.' He held out his hand. My purse sat in his fingers and regret for my earlier moodiness changed my frown to an apologetic smile.

'Oh my God. I didn't even know I'd lost it. Thank you.' I took the purse and opened it to check everything was still inside.

'Don't worry, I didn't do anything with it, except buy that speedboat, of course, but I doubt you'll miss seventy grand.' He pushed his hands into his pockets in the same way that awkward teenagers do, although he was clearly not a teen, and flicked his floppy blond hair out of his face.

'How did you know where I worked?'

'Facebook,' he said simply. 'So, as a thank you for not stealing all of your money and returning your property to you, I was thinking that you could buy me a coffee.'

I raised an eyebrow and recrossed my arms, realising that my forgiveness had been a little premature. 'Did you now?'

'Yeah, well it would be rude of you to not give something in return for me being such a good Samaritan.'

I thought about it for a moment. There were positives to going out for coffee with an alluring and persistent stranger. He was hot, there was no denying that, and apart from being overly sarcastic and cocky, he seemed all right. But Daz had taken my last surviving molecule of confidence and crushed it under the sole of his Nike Airs and the idea of possibly facing humiliation again was enough to make up my mind.

29

'You know I would, but I'm working and so I don't think I'll have time,' I said in a transparently fake apologetic tone.

'It's fine. Take a break.' Arthur's voice came from behind me. I spun around and scowled at him. 'Take as long as you need.' He smirked and leaned back in his chair.

'It's settled then,' Theo said, making for the door. 'I'm thirsty, let's go to the café in the park.'

I walked to the counter where Arthur was holding my jacket in his outstretched hand, a wicked smile on his lips. 'I hate you so very much right now,' I whisper-shouted.

'Oh, just shag and get it over with,' he replied mockingly.

With a sigh, I followed Theo out of the door for our impromptu coffee date and inside my brain, the *Countdown* theme began. It wouldn't be long until I embarrassed myself and this handsome stranger saw what a complete loser he'd worked so hard to spend time with.

It took almost ten minutes before the dreaded question was asked: 'What do you do for fun?'

My immediate answers were 'Nothing' and 'What is this fun you speak of?' But it was too early to let him know what a bore I really was.

'You know. Stuff,' I replied as we took a seat on a frigid stone bench.

'How very in-depth.' He smirked and took a sip of his decaf flat white.

'What about you? What do you do?'

'You know. Stuff,' he replied, looking at me with a grin, his lips curling up and sending creases to the corners of his mouth. He had high, sculpted cheekbones and a roman nose that made him look like an artist had chiselled him out of marble. He was at least half a foot taller than me with wide shoulders that sat beneath a green cable-knit jumper and denim jacket. 'You know, I can't help but feel like you're not the chatty type.'

'I'm not.'

'Well, I am.' He looked up at the sky and watched a flock of pigeons descend onto the square in front of us. 'You're an odd one.'

'That's the most accurate description of me I've ever heard,' I replied, the *Countdown* theme almost at the final *bong*.

'Odd and needlessly angry.'

'Oh, there's plenty of need for it. It fuels me.'

I shifted on the cold stone bench and bounced my knees to try and keep warm.

'Is this on my account or do you do this all the time?' He turned to me, placing one of his large hands on his knee; the trace of a smile just visible.

'Do I do what all the time?'

'Bombard others with hostility and take an instant dislike to people you know nothing about.'

I opened my mouth to defend myself, but I knew that what he'd said was true.

Hostility was my comfort zone.

'You can't just make me buy you coffee and then insult me,' I said, my voice thick with annoyance.

He rolled his eyes and turned back to the pigeons that were now pecking around on the ground in front of us. A male pigeon puffed out his chest and attempted to seduce one of the females; she was having none of it and I felt a strange kind of affinity with her.

'There was a time when a handsome stranger could notice a pretty girl and take her out for coffee and she wouldn't think that he had some sort of hidden agenda.'

'Ha! You see, that's where you've gone wrong.' I held up

a finger and looked into his eyes with lowered lids. '*I'm* the one who took *you* out for coffee, so clearly the secret agenda is still in there.' I poked my finger into the centre of his chest, then realised that that was far too familiar and scooted away from him slightly.

'We *do* live in the age of equality; if you want to pay for coffee I'm not going to stop you.' He swigged at his drink. The ever-present gleam of mischief that glinted in his eyes was somewhat irksome.

'Which is the real you?' he asked, his tone suddenly serious.

'What do you mean?'

'Well, the person you are being now isn't the same as the one who went out for a date with that *Love Island* contestant last night. If this version of you had been in that booth, then I'd have been surprised if Daz had left alive. But instead you just let him put you down. Why did you do that?'

I scowled at him. Who the hell was this person? I hadn't known him for more than half an hour and he'd already asked me more in-depth questions than my mother had in twenty-eight years.

I stood up, my body zinging with an amalgamation of fury and discomfort.

'Well, as lovely as this has been, I'm going to go now.' I thought about tossing my cup into the bin beside me but it was still half full and I didn't want to waste what little money I had.

'Hey, wait a minute.' He stood, holding his hands up in front of him in surrender. 'I didn't mean to upset you. I wasn't being cruel; I just wanted to know the answer. Sometimes I do this thing where I just say what I think without it going through the filter of social acceptability.'

Snap.

'I'm going,' I said, stepping away from him in the direction of the shop.

'Before you go, can I just ask you one more question?' He stepped in front of me, blocking my path and causing me to bump into him.

I groaned loudly and looked up into his face. I tried to ignore how amazing he smelled and kept my grimace intact. I shrugged dramatically and he carried on.

'Why is it that you happily went along to that date last night with someone terrible, but you won't give me the time of day? Are you one of these girls who date douchebags because they think they don't deserve better, or do you just not like me?'

My shoulders slumped as my bravado abandoned me and I sat back down on the frigid bench without uttering another word. How was it that he had me pegged already? Was I that transparent?

'It can't be because of how I look – you called me handsome.'

'*You* called yourself handsome; I had nothing to do with it.'

'Ah! But you didn't disagree.' His smile was almost a super-power, the way it ignited his face and caused something to twist inside me in return.

'Look,' I sighed, my anger now reducing to a worn-down feeling of general shittiness, 'you seem like an okay guy and you're . . . not awful in the face department, or the shoulder department for that matter. If last night's date hadn't happened, then I might be more into this, but it did and I don't think I can handle another disaster right now.'

'What makes you think that I'd be a disaster?' he asked with a frown.

I looked him up and down – and from his eyes, the colour of the ocean during a storm, to his lips that always seemed to be teasing a smile even when he was trying to be serious, all the way down to his feet that absentmindedly tapped out a rhythm on the path beneath them, there was no question that this boy would spell disaster.

'Why are you trying so hard? I'm not a nice person, I'm not much to look at and someone like you could walk twenty paces in any direction and find himself a date.' I slumped forward into my lap and rubbed my forehead with cold fingers. Something about talking to him had made me feel like crap.

'Just . . . because,' he replied simply. 'Hand me your phone.' I took it from my pocket without question and handed it to him. He frowned at the state of it before he tapped in his number and saved it into my contacts. 'The power is with you now. Sleep on it and see what you think tomorrow.'

He placed the phone back in my hand, his skin brushing my palm. He didn't notice, but I felt it all the way down to my toes.

'Hopefully I'll hear from you soon, Matilda.'

'Actually, I go by my middle name: Effie.'

'Well, Effie, I hope I hear from you all the same.'

I returned to the shop with an overwhelming sense of relief.

All I had to do was not call him and I'd never have to see him again.

Toby was sitting on the century-old leather sofa by the window with a sea of papers spread out over the coffee table in front of him. Toby was a gangly Scotsman, with once dark brown hair that was now streaked with shades of white and grey. He always wore sharp suits, colourful ties and those shiny red winkle-pickers that I'd once made fun of, but now found to be a brave fashion choice.

Arthur sat beside him in an unnatural position, his legs crossed and his whole body leaning Toby's way. I greeted Toby cheerily before directing my angst at Arthur.

'You're welcome,' Arthur said after I turned to him; my hand resting on my jutting out hip.

'Yes, thank you for sending me out on a coffee date with someone who could have been a stalker,' I replied.

'A date? Do tell.' Toby placed down his fountain pen and awaited my story with gleaming dark brown eyes that sat behind his square-rimmed glasses.

I threw up my hands and sat down on the floor opposite them.

'There's not a lot *to* tell.' I told him about Daz and Theo The Eavesdropper.

'Well, it seems to me that you've got yourself a real admirer.' Toby pushed his glasses further up the bridge of his aquiline nose. 'He went to the trouble of finding out who you were and where you worked. Is he nice? Good-looking?'

'He's . . .' I paused and thought of those cheekbones that you could shave Parmesan on and suddenly I lost my train of thought.

'I'll take that as a yes.' Toby chuckled. 'Effie, life is short. You could get run over by a taxi or hit your head on the kitchen counter and you'd be dead. You're alive now, so when a handsome lad comes along and wants to take you out, let him. You can always decide against him later.' He leaned back and looked at an oblivious Arthur from beneath his lashes. 'Life's too short to let matters of the heart slip by.'

*    *    *

I sat at the kitchen table with a freshly opened bottle of wine and a bowl of pasta steaming the glass that sat beside it.

I know you're thinking it so I might as well address the Shiraz-shaped elephant in the room. I drink too much – that is not news to me.

Am I an alcoholic? No.

Am I an alcoholic in denial? Absolutely not!

But wasn't there that study once that said that drinking red wine could lower your risk of having a heart attack? I never paid much attention to those kinds of studies anyway. One week they'd be telling you that oolong tea could increase your life expectancy by twenty years and the next week they'd come forward with a discovery that drinking too much of it made your nipples fall off.

I looked around at the dark room, lit only by a dull standard lamp in the far corner. There was a small cupboard next to the lamp that acted as a museum of my failures. Inside the cupboard sat my crumpled and torn graduation certificate that Joy had confiscated from me after I'd tried to rip it in half and set it on fire one night after a little too much Black Tower. In the top drawer were the remaining thousand or so pairs of handmade earrings from when I got it into my head to open an Etsy shop, and hanging above the cupboard on its sad little hook was the lead that I had used during my brief period as a dog walker.

I had enjoyed being a dog walker. I loved animals and the job required absolutely zero contact with other people. But the money had been a pile of crap and I'd had to stop after Gumbo, a long-haired chihuahua, managed to get loose and remained lost for a further six hours. His owner had threatened to take me to court and so I'd decided to cut my losses and end that business venture then and there.

I heard the front door open and flinched.

They were home.

I braced myself for the worried glance at the bottle that sat already two glasses less than full in front of me.

My mother and father entered carrying armfuls of shopping bags, flicking the overhead light on as they arrived and making me temporarily blind.

'Wine already and it's not even six,' Joy said as she dropped the bags onto the work surface. I blinked the stunned tears from my eyes but didn't bother with a snarky reply, even though there was a queue of them lining up in my head.

My dad mumbled something in his indecipherable northern accent. I just ignored him and carried on sipping my wine and letting my food turn cold.

'Effie, do you remember Marcus Roe from school?' Mum asked with a grin that suggested she'd been meddling.

'No,' I lied. A shiver of embarrassment shook me as I remembered the last time I'd seen him. Of course I remembered Marcus Roe. I'd been at school with him since I was seven and he'd been the first person I'd ever slept with. He was always drop-dead gorgeous and the night we'd spent together had been okay, up until . . . well, let's just not get into that right now.

'Well, I met his mother in the Aldi just now,' she carried on, clearly ignoring the tone of my voice that was urging her to forget Marcus Roe. 'Did you know he's working for the BBC? He's a casting director for all those period dramas.'

'Is that so?' I asked in a monotone drone. I *did* know this. I'd seen it on Facebook along with all the other people whose lives were actually going somewhere.

'He's coming home for a few weeks while they renovate his apartment,' she prattled on. I knew what was coming.

She was no Paddy McGuinness but I knew that a date was coming all the same. Let the *daughter* see the *blatantly set-up date*. 'Kelly and I thought that the two of you should maybe meet up and have a chat. He's single, you know.'

'He's not? What a shock!' The sarcasm almost choked me.

She sighed and pushed a box of cereal into the cupboard. 'Effie, you're never going to meet anyone if the only thing you do is sit at home and drink like one of those French bohemians.'

I lifted the glass and took two large gulps, maintaining eye contact with her over the rim. She huffed and went back to unpacking.

'His number is on the fridge. You should call him, when you stop being so judgemental.'

I wasn't being judgemental and I was most certainly not going to call him.

# Chapter Four

The next day I arrived at work, with more than a slight hangover, to find Toby, once again, sitting on the shabby leather sofa, his glasses perched atop his nose and his ever-cheerful eyes shining out from behind them.

'Effie!' he cooed in his soothingly soft Scottish tones. 'You're finally here.'

I frowned with confusion and checked my phone. 'I'm not late, am I? I thought I was meant to be here at eleven thirty.'

'Your gentleman caller is here! He's in the back with Arthur.' He seemed excited, his neck elongating as he spoke, like a peering tortoise.

I sighed and let my head loll back onto my shoulders. 'Please tell me you're lying. I'm too hungover for this.'

Toby took me by the shoulders and brought his face close. I couldn't remember him ever touching me before.

'Effie, if you don't go in there and agree to a date with that lad then I will do it myself. You don't let blue eyes like that slip through your fingers. You never know, the boy could be your seahorse.' I shook the memory away, that was a memory for another time, not for now.

'Don't you mean he could be my lobster?' I asked with a quirked brow.

'No, I *mean* seahorse. Lobsters have a bond for only two weeks before going their separate ways. Seahorses on the other hand are the Ozzy and Sharon of the animal world.'

'Erm . . . you know he had an affair, right?'

Toby waved a hand in the air and scoffed. 'But they always come back to each other. Now, off you go.' He let go of my shoulders and glanced towards the back of the shop and to where muffled chatter drifted in from the back room.

'Why me?' I threw my head back, groaned and let my bag fall to the ground.

I blew disgruntled air from my nose and walked, with purpose, behind the wall of shelves that separated the front of the shop from the hidden Aladdin's cave behind. I turned through the Classics section, taking a right at Alexandre Dumas and then a left at Oscar Wilde. Above was a balcony where we kept the antiques and first editions, and the smell of dusty old books drifted down and soothed me slightly as I arrived in the Sport section. Theo was nose-deep in a book about Muhammad Ali with Arthur picking out several others and piling them beside him.

It was one of those days when all I wanted to do was go home and take my bra off. I didn't need some hanger-on trying to force me on a date, not when I had an unopened bottle of Echo Falls and a Netflix series waiting for me when I got in.

I huffed and puffed like the wolf in the stories and marched towards him. The sound of my Dr Martens slapping against the floor caused him to turn. At first, he smiled; then he saw the look on my face and the smile was gone.

'What are you doing here?' I stopped in front of him and scowled.

He nodded towards the book in his hand and then said, 'Shopping.'

'Morning,' Arthur said cheerily.

'Don't "morning" me. This is all your fault.' I sent my scowl his way before returning it to its rightful owner. 'I thought the power was in my hands?'

Theo closed the book, the pages slapping as they fell together. 'Oh, I didn't realise that this was a private library. I must have been mistaken in thinking that people could come in here and browse, maybe buy a thing or two.'

'Effie!' Arthur whispered out the corner of his mouth.

I ignored him. 'You came here because I haven't texted you yet and you knew that I was never going to.'

'*Someone* thinks highly of herself,' Theo muttered, rolling his eyes. 'So, what if that's even true?'

'Because you told me to call you if I wanted to see you. You didn't exactly wait very long.' He clenched his square jaw and I found myself wondering how it would feel to run my fingers along it.

Stop it! Focus!

'I saw this place yesterday, when I returned the purse that you didn't know you'd lost. You're welcome, by the way. I thought it seemed interesting and came back to look around. I didn't even know if you were working today.'

I looked him up and down, trying once and for all to figure out his agenda while a hangover headache slowly unfurled behind my forehead.

'I'm not stalking you, Effie. I just wanted to buy some

books. Which I will now do, seeing as my welcome has clearly expired.' Theo took two of the books and put the rest away before walking past without looking at me.

I cast my eye to Arthur who simply shook his head before returning to the front with Theo.

I turned to the bookcase beside me and brought my forehead to the wood with a bang.

I was such a dickhead.

Why was I overthinking this? I'd gone out with Daz even though he looked like an ex-member of Blazin' Squad and had been a complete tool, so why was I turning Theo away?

I managed to get back to the main part of the shop as the bell above the door jangled. I bolted after him, the door hitting the sofa arm and making Toby start as I flung it back and ran out onto the street.

'Wait!' I called.

He stopped and turned, his jaw still set. 'Look, Effie, I think I like you, even though I'm not sure why right now, but if you want me to go away then I will. You'll never have to lay eyes on me again, but just tell me now.'

I paused, my mouth open, but no words came out.

He exhaled and took a step away from me. I felt instant, crippling regret bundle like knotted twine inside my ribcage.

I tried to force my lips closed and I willed the words that were bubbling up like vomit to fall back down from whence they came, but I momentarily lost control of my body and called out his name. He turned back to me, his eyebrows raised in anticipation.

'I finish at five. If you want, we could go for a drink. But it's not a date.'

His face pulled into a smile that I turned away from, for I knew its true power.

'I'd like that. I'll come back at five.'

I sent him a forthright nod, spun on my heel and stalked back to the shop, anxiety building in my chest like a shaken can of Coke.

I closed the door and looked up to see Toby grinning at me like a madman and Arthur clutching a book to his chest, a pissed-off look on his face. He stepped forward and handed me the book. I looked down at the copy of *An Introduction to Mindfulness* and rolled my eyes.

'When I said that we could go for a drink, I meant something with a percentage on the label,' I said as Theo held the door to Green Machine Juice Bar open for me.

'I didn't want to be predictable and take you to a bar,' he said as he perused the bafflingly complicated menu. 'Anyway it's not safe for a lady, or a man for that matter, to drink alcohol around me. My charms can become overpowering.'

I snorted a laugh and ignored the ironic wink he sent my way. 'So, the lack of wine is for the greater good of mankind then, not because you're a cheapskate?'

'Cheapskate? Have you seen these prices? A glass of wine at a Wetherspoons would be half the price of these.'

I pressed my hand to my chest and feigned a flattered smile. 'Don't I feel special. Wetherspoons, you know how to treat a girl, don't you?'

Theo ordered something called a Foghorn from the girl at the till and then turned to me expectantly.

'What are you having?' he asked.

I looked back up at the menu, which might as well have been written in Ancient Aramaic, and shrugged. 'I'll have what you're having.'

43

Theo asked me to grab some seats while he waited for our drinks and so I headed for two tall chairs by a table at the window. The sound of a blender roaring into action blocked out the noise of the strange funk music playing from hidden speakers. I tried to settle into a position that didn't look posed, but the chair was too tall and my legs were too short. Add to that the fact that I was feeling extremely self-conscious and inadequate in the presence of Adonis-like gym people, and the whole ordeal made me look like I was having extreme intestinal discomfort. The sound of the roaring blender ceased and Theo headed over with two grotesque-coloured drinks.

'Erm . . . thanks?' I said as he handed me one of the small plastic cups of purple-brown hideousness.

'This place is great. Have you been in here before?' he asked, looking around at the trendy shop filled with trendy people.

'Have you ever seen that film about the little girl who's a vampire and when she walks into someone's house uninvited, she starts bleeding from her eyes?'

'Er, yeah, I've seen that.' He frowned in confusion.

'That's how my body reacts to places that serve healthy foodstuffs. So, to answer your question, no. I have not,' I replied and took a sip through my straw. The second the viscous liquid hit my tongue I knew it was a mistake. It took all the will I had to swallow it and when it was finally on its way to my stomach, I pulled my sleeve over my hand and used it to wipe my tongue. 'What the hell is in that?'

He took a sip and let out a refreshed 'ahhh' before answering. 'Apple juice, ginger, flaxseed, celery and beetroot. It's meant to be good for de-fogging your brain after a long day.'

'It's good for force-feeding to an enemy during torture, is all this is good for.'

He sniggered to himself and took another sip. 'You're not turning your nose up at a Wetherspoons wine now, are you?'

'I'd take Donald Trump's old bathwater over this.'

'Oh my God, what a disgusting thought.' He grimaced and pushed my drink closer to me. 'Come on, it's good for you.'

'My body wholeheartedly rejects it.'

'I didn't take you for a quitter, Effie.' He cocked his head and smirked and I hated how susceptible I was to it. I lifted the straw to my mouth and gave it another try and by the third sip it was almost bearable.

'So, the guys at the shop. They're a couple, right?'

'Arthur and Toby? I wish. They're in love, but I think Arthur is the only person on the planet that doesn't know that.'

He leaned his elbow on the table and braced his head against his hand. His fingers half disappeared into the depths of his shaggy hair and I caught myself wondering if it was as soft as it appeared. I imagined that it might smell like fresh sea air and pine needles. It took several seconds for me to realise that I'd just been staring at him, my eyes glazing over as I imagined combing my fingers through it. I thought that maybe he hadn't noticed, but then I saw the self-satisfied grin on his face and knew I hadn't got away with it.

'So,' I cleared my throat and looked down to stir the sludgy contents at the bottom of my cup in an attempt to hide my blushing face. 'How come you've not got a girlfriend? Someone like you doesn't stay single for long.'

'Do you say that because you think I'm handsome?' he teased.

'Again, *you* are the one who keeps using the word *handsome*. I think you have a crush on yourself.'

'That makes two of us then.' He sent me a wink before he stopped teasing me and sat back in his chair. 'What about you? I'm sure guys are forever beating down your door.'

'Ha!' I chortled, ungracefully. 'Yeah, I've had to install a portcullis to keep them out.'

'No, seriously.'

'I thought you were listening to my date the other night? I mean, I've never been very successful in the dating world, but that last date was me literally scraping the bottom of the barrel.'

'That guy was a complete tool with bad taste in clothes and even worse taste in women. You're far too good for him.'

I smiled a little at that and tried to ignore the sensation in my stomach that felt suspiciously like butterflies.

'I think you wildly overestimate me, Theo.' I could feel his eyes on my skin, boring into me.

'I think it's you who underestimates yourself.' I looked up to meet his eyes and it felt like someone had just punched me in the chest. Silence lingered in the air for what seemed like centuries before he spoke again. 'So, you work at a book-shop. That's one thing I know about you.' He cleared his throat awkwardly. 'Do you read them or only sell them?'

I opened my mouth and almost blurted out that I did both and more, that I wrote them too, but I stopped myself. To write was to bare part of your soul and I was happy to keep that particular part of my soul hidden from everyone, for now. 'Both,' I said, taking another sip and then regretting it.

'What's your favourite book then?'

I spent a quiet moment deliberating the question as if my life depended on my answer. 'I'd probably say *Jane Eyre*.'

'I've never read that one. What is it that you like about it?' he asked.

I frowned a little at his interest. I couldn't remember the last time someone asked me a question about me. Not even Arthur had ever asked me my favourite book.

'She says this one line: "I am a free human being with an independent will, which I now exert to leave you". This was being written in the time when women were meant to shut up and get married and sit by the fire and crank out children. Jane isn't beautiful or rich and she doesn't want to define herself by marriage or by what a woman is "meant" to be, which was a radical thing to be writing about at the time. The whole story is gothic and romantic and surprising. I just really love it.'

When I finished, he just stared at me, a strange look in his eyes.

'What?'

'You change when you talk about books. You're clearly passionate about them.' He was looking at me as if he knew me and something about that made me panic.

I straightened in my seat and pulled my bag up over my shoulder. 'I should probably go; they'll be expecting me at home.'

He frowned and leaned forward, his hands resting in the centre of the table as if they were inviting mine to join them. 'Is it the beetroot? I can get you another drink. I hear the Cucumber-colonic's very good.'

'That can't be a real drink.'

'No, it's not. I just didn't want you to leave yet.'

'Thanks for the terrible drink, Theo.' I ungracefully dismounted the too-tall chair and made for the exit. It was beginning to rain lightly when I found myself standing alone

47

on the dark pavement and I cursed myself for forgetting to shove an umbrella into my already overstuffed bag this morning.

I heard the door open behind me as I paused to pull up my hood and Theo appeared beside me. 'I'll walk you home,' he said, handing me an umbrella and shoving his hands into his pockets.

I opened it up and noticed the juice bar logo emblazoned on the side. 'Dare I ask if you stole this?'

'I lifted it from inside the door, but I promised I'd return it.'

'You don't have to walk me home. I've done it a thousand times.'

'I insist,' he replied. 'So, which way is it?'

I sighed and pointed in the direction of home.

'At least let me share this with you,' I said, nudging the brolly his way.

'Don't worry about me – I'm far too manly for an umbrella. I've got some street cred to maintain.' He winked and set off. I stifled a chuckle and tried to keep up with him.

We didn't speak for a while. I was nervous that I'd already given too much away and so I just waited for him to speak. The closer we got to home the more terrified I became about what would happen when we reached my house. What was he expecting? What was *I* expecting?

Wasn't this the part in all the films where I'd invite him in and we'd have *that* conversation that made everything shift and by the end of the night we'd be irrevocably in love? Maybe that was how it worked in Hollywood, but not so much in Birmingham.

'You gonna let me in on this conversation or is this one

that you need to keep between you and yourself?' he asked, waking me from my thoughts.

'Sorry. I tend to get lost in my own brain at times.'

'So I've noticed.'

Silence again and this time it felt strained. The rain was almost gone by now, leaving a sheen on the ground that reflected the street lamps like the pavement from the 'Billie Jean' video.

'You . . . erm . . . you never told me *your* favourite book,' I said, putting down the umbrella and looping its cord around my wrist.

'Oh, it's *The Count of Monte Cristo*,' he replied without pause.

'Why?'

'It's the ultimate tale of revenge and redemption. It's a classic.'

'Agreed, it is a great book.'

'So, here we reach a predicament. You have read my favourite book but I haven't read yours.'

'You should give *Jane Eyre* a go.'

'Maybe I will.'

The bright beams of a car appeared over the slight hill of the road, the lights shining through the haze of rain and illuminating Theo's face. His skin sparkled with the water that speckled his cheeks like a thousand tiny diamonds and I couldn't help but suddenly be taken back to my days of reading *Twilight*. As the car approached us, Theo took a side step towards me to avoid being sprayed by the puddles that were forming at the kerb. The back of his hand brushed against mine and we both looked down in unison. I snatched my hand back to my side so quickly that I ended up slapping myself on the thigh with a resounding *clap!*

I bit my lip awkwardly and tried to brush it off as some kind of nervous twitch or a muscle spasm or something, but thankfully home was in view.

'This is me,' I said, pointing up at the house I'd lived in my whole life.

'Nice,' he said with a nod and I knew that he was waiting for me to say something, to invite him inside or give him my number or do anything that would imply that I wanted to see him again.

'Well, thanks again for the drink.' I held out my hand and waited for him to shake it.

'You're welcome.' His fingers closed around mine and I felt a tingling all the way down to the soles of my feet. I shook his hand twice and then made to pull away, but his fingers tightened around mine. 'Yesterday, when I brought your purse back to the shop and we went to the park, you said something and it's been bugging me ever since I heard it.'

'What?' I asked, my voice struggling to stay steady with the electricity pulsing through me.

'You said to me that you weren't a nice person and you weren't much to look at and I just wanted to tell you that what you said was complete and utter bollocks.' His face was completely straight. There was no playful twist of his lips, no jokey retort waiting in his throat, but the gleam of disappointment lingered in his eyes. I looked down at the ground, unable to endure the fluttering feeling inside my chest.

'Erm, thank you,' I replied as his thumb brushed over the backs of my fingers before his hand fell away.

'Goodbye, Effie.' He cast me one last smile and turned away. I reached for the umbrella and was about to call after him when I noticed the twenty-pound price sticker on the bottom of the handle.

'Hey, Theo?' He stopped abruptly and spun around. 'Yeah?'

'Did you buy this?'

He grimaced at being caught and anxiously rubbed his palms together. 'Yeah.'

I suppressed a smile and held it out to him.

'No, you keep it. Something to remember me by.' He made to leave again and took another step.

'Theo?'

'Yeah?' He spun around again, the hopefulness still in his eyes.

'I'm cooking myself dinner tomorrow night. If you want to join me, you can. But it's not a date!' I tried to hide the smile from my voice but I knew I'd failed. 'Seven thirty?'

He looked down at his shoes and I think I might have even seen him blush a little. 'That would be nice.'

'Tomorrow then.'

'Tomorrow.'

# Chapter Five

The sodium lights of Bobby's corner shop flickered aggressively above me as I picked out which wine I'd be drinking tonight. I looked at the top shelf and panned across, trying to find one that I hadn't tried before. I got to the third from the end before I found one and I took the neck in my hand.

'Here again, Matilda?' I squirmed at the use of my first name, but Bobby always gave me a discount and so I let it slide with him.

'Yeah, Mum's had a tough week,' I replied.

Okay, I know that this one small fact would easily put me in the running for shittiest daughter award, but letting Bobby believe that my mother was the one with the drinking problem, and not me, was one of the small ways I stopped myself from feeling like shit. Mum never came in here anyway and so there was really no harm done.

'Send her my best.' Bobby said that every time. I never did though.

I pushed the bottle into my handbag and began walking home. The sky was starting to darken as I turned onto my road, the bottle banging against my ribs with every step. I'd spent the entire day stressing over tonight and I'd been almost useless at work because every spare moment was used trying to talk myself out of it. I kept telling myself that I could always text him and tell him that I was ill or that I'd changed my mind. But every time I took my phone out and went to text him, I would think about the way he held on to my hand and what he'd said as he held it and every time, I'd put the phone back in my pocket and begin the stress all over again.

I continued down my road and walked past the pub, The Flustered Duck. It was one of those pubs that was always open and never empty. It always had at least one grey-haired, bulbous-nosed man sat at the bar, nursing a pint of bitter and despondently staring into the foam of his drink, while his wife sat on the stool beside him, sipping at a half of whatever he'd had. I looked in through the window at the early evening crowd gathered on the beer-stained floorboards. Inside there were darts being thrown, relationships being made, beer being spilled, shifts being worked and lives being lived.

I turned away and walked home.

I didn't know people who went to pubs and even if I did, they wouldn't invite me.

I'd never been a social drinker anyway. I was more of a lying in bed whilst crying kind of drinker. You know, the healthy kind.

Breathe in . . . and breathe out. In . . . and out.

I sat on my bed with my legs crossed and my hands resting on my knees, copying the pose of every meditator I'd ever seen on TV. I opened one eye and squinted down at the mindfulness book that Arthur had thrown my way and read the next step: *Observe the moment.*

What the hell did that mean?

Was I supposed to look around and breathe in my surroundings? Because there is only so much one can take from a cold, untidy room.

I looked down at the next step: *Let your judgements fall away.*

Judgements on what?

Urg, this was a waste of time.

*Be kind to your mind as it wanders.*

Okay, that's it. I've had it with this crap. I shut the book and flung it to the floor, shutting my eyes and just trying to block everything out.

The sound of the odd car drifting past or the noise of our cat, Elliot, as he yowled to be let in, floated into my ears; I ignored them.

I tried not to think about how Theo would be here in an hour and a half. I tried not to think of the way he flexed his sharply angled jaw or the strong column of his neck and what might lie further down, below that neck.

My mind began to wander, drifting to places that made my ears turn red and my heartbeat quicken.

The door flew open, smacking against the wall and making the bed quiver. I opened my eyes and frowned at the destroyer of my calm. Surprise, surprise it was my mother. She'd had a haircut. Her usually shoulder-length umber hair now sat in a trendy asymmetric bob around her square-jawed face. I knew she was waiting for me to mention it. I would make a point of not doing so.

'Something wrong with your hands?' I asked sharply.

'No, dear. Why?' she replied as she allowed Elliot to saunter past her. He climbed on top of a pile of clothes, causing it to topple over and cascade across the floor.

'Oh, so you *can* knock then. I could have been changing.'

'Oh, Effie, I've seen it all before.' She chuckled.

'Not recently!'

Joy rolled her eyes and began tidying, picking things up and putting them in places where I'd never find them. 'It doesn't matter if I see your nunny – I did make it after all.'

'This is how serial killers are made, you know.' I groaned, the last of the calm seeping from me as if it had never been there in the first place.

'Me and your father are out tonight at Julie and Jeff's.'

'I know, you've told me a bazillion times.' I lay back on the bed and stared up at the ceiling and the criss-crossing strings of fairy lights that wobbled like a spider's web thick with prey.

'Will you be drinking tonight?' she asked, a hint of disapproval in her voice.

Of course I was drinking tonight; I drank every night.

'Maybe.' She looked at me from under her lashes. She knew that *maybe* always meant *yes.* 'I've got someone coming round for dinner, by the way.'

'Kate?' she asked hopefully.

'No, not Kate,' I spat, the memory of her heinously happy face making my neck tense.

'That's very sad. She's such a lovely girl and you two barely see each other anymore.'

'Yeah, it's a crying shame.' My voice was monotone.

She turned to me with wide eyes. 'Go on then, who's coming? Is it a boy?'

She shuffled over and perched on the mattress, sitting on my foot as she did. I tutted and yanked it from under her. I had ummed and ahhed about telling her about Theo, because I knew the fallout that would come from giving her false hope. But I'd never been able to keep anything from her. We talked about everything and fought about everything, constantly smashing our heads together like two rams at the top of a mountain.

'What's he like?' she asked, her lips pulled wide in a Cheshire cat grin.

'Strange.' It was the first word that came to mind when I thought of him and his overfamiliarity.

'No different from the rest you've brought home then. What does he look like?'

'Blond, pretty, about six foot tall with cheekbones that should come with a hazard warning,' I replied as I sat up and let myself slump into a comfortable position, shoulders hunched forward, back arched. 'I think he's older than me, maybe thirty, and he's got these big wide shoulders.' I held out my hands to simulate the breadth of them.

'He sounds dishy.' I squirmed at her choice of words. 'He's just a friend then?'

I turned to her with a frown settling on my brow. 'Why? Don't you think I could pull a pretty boy with wide shoulders?'

'Well, it's just that the lads you've brought here haven't exactly been catwalk ready, have they?' She quirked an eyebrow and laughed through her nose.

'Well, for your information, *he* asked *me* out.' I stood, the anger in my stomach making it impossible to stay seated.

'He did? That's wonderful. It's about time you settled down. I was married at your age and your Grandma Prudy was married when she was fifteen.'

'I told him no.' I enjoyed the look of anger that defused her smile. 'He's coming for dinner, yes. But it's not a date.'

She slapped me hard across the knee and stood. 'Effie,

when a handsome chap asks you on a date, you say yes. You'll never walk down the aisle at this rate.'

'Oh yeah, 'cause that's my only aim in life. And why does everyone keep telling me to grab this date as if I'm never going to be asked on one ever again? I'm not desperate!' I scoffed and picked up an orange jumper from my floordrobe, pulling off my shirt and tugging on the creased knitwear.

Joy sighed and rolled her eyes. 'Don't you think you should wear something a little, you know, a little more alluring?'

'What like a negligee and stockings? I'll have a quick look for my ball gag – that'll make a nice necklace.' I watched her in the reflection of the mirror as I replenished my eyes with lines of smudged black kohl, her lips pinching as she turned and walked towards the door.

'I don't know how your father and I made you sometimes,' she said as she shut the door, the cat leaving with her.

It's not a date.

I stood in the kitchen beside the oblong table where I'd laid out two placemats and a candle that flickered inside a turquoise crackle glaze bowl. My eyes moved over to the stove where two pans bubbled angrily.

It was almost half seven; he'd be here any minute.

Dinner doesn't mean that it's a date. I told him that it's not a date. So, it's not a date.

I bobbed anxiously on the balls of my feet as I looked at the candle with a feeling of impending doom surrounding me.

Dinner doesn't make it a date, but a candle does.

I pursed my lips and blew out the flame.

But it *is* dark in this corner of the kitchen and we could do with the extra light.

I clicked the lighter and lit the wick once again.

I took a deep breath, trying to summon some of the calm that my mother had destroyed earlier.

I was at home. I was safe. I didn't have to go out into the world and pretend that I felt at ease there and I knew where the knives were, should my theory about him being a stalker actually turn out to be true.

I smoothed down my orange jumper and wondered if Joy had been right. Should I have dressed up more?

It's not a date, so the jumper and the unicorn slippers are fine. I'd just have to make sure I kicked off the slippers before he arrived.

I heard the shuffling of my mother's feet and a moment later she appeared in the doorway.

'Smells like you've put too much garlic in there.' She walked straight over to the stove, took the spoon out and tasted it before dipping the spoon back into the sauce.

'Thanks, I knew it was missing some mother's saliva. That'll give it the bitterness that I was aiming for,' I said, throwing her a dirty look as she smiled a self-satisfied smile. 'Aren't you meant to be going soon?' Not so subtly willing her out of the house.

She licked her lips and took a jar of oregano from the shelf, sprinkling some into the pan without caring that she was pissing me off. In fact, she probably did it for that very reason.

We had a strange relationship, my mother and I, one that often straddled the line between banter and bullying. We pushed and pulled at each other to see who would give first, but she'd raised me and I'd learned from the best. She had this ability to hold a grudge longer than anyone I'd ever known. She blamed this trait on being a Scorpio, once scorned never forgiven, but I knew it was just because she had too much pride. I don't know exactly when it shifted from a normal parent-child relationship to something resembling a verbal trial by combat, but I think it must have been when I hit my teens and I started having a mind of my own. It wasn't like I went off the rails or anything, I just started to develop my own opinions and ideas and that simply wouldn't do.

'Can you not?' I budged her away from the pan with my shoulder and scooped out the oregano, washing it down the sink. 'Did it at least taste good?' I asked, feeling her eyes boring holes into me from behind.

'Well, it's not how I would have made it.'

I took a deep breath and exhaled slowly, loudly.

I heard the ominous *ding-dong* of the doorbell and felt my stomach turn into an anvil as I held my breath and contemplated pretending I wasn't home.

I wasn't ready for this.

I wasn't ready for company.

I couldn't even remember the last time someone ate with me. My parents and I never ate together, because I refused to indulge Joy's two-week health food fads that often smelled like soil and tasted like it too.

I felt sick and turned around to tell her not to answer it, but she was already gone. I heard the sound of her sheepskin slippers shuffling towards the door.

I looked at the candle again and panicked.

Lose the candle. Abort. Abort!

I blew out the flame again as I heard the door open and Theo's voice floated into the house.

But now he'd smell the smoke and know that it had been lit. He'd wonder why I'd blown it out and then he'd know that I still wasn't sure about what tonight really meant.

I panicked, lighting the candle again and shoving the lighter into a plant pot as Theo appeared in the doorway, wine in hand. His eyes moved from the pans on the stove to the laid table beside me with a furrowed brow and I knew that the candle was a mistake.

'You know you didn't have to go to all this trouble and dress up all sexy for me,' he said with that aggravating smile. 'How did you know that I had a thing for unicorns?'

He looked down at my feet and I suddenly remembered that I'd failed to take off my slippers.

'Well, I didn't want to make too much of an effort. This isn't a date after all and you're nothing but an amateur stalker, so why dress up nice?'

'Amateur?' He mocked outrage. 'You offend me, madam! I think the pending restraining order and the shrine in my airing cupboard show that I am overly qualified to stalk you.'

'See, this is where a normal person would ask you to leave,' I said, reaching down and taking the wine from his hand. 'Is this for me?' I didn't wait for him to answer. 'Yes? Good.'

I opened the bottle and handed him a generous glass before taking two large gulps of my own.

'Good job you're not normal then.' He held out his glass and called a toast. 'To new friends and this non-date.'

Joy came into the kitchen and took Theo's coat, a flustered smile on her face when her hands brushed his arms. She looked at me with eyes so wide I feared they might fall out and dangle against her cheeks.

'I never expected our Effie to bring a boy like you home for dinner,' Joy began, and I turned to the bubbling pans, brow tightened. Did she have to flirt with everyone?

Literally any man she came across who was slightly

good-looking was subjected to a bout of her wanton behaviour. The guy at the petrol station, the milkman – she'd even flirted with my maths teacher at parents' evening once. You'd think that my dad would be as annoyed with this habit as I was, but I honestly think he was just relieved to be left alone for a minute or two whenever it happened.

'Why is that, Mrs Heaton?' he asked politely, sending her his winning smile. She exhaled dreamily and I was glad that it wasn't just me that it affected.

'You're . . . well, you're gorgeous. Not like the last few she's brought home.' She sneered. 'By the look of the last one you'd have thought she'd picked him up from outside Broadmoor. He had a silly name didn't he . . . Bugs, that was it.'

'His name was Thomas.' I sighed with exasperation.

'Your father told me his name was Bugs.'

'Dad called him that because of his ears. He said he looked like Bugs Bunny.' I urged her with my mind to get the hell out of the kitchen.

'Oh yes, that's right, Thomas. Great big Dumbo ears he had. He could have flown away with those things hanging at either side of his face. But he didn't need them did he – ran away from you fast enough with just his feet.'

'Thanks, Mum. Aren't you leaving?' I took a swig of wine so large that I had trouble swallowing it.

'It seems a shame to leave when there's such a handsome young man in my kitchen.' Joy smiled at Theo once again and I could almost hear his discomfort. 'She *is* capable of being pleasant you know, just give her long enough and you'll see it.'

'I'll be sure to keep an eye out.' He sipped his wine and she disappeared, taking one last look at him before she closed the door and left us in peace.

'She seems . . . nice?' He wandered over to the pans and peered inside, his chest pressing against my back and making me tense. 'What are you making me then, Chef?'

'Spaghetti and meatballs,' I replied, a sudden worry coming into my brain. 'Shit!'

'*Language!*' I heard my mother shout through the closed door.

'You're not vegetarian, are you?'

He shook his head.

'Good, because there are many pieces of cow in this meal,' I replied with relief.

'Mmmm, pieces of cow, my favourite,' he said. I glanced behind me at the candle, which I tried to extinguish with my mind as it flickered in its bowl, mocking me.

I searched for something to say, but, in the end, I just carried on stirring the food, not knowing what else to do.

'So, I've met your mum; what about your dad, does he live with you?'

'Yeah, he's probably upstairs putting on his century-old "going out" shoes as we speak. He's very strange and very northern. He pretty much lives in the computer room upstairs. He runs an eBay shop.'

He wandered over to a family photo that hung on the wall and studied my ten-year-old face.

'You were a cute kid – nothing's changed there,' he said, moving on and sitting down at the table. I slopped the food into two bowls and plonked them down in front of him.

'That sounds like date talk to me – and what is this?' I asked, sitting down opposite him and topping up my glass.

'Most definitely not a date.' He leaned forward, that

stupid grin still making him look like a fangirl's wet dream, and tucked into the mess I'd put in front of him.

'Precisely.'

It was around the third time I topped up my glass that I began to feel myself going fuzzy at the edges, and the more I drank, the better Theo looked. He was especially lovely tonight in his blue plaid shirt that matched his eyes completely, but no matter how lovely he was, I still couldn't tear my mind away from the candle that glinted beside me like an annoying fly.

He'd looked at the candle at least twice now.

He spoke as he ate his food, the conversation coming easily to him, but I didn't hear a word he said.

What the hell was I thinking, putting out a candle for a boy I had known for barely ten minutes?

Did I actually like him and I'd just not realised it?

'. . . and then the hooker and I took the frying pan full of blancmange and left it as an offering to Willem Dafoe, in hopes that he'd bless our autumn harvest,' he said, instantly breaking my internal chastisement to ask myself if I'd just heard what I thought I had.

'I'm sorry, what?'

'Great, you're listening now.' He looked up and smiled with his eyes, but I could see that he was a little annoyed that I'd clearly been ignoring him. 'It's the candle, isn't it?'

'Huh?' I replied too quickly. 'Candle, what candle?'

'The candle, you keep staring at it.'

'I know I do. Just ignore it.'

'Why? *You* clearly can't.' He pushed his empty bowl to the side and I felt grateful that he'd managed to force the food down. It wasn't my finest culinary moment.

'I just didn't want you to think that the candle made it a date.'

'Of course I wouldn't think that,' he replied. 'Literally all you've said since I arrived is that this is not a date.'

'Sorry. I just . . . I'm not used to dating or even just used to other people anymore,' I said, drinking the wine down like it was an antidote to my social awkwardness. 'I'm thinking of taking a vow of celibacy.'

'Well,' he sighed, a smile creeping onto his lips, causing dimples to form in his cheeks, 'I can't lie, I'm a little disappointed that you seem so reluctant to give me a shot. But if you change your mind then by all means show me to your room and let's get down to it. But I must warn you, you may not be able to look your parents in the eye tomorrow. I'm a bit of a screamer.'

A laugh caught me by surprise and a fine spray of red wine flew from my nostrils, dappling the tablecloth with pink dots. The wine trickled down my chin and chest before bleeding into the knit of my jumper. I went to dab it away with the tablecloth, managing to upturn my bowl into my lap, tomato sauce seeping into my groin.

'You see? This is what I mean. I'm not fit to be around other humans, let alone date them,' I said with embarrassment.

'Good job this isn't a date then.'

Theo washed up as he prattled on about something to do with a boxing match he'd watched the night before and how he'd lost twenty quid betting on it. I only half listened as I wondered what the hell he was doing here. Didn't he have someone more interesting to talk to, someone prettier to hang around with? Did he have literally nothing else to do?

'Hey, is that a treehouse?' he asked, staring out the window.

'It is,' I said, my tongue feeling too large in my mouth, like the words couldn't fit.

'Do you still use it?'

'Nope,' I replied, finishing the last of my wine and looking around for the next bottle.

'Why not?' He sounded disappointed.

'Because I had to grow up sometime.'

'Effie, no one is too old for a treehouse. Let's go, it'll be fun.'

I stood and walked to the window, my legs feeling a little wine-softened. I joined him by the sink and looked down the path at the simple wooden structure sitting in the tree at the end of the garden. 'I don't even know if it's still structurally sound. We could both end up in A&E,' I replied. I turned to look at him and found him already looking at me; his eyes soft and a gentle smile on his lips. It caught me off guard and made me inhale sharply. He didn't miss this and his smile grew.

'Come on, Effie. Live a little.' He nudged me with his elbow and dried his hands on a tea towel. 'I can't think of anyone I'd rather take a trip to A&E with.'

# Chapter Six

I went and changed my jeans for a pair with less tomato sauce in the crotch, before grabbing more wine and a blanket and heading out into the dark garden. We pulled our jackets tight against the cold and walked down the long path to the tall sycamore that stood at the end, housing my childhood treehouse in its branches.

'You didn't tell me you had your own place,' he said with mock awe in his voice as he looked up into the tree.

I was drunk by now and I could feel my guard slipping, letting the weirdness come through. 'I moved in when I was five with my, then, husband. He's a famous fireman. I don't know if you know him – his name's Sam.'

'It rings a bell, yeah.' He chuckled.

'He got custody of the kids though, after my stint in rehab for playdough abuse.'

'I haven't had a good hit of playdough in years.' He closed his eyes and breathed in deeply through his nose with feigned desperation.

'I'd offer to score you some, but I've been clean for six months now.' I smiled.

Arthur often let me babble and joke, without ever paying much mind to what I was saying, but Theo was different; he was listening and, more miraculous still, laughing.

The ladder was old and eroded but looked like it could hold us and so, with rapidly evaporating common sense, we climbed the ten foot of rusted metal to a platform that hadn't held any weight since I'd spent the night after prom sleeping in there because I forgot my keys. I clutched our second bottle of wine in my hand – we didn't bother with the glasses this time – and Theo tucked the blanket under his arm as he climbed.

I hadn't been up in so long that I'd almost forgotten what it looked like. There were three walls and an open front that looked back towards the house and a roof that hung with dusty curtains of spider webs and dried old leaves.

This had been my sanctuary, *my* place, until I'd felt like I was too old for such things and let it fall into ruin.

The entirety of the floor, walls and ceiling had been painted with whatever had interested me at the varying stages of adolescence I'd been in at the time. Flowers and stars (from my naïve girly phase), skulls and emo lyrics (from my dark days), dragons silhouetted against the sky I'd painted on the ceiling and mermaids that combed their hair on the rocks (this had never been a phase; dragons and mermaids were a way of life not a passing fancy).

'What's this?' he asked as he approached the back wall, shielding his face from the dust-covered dreamcatcher that I'd made from old straws and string. He ran his hand over the flaking paint, a flurry of paint chips falling like snow from his fingers.

I walked over and felt a swell of warmth as I remembered my fifteen-year-old self sitting here with Kate, wishing our lives away.

'My friend Kate and I made a list of the ten things we wanted to do before we finished school.' Seven of the missions had been crossed out in dripping red paint when they'd been completed.

The list had been pretty generic: *Travel the world* (that one had been left unchecked, for me anyway – unless annually disappointing holidays to Cornwall counted); *Lose virginity* (that one had been crossed out so violently after my tryst with Marcus Roe that it could barely be read); and *Stay friends forever* (HA!).

The third one that remained unchecked was *Marry Chad Michael Murray* (neither of us had managed that one. I know, it's shocking that we hadn't managed to seduce a Noughties TV heartthrob, but at least we'd had high hopes for ourselves).

'Were these your wishes or Kate's?' he asked as we took a seat on the floor and dangled our legs down into the void below.

'Mostly Kate's – a couple were mine and they seem to be the ones that aren't checked off.'

'Why didn't you do yours?' he asked, unscrewing the wine and handing it to me.

'Well,' I began, sipping the wine mid-sentence, 'travelling the world takes money, which I don't have, and Chad never called back.'

'Where did you want to travel?'

'Anywhere. I've never been out of the UK.'

'What, never?'

I nodded and took another glug. 'The curse of having

68

parents with a static caravan in St Ives means that you tend to never go anywhere else.'

I drank again. I'd already drunk too much; I was beginning to get head rush. That didn't mean I was going to stop though.

'You still friends with this Kate?' he asked.

'That's difficult to answer. She used to be my best friend. Now she's just . . .' I didn't quite know how to describe it. 'We still meet up, once every few months, but I'm pretty sure she dislikes me as much as I dislike her.'

'Why do you still bother?' he asked, his shoulder brushing against mine and making me lose my train of thought for a moment.

'Kate is the person who walks around with her head in the clouds and everything she wants falls into her path, and I am the friend who walks behind her, firmly caught in her shadow, who picks up the things that Kate tosses aside. I even dated her ex once and then it turned out that he'd only gone out with me to get close with Kate again.' I looked down at my hands when I remembered Timothy Prescott and how he'd only ever touched me when Kate was around. I told Theo about her promotion and Canada and the dazzling engagement ring. 'She's stunningly beautiful and has this amazing job where she gets to wear one of those floaty blouses and handles meetings. She has this perfect fiancé who looks like he's fallen out of a fragrance advert and she's so blissfully happy that it makes you feel nauseous to even be near her.'

He picked up the bottle of wine, sipped and handed it to me.

'So, are those the things you want?' he asked.

I turned to look at him. His breath left his mouth in wisps of white. Only then did I realise how cold it was. 'I don't know.'

'If I'm following what you're saying, then you want the high-powered office job and the boyfriend who looks like David Gandy? Would those things make you happy?'

I scoffed. 'I couldn't think of anything worse than sitting in an office all day and there's nothing wrong with David Gandy, but he doesn't do it for me.'

'Then why are you jealous?'

'Because she has everything she ever wanted and she hasn't earned it. She's landed on her feet time and time again while I fell on my face beside her.' I thought back to the time when I'd applied for all those jobs after uni and the string of rejections I'd got in return, while Kate landed the first job she interviewed for and then rubbed her success in my face. I hadn't known what I wanted to do, other than write, so I'd just applied for anything and everything. But all the jobs just seemed like a distraction from what I was really meant to be doing: writing the next bestseller. 'She's happy and I'm not and that's why I hate her.' I surprised myself with what I said. Did I truly hate her? Love and hatred were so often confused.

He leaned a little closer and I studied his mouth. The idea of kissing him crossed my mind; his lips were parted and they dithered slightly in the cold November air. The wine had made me feel soft, like a cat on a hot day, and I could feel myself warming to him.

'Show me,' he said, his breath dancing over my face in hot waves. 'If she's so spectacular, then show me.'

'I don't want to,' I replied.

'Why not?'

'Because then you'll want her; everyone wants Kate.'

He frowned. 'You've made it clear that *you* don't want me, so why should you care?'

I turned to him and looked into those ocean blue eyes. 'Because I'm selfish and I don't want to give her the satisfaction of stealing you away.' I stuttered slightly. He looked down at my lips and with a mild sense of panic I lay my head on his shoulder.

'But you don't like me,' he said, the warmth of his voice carrying his smile to my ears.

'You're not so bad, as stalkers go.' We both breathed a laugh and then I closed my eyes. 'When Kate and I were seventeen, I decided that I had a crush on Jonathan Yardley. He was one of those artsy types with a floppy fringe that stuck in his eyes and his hands were always smeared in charcoal from his lunchtimes spent in the art room. I'd told Kate about how I felt; I was stupid enough to trust her back then. Cut to three weeks later and Kate and Jonathan were the school's hottest new couple. I wanted to cut all her hair off with the blunted art room scissors, but all I did was nod and say, "I never really liked him that much anyway". I don't know why I carried on talking to her after that.'

'That was a cruel thing for her to do.' The smile was gone from his voice. 'Were you heartbroken?'

'No.' I sighed the word and lifted my head to look at him. 'I've never been in love. I think it's always turned to shit before I had the chance to love anyone.'

'Well, let me see what I can do about that,' he said, projecting charm. I let out a chortle. It was dirty and loud with the odd snort thrown in. 'Kate could be the most dazzlingly beautiful human that has ever been created, but that doesn't mean that everyone would fancy her. Beauty is subjective.' I felt his arm shift and a moment later it was around my shoulders, the warmth of it startling in the icy air.

'When you see her, you'll realise how much of a stupid thing you've just said.' I closed my eyes and breathed in the smell that rose from his jacket. My head spun with the intoxication of it.

We sat in a comfortable silence for a while as we finished the second bottle of wine, my alcohol-numbed brain was slowing now and unable to feel the same level of distrust towards Theo that I had done before. He was lying back on the floor, his eyes studying the painted ceiling above with the flashlight of his phone. The blanket lay over his legs, stopping at his stomach where his shirt lifted, showing a sandy dusting of hair around his navel. I almost reached out and touched it with my freezing fingers but I managed to stop myself and instead lay back beside him.

'Why do you like me? *I* don't even like me,' I said, resting my head on the dusty floorboards, pulling my half of the blanket over my legs and closing my eyes; the room barrelled around me and I quickly opened them again before I ended up being sick.

'Do I need to have a reason? I just do.' We turned our heads to face each other at the same time and something crackled in the air between our too close faces.

'But you don't know anything about me.'

'And *you* know nothing about *me*. Let's change that. Tell me something.' His eyes felt like spotlights on my skin; warm and revealing everything in their bright light.

'Like what?' I asked.

'What's your favourite colour?'

'Green. What about you?'

'Orange,' he replied with a nod to my tangerine-coloured jumper.

'Favourite film?'

'Don't have one.'

'Well, that's just ridiculous. What about music? Favourite band?'

'The Rosehipsters,' I said, expecting him to not know the indie-folk duo from across the pond.

'I like them too,' he said. I raised my eyebrows in surprise.

'*You* like The Rosehipsters? I took you for more of a David Guetta type.'

'What year do you think this is, 2010?' he said with a slight chuckle. 'Believe it or not, other people like non-mainstream music too.' He sighed before asking his next question. 'What did you want to be when you grew up?'

'A writer. I still do.' The words slipped from my mouth before I could remember to lie. 'I don't usually tell people, like it's a dirty secret or something.'

'Why don't you tell people?'

'Because then I have to tell them that my novel was rejected, again and again, and it hurts me to say it.' I shook away the tightness in my chest and turned back to him. 'What about you?'

'That's easy. I wanted to be David Bowie.'

'You have to answer seriously; those are the rules,' I slurred.

'I *am* being serious. I saw a documentary about him when I was about eight. He was the coolest person I'd ever seen in my life and I wanted to *be* him. I took guitar lessons, dyed my hair, I even wore blue eyeshadow for a few weeks after I first saw the 'Life on Mars' video. But alas, there could only ever be one Bowie.'

'I bet you rocked that eyeshadow.'

'You know I did.'

I rolled my head to look up at the ceiling and heaved a contented breath. 'I know what you're doing, by the way.'

'And what is that?'

'You've let me get drunk so that I'll open up to you.' I looked back at him, a strand of hair falling over my face. I held up a finger and prodded him in his chest. 'I'm onto you.'

Good God, his chest was firm. It made me want to run my hands over it, but I restrained myself. I still had that much self-control at least.

He shuffled my way and reached out a hand, brushing the hair from my face and tucking it behind my ear. My breath caught in my throat.

'Why are you so unhappy, Effie?' he asked.

I felt moisture behind my eyes and the sudden urge to cry built up in my forehead. I *was* unhappy, dreadfully so, and no one had asked me about it until now.

'Because I'm doing nothing with my life,' I replied, my voice thick with drunken emotion. 'I always thought that I'd be someone, that I'd do something important or meaningful, but the truth of it is that I've barely done a thing. I go to work, I come home, I drink too much, I fight with my mum and then I fall asleep and start again the next day. My phone goes weeks without ringing sometimes. I think that if I lived alone and I died, then I'd be one of those corpses that turns into soup on the carpet before anyone noticed that I was missing.'

I paused for breath and wiped away the tear that trickled down the side of my face and into my ear. 'I know whose fault it is. It's those coming-of-age movies where a bunch of young people go on a road trip and watch the sunrise and discover who they are. They do things that they'll remember for the rest of their lives and grow as people in the process. Well, my age has already come. It's been and gone and I've never done anything like that.'

'What would you do if you could?' he asked, his brow furrowed and his eyes reflecting my own sadness.

'Everything,' I replied. 'I want to travel and eat weird new foods in weird new countries. I want to get lost on purpose. Not in a *Cast Away*, becoming best friends with a bloodied volleyball kind of lost, but just to get away from everything.' I turned and let his image fill my eyes. 'Do you know who you are, Theo?' I asked, searching his eyes for the truth. 'Do you know the person you are? Because I have no idea who I am.'

'I think I do, but then people never stop changing so can you ever really know who you are?'

I rolled my head to the side and looked at the list that sat upside down in my eyes. 'I changed who I was to fit in with Kate and her cronies. I went to see bands I didn't like, films I didn't want to see. I drank drinks I didn't like the taste of, all for them. I turned myself into a chameleon and echoed what everyone else did and said and liked. In the process I became a nothing person and Kate left me anyway.' I realised that I wasn't just tearing up now, I was fully crying.

'Why did you do all of that?'

'I just wanted to keep my friend. I think I always thought it was just a phase and she'd come back to me when she was ready.' I blubbered.

Oh my God, I was such a loser. Not only had I spat wine all over myself and started wearing my dinner, but now I was full-on ugly crying in front of him.

'I'm sorry, I shouldn't have said anything.' I wiped the tears from my eyes and sat up, head rush making my vision blacken at the edges. I wondered if I might pass out, but then I felt his hand on my shoulder and it brought me back to earth.

'You're not a nothing person, Effie.'

\*    \*    \*

It was past eleven when we climbed down from the treehouse, our bones aching with the cold. Theo descended the ladder first and waited at the bottom, ready to catch me if I missed a rung and fell. My head spun like a top as I grappled for the ladder with untrustworthy hands. The ladder seemed to carry on forever, the ground never growing any closer, until I felt Theo's hands tighten around my waist and lower me to the grass below. I felt his hands on the skin of my hips. They were cold.

I turned around; he was closer than I'd expected him to be.

'Thanks.' I cleared my throat and attempted to look sober.

'You're welcome,' he said with eyes fixed on mine, the approximation of a smile on his lips.

The air zinged between us as we looked at each other, wondering who would turn away first, but neither of us did.

Theo exhaled quietly. He was nervous.

My palms were sweaty, my knees were weak, my limbs were heavy. Wasn't there a song in there somewhere? Wasn't there a line about spaghetti too? Oh God! Why had I drunk so much? I could barely stand without swaying from side to side and now I'd have to somehow navigate this newly formed sexual tension with diminished motor skills and a churning stomach.

I wanted to kiss him and by the look in his eye he was up for it too.

I swallowed the lump in my throat and leaned forward, closing the gap between us and looking up into his face. As far as I could see, he didn't want to run away like Daz had; he didn't want to bail after deciding he liked Kate more, but then he hadn't seen Kate yet.

He looked down at me and swallowed and I knew that he was going to kiss me.

My body suddenly went into a state of panic. My lips were chapped and dry and hadn't been kissed in months, maybe even years. They weren't ready; *I* wasn't ready. I began to squirm, my chest heaving quick and irregular breaths as Theo drew closer, his arm wrapping around my back and pulling my chest to his. His heart beat against mine, his breath filling my mouth as his lips drew to within inches of mine.

This wasn't right. I'd only just met him and only a few hours ago I'd suspected him of being a stalker. I couldn't let him kiss me.

My eyes widened as his closed and I craned my neck away from him. He paused, looking unsure, and then moved to kiss me again. I darted out of the way and placed my hands on his chest.

He frowned, pressed his lips together into a line, then said, 'Have I read this wrong?'

'I don't know. What did you think it said?' I asked, my voice high-pitched and nervous.

'Well, you were looking at me with those *kiss me* eyes and you moved towards me and I just thought you wanted me to do it.'

'Maybe I did, then maybe I panicked about it and decided that I didn't. Can't a girl change her mind?' My neck was beginning to ache, my body in such a strange position that I had no idea how I was holding it for so long.

'I'm sorry, I didn't mean to pressure you into anything. I just thought you wanted me to—'

'It's my fault, really.' I pushed against his chest and he let me go.

He awkwardly scratched the back of his neck. 'I should go,' he said, tapping an Uber order into his phone.

'I'm sorry, I have no idea what I'm doing anymore.'

I rubbed my hands over my face, my palms coming away with black smears over them and I realised that I must have just smeared make-up everywhere. I literally couldn't have been more of a train wreck.

'Oh, look,' he said, staring down at his black phone screen. 'My Uber's here.'

We both knew he was lying.

He turned and walked back into the house, not stopping until he was standing outside the front door. My parents weren't home yet. The house was dark and the driveway vacant of the ugly-ass car we shared.

'It's not here, Theo. Please, come back inside. I'm sorry I made it weird.' I almost begged.

'You didn't make it weird. It was fine. I'll see you soon.' He stepped back towards the door, going in for a kiss on the cheek and then thinking twice about it and going for a handshake.

I shook his hand; his skin was just the right ratio of softness to roughness.

Nice one, Eff, you could be having those soft-rough hands sliding all over your back by now. But no, you had to make things weird and so all you get is a handshake.

'See you soon,' I said as he turned and walked out into the dark street.

I lay in bed, staring at the ceiling and rueing the day I ever slithered from my mother's womb. My brain was obsessively combing through every word I'd said to Theo, every movement I'd made, the tears I'd cried. Every so often my face would pucker like I'd just bitten into a lemon and I'd slap my palm to my forehead over and over until the wave of embarrassment was gone.

He'd said, '*I'll see you soon.*' But when was soon? Would soon ever come or would he run for the hills like all the others before him?

I could just imagine what my mother would say when she realised that the 'gorgeous' Theo wasn't coming back. It made me want to crawl under the blankets and die of suffocation or, even better, like in those sci-fi films where someone cancels out their own timeline, just cease to exist at all.

I flicked on my phone. He hadn't texted.

I opened up the chat and began typing before realising that I had no idea what to say and deleting it all.

I'd wanted him to kiss me. Why hadn't I let him?

That kiss could have been so much more than two near strangers acting on impulse and two pairs of lips pressing together.

It could have been fireworks and thumping hearts and hands in hair, but all it had turned out to be was a whole lot of awkward and a lie about an Uber.

# Chapter Seven

I'd wanted a cat for as long as I could remember, but for some reason or other, that childhood wish had never come to be. Cut to a year after uni when a beautiful, yet slightly dishevelled, tomcat turned up in the back garden.

He was perfect, with black and white tuxedo fur and a black patch that looked like a Salvador Dalí moustache below his nose. He came every day, sitting for hours on the patchy lawn and meowing loudly at the French doors when he saw people moving around inside. After a month, I took him to the vets to have his microchip scanned, but he didn't have one and after he refused to leave, I claimed him for my own. But like most good things, he turned out to be too good to be true.

I named him Elliot, for no reason other than it suited him, and he fitted in perfectly; for a while. It was about three weeks later that I realised Elliot was the best con artist I'd ever seen. He was cute, yes, but the vengeful little bastard had a thing for attacking people's ankles as they slept at night; creeping into their room soundlessly and sliding under the covers like a furry ninja before embedding his talons into the first bits of flesh he found. Not only that, but he waited until he was fully accepted as a member of the family before letting his habit of peeing in people's shoes be known. He would perch atop the shoe, boot or slipper and pee, soundlessly, into the footwear and then wait nearby until someone naïvely pushed their foot in, watching with glee as they flailed around in disgust. In addition to this, he was a serial cheater, meandering off to his other family four doors down when he got bored at home.

'*Typical man*,' Joy would say when he didn't come home.

When I woke, head heavy with the remnants of the two bottles of Châteauneuf-du-Pape we'd drunk last night, Elliot was back. He lay on my chest and stared down into my eyes like a judgemental deity, as if he too knew how much of a fool I'd made of myself the night before.

'Don't look at me like that,' I said, my voice coming out all croaky. 'It wasn't that bad.'

Elliot looked at me with unblinking yellow eyes and he seemed to say, '*It was a car crash, my dear. The boy will never come back.*'

'He *will* be back,' I said unsurely.

I rolled out of bed, flinging Elliot to the floor as I threw back the duvet; he landed gracefully on all fours and sauntered off onto the landing. I groaned and walked over to the mirror where I proceeded to wipe last night's smudged eyeliner from my ashen cheeks using only saliva and the ends of my fingers.

I stopped and looked hard at my reflection, hating everything I saw with unbridled passion.

'Why didn't you just let him kiss you?' I asked my reflection, my infuriating face just staring back at me. I looked down at my phone, which was charging on the floor, and pressed the home button with my toe.

No messages.

I'd blown it.

My thumb hovered over the 'new message' icon and paused as it waited for confirmation from my brain. I opened the new message and went to type, but what the hell would I say? 'Sorry I'm such a train wreck. Come back, I'm begging you!' I made a deep guttural sound in my throat and locked my phone.

I looked around the room and saw last night's clothes strewn across the pile of clothes from the day before that. I'd never been an organised person, but in the last few years all concept of tidiness had seemed to erase from my brain.

The small amount of space that I had was mostly taken up by one large wardrobe, the doors of which hung open constantly, the clothes spilling from it like wardrobe vomit and cascading down onto the floor. There lay a path that weaved its way through the landscape of hills and valleys of detritus, which led safely to the door, but that was about all that could be seen of the pine-effect laminate beneath.

I checked my phone again, making sure that it wasn't on silent, and wondered if I should text him.

The sound of knuckles rapping on wood came and a moment later the door, already ajar, swung open to reveal my mother's beaming face.

'Good morning!' she trilled, instantly picking up a shirt from the floor and folding it. She looked around for some-where to place the neatly folded square of fabric then, when none could be found, placed it on top of a pile.

'Your father and I are very impressed with that Theo.'

'Dad didn't even meet him,' I said as I peeled off my PJs

and stood there casually in a sports bra and a pair of knickers with sagging elastic.

'He saw him on the security camera,' she said, continuing in vain to tidy.

'That's not creepy at all,' I replied. My dad had had a camera fitted in the back garden a few months ago. He told people that it was because his storage shed got burglarised, but what he didn't tell them was that the two culprits were a pair of footloose squirrels. I don't know why he thought a security camera would deter the squirrels, but then, many of the things he did confused me, so I didn't ask. 'Well, don't get too excited because he probably won't be back.'

'Why? What did you do?' Joy ceased her tidying and turned to me, her eyes wide.

'Mother, the sooner you learn that I am unlovable, the easier it will be for you to come to terms with the fact that I will die a spinster.' I looked back at myself in the mirror and scowled at myself.

Joy tutted and turned back to her tidying. 'Well, that's a damn shame. He was a very lovely boy *and* he's doing well for himself by the looks of that bottle of wine he brought here last night.'

'Yes, Mother. I know! But I made a fool of myself and then he ran off, so that's the end of that.' I felt a pressure build behind my eyes and knew that a headache would soon follow.

I know I'd never been pleasant, but was I really so unbearable that they all had to run away in the end? I mean, I couldn't be that bad. Even Hitler had a girlfriend.

I picked a pair of jeans up off the floor and attempted to put them on, I managed to get them just above my knees before I accepted defeat and threw the too-small trousers back onto the pile.

'Do I have a big bum?' I asked, cupping my cheeks in front of the full-length mirror and frowning at them over my shoulder.

'No,' Joy said after a long pause. 'Your bottom is normally sized. Your thighs, on the other hand, are larger than average.'

'Oh gee, thanks.' I quickly picked up a pair of baggy patchwork trousers – from my lingering hippy phase – and hid my newly embarrassing legs.

'What did I say now?' Joy flung her arms out into the air at either side.

'Well, it's fine to have a big ass. Kim Kardashian, Beyoncé, Jennifer Lopez, they all have big butts and they're all fucking gorgeous.'

'Language!' Joy said, although I knew that she was now cottoning on to the fact that the swearing was here to stay. 'What's wrong with sturdy thighs?'

'Sturdy?!' I gasped as if *sturdy* was a dirty word. 'Sir Mix-a-Lot's song didn't go "I like sturdy thighs and I cannot lie"!'

'You're being ridiculous.'

'Am I?'

'Effie, your thighs are big and your hips are wide, but that doesn't mean you're not beautiful.'

I didn't answer and instead pulled on a long baggy jumper that covered most of my body down to the knees, before storming past my mother and causing one of the piles of folded clothes to fall back into the gap she had just made; trying to restore order to the chaotic room.

I clunked down the stairs loudly, my frustration echoing through the hall for all to hear, when the doorbell rang. I rolled my eyes and walked to the door, letting it swing open to reveal the 'piss off' face that I was wearing. But as soon as my eyes adjusted to the glare of sun behind the visitor, my heart leapt and I suddenly felt sick.

'Hey, I brought bagels.' Theo stepped inside and thrust a paper bag into my face.

'What are you doing here?'

'I told you. I brought bagels.' He wandered into the kitchen as I closed the door and jogged after him. He pulled one from the bag as he walked to the counter and took a bite.

'Do you think you could give me a little warning next time? I don't have any make-up on.'

'You look great, love the trousers,' he said around a mouthful of cold untoasted onion bagel.

'Shut up,' I replied, tearing the bagel from his teeth, slicing it in half and jamming it into the toaster. 'I could have had one of my many, *many* lovers over or I could have been meeting with my coven.'

'I would have been happy to join in with both of those things.' He smiled with bread-spackled teeth and some of my frustration disappeared. 'Anyway, now that you're finished moaning, I have big plans for us today.'

'What plans?' I asked as Joy trotted into the kitchen with a beaming smile on her face.

'Is that Theo I hear?' She threw her arms around him like an old friend. 'Effie said that you were gone for good, but it would seem she hasn't scared you away just yet.' She winked at me over Theo's shoulder and took a deep inhalation of his shirt. I shuddered and turned back to the toaster.

'Try as she might, I'm difficult to scare,' he said, letting go of Joy and taking a seat at the table as if he'd been visiting for years.

'What do you have planned for today then?' Joy asked, sitting opposite and pouring him some coffee.

I *had* planned on spending the day sitting in various places around the house, waiting for an appropriate time to open the wine, but Theo had put rather a dent in those plans.

'Effie and I have an appointment,' he said with a smile. The toaster popped and I grabbed the slices, burning my fingers in the process, before tossing them onto a plate.

'We do?' I asked, grabbing the butter from the fridge and handing it to him. 'What appointment is this?'

'It's a surprise.' He winked and smeared an inordinate amount of butter onto his breakfast before crunching through his bagel with ravenous teeth.

I dressed quickly into tight jeans that made my thighs look proportionate to the rest of my body and a hoodie, before pulling my knotted hair up into a ponytail and sliding my feet into a pair of pumps.

I leaned into the mirror and looked my reflection in the eye.

'You will not be a dickhead today, Effie. You will be nice to him and if he tries to kiss you, you will let him. Understand?' I nodded at myself and took a breath. 'You're lucky he even came back at all.'

When I resurfaced downstairs, I found Joy leaning across the table, her chin resting in her palm and her eyes smiling softly at Theo as he told her about his job.

'It sounds fascinating.' She sighed dreamily.

Theo turned and smiled when he saw me standing in the doorway. It felt strange to have someone smile when they saw me; they usually just grimaced or simply left the room. He swiped the crumbs from his chest and stood, much to the disappointment of my mother.

'You ready?' he asked.

I nodded and before Joy could invite herself along, we were out of the house and into Theo's car. It was one of those fancy red Nissans that isn't quite a 4x4; I tried to pull a Shania Twain and act unimpressed.

The seats were comfy and it smelled like coffee and new plastic.

He turned his key in the ignition and sent me a smile.

'So, where are we going?' I asked.

'I told you, it's a surprise.'

Theo plugged his phone into the tatty AUX cable dangling by the gearstick and a few seconds later I heard The Rosehipsters trilling from the speakers.

I looked over at him and smiled. There was no sense of awkwardness in him today, as if our almost kiss had never happened.

'I'm sorry about last night,' I said quietly. 'I drank a bit too much.'

'I think we both did,' he said, with a dismissive swipe of his hand. 'Ready for an adventure?'

When Theo had said the word *adventure* I'd pictured skydiving and assault courses. I thought maybe we'd be trekking through a forest or exploring some caves. But when the ugly grey building came into view and he parked by the doors, I felt my sense of adventure evaporate.

'The gym?' I asked with curled lips.

'Not just a normal gym, a boxing gym,' Theo said smugly.

'Boxing?' My mouth hung open with dismay. 'What part of you was under the impression that I did any kind of physical exercise, let alone exercise that could result in me losing a tooth?'

'Have you ever even been to a gym before?' he asked as

87

he pulled two bags from the boot of his car and slammed the lid shut.

'Of course not! The mere suggestion is an insult.' I exhaled with angst, crossed my arms and pushed out my hip.

'Maybe you'll enjoy it and become a gym buff. Weren't you just complaining on the way here about your mum saying you had . . . what did you call them . . . robust thighs?'

'Sturdy!' I corrected him, my face turning beetroot red. Theo walked towards the entrance and tapped the electronic key over his shoulder. The car doors clicked shut.

'Well, *I'm* going in and I have the keys, so you can wait out here in the cold or you can come inside,' he called as he walked through the sliding doors.

The inside of the gym was everything I had feared and more. The walls were painted with varying shades of grey and blue and the air was thick with the scent of sweat and aggression.

I walked embarrassingly close to him through the fluorescently lit hall, using him as a shield against the sweat-soaked men beating the crap out of each other in the ring. A skinny man, with a sagging purple bruise around his left eye and with his lips pulled tight over a black gum shield, ducked the punch of a guy who was built like Michelangelo's *David* and who moved with such speed and grace that it looked like he'd choreographed the whole thing in advance.

'What were you saying last night?' Theo asked, his stride confident; he'd been here before.

When I didn't reply he answered for me. 'You said that you hadn't done anything new in years. Well, here's something new.'

'When I said that, I meant things like tobogganing or strawberry daiquiris, not . . . this.'

We walked further to where several punching bags hung from the ceiling. The sounds of grunting and impact as many fists *thwacked* against them echoed through the hall. Every person here seemed to have an injury of some kind, a bruise or a cut or, in one man's case, a bright stream of blood that trickled down from his cheek and pooled in his collarbone.

'I'm not dressed for this and I'd rather my blood stays inside my body.'

'I have some things you can wear,' he said as he came to a stop outside the changing rooms.

'You have spare women's gym clothes hanging around your house?'

'Yeah, well the women's ones just make my arse look better.'

'Ha!' I said, straight-faced and without an ounce of humour. 'But really, whose are they?'

'Oh my God, Effie,' he said with rolling eyes. 'Just go and put them on and meet me back here.' He thrust the bag into my hands and went through the door to the men's changing room.

A brightly lit vending machine hummed menacingly beside me as the bag of a stranger's clothing lay heavily in my clammy hands.

I sucked in a mouthful of sweat-sodden air and forced myself forward.

The changing room was my nightmare made true: a large room with no corners to hide in, with a series of benches running down the centre and no cubicles. From the moment I'd stepped inside I was greeted by several naked women, all of whom seemed to have no reservations about stripping completely nude in public. There were no rippling thighs, no flailing bingo wings or jiggling stomachs. I did not fit in here. I quickly averted my eyes and scurried to a bench where

I dropped the bag and sat down on the sticky wooden slats. Then I remembered the naked, sweaty women and quickly leapt up, trying to ignore the way my jeans peeled away from the bench as I stood.

The room smelled of self-confidence and cotton-fresh deodorant spray. It clung to the inside of my throat like a mouthful of chalk dust and made me want to dry-heave.

I steadied my breaths and unzipped the bag, finding inside a freshly laundered bundle of clothing. I pulled them out, causing something to clatter to the ground as I looked through them. My hands were shaking. I needed to calm down.

I turned to pick up whatever had fallen, but one of the naked women had already done it and now stood beside me, boobs exposed and arm outstretched, holding a purple water bottle.

'You dropped this, Jenny,' the naked woman said with a smile. Her lip was split and it glistened with whatever clear substance it was oozing. I couldn't help myself from looking down at her breasts while I spoke, staring into her rose petal nipples like they were eyes.

'Thank you,' I said, taking the bottle and wondering why the woman had called me Jenny. I turned the water bottle over in my hand and saw the name scrawled in eroded Sharpie on the side.

Who was Jenny and why would Theo have her clothes at his house?

I pushed the bottle back into the bag and picked up the clothing before going into the toilets and changing in there. I pulled on a pair of purple spandex trousers, which groaned as they stretched over my 'sturdy' thighs, a racerback vest and a zip-up hoodie that smelled of expensive perfume and femininity.

Maybe Jenny had been a roommate or maybe she was his ex and he was dressing me up in her clothes like some sort of reverse Norman Bates.

I went back out into the changing room and stuffed my clothes into the bag before pushing it into a locker and walking back out into the gym with the confidence of a newborn lamb.

'I thought you might have decided to walk home.' Theo's voice came from where he leaned against the vending machine. He wandered over to me and flashed that smile. It was still hard to believe that anyone could be continuously happy to see me. He must have very low standards.

He wore a baggy vest and shorts that stopped just above his toned calves. He looked like he fitted in here, like he'd fit in anywhere.

I looked down at myself. The clothing was figure-hugging, leaving little to the imagination. I folded my arms over my stomach and bounced fretfully on the balls of my feet. He placed a hand on my shoulder and squeezed. 'Come on, Balboa, I've got us a corner over here.'

I shuffled along after him, looking more out of place than a goth at a fairy princess party, as he led me to the mats. He threw over a pair of gloves and began strapping pads to his hands.

'You want me to hit you?' I asked with fear in my voice. 'I struggle getting through a single day without injuring myself in some way. Yesterday, I got nail varnish remover in my eye. God knows what will happen if I actually try to hurt you.'

'I've only known you for four days and, in that time, I've seen that you are pretty much the angriest person I've ever met,' he said.

91

I opened my mouth to protest, but realised he was completely right and so I just shut up instead. 'You're angry about your date with Daz. You're angry with Kate and your parents and your lack of money.' He reeled them off like a shopping list. 'You're angry about me bringing you here and you're angry that I've pointed out that you're angry. So, you're going to hit me as hard as you can, and as many times as you can, and we'll see what we can do about that anger.'

'I don't know what to do,' I said meekly.

He showed me how to stand, left foot forward, fists raised in front of my face, and then he braced himself for impact.

'This is so stupid, Theo,' I moaned, looking over my shoulder at the other people in the room.

'Why? Are you a pacifist now?'

'I just think this is stupid and I don't want to do it.' I flung my hands to my sides like a petulant child.

'Why not? Because someone might see you?' He looked behind me at the others I'd been glancing at. 'Those two in the ring aren't looking at you. *That* woman isn't looking at you.' He looked back at me and raised his pads. 'No one is looking at you.' It wasn't meant as an insult, but it felt like one. 'But I am. I'm looking at you, Matilda.'

'Don't call me that, please,' I replied, my teeth on edge.

'Why, Matilda? Does it make you angry . . . Matilda?' He spat my name like an insult and it annoyed me more than I wished it did. 'What would Kate think if she saw you here refusing to participate? Would she be disappointed in you?'

'I don't give a shit what Kate would think about me,' I spat back and flexed my fists inside their gloves.

'Kate wouldn't have time to come here anyway, what with her promotion and the move to Canada.' I knew what he was doing, but what annoyed me the most was that it was working, perfectly. 'Anyway, she probably couldn't haul herself out of her front door, not with that diamond ring weighing her down.'

The edges of my vision began to fuzz as the centre of Theo's right hand pad took the shape of Kate's face and without warning I lunged at it, my glove singing as it hit the plastic coating.

'Good!' Theo smiled. 'Do it again.'

I didn't need to be riled up this time as punch after punch landed against Theo's pad. There was barely a second between blows as I pounded the anger from my fists, the tension in my neck easing with each *thwack!*

The sweat began pouring from my skin, my hair gluing to the side of my face as I attacked him.

I thought of Kate and everything she had and yet did not deserve. I thought of Daz and all of the others before him who had made me feel small, insignificant, ugly. I thought of my mother, bending me until I snapped and then saying that *I* was the argumentative one. I thought of my father, forever upstairs with his computer, tucked away from the real world and concerning himself only with 'Buy It Now' offers and customer feedback. I thought of Elliot and the pair of perfectly good Dr Martens that he'd sullied only two days previously with his annoying peeing habit.

I thought of Theo and how much I wanted to be like other girls. I wanted to feel confident enough to let him touch me, kiss me. I wanted to flirt easily and make easy conversation without having to overthink everything I said for fear of making a fool of myself. I wanted to stop lying to myself. I wanted him, but something in me wouldn't let myself admit it.

And I thought of the manuscript, lying unwanted and

unread in the dust and the pile of rejection letters beside it. And the people who hadn't been able to see how much I wanted them to want what I'd written. And as all of those thoughts fell into my head, the punches came and didn't stop coming. My anger was my fuel and it was plentiful. I felt a tear drop onto my cheek and roll into the crease of my nose. I swiped at it with my glove, smearing it over my face.

'Effie, are you okay?' Theo's voice came but it couldn't pierce my bubble of fury; my gloves slammed into the pads, drumming out a rhythm of rage. The tears were coming faster now, blurring my vision, streaming down my cheeks. 'Effie, stop!'

'You wanted this!' I shouted, not caring that I'd roused the attention of almost everyone in the room. 'You wanted me to feel this.'

'Effie!' He dropped his hands and stepped forward just as my fist sailed through the air, caught his jaw on the right-hand side and sent him reeling. He stumbled backwards, the shock of the impact etched into his face, before he fell down onto the mat beneath him.

The trance was broken, the haze of anger disappearing instantly as Theo passed out and lay limply on the ground.

# Chapter Eight

I paced anxiously for a few minutes until Theo woke. A South African gym instructor knelt beside him with an ice pack pressed against his darkening jaw. When Theo finally opened his eyes, I knelt down and hovered over him.

'You all right there, mate?' the instructor said in his thick accent. 'The first thing I ever taught you was to never step into a punch undefended. You clearly didn't listen because you dropped like a sack of shit.'

'Mason?' Theo groaned, his eyes lolling in their sockets. 'It's been a while.'

'It has. You could withstand more of a beating when I saw you last. You've gotten soft,' he replied.

Theo tried to laugh, but it came out like a puff of air.

'You know each other?' I asked, my voice faltering as I spoke.

'I used to be Theo's personal trainer about ten years back,' Mason said, helping Theo sit up.

'Effie.' Theo smiled my way. 'You were better at that than I thought you'd be.'

'I'll say,' Mason said with a grin. 'If you ever want to train properly, then let me know.' He took a card from his pocket and handed it to me. I smiled and then looked back down at Theo whose jaw was swelling and turning purple before my eyes.

'I'm so sorry,' I said. I lifted my hand and gently touched the unharmed skin around the bruise; I really had done a number on him. I felt the roughness of his stubbly cheek as my fingers moved over the dappling of multicoloured bristles. My eyes lingered on his lips, which were slightly parted. I suddenly realised what I was doing and quickly stopped.

'Is my modelling career over?' he asked. 'Will I ever be on the cover of *Vogue* again? Tell me straight, I can take it.'

'I think you'll be just fine,' I replied with a smile. It felt strange; my face wasn't used to it.

Theo sat with the ice on his face while various gym-goers congratulated me.

'Thank you for this,' I said as he flexed his jaw and sized up the damage. 'It really did help and I kind of enjoyed it.'

'I'm sure *you* did.' His voice muffled by his partially paralysed mouth.

'Do you forgive me?'

He looked over at me with what I thought was a smile, but couldn't quite tell, and nodded.

I decided that Theo shouldn't drive and so I took the keys with the intention of driving back to his and then getting a taxi home. As we were walking towards the exit, Mason jogged up to say goodbye.

Theo leaned on me, his head still a little muddled from my *Rocky* re-enactment. I liked the way his body felt as it pressed against mine, the solidity of him, the scent of cologne and coffee that drifted over from his jacket.

'I was meaning to ask how you're doing these days?' Mason said, his sweating brow glistening in the midday light.

'I'm doing okay thanks, mate.' Theo straightened up and cast Mason a look as if there was something he didn't want to talk about. 'Much better, thanks for asking. Listen, I've been wanting to get back into this for a while. I feel like it's time to make a comeback. I'll be in touch soon.'

'I'll track you down if you don't,' Mason replied before jogging back inside.

When we were back in the car, Theo leaned his head against the window and sighed.

'Why did you quit?' I asked, settling into the driver's seat and turning the key. The engine hummed almost soundlessly as I adjusted the seat.

He didn't look at me when he answered. 'You know . . . life.'

'What happened?'

'Can we just go home, please? I need some paracetamol.'

I parked Theo's car outside his apartment building and helped him to the door. I knew the building well. It was one of those architect's fantasies that had popped up on the city skyline over the past ten years and resembled more of an art piece than a building.

It looked like it had been designed by the inventor of Tetris and inside the lobby, everything sparkled like mirrors.

A doorman greeted us and then looked at Theo with concern. 'Mr Morgan, are you all right?'

'Yes, thank you, Ben. I've got myself a feisty one here.' Theo jerked his head in my direction before stepping into the lift. I paused in the lobby, unsure if he wanted me to go with him or not. 'You coming?' he asked, pulling a key from his pocket and sliding it into the wall. I jumped inside as he turned the key beneath a plaque bearing the number eighteen and the doors closed.

'Don't tell me you have one of those apartments where the lift opens straight up into the hallway.' I stared with wide, excited eyes.

Several seconds later the doors slid apart and, sure enough, I found myself stepping out into a hallway that looked like it had been ripped from the pages of an interior design magazine.

'What the hell?' I pushed through a door into a massive open-plan living room with one of those trendy kitchens that's right there in the room. 'What the hell were you doing coming to my house when you live here?' The room was painted an on-trend grey with exposed brick in places and copper light fittings. The sofas were plush, grey and gorgeous and there were books lining the walls and artistically fanned magazines on the aged oak coffee table.

It didn't look lived in; it was too perfect.

'Dad owns three identical apartments in this building and he lets me live here while I work for him in Birmingham. The downside is that I have to keep it spotless and I get kicked out every so often so that people can come and view it.'

'I'll take it,' I said as I threw myself backwards into an armchair that was so soft it almost swallowed me whole. 'I'll give him everything I have, which is around thirty pounds – that'll cover it right?'

Theo chuckled and grabbed two cans of Coke from the fridge. He pressed one to his jaw and then handed the other to me. I cracked it open and gulped down half the can before feeling the urge to burp and placing it on the table. I managed to style out the burp as a cough and regained my composure.

'Your dad's in property then?' I asked.

'Kind of,' Theo replied as he sat down on the sofa. 'It's an investment really. His main business is antiques. He buys them and I help him sell them on at auctions.'

The apartment had very few personal items, except the books and a pile of games beside a console.

I looked down at the stranger's trousers that still groaned around my thighs and wondered if I should ask or not.

It was far too early for me to be getting jealous.

'Who's Jenny?' The question burst from my mouth before I could stop it and hung in the silence for a few seconds longer than was comfortable. I saw the question hit him, like the name *Jenny* had physical weight that landed on him like a boulder. 'I found her name on some of the things in the bag.'

His eyelids flickered and his breaths deepened.

I wished I hadn't asked.

'You don't have to answer,' I said shifting awkwardly in the armchair.

'No, it's okay.' He sat forward and wrung his hands. 'Jenny was my girlfriend all through school and then she was my fiancée.'

'And what is she now?' I asked.

'Nothing,' he replied. 'She broke it off.'

'Why?' The thought of anyone passing up the opportunity of being with Theo was too ludicrous to contemplate. Then I remembered how hard I'd tried to push him away and realised I was a hypocrite.

His nose wrinkled as if he'd smelled something bad and he shook his head. 'That doesn't matter.'

'Okay,' I said.

Neither of us spoke for what could only have been a few seconds, but felt like a year or two, until Theo stood and walked over to the kitchen counter.

'I almost forgot, what with the head trauma and all, I have something for you.' He rummaged through some papers and pulled out a tatty sheet with scribbled words all over it.

He handed it to me and sat back down as I attempted to read what he'd written. His handwriting was atrocious.

'What is this?' I asked.

'Last night, when I finally got you drunk enough to open up, you started telling me about all of the things you felt you'd missed out on. So, when I was lying in bed, thinking it over, I remembered that list that you and Kate made and I thought we could make another one.'

My brain managed to decipher his scrawls and when I got used to it I saw that there were thirteen missions.

'I thought that we could do some of those things together, if you wanted,' he said. I looked up and wondered if he was being serious.

'A list? What, do you think we're in a romcom or something?'

'Of course not, because then you'd actually be pleasant.' He smiled and all trace of his earlier discomfort was gone. 'What's your other option: sit in your room and get drunk?'

'Sounds good to me,' I said, putting the list down on the table and leaning back.

'Effie.' He sat forward and took my hand, every muscle in my body tensed. 'I know that you and the wine are great friends, but it can only make you happy for so long.' He picked up the list and put it in my hand. 'Have you even read it?'

I rolled my eyes and read:

1. *See a sunrise*

2. *See a live band* I *actually want to see*

3. *Leave a mark*

4. *Fall in love*

5. *Move out*

6. *Do something unexpected and outside comfort zone*

7. *Eat something new and strange*

8. *Get lost on purpose*

9. *Do something that matters*

10. *Stop holding grudges*

11. *Achieve a dream*

12. *Learn to love myself*

13. *Earn more money*

'They're all things you said your life was missing, so why not do them? We can already cross out number six, because we just did it.'

My eyes moved to the bruise that was still developing on

his jaw and a feeling of achievement filled my chest. He'd been right. I had enjoyed myself, even if I had knocked him out in the process.

'Okay,' I said.

His smile widened until he grimaced and held a hand to his jaw.


'Here,' Theo said pushing a tenner into my pocket and walking me towards the lift door. 'For your taxi.' I sent him a grateful smile and moved towards the lift, my legs aching from sitting in an odd position on the sofa and watching TV while Theo nursed his jaw with a bag of frozen sweetcorn.

'Thank you for today,' I said with a new-found lightness in my stride. 'I had fun, apart from the GBH.'

He leaned casually on the wall, his eyes heavy with tiredness and the ache of his injury.

'Again, I'm sorry for your jaw.'

'Don't worry about it,' he said as he jabbed the button beside the door and the sound of the lift springing to life hummed through the chrome doors.

This was the moment; I could feel it. If he tried now, it would be perfect. I stayed close to him and urged him to kiss me.

My heart thumped in my ears as he stepped forward and his face moved towards mine. My breath caught and I quickly moistened my lips as he drew so close that I could smell the Coke on his breath.

But at the last second his head moved to the side and I realised that all I was getting was a hug. His hands spread wide over my back, pulling me towards him, and I found myself curving into him. Something pleasant fizzed in my chest and a flush of heat burned my cheeks.

'Listen, I've got to go out of town tomorrow.' He drew back, his hand remaining on my shoulder, the weight of it – half on the fabric of my borrowed shirt, half on bare skin – made me unable to focus on anything else. 'I'll be a day or two, but don't think that that excuses you from carrying on with the list.'

'Where are you going?' I asked with furrowed brows and a hollow feeling opening up inside of me.

'I'm going to a house clearance to get some new pieces to sell on. It's at this big old manor house out in the country-side so there'll be tons of snotty-nosed toffs milling around and trying to outbid us.' The clunk of the lift signalled its arrival and the doors slid open.

'Okay. I'll see you then.' I stepped inside the lift and it felt like that scene in the cartoon movie where the old woman leaves the baby fox in the forest. I was the fox, pathetic and unable to take care of myself and Theo was the old woman, leaving me to die in the wilderness.

'See you,' he said and began to walk away.

Just before the doors closed completely, he turned and called, 'Hey! I'll miss you.'

I smiled and felt the blood rush to my head. 'No, you won't.'

I caught a flash of that dangerous smile before the doors came between us and the image stayed burned into my eyes until I reached the ground floor.

I sat in the kitchen with a half-empty bottle on the table. My feet rested on the seat of the chair beside me as I leaned back casually against the wall. He'd said that he'd miss me. Was that true or had it just been for effect? Either way it had brought a smile to my face.

The sound of some indie cover of a Tom Petty song played from my phone and I swayed my wine glass from side to side, in time with the beat. Something had changed today, between Theo and me. Yesterday he had been somewhat of an annoyance to me, whereas now, whenever I thought of him I became slightly lightheaded. Was this normal or was I coming down with something?

At that moment, Joy walked into the room and opened the fridge. She took out several items and placed them on the work surface. I often envied my dad's ability to avoid all human contact in a house this small. He was so good at moving around unseen that I could go full days without seeing him, yet I knew from the sound of tapping computer keys through the door that he was there.

'Are you going to eat anything today or have you evolved to sustain yourself purely on Echo Falls, darling?' Joy said disparagingly.

'It's made of grapes isn't it?' I replied. 'I'm just making sure I get my five-a-day.' Why should I bother with food when wine had all the calories I needed?

'Well, I'm making chicken and leek pie if you decide to soak up some of that alcohol with actual food.' She sighed. She clearly had a problem with my heightened levels of alcoholism, but I lived to displease her and so I took another swig.

'Isn't it compulsory for writers to drink?' I asked. 'Edgar Allan Poe, F. Scott Fitzgerald, Ernest Hemingway, they were all alcoholics and they did all right for themselves, didn't they?'

Joy spun around and cocked an eyebrow. 'Yes, my dear, but you also need to put actual pen to paper to give your alcoholism some semblance of legitimacy.'

She had a point; I had to give her that one. Although her comment was rather outdated. It wasn't so much pen-to-paper as fingertip-to-keyboard these days. But whichever way you said it, I still wasn't doing it. There's nothing like a pile of rejection letters to make you never want to write again.

I bristled in lieu of a response and took another swig.

I was an irritant in my mother's life, like a particularly abrasive hand soap. We rarely had a conversation that wasn't a battle of some kind. The prize was never known, the stakes uncertain, yet we still battled.

I don't know if it was the same between fathers and sons as it was between mothers and daughters, the battle to establish hierarchy, the war for head of the house. I suppose it is, especially if said son or daughter is grown and ready to run their own house but can't leave their parents due to monetary restrictions. One day, I assumed that it would come down to some sort of gladiatorial battle in the garden, a fight to the death when one of us would prevail and gain control over the pressure cooker and the TV remote.

'How was your day, Mother? Get a lot of menial chores done?' I asked, the wine making me brave.

'Actually, I did. Thank you. But you'd know nothing about that, would you?' she said with a razor-sharp tongue and I wished I hadn't drunk as much wine; that way I'd have been able to come up with a good retort.

# Chapter Nine

I stared at my lunch with curious revulsion.

Theo had left me in charge of myself, a task that I had never boasted to be an expert at, and had told me to carry on with the list. I didn't feel too confident about finding a band to see alone or getting up before my shift to view the sunrise. And so, on my lunch break, I'd gone to the nearest supermarket and picked up the weirdest food that I could find in an attempt to tick off mission number seven: *Eat something new and strange.*

I'd pondered over the unfamiliar items of the World Foods aisle and had almost opted for a jar of kimchi – fermented cabbage that looked like stringy hangover vomit – but as I wandered past the fish counter, my eye had been caught by something so strange that I'd hastily shoved the kimchi onto a shelf and bought that instead.

When I'd returned to the shop, I'd found Amy riffling through the magazine section.

Amy is this girl who comes by every other week to pick up the latest copy of *Writer's Inspiration* magazine. She's a writer who tells everyone about her plot, her characters, her worries and doubts. It's quite exasperating really, but she's a customer so I'm forced to smile and nod while she prattles on about scene structure.

I'd made a terrible error of judgement when I'd told her that I was also a writer, or playing at being one anyway. Ever since then she'd latched on to me like I was some kind of role model or something. I couldn't think of anyone worse for her to look up to, unless being a drunken failure was what she aspired to be.

Her eyes seemed to gleam with the sparkle of a mind always gathering information for the next paragraph, a gleam that I'd lost a long time ago.

She was nineteen and naïve; life hadn't yet rubbed away her sparkling enthusiasm. Her eagerness reminded me of my own, or lack thereof, and every time I saw her keen little elfin face it made me remember just how much I'd given up on my dream.

'How's the book coming?' I asked as I slid her purchase into a paper bag.

'Great. I'm on the second in the trilogy now.'

Oh yeah, I should have said, Amy writes tons.

She's already completed two short novels and is now halfway through a trilogy. She doesn't let the rejections knock her down though; if anything they spur her on to write more.

Her eyes glinted at me from behind her thickly rimmed glasses that suited her so well they just looked like an accessory.

'You still writing?' she asked, her brow creasing as if she pitied me.

'No.' I took her money and sorted her change. 'There's only so many times you can hear that you're not good enough.'

She took her bag and pocketed her change. 'Just remember that George Orwell and Stephen King were both rejected. Everyone has to start somewhere.' She took a mint imperial and popped it into her mouth before leaving with that same irksome skip in her step.

At least that was over and I had a fortnight of peace before she came back and reminded me of the extent to which I'd given up.

I took my lunch to the least frequented section of the shop, the sad little Local History corner. Barely anyone set foot in there and so it was the best place to eat, undisturbed. I made myself comfortable against the shelving and crossed my ankles.

Popping the lid from my 'lunch' caused a vinegary scent to rise from the little polystyrene tub. It smelled like that weird foam that the sea makes sometimes – it wasn't particularly appetising.

The guy at the counter had called it Seafood Salad, but I failed to see where the salad part came into it. All I could see were oil-coated octopus tentacles, white rings of leathery squid and mussels that looked like shrivelled little vaginas.

I took a photo and sent it to Theo. If I was actually going to eat this monstrosity and complete this mission, then I was at least going to have photographic proof.

I placed a tentacle in my mouth and it took all the will I had to chew it. The taste wasn't too bad. The texture, on the other hand, was something I guessed I'd have to acquire a liking for.

I heard Arthur heading down from his flat above, his feet clunking heavily on the creaking stairs. I looked up into the anti-theft mirror and watched as he anxiously paced behind the till, his hands drumming out a rhythm on his thighs.

I was about to shout out to him and ask him what his deal was, but then someone came in through the door and I no longer needed to ask.

Toby stood in the doorway with his old battered grey briefcase in one hand and a paper bag clutched in the other.

I shuffled back and made myself comfortable as I watched them in the convex reflection of the mirror. Watching those two was like the longest-running will-they-won't-they sitcom coupling of all time. It was obvious for all, except the two numpties involved, that they both liked each other and yet neither of them had the nerve to make the first move.

'There are a few things I need to check over with you, before we put this whole issue to bed,' Toby cooed in his soft Scottish tones. 'I brought lunch; you can share it if you like.'

I saw Arthur's blushing smile as he walked out from behind the counter, put up the *Closed for Lunch* sign and joined Toby on the sofa.

I watched them quietly, not really thinking about how creepy I was being. Toby accidentally brushed Arthur's arm and Arthur leaned over and flicked a crumb from Toby's tie. It was all I could do not to giggle with excitement.

Was it finally happening?

Arthur had never wasted time in getting what he wanted, but this charade with Toby predated our friendship. I couldn't work out why he was dancing around the subject when all he needed to do was say one word and Toby would be his.

Maybe that was always the case when you knew that something was going to be special.

I thought of Daz and how willingly I had run to that diner and how I had known from the get-go that he was going to be a tool. Yet I had gone there expecting opposites to attract and sparks to fly, but then an adolescence filled with Taylor

Swift songs and Nicholas Sparks novels had led me to have unrealistic expectations about love. Love was never like it was in the songs or the stories; love was disappointing and painful, but some sadistic side kept hoping that I'd eventually stumble upon the love of my life. My soulmate. My lobster – I mean seahorse. Who knew, Theo could be my blond-haired, blue-eyed seahorse, but when he'd come along, I'd done nothing but try and scare him off, almost breaking my own neck trying to get away when he'd attempted to kiss me. Maybe it was natural – when you could feel a hard fall coming on – to jeopardise your chances or try and talk yourself out of it, just so you wouldn't get hurt when it all inevitably went tits up; like those animals that flee when they sense a natural disaster coming.

Was that what love was – a natural disaster?

They talked about accountancy, but after a while they got waylaid with talk of travelling and days spent in the sun. Toby was telling Arthur about his cousin's house in Prague when I realised that I'd eaten the entire pot of seafood, leaving nothing but a pale yellow swill in the bottom.

I snapped another picture of the empty tub and sent it to Theo.

Mission 7 – complete!

He texted back quickly:

I'm going to trust that you ate that and didn't just chuck it in the bin. XXX

I studied his text for a few minutes, my eyes lingering on the three kisses at the end and wondering if he had really meant to send them or if it was just a force of habit.

I'd been sitting/eavesdropping on Arthur and Toby's date for half an hour when I realised that I could no longer feel my legs. I clambered up as quietly as I could, using the shelves to pull myself higher until I was standing, my legs feeling like they might buckle under me.

I took a tentative step forward and rolled my ankle. I cursed under my breath.

'Effie?' Arthur called and I knew the jig was up.

I stepped into view, the pot of seafood swill clutched in my hand on its way to the bin.

'How long have you been hiding in there?' Toby asked with an inviting smile. Arthur, however, looked incredibly pissed off that I'd crashed his date.

'I know this looks creepy but I promise I wasn't listening,' I lied. 'Just pretend I'm not here.'

I hobbled over to the bin, my legs prickling with pins and needles. I felt my phone buzz in my pocket and reached down to look. It was a photo from Theo of him posing beside a huge taxidermy owl.

What do you think about this for the treehouse? he'd written.

I smiled and replied: I love it. We can put it in the sunroom in the east wing.

I had planned on binning my pot of disgust and then getting out of their hair, but as per usual I didn't quite manage it. As the feeling began to return to my legs, I became aware of a tightness around my ankle. I took a step to relieve it, realising too late that it was the card machine cord and causing everything on the counter to clatter to the floor. I tumbled with the rest of the rubbish and landed face down in the octopus juice, groaning as I felt it seeping into my hair.

'Effie, are you all right?' Toby ran over to the counter and pulled me out of my mess.

I used my sleeve to wipe the gunge from my cheek and turned to see Arthur staring at me with annoyance.

'I'm fine, go back to what you were doing. If the world stopped every time I fell down, then nothing would ever get done.'

'Good God, what is that?' Arthur scrunched up his face and eyed the fish juice that lingered on the floor in an unsavoury puddle.

'It's probably best if you don't know,' I replied as Toby handed me a tissue and I mopped up the viscous liquid.

'I'm going to have to go and find an air freshener. It smells like a hooker's gusset in here,' Arthur said before jogging up into his flat to find something that would overpower the stench.

'I'm not going to wonder how he knows that,' I said, tossing the sullied tissue into the bin and smiling at Toby. I'd always liked him. He was gentle and soft-spoken; a stark contrast to Arthur.

'You know that this accountancy business is only a ruse to get you here, right?' I lowered my voice, watching his reaction as I spoke.

His lips curled, his eyes creasing at the corners.

'Oh, I know. Only someone who knew exactly what they were doing could have made that many perfect mistakes.' He pushed his glasses further up his nose and smiled my way.

'You going to tell him that you know what's going on?'

He leaned in close, as if about to tell a secret, and said, 'And spoil all the fun? Never!'

'Why a person does that to themselves I will never know!' Joy blurted from the safety of the sofa. It was where she always sat, the upholstery faded and sagging from years of scrunching herself up into the same corner. The newly cut angle of her hair brushed against her neck as she spoke.

I still hadn't mentioned her new haircut and I knew it was eating her up inside.

My father had made a rare appearance downstairs and he had managed to stay conscious for all of twenty minutes before dozing off into a blissful slumber; soft snorts sounding from his wide nostrils. His head lolled, his thickly bearded chin bobbing against his chest as he breathed. He was looking old these days. His red hair was slowly turning snowy, his hands beginning to look more and more like my grandad's had as the days went by.

I craned my neck from the armchair in the window to look at the television screen and the person my mother was complaining about. The girl was pretty, in a rock star kind of way, with darkly lined eyes, sultry red vampiric lipstick and from her septum hung a small silver hoop.

'I mean you may as well cart her off to Spain and enrol her in a bull run with that thing hanging out of her nose.'

'I like it,' I said before turning back to the window and staring at the road.

I often found some kind of dark thrill in actively disagreeing with my mother. I would sometimes fully agree with what came out of her mouth and yet I would still say that I disagreed, simply for the pleasure of disagreeing.

'You'd never get that done would you, love?' Joy asked before loudly slurping at the tea in her Michael Bolton tour mug; the sound set my teeth on edge. 'I know you wouldn't. We didn't raise you to poke holes in your face – did we, William?'

My father woke from his reposed position in the reclining chair. He looked around puzzled for a few seconds, agreed with his wife without knowing what he was agreeing with, and then swiftly fell back to sleep.

'I don't know, I think it would suit me,' I said, the pathetic feeling of power making me feel alive for a moment. I would never actually get a septum piercing, for the simple reason that I couldn't pull it off, but hearing the mild terror in my mother's voice was all I had really set out to achieve.

'Well, we'd be very disappointed in you – wouldn't we, William?' Joy raised her voice on his name and, just like before, he was roused, quickly agreed and fell back to sleep.

'How would I ever live with myself?' I muttered into the coarse maroon fabric of the chair. I looked down at my lap and lit up my phone, opening Theo's texts and grinning to myself at the numerous photographs he'd sent me throughout the day. He'd sent one at around three o'clock of him posing in a pith helmet and then another at five of the drive-thru dinner he'd eaten in the car on his way back home. It had been a long time since someone had thought of me enough to send me more than one text per fortnight. I was sure that my phone would soon have a breakdown over its sudden increase in usage. I opened a new message and began typing.

I miss you.

I stared at it for a minute or two, my thumb hovering over the send button.

For a moment I thought that I might send it, but my thumb moved down to the backspace button and deleted it.

'Look at that dress,' Joy said with a maniacal look in her eye. 'Who told her she had the right to show the world those legs?'

I rolled my eyes and wondered if she'd always been this judgemental and I'd just not noticed or if she was slowly ageing into a bitter old bigot.

I looked down, opened the Facebook app on my phone

and began trawling the news feed. There were the obligatory reposted videos – one of a man rescuing a cat with its head stuck in a tin can and one of a lipstick that could withstand eating, drinking, kissing and nuclear weapons. There were a few posts from Arthur's business page about November deals and a number of those infuriating public diary posts, usually by someone on some kind of torturous diet, who saw fit to inform every fucking person in the entire fucking world about their low-calorie, high-protein lunch. I scrolled further and saw a fresh new selection of posts that made my stomach churn.

A picture of a newly built detached house on the outskirts of York came onto the screen. A smiling couple stood before it next to a SOLD sign; a shiny new Vauxhall gleamed in the driveway. I recognised the man in the photo as Andrew Golding. He'd sat behind me in French class and was forever fiddling with the groin of his trousers. I hoped he'd grown out of it by now.

The next post was one from Kate. A photo of her plane ticket to Toronto sat, artistically lit and surrounded by strategically strewn fairy lights, beside a glass of prosecco. The caption read: *'Can't wait to fly out to Canada, eh. #Blessed.'*

I swallowed down my bile – both verbal and physical – and pressed the lock button on my phone. I suddenly felt ashamed and like my skin was too tight. My stomach churned like I'd just eaten an out-of-date prawn and all I wanted to do was vomit it back up.

What was I doing with my life, sitting in a cat-hair-clad armchair, picking at my too-long toenails and gawping at other people's successes? Where the fuck were my successes? Surely the laws of probability would bring at least a mild victory to me soon.

My phone buzzed, making me jump, and I saw a message from Kate open up on the screen. My smile disappeared.

The text read:

Hey guys. As you all know, I'm moving to Toronto for a few months for an incredible job opportunity and Callum is throwing me a going away party. You're all invited so dress up in your best clobber and get yourself to ours on Saturday at six. K xxx

I locked my phone and pushed it down between the arm of the chair and the cushion. I couldn't think of anything worse than going to a party to celebrate everything that Kate had somehow managed to achieve. I had nothing to brag about, nothing to be proud of. All of my pride had languished and died long ago and so, the thought of stepping into a room of sparkling, Gucci-clad overachievers was not something I relished.

I wondered what Kate was doing right now.

Probably bathing in rose petals, her beautiful fiancé between her legs and her lips pressed to the rim of a flute filled with champagne more expensive than the shitty car that I shared with my parents. My chin rested on the back of the chair as I watched Elliot groom himself lewdly on the driveway. He looked up at me, his stare boring into me like drills into my soul.

*'I'll tell you what she's not doing,'* Elliot's yellow eyes seemed to say, *'she's not sat with her parents sending almost text messages and watching her cat lick his own balls.'*

# Chapter Ten

A powdery cascade of dust fluttered down from the top shelf and into my lungs as I rearranged the Romantic Fiction section atop a teetering stool. I spluttered the dust mites from my windpipe and wiped the cover of a book on which a couple embraced before a setting sun. The quoted review read, 'A romance for the ages.' I scoffed and read the blurb before shoving it back between Cecelia Ahern and Jojo Moyes.

I tried not to think about the characters that lay unread beneath my bed. I'd created them, breathed life into them. I'd rejoiced when they prospered and cried when they died, as if I, the author, had no control over them.

I loved them like they were my children and I'd sent them out into the world to flourish, to grow, to be loved by people everywhere; but they had only returned ruined and rejected.

I hopped down to the ground, felt a burning pain in the balls of my feet and told myself never to do that again.

Jumping is for young people, Effie.

'Romance is done. Does the True Crime section still need

doing too? I think I need a little murder and espionage to get rid of this sickening lovey-dovey feeling I have inside of me,' I said as I slumped down onto the sofa beside Arthur. When he didn't answer I turned to him with a frown and found him staring off into the depths of the shop with vacant eyes. 'Arthur, you okay?'

I prodded his shoulder with my index finger, the haze of deep thought evaporating.

'Huh?' He turned to me and noted the duster in my hand. 'Oh, thanks. I've been meaning to do that for a few days now.'

'I know, but you've been far too busy making fake mistakes on your tax forms to fit in any dusting.' I rolled my eyes and leaned my head on his shoulder. It was bonier than Theo's. 'Just ask him out, Arthur. He knows. Everyone knows.'

'He does?'

'He knows,' I repeated, feeling his muscles tense beneath my cheek. 'He knows and he still came anyway, which can only mean one thing.'

'I don't know what's wrong with me.' He sighed and leaned his head on top of mine. 'I've never been like this before. You remember that carpenter who came in to fix the shelves? I had him wined, dined and tooth deep in the pillows before he'd even finished the job.'

'That you did,' I replied, 'but you didn't love the carpenter; you didn't even know his name.'

'Do you love this Theo?' he asked, the sudden change in topic giving me metaphorical whiplash.

'I think I could,' I said, 'given enough time. But you two have had six years. Time's running out to make a move, Arthur.'

There was a pause in the conversation as we both sat in

the silent shop. The street outside was silent with the mid-afternoon lull, as we both drifted into a state of catatonia.

The bell above the door clanged and we both rose an inch or two out of our seats. The duster fell from my hand and a quiet whimper came from Arthur.

'Sorry, is this a bad time? I can come back when you're less run off your feet,' Theo said as he closed the door behind him; his face breaking into a smile when his eyes found me.

I stood up with the full intention of hugging him, but once I was up and staring into his face, I wondered if I should or not. I wanted to. I'd missed him more than was appropriate after knowing him for only a week, but I stopped myself and instead just rose and stood awkwardly beside him.

'Hi,' I said, my voice wispy and fragile like a schoolgirl's. 'I didn't know when you'd be back.'

'Well, here I am after so much not-so-popular demand.' He held out his arms, as if to announce his presence.

Every time I was confronted by Theo after some time apart, I assumed that he would have lost interest or some of that sparkle would have waned, but there it was in the bottom left-hand corner of his eyes.

Arthur leaned over me and said hi before we all slumped back down onto the sofa and melded into its vintage leather comfort. Theo stretched out his arms and yawned. He looked at home in any place, relaxed, at ease and not worrying about what everybody in the room was thinking about him. I envied him in that way; in many ways.

'So, how is the list coming along?' Theo asked.

'I ticked off the weird food one and then kinda ground to a halt,' I said.

'What list is this?' Arthur asked.

'Just some strange new kind of therapy that Theo's forcing me into,' I replied and filled Arthur in on everything.

'You got her to go into a gym?' Arthur asked, aghast.

'I certainly did, the evidence of which is still on my face.' Theo tilted his head to reveal the deep purple bruise that covered his jaw and bled down onto his neck.

'Next thing you'll be telling me that you got her to agree to go to Kate's party.' Arthur said with a laugh.

My heart fell into my stomach. I wasn't even going to mention it to Theo because I knew he'd make me go.

'She conveniently told me nothing about this.' Theo turned to me with judgemental eyes.

'Specifically, so you wouldn't try and talk me into going,' I said, sending Arthur the stink eye.

'Remember number ten on the list, Eff,' he said. 'Stop holding grudges.'

'Ha!' Arthur laughed. 'Good luck with that one.'

That evening, Theo and I sat in the treehouse and shared a margherita pizza from the shop on the corner. We'd popped into the off-licence and he'd bought a can of lemonade while I'd opted for a pre-mixed can of whisky and Coke. 'Life on Mars' played from the speakers of Theo's phone as we devoured the pizza and sang along.

I watched my mother as she washed up at the kitchen sink, her eyes continually glancing up at us.

'I don't mean to alarm you, but I think we're being watched,' I said, looking to Theo and motioning to my mother's prying eyes.

'Yeah, I noticed that too.' He lifted a hand and waved to her, his smile wide. She blushed and waved back.

'I need to get out of this house,' I said with a sigh. 'I would love to be able to do something without having to tell someone what I was doing or where I was going or how long I'd be.'

'Yeah, you could always live on your own like me and go days without actually speaking a word,' he replied.

'I would, but some of us aren't lucky enough to have parents who own property.'

'True. I did get lucky there.' He finished the last piece of pizza and closed the box, lying back and using it as a cheese-scented pillow. I watched him close his eyes and take a deep, lingering breath. His chest rose and fell to the steady beat of the breaths that whooshed from his nose. He was startling to look at, his hair falling down and brushing his lashes, his lips parted and ready to kiss, had I the nerve to lean over and do it. He looked like an effigy, serene.

I don't think I'd ever felt serene.

His fingers drummed against his stomach as the song changed to 'Heroes'.

I turned back to the house, the heat gradually dissipating from my face. The kitchen window was empty now. Clearly Joy had had enough of spying for today.

Elliot sat below on the grass, his tail whipping from side to side as he watched something moving among the blades. The treehouse was almost ten feet off the ground, a long way to fall, but that had never stopped me from hanging my legs over and pushing my luck.

I thought back to when I'd been around ten years old. I'd just had an argument with Kate and I'd lost my temper with my mother, so I'd spent the whole evening crying in the treehouse. I'd sat where I was now, my chubby ten-year-old legs dangling down, and after an hour or two I fell asleep. I woke with a sickening flip of my stomach as I fell down, down onto the grass below, my radius snapping like a breadstick.

At the time, it was the worst pain I'd ever felt, then I grew up and realised that life was a greater pain still. Since that moment, when I had found myself spiralling downwards like Alice into the rabbit hole, I had begun to think a lot about death.

I didn't think about it in any overly serious way, I was just curious. Like, do people who die in their sleep ever know they've died? Did people die instantly when they were decapitated or did their brains carry on working long enough for them to see their own bleeding neck stem?

'If you died right now, like if a lump of space rock fell and skewered you to this treehouse floor, what would you want your epitaph to say?' I asked.

'You know, I was just thinking the exact same thing,' he replied, opening his eyes and turning his head to me.

'Really?' I asked lying down on my side, head propped up on my arm.

'No, because I'm not insane,' he answered.

'No really, what would you want people to read on your tombstone for decades to come?'

'You mean before they tarmac over me to make a new car park?' he asked.

'You're taking all the fun out of this.' I tutted.

'Far be it from me to take the fun out of epitaphs,' he said with a smirk. He thought for a moment and then said with dramaticism. 'Theodore Alwyn Morgan. I don't know where I'm going from here, but I promise it won't be boring.'

'What does that say about you?' I asked, my brow knitted.

'That I'm optimistic and, seeing as the great man said it

himself, it shows my profound love for David Bowie. Your turn.'

I'd thought about this before, many times. I didn't need a minute to think. 'Matilda Effie Heaton. I'd say I did the best with the time I had, but it's wrong to lie on tombstones.'

'How inspiring.' He turned his face back to the ceiling, his eyes closing again. I lay my head down on the floor beside his and closed my eyes too. It felt oddly calming to feel nothing beneath my feet, as if I were floating. Maybe this was what serenity felt like.

The song changed to 'Bette Davis Eyes' and I felt Theo tense beside me. He flipped over and quickly skipped the song.

'Hey! I like that one.' I tutted in annoyance and let my eyes fall closed again.

'Sorry,' he apologised, but didn't change the song back.

After a long silence I opened my eyes and turned my face to him; his eyes were still closed.

'So,' I said, 'Alwyn, huh?'

His lips curled up into a crooked smile. 'Shut up, Matilda.'

Saturday arrived like an uninvited house guest when you have Netflix on pause, your PJs on and popcorn heating in the microwave.

I'd burrowed down to the deepest depths of my floordrobe and pulled out anything that could pass as 'dressy'. I hadn't been *out-out* since my freshers' weekend at uni and that had been a night to forget; cajoled into an awkward quintet of strangers, newly sharing a flat, forced to go out and get shitfaced in the pursuit of 'bonding'. Cut to me, three hours in, about seven tequila shots and a stolen purse later, sitting on the toilet of a shitty bar and crying into my hair while the sound of 'Backstreet's Back' from the DJ's Throwback Hour thumped through the wall.

I was less of a *go out and party* and more of a *stay home with the cat* kind of girl, so naturally my party wear was rather thin on the ground, literally.

I picked up a floral skull dress from my emo phase and held it up against myself, frowning at my reflection and throwing it back into the pile.

Theo had pulled out the trump card, which had been *The List*, and I'd been unable to refuse to go to Kate's party. I'd promised to go along with this bucket list saga and backed myself into a corner. My phone buzzed from atop the groaning bookshelf beneath the window. I grabbed it and read the text; it was from Theo. He was on his way.

'Shit!' I shouted and threw the phone forcefully into the pile of clothes.

'Language!' My mother's voice came from along the landing, quickly followed by her skulking footsteps heading towards my open door. 'What's wrong now?'

'I have no clothes,' I groaned.

'Don't give me that nonsense!' Joy chided. 'You can't move in this room for clothes.'

'Let me rephrase then, I have no clothes that I don't look like a basking hippo in.'

'Oh, do shut up!' Joy picked up a shirt from the pile. It was black with a red rose floral pattern, a laced-up front and flared sleeves. 'What about this?'

I snatched it from her, with a little more aggression than was intended and held it up. 'I look like a boozy housewife.'

'Effie, it's only Kate's party.' She crossed the room and squeezed my shoulders. 'She's your oldest friend. She won't care what you wear.'

'But *I* will. She'll look like a Greek goddess as usual and I have to at least try and keep up.' I picked up a pair of skin-tight black jeans, decided to couple them with the drunken mum shirt and grabbed my criminally underused heels from the windowsill.

'It's not a competition of who can look the best, you know,' Joy said naïvely as she wandered back to whatever she'd been doing before.

'Yes, it is,' I mumbled to myself. 'It's always a competition.'

The smooth motion of the ascending lift made me feel sick as I stared at myself in the burnished doors. Theo stood calmly beside me looking like he'd just come from an audition for James Bond, the bruised jaw helping to add to the devil-may-care narrative. He wore a blue suit with a skinny purple tie. He'd clearly gone to more effort than I had.

I saw him turn to me in the reflection of the door.

'So, is this a date?' he asked.

'I hadn't thought about it,' I replied. I'd been far too busy having an anxiety attack over this party.

'Well, you're going to have to decide because I need to know if it's appropriate for me to tell you that you look beautiful.'

I blushed and looked down at the black suede of my shoes.

'I mean, the outfit is really nice but what I like most is the greenish tinge to your face and the way you keep swaying like you might pass out.' He smirked.

'You're the one who dragged me here. Which means that my nausea is at least fifty per cent your fault.' I smoothed down my clothes and scrunched my hands in my hair in an attempt to give it some life. 'Let's just hope that Eloise "Fucking" Kempshore isn't here.'

'Who's she?'

'Don't worry. You'll know her when you see her.'

I clenched my fists at my sides and took a deep breath, closing my eyes and trying to slow my racing heart.

I felt a warmth in my palm as Theo slid his hand into mine and gave it a squeeze. I looked up into his eyes. I could feel my cheeks burning. His thumb traced a line up and down my index finger and the sensation made my stomach flip. It really wasn't helping the nausea.

'You don't need to worry,' he said. 'If it truly is as terrible as you think it's going to be, then we can just take advantage of the open bar and sit on our own.'

If I hadn't felt so sick, I might even have smiled.

The lift made a quiet *dinging* sound and I looked at our slightly warped faces in the door.

'If I fall down or embarrass myself, then please do the kind thing and just shoot me dead,' I said with a shuddering sigh.

The doors slid open and the terrible sound of jazz muzak filled my ears.

'Breathe,' he said quietly 'and remember that wine is only a few moments away.' He loosened his grip as I stepped out into a blindingly white hallway and his hand fell from mine.

'Good to know,' I replied, retaking his hand and squeezing it tight. 'I'm gonna need this.'

I'd never been to Kate's penthouse apartment before; we tended to keep our meetings to neutral ground like coffee shops to limit the time we had to spend together. She'd lived here for less than a year, which could clearly be seen by the show-home cleanliness of the place. I supposed she had a maid to clean for her. I couldn't see Kate on all fours shampooing the carpet and messing up her manicure. I guess life must be very different when you earn enough money to be an insufferable show-off.

It was an open-plan affair with floor to ceiling windows running down the entire side of the building, opening out onto a balcony that was clearly never used, which I'm sure was down to them not wanting to let the air in to muddy their sterile living conditions. It was huge with an overdramatic modernist staircase, which led up to the second level and sat in the centre of the room like some kind of installation art. Everything was in varying shades of cream or white, some with a smattering of sequins or diamantes, you know, just to make the place glisten a little more than it already did.

The room fitted the occasion perfectly. It was clean-cut, stylish and wildly indulgent; much like the people filling it.

'Wow,' Theo said with wide eyes that sparkled with the reflection of the room. 'It's horrible. Impressive, but horrible.'

I agreed, but that didn't mean I wasn't jealous. Jealousy was my vice, always had been and always would be. I wished that I owned this sparkling, sterile apartment, simply so that I could sell it and spend the money on a nice one.

The sound of lips smacking and 'mwah, mwah' could be heard as one cheek was pressed to another in the French way of greeting an old friend.

I *would not* be doing the same.

I was not French and I saw no friends here.

My eyes darted from one face to another, searching for people I knew and should therefore avoid like the bubonic.

I felt a premature rush of relief when I didn't recognise any of them, until I saw the pearly whites of a grinning Eloise 'Fucking' Kempshore rushing towards me; a phone in one hand and a Martini in the other.

'Effie Heaton!' She giggled as she spoke, her words dancing up and down, riding the laughter in infuriating waves. 'How long has it been?'

I quickly swallowed the venom that was creeping its way onto my tongue and stretched a forced smile across my perspiring face. Eloise's eyes skirted over Theo, dismissed him and moved back to me.

'Eloise! It must be seven years at least.' I allowed myself to be pulled into an affectionless embrace and gritted my teeth as Theo's hand fell from mine, leaving a cold absence where it had been.

I felt Eloise's shoulder blades poking through her skin as I rested my hand on her scrawny back. Her hair smelled expensive, like one of those shampoos that have non-fragrance names like, *Pearl and Cotton* or *Jade and Diamond*. What the hell does a pearl smell like anyway?

Eloise let me go and, as soon as I was free, I reached for Theo's hand again and held it like a life ring in the middle of the open ocean. 'How have you been?' Not that I gave a rat's ass.

Eloise had been my Regina George and Kate had been her Cady Heron. Eloise had pulled Kate into The Plastics and away from me. She'd made my life hell for years, Kate holding her tongue and allowing me to be torn to pieces, and now here we were, hugging and pretending we hadn't wished each other dead only a few years earlier. What was that I could smell . . . ? Oh yeah, bullshit!

'Oh!' She gestured dramatically, like an old-time thespian. 'Life is good. I'm working for Talbot and Tallow as a publicist.'

'Talbot and Tallow, the publishing company?' My heart sank.

'That's the one.' She took a sip of her Martini. 'Only last

128

week I was on a book tour with Benedict Cumberbatch promoting his autobiography.'

'I didn't think you were a big book person.'

'Ha!' She startled me with her aggressive single laugh. '*I* don't read them. I just make other people think that *they* should.'

I felt my nostrils flare and Theo's hand tightened around mine.

Happy thoughts, Effie. Happy thoughts.

'Sounds amazing,' I said through set teeth. 'How did you get into that?

'My uncle is a senior editor there, so he put in a good word. Not that I needed it.' She grinned and flicked her platinum blonde hair over her skeletal shoulder.

'How lucky.'

'Not really. It's easy to think of achievements as luck, but then that would just be me belittling myself, you know? People make their own luck in life, their own opportunities. If we didn't, then where would we be?' She laughed. 'Still working as a barista and living in our parents' houses.'

I hate you. I hate your laugh. I hate your hair that smells like pearls. I hate everything about you.

'Yeah, imagine that.' I clenched my jaw and tried to ignore the sinkhole of despair that was opening in my chest.

'What about you, Eff? What are you doing these days?' Eloise asked taking a sip and pressing her sienna-stained lips together. I winced at her use of my nickname; she hadn't earned the right to forgo the last two letters of my name.

My mouth turned dry.

My tongue turned to paper.

I couldn't tell her the truth and I hadn't thought ahead and prepared a lie.

This was it. This was the moment when they would all find out that the loser I'd been at school was never a phase I had grown out of.

At that instant Theo leaned over, his hand outstretched towards Eloise. 'I'm Theo, by the way. I thought it only polite to introduce myself.' Eloise didn't notice the dig. It gave me a momentary sense of relief from my all-encompassing fury.

'Nice to meet you,' she lied, looking at him like he was the skater boy from the old Avril Lavigne song.

'Yeah, I know it is,' he said. 'Effie works for my family business as an antique dealer.'

I breathed a sigh of relief.

Eloise opened her mouth to say something when I heard my name being called from behind. I turned to see Kate walking towards me, my stomach sinking and panic rising in my chest when I realised that there was no hiding Kate from Theo now. In a few short moments he would finally see her in all her beauty and he'd realise he'd settled for corned beef when he could have been having fillet steak.

Kate was immaculately put together in a way that I never would be. Her hair hung in glossy curtains, framing her face like a Vermeer. Not a hair sat out of place as it shone in the subdued mood lighting of the room. Her skintight dress hugged her slender figure like it was a purple second skin and showed off her long, tanned legs. I imagined myself in that very dress and shuddered at the thought of exposing my short, congealed goose-fat thighs and corpse-coloured skin.

'Effie! I didn't think you'd make it.' Kate arrived beside me, her heels making her a full foot taller. She dawdled for a moment, clearly not wanting to hug me in front of her fancy friends and muddy her dress with my mediocrity.

Instead she turned to Theo. 'And you brought a date. Hi, I'm Kate.'

'Theo Morgan. Effie's told me a lot about you.' He shook her hand and my grip tightened on the other one, which was still clasped in mine. I was a lion defending its kill.

'Only good things I hope.'

'The best,' Theo lied.

I had known Kate for almost the entirety of both of our lives and so I always knew when Kate fancied someone. And Kate most definitely fancied Theo.

I pulled the hand that I was holding around my waist, moving him closer. Theo looked slightly confused for a second before playing along and holding me by the waist.

'Where's Callum?' I asked, quickly reminding Kate of her fiancé.

'He's sorting something in the kitchen, I think. We've been having some work done. The stonework surfaces are too easily stained so we're having them changed.'

To what, I wondered, gold?

'Oh, here he comes now,' Eloise said, pointing to the bobbing dark-haired head of Callum, which was moving towards us.

'He's been a little stressed recently, what with the wedding and me moving away for a few months. We won't even be able to have a honeymoon before I leave,' Kate said.

'Honeymoon?' I asked, confused. 'Don't you have to get married before you go on a honeymoon?'

Callum arrived at Kate's side and he placed a kiss on her cheek.

Callum was gorgeous, obviously – Kate would settle for no less. But I had never liked him; he always got my name wrong.

'Hey, Elsie,' he said with a grin. I couldn't work out if he was dumb or if he was doing it on purpose.

'Effie,' I corrected him, sounding out the syllables. 'My name's Eff-ie.'

I'm sure he would have apologised, had he not been too preoccupied by wrapping his arms around Kate and nuzzling her ear.

I felt a little vomit rise up in my throat.

He moved his hand to rest on her perfectly toned stomach and my eyes found the gold band around his ring finger. 'Did you already get married?'

Kate smiled and blushed with joy as she nodded and held out her bejewelled hand. 'Yesterday! Can you believe it? All those years of sitting in your old room cutting pictures out of magazines and planning our big days and now mine's been and gone.'

It took a moment to sink in and when it did, I felt the calmest I have ever felt in my entire life. It was almost as if I would never feel anything again. It was wonderful.

Then it ended and I forgot how to breathe.

'Yeah!' I stepped forward, letting Theo's arm fall away. This was between me and her. 'Except, when we planned our wedding days, we included each other in them.' Theo shifted awkwardly and took a step back as if he was afraid of what I was going to say.

'Oh, Eff, it was such a small ceremony. We wanted to get it done before I went away,' Kate said, her head tilting as if she was talking to a child.

'So, you already had this planned when I met you for coffee the other day? What was all that crap about you finding a place for me, then? Why bother lying if you knew I wouldn't be there, Kate?'

132

'Well, I . . . I . . .' Kate stammered.

'You didn't invite me to your wedding.' I said the words again, as if clarifying it to myself. 'How long were we friends, Kate? I mean *real* friends, not this ridiculous pantomime we've been doing recently. Fifteen years? That's about right, yes, fifteen years of being as close as two people can be and you didn't think that that made me worthy of an invitation to your wedding?'

'Effie, it was such a small day.' I saw a look of genuine distress on her perfectly contoured face. It didn't make me back off; in fact it made me lunge in for the kill.

'It was such a small day and I am such a small person. I don't matter enough to even get a text about it.' I felt this final betrayal lodge in my throat and stick there like dry bread. Years of bottled-up emotions and unspoken words were suddenly set free; the cage door unbolted, the words set loose.

'You know what? I'm glad you didn't invite me, because now we can finally put an end to this fake friendship.'

'Effie, please, people are staring.' Kate shot me a look of embarrassment and smiled awkwardly at the people that had gathered around us, silently eyeing us with interest.

'I don't give a crap if they're staring or not!' I spat. 'I've known you longer than anyone in this room and yet I bet some of them were at your wedding.' I held out my arm and gestured to the wide-eyed people around us. 'None of them comforted you when your dad left. None of them sat in hospital with you when you had your appendix removed. None of them came and picked you up at 3 a.m. after you'd been clubbing and got lost in town. But *they* were all there, because *they* fit into what you want your life to be and sad, penniless, sloppy little Effie doesn't quite suit the aesthetic.'

Kate had gone silent, her teeth on edge, her eyes fighting back tears; she always cried when people shouted at her. I bet most of *them* didn't know that.

A waitress arrived with a tray of drinks, presumably to try and defuse the tension with Veuve Clicquot. I reached over and took a glass, swigging half of it down before speaking again. 'Well, thanks for the invite, Kate. I'll make sure to take advantage of the free bar. Think of it as a going-away present and after tonight you'll never have to pretend to be my friend again.' I turned to Callum who, by the look on his face, clearly hated the air I breathed. 'Enjoy being her everything while it lasts, Callum. I certainly did.'

With that I pushed my way through the gawping crowd, managing to snatch a bottle of wine from a waiter and make it out onto the balcony before ending the fight with my tear ducts and letting my mascara run down my cheeks.

# Chapter Eleven

Theo didn't follow me outside and I was glad of it. I sat on the stone wall of the balcony with the bottle of Shiraz in my hand and my legs dangling over the abyss. The sound of the party regaining normality came muffled through the glass behind me. A few minutes after I stormed out onto the balcony, a young waitress, who fitted in there as much as I did, brought me several glasses of champagne and gave me a reassuring pat on the shoulder. I could see her checking up on me, every so often, through the gossamer curtains. Probably to make sure I hadn't fallen off the building.

I wondered how high up I was – two hundred, three hundred feet? I'd never been very good at estimating.

I looked down, the ground nothing but a speckle of lights and an echo of sounds made fuzzy with the Shiraz that was doing its job of numbing me.

I would have stormed out and gone home, had I been safe in the knowledge that there was wine there, but I knew there wasn't and payday wasn't until Monday, so I'd stayed.

I wondered how long it would take to reach the ground,

should I choose to push off with my heels and fall through the air.

Would I die when I hit the pavement below or would I just be horribly paralysed? I wondered if the fall would feel like when you hang your head out of the car window and the air rushes into your mouth so fast that you can't catch your breath. If it *was* like that, then would I suffocate before I reached the ground? Would Theo use the epitaph I'd told him back in the treehouse?

I lifted the bottle to my lips. I'd found no use for the glass that the waitress had brought me; bottle to mouth was much faster. I pulled it away from my lips too quickly and the red liquid spilled and formed a puddle in my crotch, seeping into the denim like blood. Great, now people would think I was having an ill-timed period.

I glanced back at the people milling around inside behind the curtains and glass doors that separated us. There were so many of them. I wouldn't be able to fill that room with my friends, even if it was a quarter of the size. I noticed three empty champagne glasses lying smashed on the floor and wondered who'd broken them, before remembering that it had been me after I'd downed them.

There was a centimetre or so of wine left in the bottle. I tipped it up and swallowed, before tossing the empty onto the ground behind me. It didn't smash, just rolled over the uneven paving and made that tinkling noise that you don't think you'll grow so accustomed to hearing on a daily basis.

I'd known I had a problem a few years ago when I woke up at four in the morning, still in the bath, empty bottle of wine on the tiles, the glass sunken to the bottom of the tub and pink-tinged water cooling around me. The only thing that had stopped me from drowning was the inflatable neck pillow.

I'd tried to stop once or twice, but life was too sharp, too loud without it.

I swayed slightly, the wind making me teeter on the edge of a dramatic demise.

I mumbled to myself as I wiped at the wine in my crotch, grumbling unspoken arguments with Kate as I did.

'Is this a private conversation or can others join in?' Theo's voice came from behind me. A moment later he hopped up to sit on the wall, his body facing the safety of the balcony floor and not the empty chasm of the night. He had a half-empty bottle of beer in his hand and his tie had been loosened.

'I thought you would have left already,' I slurred, looking out at the sparkling lights of the city that fuzzed like fireflies in my drunken eyes.

'And miss Jeremy Kyle live? Never, it's far more exciting in real life.' He was trying to joke and pretend that everything was okay, but there was no hint of a smile in his voice. 'No, I was busy being talked at by Kate.'

'You in love with her yet?'

'Oh yeah, 'cause I'm a sucker for bitchy, shallow women.' He took my chin in his hand and turned my face to his. 'Are you all right?'

I ignored his concern. 'You spent half an hour talking with Kate?'

'And others. I thought you'd want to be alone with your old pal, Shiraz, for a while. Some guy called Marcus came up to me and told me he knew you at school.' He rolled his eyes. 'My God, he likes the sound of his own voice, doesn't he?'

'Marcus Roe?' I asked with panic in my voice. Theo nodded. 'What did he tell you?'

'Nothing. Why, is there something to tell?' he asked with a curious gleam in his eye.

'No. Absolutely nothing – shall we move on?' I replied and turned back to the view, trying not to picture the last time I'd seen Marcus. I needed to get out of here without him seeing me.

Theo sighed and swigged at his beer. I watched him from the corner of my eye.

He fitted in here. He was beautiful, just like them. Beautiful things belonged together, not with me.

But for some reason he was out here talking to me and not in there fighting for a moment alone with Kate. There could only be one explanation: I was his bad pancake.

There was always one pancake that was a mess.

The one that falls apart, sticks to the pan and burns. It ends up being an ugly, sticky mess and all you can do is throw it in the bin and end its misery, before moving on to the proper thing. He might think he was falling for me now, but in a few weeks the novelty would wear off and he'd be gone.

'You think you're going to fall in love with me,' I said, my half-closed eyes meeting his.

'It might have crossed my mind,' he replied. I drew closer and grinned.

'You think I'm just having a rough time of it and, once you save me, I'll be the perfect girl and I'll stop being so bitter and angry and sad all the time. I'll stop drinking and I'll get myself a proper job. But I can't stop being all of those things because that's who I am. I can't stop drinking because it's all that gets me through life and I can't get a better job

138

because I can't do anything of value except write and no one even thinks I can do that.' I reached out for the wine, then remembered that the only bit that was left had soaked into my trousers. For a second I seriously considered taking them off and sucking it from the fabric.

Theo looked down at the ground and sighed loudly. 'You know, this woe-is-me attitude is getting kind of old, Effie. You have a lot more than some people. You should treasure what you have.'

'Go on then, Ghost of Christmas Present.' I moved closer, my hot wine-scented breath dancing over his face. 'What do I have?'

'You have parents who love you, a place to live, a job that you enjoy. You're healthy, intelligent and beautiful and you're only twenty-eight. Your life hasn't passed you by yet.'

'If you say so,' I said. His face was so close that he became nothing but a blur of blond hair and cheekbones. 'You know, I realised something just now. This whole time I've been thinking that other people were the problem. My mum, my dad, Kate, Eloise "Fucking" Kempshore. But they're all getting on just fine. They're all navigating life like they were born to do it and I'm the one floundering. So, I must be the problem. The problem is me.'

'You're not a problem, Effie. You're just in a terrible place right now.'

'So, why are you wasting your time with me?' I asked and motioned to the room of beautiful people on the other side of the glass doors. 'I'm sure there's someone more appropriate for you in there, someone beautiful, someone that's not a train wreck.'

I saw his nostrils flare. He exhaled slowly before turning

to me with angry eyes. 'Exactly how shallow do you think I am, Effie?'

'What is it about me that you find so irresistible? I have manly upper arms and sturdy thighs and terrible posture and those are only the problems that I have on the outside.'

'You really don't see yourself, do you?' He looked down and released a heavy breath, exasperated. His tongue poked out to moisten his lips and I got the sudden urge to kiss those newly moistened lips. He sighed and opened his mouth to speak, but before he could say anything I leaned across and pressed my mouth, painfully, to his.

I kissed him, sloppily, angrily. He tasted of the bitter beer he'd been drinking, mingled with the full wine flavour plastered all over my tongue.

He fought against me, pushing me back with his hands.

I pulled away. His lips were red from the force I'd used.

He stared at me; he looked upset, angry even.

'I had to do it just once. You won't be back now that you've seen the real me.' I leaned forward, the momentum making me sway dangerously close to the edge. I thought I might fall, that this might be my final night, that I might have had my last taste of wine, my last taste of him, of anyone.

I felt a horrible pulling feeling in both of my shoulders and before I knew what was happening, I was being dragged backwards and placed, not too gently, on the balcony floor.

Theo knelt down beside me and took my face in his hands.

'I'm fed up of you making decisions on my behalf, Effie; they aren't yours to make. And stop telling me that I'm like every other guy who's ever been a dick to you – it's insulting. Now, I'm taking you home before you fling yourself to your death.' He pulled me up to standing. A tear fell down onto my chin; I wasn't even aware I was crying. The rush of blood to my head made me feel dizzy.

'You act like you're this great guy, but you're not,' I slurred. 'You seem like it right now and you'll fool me for a little while, like all the others have, and then, somewhere down the line, you'll end up getting bored of me or deciding that you like someone else better and I'll see that you're just like the rest of them.'

Theo's jaw was pulled taut, his eyes hard and boring into me from several paces away.

'Firstly, that's a very sexist generalisation. Secondly, thank you for telling me that I'm not just a fickle cheater, but that I'd try and manipulate you into a relationship before I revealed that about myself. It's all very flattering.' He scoffed and shook his head in frustration.

'It's true.' I raised my voice to an almost shout and curtains began to twitch around the windows. 'You're gonna end up being just another rung on the ladder of disappointment that I climb on my way to spinsterhood and I dunno if I can be bothered with it anymore. I might swear off men, become a lesbian, but then I'd probably have the same luck with women.'

'Stop it, Effie.'

'There must be a reason why you're on your own. You're single-handedly the hottest person I've ever met, you're funny and intelligent and kind.' His eyes seemed to redden with anger as his jaw flexed, but still I kept pushing. 'I know why *I'm* single. I mean, just look at the state of me. But shouldn't you be married by now, or at the very least engaged? Everyone else seems to be, so, if you're such a great guy, why aren't you?' I took a step forward, the quick motion making the blood rush back to my head. There was a cutting remark sitting on the tip of my tongue, but as I went to say it, the edges of my vision began to turn fuzzy and before I could warn him, my legs buckled, I hit the floor hard and everything went black.

I woke to the smooth forward motion of Theo's car and the sound of country music on the radio.

'Why are you listening to Dolly Parton?' I asked, my voice slurred and slow.

He sighed from the driver's seat, clearly annoyed that I'd woken.

'Because I like her music,' he said with an angry twang in his voice.

'Don't you listen to anything that was recorded this century?'

I saw his jaw muscles tighten and release as he flexed his bruised jaw, but he didn't respond.

'I'm sorry I kissed you and made a fool of myself and almost threw myself off a skyscraper.' I looked over at him; his knuckles were white as he gripped the wheel.

'I don't blame you for being angry with her, Effie. She did a shitty thing and she's not a nice person and I don't blame you for getting drunk either. But you can't answer shitty behaviour by being even shittier. The next time you kiss me, if you ever do, you'd better mean it. I don't do this often and I wouldn't be putting up with all this shit if I didn't really like you. So, stop thinking that I'm too good for you or that I'm only hanging around with you because I have some sort of Prince Charming complex. I like you – is that so hard to understand?'

I opened my mouth to answer but what came out were not words, just vomit.

I threw up into my lap in an attempt to spare Theo's car, but there was so much of the burgundy spew that it rolled down the sides of my legs and began seeping into the seat beneath me.

I apologised as he groaned and I promptly passed out again.

# Chapter Twelve

Please God, let it all have been a dream.

My eyelids peeled back like sandpaper as they opened to a blurred, abstract image of my room. I lifted the covers and saw that I was in my underwear; hopefully I'd not been with Theo when I'd decided to strip off, otherwise I may well have given what must have been the least sexy striptease of all time. Oh God, my head!

My mouth was dry, so very dry. I unattached my tongue from the roof of my mouth and tried to moisten it. Turning to the side, I found a blister pack of paracetamol and a pint glass of water. I had no idea how they'd got there.

I put two pills onto my dry tongue and downed the whole glass, instantly regretting it and feeling a horrible churning in my stomach.

I had never been one of the lucky ones who forgot portions of their drunken nights. No, I always remembered everything. Everything I did. Everything I said . . . eventually.

Oh God! I'm dying. This is it, this is how I go.

I rolled over and pulled the covers over my head, pushing

the quilt into my mouth and biting down hard in an attempt to fight the memories of my outburst with Kate, of how all those people had looked at me, of Theo and how I'd . . . Oh my God! I kissed him and then threw up in his car!

It was early and I was sure that everyone else would still be in bed, so I tentatively made my way to the shower. I passed the top of the stairs and recalled how Theo had carried me to bed, Joy leading the way and apologising the whole time. My body trembled all over. Whether that was from the anxiety of what I'd done or from the near alcohol poisoning that I seemed to have inflicted upon myself, I don't know.

I showered – washing the vomit and shame from my hair – got out of the shower, promptly threw up on my feet, showered again and returned to my room. When I shuffled back to bed, I found Elliot curled up on my pillow. I smiled and lay down as if he wasn't there, nestling my head into his soft fur and hoping he'd stay put, but Elliot didn't like me to be comfortable and so he slid out from under me and lay down on my chest, purring loudly while his claws pulsed. His claws stung but I didn't stop him; if anything the pain kept my mind off what I'd done.

For years I'd imagined how good it would feel to tell Kate what I really thought of her, but now that it had actually happened, I felt nothing but regret and an overwhelming sense of humiliation.

I'd done a good job of hiding my life from those I'd gone to school with, rarely updating my profiles and only adding highly doctored and painstakingly selected photographs, but I had shattered that illusion last night. Eloise 'Fucking' Kempshore and Marcus couldn't have been the only ones there who knew me, but I hadn't stuck around to find the others.

A memory of my feet dangling over a vast drop and Theo's disappointed face looking back at me caused me to smack myself hard on the forehead and groan sadly at Elliot's aloof face.

'Stop looking at me like that!' I said to him. His yellow eyes stared down hard into mine.

*I thought you liked everyone looking at you; you certainly put on a show for them all last night,'* he silently replied.

'Shut up!' I shoved him from the bed and he landed with a thump on all fours. He lingered for a few seconds, staring into my eyes with a wisdom far beyond his species and for a disconcerting moment, I thought I saw him shake his head in shame before sauntering from the room.

I grabbed my phone from the nightstand and saw that there were no messages, no calls, not even a junk email.

I flung it into the mountain of clothes and rolled over, pulling the covers over my head and eventually falling back into an uncomfortable sleep.

It was one in the afternoon when I woke again and, this time, I felt much better. The moisture had returned to my eyes and my head felt less like a battered piñata.

I hauled myself up and got undressed. Everything hurt. Why did everything hurt so much?

I looked down at my side where a light purple bruise bloomed on my hip and a graze sat, crusted with blood, on my elbow.

I must have hurt myself more than I realised when I'd passed out on the balcony.

How I hoped that Marcus Roe hadn't seen Theo carrying me out. Why was I always so drunk when Marcus was around? Why was I always so drunk, full stop? You'd think I'd have learned by now that wine led to a hangover day of doing nothing but regretting my life decisions. But I'd grown so used to hangovers by this point that I more often woke with one than without one. My entire life was one giant hangover.

I pulled on an old grey sweatshirt that Dad had bought me from some godforsaken steam railway I'd been dragged to and a pair of ripped blue jeans. I slid my thick-sock-covered feet, which still ached from their unfamiliar night in heels, into a pair of clunky boots and pulled a black beanie over the tangled mess that sat atop my head.

I slid my phone into my pocket – it was still void of any kind of correspondence – and gritted my teeth before descending the stairs.

I didn't make eye contact as I entered the kitchen where Joy sat reading the paper and my dad stroked Elliot while eating a cheese sandwich. Elliot waited patiently for the grated chunks of cheese to fall, catching and swallowing them before they had time to reach his lap.

'Can I borrow the car? I've people to apologise to,' I said, opening the fridge, taking out a carton of apple juice and pushing it under my arm.

'I should think so,' Joy said scornfully without looking up from her paper. 'I wasn't proud of you last night, dear, neither of us were. Isn't that right, William?'

'Yes, dear,' he replied without looking up from his sandwich.

'Join the club,' I said, snatching the keys from the hook beside the door and turning to leave.

'That Theo is a wonderful boy,' Joy shouted. I stopped but didn't turn around. 'He brought you home and put you to bed last night. He even sat with you for a while to make sure you didn't choke on your own vomit.' I didn't remember that part. I must have fallen asleep the moment he placed me down. 'And you did nothing but complain, as usual, telling him that he was carrying you too fast and then stripping off in front of him like a woman no better than she should be.'

Oh God, so I hadn't been alone when I'd cast off my clothing. At least I'd left the underwear on.

'If you want him to stick around, Effie, you'd better start showing him some kindness.'

I didn't reply. I just added her words to the pile of other disappointments that sat across my shoulders and left the room.

I pulled up outside Theo's building and sat in the car for twenty minutes before going in.

I told the doorman – I remembered Theo calling him Ben before – which apartment I wanted and he rang ahead to see if Theo would accept my visit.

My stomach flipped with a mixture of worry and the hangover that I was quietly nursing. As soon as Ben lowered the phone, he ushered me into the lift and turned his key in the lock. The doors slid closed and the upwards motion made me feel like throwing up again, but the super sweet apple juice had calmed my stomach and the worst of it was over now.

When the doors slid open, I stepped into the hallway and took a deep breath. Theo hadn't come to meet me, but I could hear the sound of a video game being played from the next room. I wandered through and found him battling some sort of undead samurai warrior from the comfort of his sofa.

'Um, hi.' My voice was quiet and barely crested above the cries of pain as the game heroine died. He placed the controller down on the table and turned his head, his eyes not meeting mine. 'I wanted to . . . um, to apologise for last night.'

He stood, hands in pockets, and walked over to me. His eyes were hard, hurt; his lips pressed into a line. He looked tired. Light grey circles hung around his eyes.

'I'm so, so, incredibly sorry,' I said as I desperately tried to meet his gaze. 'I'm sorry that I get like that and say terrible things and embarrass myself.' I took a breath and tried to steady myself. 'I knew that Kate and I were finished. But the truth of it is that, even though I knew, I'm still a little bit heartbroken about it. I loved her like my sister and now we're nothing. That just got a little much for me last night.' I took a breath and felt a tear roll to the end of my nose. I pulled my sleeve over my hand and dabbed it away. 'I remember what you said about me thinking you're too good for me – you got that exactly right. I don't want to let myself get my hopes up if you're going to figure out that this isn't just a phase for me, this is who I am. I mess things up, I ruin everything and I drink too much. That's just how I was made.'

I felt the tears falling thicker, faster and all I wanted to do was feel his arms around me. I stepped forward and laid my face against his chest as I let my tears soak into his *Buffy the Vampire Slayer* T-shirt. I breathed in his scent and waited for him to put his arms around me; he didn't.

After enough time had passed for me to smear snot all over him, he pulled away but didn't meet my eye as he brushed the tears into the fabric of his shirt.

He backed away another step, his eyes looking over my shoulder, at the ground, at his hands; anywhere but into mine. He turned abruptly and walked over to the fridge, took out two bottles of water and threw one to me. It bounced from the heels of my hands and struck my chin before falling to the floor with a sloshing thud. 'Come on,' he said, turning off the TV and grabbing his jacket from a hook on the wall, 'we're going out.'

The receipt from a valet service sat on the dashboard and gently fluttered in the warm air that filtered in through the fans. I guess he'd wasted no time in getting the contents of my stomach cleaned from his car upholstery.

I tried to push the fragmented image out of my brain, of Theo looking at me with disappointment, of the diffused light from the overhead street lamp that glistened in the viscous pool in my lap.

I stared out of the window and watched the grey ugliness of buildings give way to open countryside that zoomed by in a blur of verdant green dappled with the russet hues of autumn. I had no idea where we were going, but I didn't really care either.

I felt like something had changed, like the Kate-shaped anger I'd been carrying for so long had finally fallen away and now all that was left was a hollowness where that anger had sat.

Maybe I'd been hanging on and I hadn't even known it.

I'd been waiting for us to fix things, to be important to each other again, but last night had removed all chance of that. I felt lighter and heavier at the same time, freer, more numb. It didn't feel good, but then it didn't feel bad either.

Theo and I didn't speak for the duration of the journey. The only sound that could be heard was the anxious grinding of my teeth and the sultry sounds of Johnny Cash droning from the speakers.

It was a depressing song that I'd heard before but I didn't

know the name of. The lyrics were about needles tearing holes and crowns of thorns. It fitted the mood perfectly.

We began to slow after a while and Theo pulled into a gravelled car park, stopping beside an out-of-order pay and display machine.

'Where are we?' I asked, my throat scratchy from underuse and vomit trauma.

He pulled two small sheets of paper from his pocket and handed me one. They were copies of the list. He pointed at mission number eight.

'We're getting lost?' I asked, not really in the mood for a ramble; I wasn't wearing my comfortable Docs.

'We are,' he answered, his voice devoid of friendliness. He took his water from the dashboard and climbed out, slamming the door a little too hard.

Outside the car, the wind seemed to alternate between gusts of comfortable coolness and a biting bitter cold that cut straight through my clothes. I shivered and trotted after Theo, who was already nearing the line of trees at the edge of the crunching gravel. He didn't wait or even check over his shoulder for me as he cut through the trees and ascended a hidden path.

'Theo, wait!' I called, but either he didn't hear me or he ignored me.

I stepped onto the path that was one smattering of rain away from being a muddy bog and climbed the dramatic, sudden incline of a concealed hill. My thighs burned with the exercise and my chest stung with the freezing air that turned my lungs to ice as it passed through.

Theo was a good way ahead, his body silhouetted against the sky as he neared the end of the covering of trees. I mustered all of my strength and ran the last few metres until

I too fell through the trees into the open space. My feet landed on springy grass that covered the range of hills that stretched out as far as I could see, chopping through the landscape all the way into the horizon. The furthest hills disappeared into the light fog that hung in the distance, the last ones nothing but ghostly spectres in the haze of the horizon. To either side sat a small town and the glint of cars passing along invisible roads sparkled like stars, the sound of their engines only a gentle *whirring* in the quiet. The fields that stretched out on both sides were blocks of colour, a cubist artwork made up of the changing colours of the season. Theo hadn't stopped to take in the view; in fact he was so far in front that he would no longer be able to hear me if I called. His hands were shoved into his pockets, his shoulders hunched against the cold.

He was still angry with me. He screamed it with every movement his body made. He was good-natured, had a sense of humour and was extremely skilled at charming anyone into anything with just one smile, but one thing he wasn't good at was hiding how he really felt.

I hated myself today more than I had done in a while. I might not have seen it straight away when he forced his way into my life, but Theo was the best thing to happen to me in so long that I couldn't remember the last good thing that had happened before him, and I'd treated him with all the respect that Elliot showed any pair of shoes.

Did he still like me or had the *Countdown* theme finally hit the last *bong*?

I jogged after him, my lungs burning more and more with every step.

The wind rustled the leaves of the trees, which glowed with the smouldering autumnal colours that made them look like fire, dancing in the same breeze that rippled the grass like the surface of water.

I jogged to keep up with Theo, but he wasn't waiting up for me and it was over an hour before either of us spoke. Theo had stopped to take a drink and stroke the dog of a passing walker – a giant panting Bernese mountain dog that spent enough time dribbling onto Theo's shoes for me to catch up.

'Well,' I panted as the dog and its owner passed by, 'I think we can well and truly tick this one off the list. I haven't got a bloody clue where we are.'

Theo slowed and turned around, his face reddened by the aggressively cold wind. He shook, either from the cold or the anger that was so clearly etched onto his face. He parted his lips as if to speak and I steadied myself for what I feared would be the beginning of a goodbye, but all he did was take a swig of water. When he was done, he crushed the empty bottle in his hand and shoved it into his pocket. He turned his back to me and began walking again.

'Theo!' I called, my throat hoarse. 'Theo!' He carried on walking as if I hadn't uttered a word. 'Theodore Alwyn Morgan, stop walking right now!' He stopped and turned, his eyes coming to rest an inch or so above my head. 'Are you ever going to speak to me again?'

Silence.

'I apologised to you. I told you that I'm sorry. I make a mess of everything – that's what I do. That's what I've always done.' I was on the verge of crying again. For God's sake, Effie. Stop crying, you're not a crier! 'I fail at things – that's *always* what I do. You knew this about me when you met me.'

He scoffed loudly and stepped towards me. 'I don't know

how much apologising you've done in the past—' he drew his hands from his pockets and held them out in front of him in frustration '—but an apology is where you admit that you are in the wrong and take some responsibility for your own actions. All you've just done is give a list of excuses.' He took another step closer. His brows knotted in the middle, his nostrils flared. 'It isn't some higher power that's been willing you to fail that made you do all of those things last night. *You* did and *you* said all of those things.' He took a breath before beginning again. 'It's like, no matter what I say or do, you won't accept me and it's not because of anything I'm doing wrong. It's because you think so little of yourself that you think I'm going to break your heart and leave, so you won't even contemplate letting me have it.'

'I know. I'm sorry.' I stepped closer, his image nothing but a blur in my slick eyes. 'You're right about everything. I acted like a child. I drank too much. I made a fool of myself and I insulted you. I'm sorry.'

'I don't do *this*.' He gestured to me and then to him. 'I don't date. I don't chase girls. But for some unknown reason I just don't seem to be able to leave you alone, no matter how hard you try to push me.' He moved as if about to take my hand, then thought better of it. 'The world isn't against you. You could be happy. *We* could be happy, but if you insist on drowning yourself in this ocean of self-pity then I won't let myself be dragged under too.'

I knew then that I'd pushed too far. I knew then that I could lose him.

I stepped closer again. 'Look at me.' I placed my hands on his cheeks and gently angled his face downwards; he winced when I touched the bruise that still stained his jaw. 'You haven't looked at me all day and I need you to look at me.

I need you to see me.' He rebelled for a moment or two more until his blue eyes finally fell on mine. I knew now why he hadn't looked me in the eye all day, because the instant he did he softened. 'I can't tell you that I'm suddenly going to see my own worth, because that problem was there long before you arrived. But I *can* tell you that I'm not going to act like that again and I'll stop trying to push you away. Starting now.'

I saw, in the way that his mouth hung ajar with unsaid words and his eyelids flickered, how much this meant to him. How much *I* was beginning to mean to him.

I felt the heat bloom in my chest again and it was the closest I'd ever been to loving someone. I looked at his lips, parted and shivering slightly from the cold, and took hold of his collar, pulling his face to mine. I could feel the resistance as he pulled back.

'Stop.' He held up a hand to keep me back, his palm landing on my collarbone. 'I asked you not to do this until you meant it. Don't do this if it's just an easy way to get me to forgive you.' His voice was quiet, his breath hot as it hit my face.

'Forgive me or don't. Either way, I still mean it,' I said before I pulled him closer, my lips finding his, my fingers gripping his collar tightly. His lips were warm, soft, and all I could focus on as he placed his hand on the small of my back and pulled me towards him. Fireworks burst inside my chest as his fingers traced a line up the back of my neck and found their way under my beanie and into my hair. He paused for a moment and pulled away an inch. I opened my eyes and felt the disappointment that it was over. I felt like I could carry on kissing him forever. He smiled a blurred smile, his face too close to be in focus, before returning and kissing me again.

155

Suddenly the air wasn't so cold, the wind not as harsh. Everything around me evaporated; except him.

We may have been physically lost, with the sky darkening around us and no idea of where we'd left the car. But for the first time in a very long time, I didn't feel lost at all, not even a little bit.

The thing about kissing someone new is that once you've started it's pretty hard to stop. We found our way back to the car, with some difficulty, and Theo drove us back to his. As soon as we set foot in the lift, we started where we'd left off on that hillside. We fumbled through the apartment, blindly in search of the sofa.

I banged my knee on the coffee table and let out a yelp as Theo stripped off my coat and let it fall beneath our feet.

I think it was pretty safe to say that I was forgiven as he cradled my face in his hands and kissed my lips, my cheek, my neck, my collarbone. His weight was stifling as it pressed me to the sofa. I could barely breathe, but I would gladly suffocate if it meant that he was touching me.

I should have been focusing on him, on the way his body pressed against mine, on the way that he breathed me in like he was gasping for air and I was the oxygen that he needed, but all I could think of was that I hadn't shaved.

I'd done the basic – ankle to knee and armpits – but not the 'first time with someone new' shave. I wanted him to carry on and get lost in the moment. I wanted to let his hands continue their timid exploration beneath the hem of my sweatshirt. I wanted all of him, now. But I didn't want our first time to be sloppy, unprepared for. I wanted it to be what all the other times hadn't been.

'Don't you think this is a little fast? I mean, only this

morning you could barely look at me,' I said, my breathing slowing.

'Fast?' he asked, clearing his throat. He pulled back a little further, his eyes refocusing as he climbed off me. 'You're right.'

I sat up and smoothed my hair down; I seemed to have lost my hat and both of my shoes in the scuffle.

We both took a beat to regroup and shake off the hormones that had made us both regress to our teenage years.

'Do you want a drink?' he asked, adjusting his clothes, heading over to the kitchen and pulling a bottle of wine from a rack.

'Not wine,' I called. I really had meant what I said. I wanted Theo and I to work out and if that meant drinking less then that's exactly what I would do.

He raised his eyebrows in surprise and pushed the bottle aside. He brought me a glass of water instead and sat down beside me, his leg touching mine.

Trying to keep myself from touching him, from leaning over and kissing him again, was an exercise in my own self-restraint. I began fiddling with the hem of my sweatshirt to try and take my mind away from him.

He pinched the bridge of his nose and squeezed his eyes tight.

'You okay?' I asked.

'Yeah.' He stretched his eyes wide and blinked several times in quick succession. 'Just a headache.'

He grabbed the remote and clicked on the TV. He made himself comfortable and began flicking through a list on the screen. 'I was thinking that we could watch some films together. You don't have a favourite film and that's just too upsetting for me to even contemplate, so we need to find it.'

The list was a geek's paradise. Anything that involved spaceships, sword fights, superheroes, wizards or aliens was on it.

'I'm getting the vibe that you're a little bit of a nerd,' I said with a smirk. 'Am I dating a nerd?'

'I don't know,' he said as he turned to me, 'are we dating?'

I turned red and looked down at my hands in my lap. 'I don't know ... I mean ... if you wanted to we could ... but it's fine if you—'

His fingers were under my chin as he guided my mouth to his.

His lips remained on mine for a moment before sadly falling away. 'Feel free to take that as a yes.'

# Chapter Thirteen

There comes a time in every child's life when they imagine killing their mother.

It can sometimes be only a fleeting daydream in which you smother her with a pillow or push her from a window. Other times it can be a high-budget brain production, starring A-list celebrities and with special effects that would rival even Michael Bay.

That morning Joy had woken me at six thirty by storming into my room, without knocking, and placing a pile of laundry on the bed, which I was still in, I might add. That had been her first fatal mistake. The second mistake had been to inform me that I looked tired and that it wasn't healthy for a person my age to not be in a routine. The third had been to go outside and start painting the shed when Theo and I were out in the treehouse, just so she could keep an eye on us like we were four-year-olds on a play date.

'Can't we go to yours?' I asked under my breath as we watched Joy paint the shed a grotesque shade of green.

'Some people are viewing it today. I can't go back until

six,' he replied, staring disgustedly at the colour being smeared over the boards.

'I'm suffocating here.' I grasped at my throat because the metaphor was literally choking me. Joy sighed with satisfaction and stepped back to view her handiwork. 'What is that colour even called? It's giving me cataracts.'

He looked at the shed as if it was about to make him gag. 'I believe it's called Mint Green.'

Joy turned her face up to us and shouted, 'What do you think?'

'Great job, Mrs H,' Theo called, being polite as usual. She smiled and wandered inside to wash her brushes.

'You don't have to lie to her, you know,' I said, looking away from the shed before it made me go blind.

'There's nothing wrong with being polite – you should try it some time.'

'I once heard someone say that there are two types of conversation: polite and true. Politeness is the same as lying.'

'If the truth is negative, then why say it?' he asked, leaning back on his hands. 'What's the worst that can come from lying about the colour of that shed? For example, I didn't tell her I liked the colour, I told her she'd done a good job of painting it. That wasn't a lie; it was just an omission of the truth.'

'That's the same as lying.'

'If she's walked away happy, then what does it matter?' he asked.

I rolled my eyes and looked down at my phone and glanced at the time. It was after five. The itch to open a bottle of wine came again, intense like a fire in my gut. I took a deep breath and tried to shake the thought but it stuck 'like shit to a cinder' as my dad always said.

I leaned back on my hands, the dust from the floor sticking to my nervously sweaty palms. Theo copied my pose and a few moments later I felt his fingers falling over mine. I couldn't help the smile that came to my lips, the red that flushed my cheeks.

I knew that yesterday had been the start of something new for us both. That he'd said that we were dating and sealed that promise with a kiss. But as I looked at him, every dazzling inch of him, I found it impossible that I could now call myself his girlfriend. His thumb made gentle circles over the back of my hand and a breath, almost a sigh, fell from my lips. I imagined leaning over and kissing those lips that were all I could focus on. I imagined his hands at my neck and his weight pressing down on me. I imagined feeling his skin against mine and I felt my heartbeat in my skull.

I leaned forward, the distance between us too much to bear. I reached a hand up to his jaw and let it slide to his hairline. He leaned in to it and he set his sights for my lips. I inched closer, his lips so close I could almost feel them . . .

'Effie?' Joy's voice came from below. The magic was broken; the hormones dissipated and were quickly replaced by fury. I looked over the edge. Her annoyingly cheerful face beamed up at me from the foot of the ladder, her phone pressed to her chest.

'What?!' I almost bellowed.

'What is the name of that singer I like?' I barely heard her words over the grinding of my teeth. 'The girl with the ginger hair.'

'Jess Glynne,' I barked. 'Anything else?'

'No, dear. I just wanted to tell Julie.' She took the phone from her chest and began jabbering back into the microphone.

I leaned back and loosed an angry breath. Oh, for a place of my own where my mother didn't destroy every fleeting moment of happiness.

I looked over at Theo who smirked as he took an apple from the stash we'd brought up and bit into it.

I couldn't help but envy that apple. His lips pursed against the skin, his teeth biting down on the flesh of it. If my bloody mother hadn't interrupted, then I could have been that apple.

'What are you doing next weekend?' he asked, apple juice trailing down his chin.

'Working at the shop – why?' I asked leaning over and wiping it away with my thumb.

'I'm going down to see my family and wondered if you wanted to come with me?'

'Have we reached the "meet the parents" stage already?' I asked, feeling slightly nervous.

'You don't have to come. I know it's a bit soon, but the offer is there if you want to.' He looked at me with hopeful eyes.

The idea of spending three whole days away with him was something I didn't want to turn down.

'I'll ask Arthur if I can have the time off.' I smiled, leaned over and kissed him, the sweet tang of apples sticking to my lips.

'I can't stay late tonight,' he said disappointedly. 'I've got loads of work to get done by tomorrow.'

'Don't leave me alone with them,' I begged. 'I'll have no choice but to sit with them and watch some inane drivel like *The Midlands' Best Tearooms* or *Gardening for Geriatrics*.'

'I'm sorry, m'lady, I must abandon you to your fate. But don't worry, you'll have a few days away from them to look forward to.'

\* \* \*

I watched my parents from the armchair in the window, their faces illuminated by the blue glow of the TV screen. They were creatures of habit, watching the same mundane sitcom week after week and laughing at the jokes they'd heard a thousand times before or watching a documentary on farming and getting the idea into their heads that they would like to become farmers, even though they wouldn't last five minutes once the rain started or they got a little cold.

They had been born normal and had remained so their whole lives. In fact, they would probably still fit perfectly into the mould that forged them. I wasn't cast from the same mould; I hadn't even seen it. I had been hand sculpted by a half-witted amateur with a tremor.

I had no idea how I had been the product of those two, sitting there smiling and nursing their cups of tea while I sat in the corner, a grimace on my face and a glass of wine, half drunk, in my hand.

I know, I said I wasn't going to be drinking as much, but you can't expect me to go cold turkey now, can you?

At my age, my mother already had her own house and had been working full-time for seven years; I knew this because she told me every bloody chance she got.

She hadn't gone to university, but then not many had in those days, and she'd instead begun working as a seamstress in a shop that sold wedding dresses, the shop she still worked in to this day. She met William when she was nineteen and she'd married him by twenty-two. They'd worked hard to earn the money to get themselves a house and by the time she was twenty-five they were settled and stable in a way that my generation had no hope of being until we were in our late fifties.

She thinks it's so easy to go out and do the same things

163

she did: to get a job that pays well, to get married and buy a house. But what if the jobs are all gone or they don't pay well enough? I knew I had a cushy deal at the shop, but the pay was garbage. Even if I started saving now, I wouldn't have enough to move out until I was ancient and by that time, my parents would be dead and I'd already have their house anyway. There were other ways of moving out, of course. Marrying a rich twat like Kate had done, not that she'd needed the extra money. But what if you don't want to get married and have to settle for the money that you make yourself and not your spouse's? And what if the housing prices are so high that the only way anyone can even dream of owning one is if a family member dies and leaves it to them?

If you were born in those fateful years between 1981 and 1996, you were branded a *Millennial* and blamed for ruining everything from the napkin industry to golf. We were laughed at for our collective love of avocado on toast and gym memberships and for our obsession with houseplants. But, in the end, maybe we will need those impeccable biceps and that impressive stamina to pelt those people bitching about us for ruining everything, with said avocados and houseplants.

We were told that we want too much by the generation that got everything they ever wanted and were called *The Snowflake Generation* by people who thought we couldn't handle anything. Well, what I say to that is, try living with your parents into your late twenties, with no hope of moving out, and see how much you can handle then.

It was a vicious cycle – every generation hated the one that came after it and blamed the one that came before. So, it was natural, in a way, for everyone to dislike my generation. But

I didn't know if other generations had been hated with the passion that seemed to fall the way of Millennials.

I'm sure that Joy hadn't dreamed that she'd have a daughter like me or that I'd still be living with her at twenty-eight years old.

I know what she'd have wanted. She never told me but I always knew, and it was nothing like what she got. She'd rather I was thinner and flirtier, with fewer anger management issues and less of a drinking problem. She'd rather I was like Kate, living a fake existence in a fake apartment with fake friends fluttering fake eyelashes, where everyone smiles all the time and all the bad things are pushed away so that they didn't discolour the ivory rugs. She'd wanted someone who hid their problems and acted like everything was fine. Well, I was never a very good actress. I failed Drama. Twice.

She'd rather I was into something academic that she could boast about to her circle of friends who met up every Monday night at the exact same place where they ate the exact same meal, week after week. She'd have wanted me to have skipped the goth and hippy phases and gone straight through to preppy; that way we could have shopped together at Joules or Cath Kidston and bought matching wellies that we'd never wear because God forbid we'd actually go somewhere with mud. If she'd had it her way, I'd have married a doctor or an accountant by the time I turned twenty-two and I'd have walked down the aisle in the same dress she'd worn all those years ago.

It's a shame she got none of that.

Like most people in my life, I'd disappointed her. She did well to hide it, but if you're anything like me, you can smell disappointment a mile away.

Maybe Theo's family would be different. Maybe I'd be

exactly who they dreamed their boy would end up with. Maybe this could be my chance to play at being the girl I'd always wanted to be, the one who giggles during small talk and knows what to say to carry on a conversation instead of stopping it dead. Or then again maybe not.

# Chapter Fourteen

I stood at the window. The sun was rising on a new day and I saw it with clear, open eyes.

Something in me seemed to have woken up since my outburst at the party and my argument with Theo.

What he'd said on that hill a few days ago about me blaming everything on a higher power that forced me to fail had jolted me awake and made me realise what an idiot I was being. Whenever I'd messed up, missed out, said the wrong thing or just plain ruined everything, I hadn't placed the blame with me. But it wasn't a force that made me mess things up. It wasn't some vindictive god that enjoyed seeing me squirm. The fault was mine and mine alone.

It was as if the last seven years had seen me breathing on autopilot, the air doing what it needed to sustain me and nothing else, but now I felt it. I felt the air filling me up, igniting something inside me and oxygenating the blood that pulsed round my body so quickly when I thought of him.

The door to my bedroom opened, the fairy lights overhead rippling as Joy walked through the door with bleary eyes.

'Time for up, Effie!' she said, walking to the bed and shaking the bedpost three or four times before seeing that it was vacant.

'Morning,' I said, my voice ethereal and calm.

Joy started, her eyes wide and confused, her mouth hanging ajar in dismay. 'You're . . . you're awake!'

'Yes, I watched the sunrise this morning. I've never seen one before.' Mission number one . . . CHECK! I turned back to the window and smiled contentedly when I saw Elliot sprawled atop the car, asleep.

'Are you ill?'

'Nope. I'm fine.' I turned and walked over to her, giving her a hug before going to have a shower and leaving her, disorientated, in the overstuffed room.

I arrived at work to find Arthur and Toby sharing a coffee and looking through a travel guide of the Czech Republic. They barely noticed me when I walked in; they were too busy blushing and smiling at each other.

'Good morning,' I trilled in a sing-song voice that sounded nothing like my own.

Arthur looked up, his bottom lip jutting out, his brow knitted in a frown.

'What's wrong? Are you ill?' he asked with genuine concern.

'No, why is everyone asking me that?' I placed my bag in the corner, thought about taking a complimentary mint imperial, then decided against it and took the box of new arrivals to the shelves.

'You look good,' Toby said with a smile that implied I'd been up to something naughty. 'I tell you what, that boy's been good for you. There's nothing that broad shoulders can't fix.' He sipped his coffee and smiled to himself, as if reminiscing on a particular pair of broad shoulders. Arthur looked at his own regularly spaced shoulders and frowned in disappointment.

He left Toby perusing a map of Prague and came to pass the books up to me as I climbed the creaking stepladder.

'What's Toby doing here?' I lowered my voice and asked with a smirk. 'Did you lie about your accounts again? I'm not sure you can keep using that excuse for much longer.'

Arthur breathed a laugh and passed me a handful of thrillers. 'No, I actually came clean about the tax returns.'

'He knew already, didn't he?'

'He did. We ran into each other at the supermarket and neither of us had eaten, so we had dinner together.'

'And you confessed your undying love.' I sighed dreamily, holding my hand dramatically to my chest and squeezing my eyes shut.

Arthur shushed me and smacked me hard across the thigh with a John Grisham. 'You've been spending too much time in the Mills & Boon section.'

'I'm happy for you,' I said, leaning down from the stepladder and kissing him on top of his head.

When I drew back, I saw him staring at me, brow furrowed, eyes wide. 'What the hell happened to you? You're . . . happy. You're never happy.'

I shrugged and continued stacking the shelves.

'It wouldn't happen to have anything to do with the call I got from Theo this morning, would it?'

'He called?'

'Yeah, he asked if you could have the weekend off to go to Wales and meet his family. Moving a bit fast, aren't we?'

'What if it is?'

'I like this new you. Let her stay.' He leered a one-sided smile. 'So, are you going?'

'Of course I am.'

'A weekend away, huh? Have you . . . you know, done the deed yet?' He shrugged.

I stopped stacking, suddenly feeling like being sick. I hadn't even thought about that. 'No,' I mumbled, keeping my eyes firmly on the books I was arranging.

'Well, don't do anything I wouldn't do.' He grinned and turned back to his reclining accountant, whose nose was still between the pages of his travel guide.

What Arthur wouldn't do? That didn't leave me much.

'Oh, Effie, before I forget,' Arthur said, retracing his steps back to me, 'when you get back, we need to have a chat.'

'That sounds ominous. Should I be worried?'

He shook his head. 'I don't think so.'

I slumped my shoulders and frowned his way. 'Can't you just tell me now? I'm going to worry until you do.'

He grinned. 'That's the thing about working in a bookshop. You get a flair for dramatic cliffhangers.'

That evening I left work half an hour early and made my way to the nearest department store and to the lingerie section that was on the third floor, tucked away in the back corner like some sordid little secret. I perused something I liked, a dark purple set with just enough lace to look like I wasn't trying too hard. I looked at the price tag and recoiled.

Did I really need these?

Maybe I could just buy the bra and not the matching knickers, but then I thought of what I had at home: several pairs of decade-old full briefs with little holes in the front for my pubes to poke through like a hairdresser's highlighting cap.

No, I definitely needed them both.

It pained me to tap my card to the reader but I told myself that it was for the greater good as I headed out to the nearest chemist.

On the way I passed by a beauty salon and I considered getting a spray tan, lest I vaporise the poor boy's eyes with my blindingly white skin, should he use that smile to lure me out of my clothes.

I'd had one before so I knew the drill and I had enough time to fit it in.

Then I remembered the indignity of standing topless in front of a complete stranger in a too-tight paper thong that cut me in half like a human sausage.

I remembered having to waddle around the room while I dried and the cloying feeling on my skin for days afterwards. No, if he was going to touch me, I wanted to feel it and not through a layer of tan-coloured coating.

Not to mention the bed sheets I'd had to throw out when I'd woken up and found them smeared in brown, like some kind of knock-off Turin Shroud.

No, I didn't want to stain the Morgan family's linens.

I carried on walking.

I stepped through the door of Boots chemist and immediately began scanning the aisles for anyone I knew before heading to the family planning section.

I grabbed what I needed and was on my way to the till when my shoulder collided with someone. I managed to grip the box of condoms enough for it not to fall to the ground. I spun around to apologise, but when I saw who it was, I felt my throat close up, the blood draining from every part of my body and pooling in my cheeks.

Marcus Roe.

Why was this happening to me? What kind of sick monster had I been in a previous life to deserve this?

Maybe he wouldn't recognise me; I didn't look anything like I had when we'd shared our . . . encounter.

'Effie Heaton?' He raised one brow and smirked.

Fuck!

Shit, he'd aged well. He had long brown hair that was tied in a topknot on the crown of his head and a short beard that looked like it had just been trimmed.

'Marcus. How have you been?' I asked, shoving the box up my sleeve.

'I'm great, living in London now but I've come home for a visit.' He stepped forward, his long Sherlock Holmes coat swishing behind him.

'Yeah, our mums met the other week.'

'That's right. You're still living at home, aren't you?' he asked.

'Yeah,' I begrudgingly admitted and felt the familiar shame flood through me.

'I was speaking to your friend at Kate's party. Theo – he seems like a nice lad.' I'd forgotten how condescending he sounded when he spoke. *Lad*. Theo was older, wiser and much less punchable than Marcus was.

'Yeah, he's great.'

'Are you dating? It's just my mum mentioned that Joy said you were single.' His mouth donned a self-gratified smile.

'Early days,' I replied.

We stared at each other for a moment, our brains clearly replaying the exact same memory; his lips curling, my gag reflex flexing.

'Excuse me, miss.' A woman in one of the shop's white uniforms approached me with a puckered look on her face.

Thank God, a distraction. 'I'm going to have to ask you to remove the unpaid-for item from your sleeve. Otherwise I will be forced to let the authorities know.'

My heart dropped. 'Oh no, I'm not trying to steal anything,' I assured her. I smiled at Marcus. His brow knotted.

'Miss, I clearly saw you place something in your sleeve. Hand it over to me or I'll have to alert the security guards.'

*Please, please fuck off,* I begged her with my mind.

'Listen, I was always going to pay for them. Just don't make me get them out here,' I said through gritted teeth, my eyes motioning to Marcus.

She didn't get the hint.

'Miss, this is your final warning. Please remove the item from your sleeve.'

'Oh, for fuck's sake. Fine!' I pulled the condoms out and lost my grip on them. The box sailed through the air, hitting the toe of Marcus's brogue with a soft *thud*.

He bent down and picked it up, glancing at the packet and then looking to me with a one-sided grin. 'Latex free, huh?'

My cheeks burned like the surface of the sun as I glared at the woman with such hatred that she stepped back a few paces.

I snatched the box from his hands and didn't look him in the eye as I said goodbye. 'Well, this has been just fantastic. Let's do it again sometime.'

I turned and walked towards the tills as Marcus called one last thing after me.

'Maybe do it on an empty stomach this time!'

I looked at the ground and wondered why a sinkhole never appeared when you needed one.

*   *   *

I sat on the cold bathroom tiles nursing my bloody leg and cursing the discarded razor that lay halfway across the room with a chunk of my shin between the blades. I may as well have nicked an artery with the amount of blood that dripped down my leg onto the floor.

I dabbed at it with a tissue, managing to mostly just smear it across the teal tiles, making them an attractive purple colour.

I knocked my forehead against my knee and squeezed my eyes shut, trying my best not to picture Marcus Roe and his stupidly handsome grin.

Marcus and I only seemed to deal in disastrous interactions, but my disasters were not limited to him when it came to my sex life, oh no. There was a compendium of stories involving my previous lovers that I had locked away inside my brain, in a box, before submerging that box in concrete and casting it into the black hole of my mind. But occasionally it would find its way back out of the black hole to torture me, and tonight was one of those occasions.

I took my mind back to my seventeenth year, to when I'd had a few too many drinks at a party. It was at the house of someone from my year, but I'd never spoken to them due to the gargantuan distance between our levels of social status. I had only managed to get an invite because Kate had insisted on me tagging along; we were still trying to save the dying relationship in those days. I'd stood by Kate for most of the night, watching her effortlessly mingle, flirt and laugh, while I quietly drank too much and fretted about the hangover I'd have the next day. I drank until the ground began to swim beneath me, my eyes lolling shut. I wasn't the alcoholic back then that I was now, so a glass or two of cider and several shots of some unknown concoction was enough to lull me to the edge of unconsciousness.

That's when Marcus Roe came into the picture. Every school had a Marcus Roe: seriously good-looking, could charm the crown jewels from the Queen herself given half the chance.

He had the long dark hair, pierced ear and skater look that was the peak of hot back then, and for some reason all he wanted to do was talk to me. Back then I thought that someone had finally *seen* me. That he'd spotted me across the crowded room, stopped, and his world had fallen away until all he saw was me. Now I think it's more likely that he saw the drunkest girl in the room, and decided that I was his best shot at a quick shag.

I was still in the midst of a fully fledged emo phase back then, with a heavy side-swept fringe, black skinny jeans tucked into high-top sneakers and about eight quids worth of kohl stick smeared around my eyes. He'd made me a coffee and we'd sat in the kitchen while we both sobered up. It was our first conversation ever and it was going well. He'd asked if I wanted to go somewhere more private and, when I agreed, he'd led me up to the attic that had been renovated into a bedroom that was bigger than any of the rooms in my house.

He'd kissed me as soon as the door closed and it was a hungry, passionate kiss that I'd seen in films but never thought actually happened in real life. I felt fire inside me as we clumsily undressed and went over to the bed. The alcohol numbed any sense of self-consciousness that I most definitely would have felt, had I been sober. He climbed on top of me after I'd lain down on the Egyptian cotton bed sheets and I'd let him take the lead. He was bound to be more experienced than I was at this sort of thing, especially seeing as the only reference I had for sex was when I'd accidentally leaned

175

on the remote at two in the morning and had a brief but scarring introduction to the adult channels.

Everything was going well until he rolled over and pulled me on top of him. I looked down at him, his pretty-boy face morphing into some sort of melting plasticine mess in front of my eyes, and then I'd felt the vomit rush up my throat like water from a fireman's hose. It covered him from head to pubes in one fell swoop. He'd flung me off and run, cursing, from the room.

I lay on the vomit-strewn bed, the pain of my first time still blooming between my legs, naked and with the sound of laughter from downstairs creeping into my ears.

I fell asleep and when I woke, I found myself lying in Kate's bed. My hair had been washed in a bowl of water that sat beside me and I'd been wrapped in a fluffy pink dressing gown before being bundled into bed. On the nightstand I found a pack of aspirin and a bottle of water and lying next to me was Kate, soundly asleep and making those strange laughing noises that she made whenever she was in a deep dream. The next morning I'd gone straight to the doctor and ordered an STD test and the morning-after pill and promised myself that I would never again be so goddamned stupid.

Still sitting on the bathroom floor, I dabbed the blood from my leg and examined the wound. The gouge was deep, right on top of my shinbone, and it pulsed with that very specific stinging pain that only a razor seems to bring.

After Marcus I'd been terrified of the next time that I might find myself in the throes of passion, but I needn't have worried because I wouldn't find myself there again until I was twenty and I got my first proper boyfriend. His name was Alex and he was a regular at the café I worked at to fund my university diet of pasta and orange squash. We dated for a month before I plucked up the courage to sleep with him and when I did, I discovered that I was clearly never destined to be a sexual being. After the panic of the morning following my last encounter, I'd made sure that I was prepared, buying the condoms and making sure that I knew how to put them on properly. But even this was a mistake, because it was about three minutes into the act that I discovered my latex allergy and, lo and behold, the next day I was back at the doctor's surgery.

The third disaster was a disaster of a different kind. This time the only input I had was choosing the wrong person to go home with. Alex had broken up with me three months earlier after finding out that I wasn't going to be the all-you-can-eat nookie buffet he'd been searching for and I again found myself in a state of singledom. I met Daniel Wilcox in the university café. We were reading the same book and I managed to give away almost the entire plotline because I was reading ahead of him.

He was nice, moderately attractive, with a posh accent that made me feel like I was aiming high. He was . . . fine. He was a great cook and he invited me back to his for a meal. It was going great. I was beginning to think Daniel was the boy I'd take home to meet my joyless mother and my mono-syllabic father and my deeply judgemental cat. Maybe Elliot would even welcome him into the family by christening his shoes with hot urine. But that was not to be, because as I lay there, looking up at Daniel's swirling Artex ceiling, my head bouncing against the wooden headboard, Daniel opened his mouth and shouted with passion, '*Ride me like a seahorse!*'

It didn't make sense. Why did he have sexual feelings towards seahorses? I remember lying there and waiting what seemed like an eternity for him to finish and once he was done, I grabbed my things and ran out of his flat, dressing myself on my sprint down the stairs.

I stood up from the bloodstained bathroom floor and threw the tissue into the toilet before staring at myself in the full-length mirror. I turned this way and that, watching the shadows move over the curves of my body and judging every dimple, every hair, every inch. I knew I was too critical, that the way I body-shamed myself was stupid and counter-productive, but I couldn't seem to help it.

Everyone who was heralded as beautiful was thin and tanned and didn't have those little dimples of cellulite beneath their butt cheeks. They didn't have pale skin or red hair or wide hips. The world had decided what beauty was and they had plastered it all over TV, the internet and the news. But what about the rest of the people who didn't fit into the criteria? Were they destined to be shunned as fugly for their whole lives or was the criteria simply bullshit from the get-go?

Theo had told me I was beautiful and I hadn't believed him, not because I thought he was lying, just that he was maybe confused or partially sighted. I remembered mission number twelve on the list . . .

*Learn to love myself.*

That one seemed to be the hardest one for me to imagine completing.

The next morning, the tingle of excitement in my stomach woke me early enough to sit and panic for a couple of hours before Theo arrived. I packed my things, kissed my parents goodbye, searched for Elliot but couldn't find him and then sat at the kitchen table, the loud tick of the wall clock echoing in my bones as each second passed by. I made a coffee in the chipped Rosehipsters mug that had been my pride and joy since Kate had given it to me for Christmas ten years ago; back when Kate cared about who my favourite band was and other trivial things like that.

I felt a pang of something unpleasant in my stomach as I took a sip and tried not to think about my outburst at the party. Surprisingly, we hadn't spoken since.

I pulled my phone from my pocket and opened up Kate's Facebook page. The latest post was a shot of her smiling next to her colleague in the airport bar, beer foam clinging to her top lip. I searched Kate's pixelated eyes for some sign of unhappiness, some sense of loss akin to the one I was feeling, but I found nothing.

Kate wouldn't miss me and, if I was being honest with myself, I wouldn't miss Kate. The Kate I grieved for had ceased to exist years ago and the anger of that loss had clung to me ever since, but now Kate was gone and it was time for me to let go. I scrolled through the feed one last time, seeing the shots of happy, successful people who had slowly ground me down to nothing over the years and, with a mingled sense of foreboding and relief, I opened the settings and let my thumb hover over the screen. I took a breath and checked myself, before lowering my thumb and deleting my account. A message popped up, saying that my account would be kept for a month, should I change my mind. I hoped I wouldn't.

Once it was gone, I pushed the phone into my bag and felt a smile form in my cheeks. I felt like I'd just smashed the crooked magic mirror that had caused only pain and now I could forget about all of those shiny happy people and focus on what was important, what all of *those* people had been focusing on all along, instead of jealously wanting what others had.

I heard the *thrum* of a car engine pulling up outside and my heart leapt.

I opened the door before he had chance to knock, his fist hovering in mid-air. He smiled as I leaned forward and kissed him, the smell of washing powder and mid-price aftershave filling my nostrils as I pulled him close. When I released him, his smile was still intact, if not a little bigger.

'Are you ready?'

There's something strangely exciting about a motorway service station.

The smells of junk food and coffee that mingle in the air and waft into your face the second you step through the automatic doors.

The panicked search for the toilets as you run, legs pressed together, until you see them.

The racks of CDs that you momentarily feel will enhance the rest of your journey before you see the extortionate price tag and fling them back with disgust. We'd stopped at the first services that we could find and Theo and I had separated at the toilet doors. I now found myself standing before a rack of junk food, cradling a bottle of Coke in my arm and wondering what Theo would want.

I knew quite a bit about Theo by now.

I knew that he was a closet nerd and that his love of Bowie bordered on obsessional.

I knew that, when it came to takeaways, he preferred Italian and had never developed a liking for Indian food.

But I had no idea which junk food he'd want.

Was he a fruit or a mint kind of person? Dark chocolate or milk?

'Don't think too hard, you'll hurt yourself.' I heard him before I saw him.

'Peanut or plain?' I asked, holding out a bag of each flavour M&M's.

He pointed his finger at the plain one. 'The peanut ones could potentially kill me so let's stick with plain.'

'You're allergic to nuts?' I asked, adding it to the information file I was building on him.

'Didn't I mention that before?' he asked, absentmindedly perusing the shelves.

Theo was paying for petrol and so I insisted on paying for the snacks. I went to the till and winced as I handed over a ridiculous sum of money to the dead-eyed boy with the receding chin behind the counter.

I pushed the bags into the pockets of my jacket and walked out to join Theo in the atrium, the smell of coffee making my mouth water.

He took my hand and laced his fingers through mine.

It was surprising how quickly I'd grown accustomed to being touched. It was difficult to remember more than four times in the last year when anyone had touched me on purpose and one of those was a nurse taking a blood test. Of course, Joy and I had shared physical contact during this period of time, but those moments were reserved for 'mama hug meltdowns'.

It was still early and the air held that early morning mist that made even the mundane car park look atmospheric.

As we stepped towards the exit, a woman entered through the automatic doors.

Theo looked up, his smile falling as he locked eyes with her. He quickly looked down, avoiding her gaze.

Every one of his muscles stiffened as his body steered me towards the door.

'Theo?' The woman looked up and froze.

He winced and slowly turned.

'Hey,' he said with feigned enthusiasm.

She smiled in disbelief, propelling herself forward and flinging her arms around his neck.

His hand fell from mine and he lifted it to her shoulder, as I stood beside him waiting for an introduction.

She stepped back and held his face in her hands. The action was intimate. It made my toes curl.

'I can't believe it's you. You're looking good, *really* good,' she said. 'How is everything these days?'

He took her wrist in his fingers and gently let it fall away. 'Fine, I'm fine.' He said it in a way that suggested he was anything but fine.

The woman had warm brown skin and stunning hazel eyes that reminded me of Elliot's. She had the toned, athletic body of a goddess and her hair sat in a halo of black curls around her head. She was sickeningly beautiful.

I looked at Theo from the corner of my eye and I could almost hear his teeth snapping as they pressed themselves together.

'And who's this?' She turned her feline eyes to me.

'This is my . . . Effie,' he said, his voice cracking in the middle of the sentence. 'Eff, this is Jenny.'

Oh fuck.

No, not her. Not someone who looks like that!

So, this was the one who got away.

This was the girl Theo had loved since school, the girl who became his fiancée.

Why did she have to look like that?

Why couldn't she have had a face like a dropped apple crumble or at least just have had the decency to be having a bad hair day?

She was beautiful. Just like Theo.

They must have entered rooms to angelic choruses when they were together.

My God, the child beauties they would have made.

'Nice to meet you,' I said timidly.

The doors slid open behind her and a man entered with two giggling identical girls.

The man placed a hand on her shoulder and smiled at us.

'Hi there,' he said in a cheery tone.

She looked Theo up and down before speaking. 'This is my husband, Matt, and these are our girls, Lucy and Leila.'

Theo seemed to wince as Matt extended his hand to him. A moment or two passed where I was unsure that Theo could remember how to move, how to breathe. But then he reached forward and shook Matt's outstretched hand, his eyelids flickering at the unwanted physical contact between the hand that used to hold Jenny's and the hand that held hers now.

She looked back to Theo and their history lay heavily in the air between them.

I looked down at the twin girls who hid shyly behind their mother's legs; they couldn't have been any older than three. Matt stood beside her with one of those contagious smiles on his face. I knew I would have caught it, had I not been occupied by my current anxiety attack. He was tall and broad-shouldered, with blond-brown hair and blue eyes; if nothing else, Jenny definitely had a type.

'Hon, I'm gonna take these two to the toilet before we need to find a mop,' Matt said, smiling at Theo and I and cajoling the two girls away.

Theo watched him leave, while Jenny watched Theo and I watched Jenny, watching him. We were a train of wandering eyes that spoke our secrets for us.

'So, where are you off to?' Jenny asked.

He cleared his throat and rubbed the back of his neck. 'Eff is coming to meet my family.'

She grinned widely. 'How are they? How's Tessa?'

Of course, Jenny already knew his family. She probably used to have nights out with his sister and knew all the family secrets. I was so far behind.

'Good, they're all good,' Theo replied.

'I called Tessa not long ago. My boss wanted a sculpture for the office building and I thought I'd give her first dibs but she never got back to me.' She tilted her head as her eyes moved over his face.

Stop it, eyes down, woman! You chose Matt.

'You still boxing?' she asked.

'No,' he said forthrightly. 'You?'

She laughed. 'No, but then I was never the one who was going places with it, was I?' I moved closer and slid my hand into Theo's.

He flinched like I'd startled him; like he'd forgotten I was here. He shook off my hand and it fell back to my side. I swallowed the rejection and gritted my teeth to stop it coming out in the form of words I'd regret.

'We'd better get going, hadn't we?' I said, a little too angrily.

Theo looked up from the ground as if I'd broken his trance and nodded.

'Yeah, long way to go,' he said.

She looked sad, as if she wanted to cry. 'It was so good to see you.'

'Yep,' he replied.

'Maybe I could give you a call sometime and we could catch up?'

'Maybe,' he said and started walking towards the exit.

184

Jenny nodded me a goodbye and walked away as Theo took my wrist and led me out into the car park.

'Sure, take my hand now that your ex isn't looking,' I said, tugging my arm away from him.

He didn't stop walking, marching straight up to the car and climbing in. When I joined him both of his hands were white-knuckled around the steering wheel and his head leaned back against the seat.

'Did you want to appear single – is that it? Because, if you didn't notice, her husband and twins were *right there.*'

He didn't answer, his breaths whistling out of his nose.

I knew it would only be a matter of time before he became embarrassed of me and why wouldn't he when the last woman he was with looked like that?

'It wasn't like that, Eff. I swear,' he replied after letting his nerves settle.

'Then what *was* it like? Because from where I was standing it looked like you didn't want to be seen holding my hand.' I seethed. 'And what was that, introducing me as *"my . . . Effie"*?'

'It's complicated.'

'Oh, don't give me that *"It's complicated"* bullshit.'

'I planned on marrying her!' His voice rose to an almost shout. He rubbed his hand over his face and spoke normally again. 'I planned on having kids and late-night arguments with *her.* My entire life was set and planned and all of those plans included Jenny.' His words were clipped and furious. 'The wedding was planned, the honeymoon booked, then she was gone and all of those plans died.' He smiled a joyless, hurt smile. 'She *still* went on the honeymoon though; I believe that's where she met Matt.'

I looked over at him, my eyes slick with jealous moisture.

He stared straight on through the windscreen; his pupils were pinpricks.

'Why did she leave you?' I asked.

'That doesn't matter.' He looked down at his knees. 'What *does* matter is that she bailed when I needed her most.' He turned to look at me, his nostrils flaring. 'Yes, I still feel something whenever I think about her, but mostly it's an overwhelming feeling of betrayal. Think of what you feel towards Kate, then times that by ten and you're halfway to understanding what I feel towards Jenny.'

I'd never seen him rattled before. He wasn't in control here; he'd let the mask slip.

'Is there something you're not telling me? Something I should know? Because every time I broach the subject of your past you clam up and give me the vaguest answer you can muster,' I said.

'No,' he replied unconvincingly, 'I've never lied to you and I'm not going to start now.'

Something he'd said to me recently popped into my mind. *That wasn't a lie; it was just an omission of the truth.*

Was he omitting the truth now? Or was I just on edge from meeting the ex-love of Theo's life?

What could she have done to make him so angry, to make him seethe like he did?

I knew from Kate how much you had to love someone to feel that amount of anger.

Would he ever get that angry with me?

# Chapter Fifteen

I sat, tight-lipped and silent, in the hours that followed, as my anger flared, burned and then dissipated. The old me would have thrown an *EastEnders*-level hissy fit and got a taxi home, no matter the expense, just to make a point. But the new me was less of a drama queen. I had been furious back at the service station, but the more I thought about Jenny and what it must have felt like to have her leave him out of the blue, I began to understand his reaction a little more. I wasn't exactly the best at gracefully handling stressful situations, so who was I to judge him?

My life had ceased to suck from the moment I'd let him in (metaphorically of course, although hopes of 'letting in' of another kind would, with any luck, come up during our weekend away) and I wasn't going to let petty jealousies ruin that.

That being said, I would still wait this one out with resting bitch face until I got an apology.

I looked over at Theo. The muscles in his forearms stood proudly as he held the steering wheel. His eyes stared angrily through the windscreen.

We hadn't spoken since Jenny had stumbled in and ruined our sense of adventure and guarded secrets had started to make the air turn sour.

I shifted uncomfortably in my new underwear. Why was it always a choice between sexy and comfortable? Why couldn't they make a pair of pants that were both perfectly suited for a movie marathon and being torn off in the throes of passion? I tried to manoeuvre myself without him noticing, plucking the lacy purple garrotte from my butt crack.

The motorway eventually turned to winding tree-lined roads, flanked on both sides by hills and mountains, and when we passed the *Welcome to Wales* sign I began to feel the nerves building.

I'd never met a boy's family before and the idea of it made me feel sick.

Would he be as embarrassed when introducing me to them as he had with Jenny?

I knew he had a sister, Tessa, a sculptor who still lived at home. At least I would get on with her, I hoped.

I knew little of his parents, but they couldn't be any worse than mine. I wanted them to like me, but people generally didn't take to me easily.

We'd been driving for hours when we found ourselves on a winding road beside a huge lake and Theo surprised me by pulling into a car park.

'Where are we going?' I asked, stretching my aching legs and looking around.

He parked up and turned to me, the anger still simmering behind his eyes. 'Come with me.'

I slid my feet back into my boots and climbed out of the car with the grace of an ageing wrestler.

He was at my door before I got the whole way out, his

hands finding my shoulders and, before I knew what was happening, he pulled me into a hug that felt kind of urgent.

He pulled away but left his forehead resting against mine as he spoke. 'I'm sorry about what happened back there. I didn't mean to drop your hand, I just kinda freaked out. I know what that must have looked like to you but I don't want her anymore, I swear. Forgive me?'

The breath caught in my throat at our proximity, at the smell of him that filled my nose, at the way his hands held my neck gently on both sides. I looked into the blur of blue that was his eyes and the air returned to me.

I thought back to when he'd had to pull me from that balcony and carry me to bed after my outburst and I made the decision that we were now even.

'Maybe,' I replied. 'It's a shame that I didn't do something similar and lose my mind in front of someone *I* used to love . . . oh wait.'

He smiled and pulled away, opening the boot and sliding on his coat. He took out a small backpack and donned it.

'What's going on?'

'You see that?' He pointed to the left at the mountain that rose from the ground like a titan. I nodded and turned back to him. 'That's called Cadair Idris. It's meant to be the seat of Idris.'

'Elba?'

'No, not Idris Elba. The mythological Giant Idris,' he replied with a chuckle.

'That still doesn't explain why we're here.'

He slammed the boot shut and walked over to me. 'We're climbing it.'

'We are what now?' I asked.

He reached into his pocket and pulled out the list. '*Leave*

189

*a mark*. What better place to leave one than at the top of a mountain?'

'I'm pretty sure I meant a metaphorical mark.' I crossed my arms in protest. 'I don't know how to climb a mountain!'

'Well, I do.' He handed me a thermal coat that wasn't mine. I wondered if this had been Jenny's too. 'I've climbed this mountain dozens of times. Come on, live a little.'

I pulled the coat on and turned to look at the mountain. 'How high is it?'

'Around nine hundred metres,' he said casually, locking the car and taking my hand. 'Come on, if we die, we die together.'

'How comforting,' I said as he pulled me along towards the incline.

I tightened my boots and sighed. I was not wearing the right pants for mountaineering.

Three hundred metres up and I was about ready to drop down and make wherever I fell my grave, but I was doing better than Theo who, after boasting about his mountaineering skills, was lagging pitifully far behind.

I sat down on a mound of turf and waited for him, my chest heaving with a satisfying kind of burn.

'Just build me one of those cairns made of little stones and tell my parents where you left me,' I said when he finally arrived.

'I'll be sure to do that. I'm pretty sure your mum won't hold it against me. She likes me too much,' he panted.

'Yeah, and they'll be glad to have the house to themselves.' I lay back, my skin beaded with sweat. I dreaded to think what I looked like. I glanced over at Theo. The sweat glistened on his skin like he was a fictional sparkly vampire and there

I was, frizzy-haired and red-cheeked and with a sweat-soaked bra that was making my boobs itch. He sat down beside me and opened the backpack, taking out some water and a blister pack of paracetamol.

'Another headache?' I asked as he popped two pills from the pack and swallowed them down.

He nodded. 'Come on, there's six hundred metres to go yet,' he said, standing and setting off again.

'You'll be the death of me, Theodore Alwyn Morgan,' I said as I slowly unlocked my knees and followed on.

I had never been the Bear Grylls adventurer type. My body, mind and temperament were much better suited to indoor activities, be that attempting to write or drinking a bottle of Shiraz in a darkened corner. Even the things I did do outside the comfort of my house were always done inside the tree-house, thus technically rendering them indoors.

But as I stood three hundred metres up the mountain, looking out to what I thought might be the ocean stretching out in the distance and blending seamlessly into the sky, I thought that I maybe needed to try and be a bit more Bear Grylls.

It seemed that I'd got the hang of mountaineering by late morning and I was now thoroughly enjoying it. I somehow instinctively knew where best to place my steps and which areas to avoid and I'd taken it steady to conserve my energy, but even so, Theo was still lagging quite far behind. About two hours ago I had asked him if he wanted to tap out and turn around, but he'd insisted that we carry on to the summit. I did worry what might happen if he collapsed. I'd never called an ambulance before, let alone an air ambulance, and I didn't fancy my chances of carrying him back down. I was surprised at how much better I was at this than he was, seeing as I'd never done anything like this before and he was a muscular form of physical perfection.

I don't know what he was trying to prove to himself, but whatever it was he was determined to prove it.

I sat down and waited for him, his figure slowly growing larger.

Life was completely different up here, completely separate from how it was *down there.* It was hard to believe that, miles away, life was still happening. Cars were still honking and people were still jabbering into their phones, yet here I was and it was like they didn't exist at all.

The moon and the sun shared the sky, the sun blazing, although giving off very little in the way of heat, and the moon waiting patiently for its turn to take over and rule the sky alone.

A bird, red in colour and with a forked tail, swooped into the wind gracefully, riding the air like a leaf. It was not the fat pigeons with deformed feet that I was used to seeing; it was altogether less depressing, more beautiful.

I didn't know Wales. I'd only been here twice when I was younger and never to this part. I'd only really seen two places in the world in great detail: where I lived and the static caravan in St Ives, and I suppose the journey between the two. I had never pondered the beauty of Cornwall; I'd stopped seeing it after those first few scarring years of living in such close confinement with my parents for two weeks every summer. My parents had gone on walks, but I had always stayed behind with a copy of *The Hobbit* or some such book, so that I could read about walking but not have to do any.

Theo was almost within hearing distance now. His heavy panting was just audible over the rush of the wind in my ears.

I *had* done rambling once before, but I hadn't enjoyed it. It had been while I was in Brownies (a club that I had been forced to join because my mother had once been one – I had hated every millisecond) and we had been taken to some forest in the arse end of nowhere to earn our orienteering badges. I couldn't have given less of a shit about orienteering until about three hours in when I found myself hopelessly lost and crying and wishing I'd listened when they'd explained how to do it. Needless to say, I didn't earn the badge.

I wasn't in Brownies for long before I got kicked out. That's right, I was defying authority even at the tender age of eight. What heinous crime did I commit, I hear you ask? I hit Lauren Gardner over the head with the flag during church parade because she called me a 'Ginger Minger', that's what. I got a bollocking and was asked to leave, but Lauren got three stitches in her scalp and never spoke ill of me again, so I took that one as a win.

Theo arrived beside me and bent himself double, holding on to his knees for dear life. Sweat dripped from his brow into the grass beneath.

'Are you sure you want to carry on?' I asked, genuinely concerned by the way his breaths rasped in his throat.

'We are climbing this mountain even if it kills me,' he wheezed. 'Come on, there's something up here I want to show you.'

I don't know how far up we were when we found the lake, but it took what little breath I did have away.

Nestled into the cresting peaks was a clear blue lake that looked otherworldly up here. Theo told me its name, Llyn Cau, but I let him do the honours of pronouncing it. I liked how his voice shifted when he said the Welsh names of things, his mouth remembering the accent like muscle memory.

We sat beside the water and ate the sandwiches that Theo had packed, the sun glinting on the water.

'They say that if you fall asleep on this mountain, you'll wake either a poet or a madman,' he said, taking a segment of orange and bursting it between his teeth.

'Why have you climbed this so many times? Wasn't once enough?' I said, my mouth full of bread and cheese.

'I used to come up here with my mum. She liked hiking and I used it as training.'

'Training for what?' I asked.

He barely paused for breath before answering, but I saw something shift in him, subtle and almost unnoticeable. His muscles stiffened, his jaw set slightly, his pupils grew small.

'I had hopes of becoming a professional light heavyweight boxer. I had a few junior belts and I'd just qualified for Team GB for Rio. I was on my way to becoming quite the big deal.' He looked down at his orange, decided he didn't feel like eating anymore and placed it back in the rustling plastic bag.

'What happened?' I asked, placing my sandwich down too, although I was still hungry. He stared over the water, his eyes misting with a memory that he didn't feel like sharing. I looked down at his hand spread over the grass and placed mine on top of it.

He turned and looked at me like he'd forgotten I was there. 'You don't have to tell me if you don't want to.'

'I'll tell you all about it, just not here.' He picked the orange up again and pretended that everything was fine. I was beginning to worry about how good he was at doing that.

The final ascent to the summit was a climb through loose rocks and shingle that tumbled beneath our feet as we climbed. The wind whipped my hair in front of my face and rendered me occasionally blind. It was a struggle to push on through the final few metres, my legs aching, my heart pounding in my head. But when we got to the rectangular stone block that signalled the summit, I felt an overwhelming sense of achievement.

Theo held on to the stone as he panted and wiped the sweat from his forehead before it had chance to freeze in the bitter wind.

The view was like nothing I'd seen before, as if I was seeing the earth from heaven.

'We did it,' he said, a look of fulfilment on his face as he threw his arms up above his head and let out a *whoop* that ricocheted around us, echoing for an age before disappearing.

I pulled my phone from my pocket and snapped photographs of the view, just so that when I woke up the next day, I would have proof to show myself that I actually did this.

'And you thought we would die up here,' Theo said.

'Let's make it down before we celebrate too much,' I replied.

I felt his gaze upon my face and when I turned, I saw that he was staring at me.

'What?' I asked, wondering if I still had half my cheese sandwich smeared over my cheek.

He took my phone from my hand, turned it to front-facing camera, leaned in and kissed me.

I barely heard the artificial click of the camera as he pulled me towards him. I barely felt the wind. I barely even remembered who I was until he pulled away and smiled down at me, pushing my phone back into my pocket and letting out another *whoop!*

In that moment, I think I was the happiest I've ever been.

\* \* \*

Just below the summit was a crumbling building known as the summit shelter. We went inside. The roof was filled with holes and bugs that skittered above us. Theo took my hand and led me to a spot on the wall where he pointed out a stone that had been carved with angular graffiti. It read:

*Theo and Megan Morgan were here 2011*
*Y dringo ydy popeth/The climb is everything*

I ran my fingers over the letters, a layer of dust coming off onto my fingertips. Theo cleared his throat and I turned to see him holding out a Swiss Army knife.

'Go on then, leave your mark.' He placed the knife in my hand. 'Just be careful, I know what you're like and we don't want to call out the air ambulance.'

I took the knife, carved my name on the stone beside Theo's and took a photograph.

'May I do the honours?' I asked, holding out my hand. He placed the list into my palm, along with a little silver pen that he pulled from his Swiss and I crossed out the mission.

The encroaching feeling of anxiety grew like a balloon in my chest as we passed the threshold into Theo's hometown. It had taken most of the day to travel up and down Cadair Idris and then it was an hour and a half drive to get to the town where Theo had been born.

'How come you don't have an accent?' I asked, my mouth full of gummy Haribo rings. I'd always had a problem with accents, not because I didn't like them, but because if someone had a particularly strong one, I found it almost impossible not to imitate them.

'What do you mean I don't have an accent?' he asked,

letting the strong sing-song Welsh accent form around his words.

I laughed.

He cleared his throat and continued in his usual voice. 'I was born in Wales but then my dad's business took him to England and we moved there when I was four. They kept the old house and as soon as they could move back home, they did. I stayed in England to finish school and because that's where Jenny was. After that fell apart, I kind of bungeed between the two, doing Dad's work in Birmingham so that they could continue to live here.'

'Wouldn't you rather live out here too?' I asked.

'Would you be here? Because if not, then no, I wouldn't.' He smiled to himself. He was the unbeaten champion of charm. I wished I was more immune to it.

'Will they like me? Because, you know, people don't generally tend to,' I said, the worry seeping back in once the thrill of the charm had gone.

'Hopefully, just don't break a priceless antique or insult them and I'm sure you'll be fine.'

See, I knew that he was joking, but still the possibility of me tripping and landing on a priceless Wedgwood urn and then offending them by telling them it was ugly anyway, was not that far-fetched.

# Chapter Sixteen

My family had never been rich. Even the relatives going back hundreds of years had been either scraping by or in the poorhouse and, although we weren't quite as near the breadline as they had been, we hadn't moved very far up the financial ladder. I had lived in the same house since I'd been born; a run-of-the-mill semi-detached suburban with two bedrooms and a medium-sized garden. I'd always loved that house, modest and cramped as it was, but as we approached Theo's childhood home, I saw that *modest* and *cramped* were words that had never been mentioned in the same sentence as the Morgan house, if you could even call it a house.

'Your house has gates,' I stated, eyebrows well and truly raised. 'Are you, like, millionaires or something?'

'Not quite, but we have enough to afford gates.' He leaned over and popped the glove box, taking out a small black key fob. He opened the window and passed the fob over a reader before the gates opened in front of us like a very middle-class version of Jurassic Park.

'You failed to mention that you live in a gated mansion.'

'That's probably because *I* don't actually live here anymore and I'd have sounded like a dick if I'd mentioned it,' he said as he slowly drove down the rhododendron-lined driveway, the few leaves that were left speckled with rain. I began to feel our mountain lunch repeat on me as we neared the end of the drive and the bushes fell away to reveal an immaculately kept lawn; it was one of those that had been mown into that fancy two-tone stripe pattern and it stretched out to a lake that lay just behind. The house itself was small for a manor house, but a manor house all the same, complete with sculpted creatures adorning the roof and a shiny old Land Rover sitting in the driveway.

Theo parked the car and turned to me abruptly.

I noticed then that a sheen of sweat clung to his brow and his usually warm complexion had turned slightly pallid. 'So, a quick crash course in how this is gonna work. My dad, he will insist you call him Rhys, is going to mention Great-Uncle Alwyn almost immediately after meeting you. He's then going to mention him a few more dozen times before we leave, so just a heads up on that. My sister, Tessa, tends to be a bit absentminded and will probably act like you are the Antichrist until you prove her wrong.'

'What about your mum?'

'Oh, don't bring her up.'

'Why?'

'Because she's dead.'

I recoiled.

Was I being an idiot or had he never mentioned this before?

I scanned back through all the conversations we'd ever had and tried to find the moment when he'd told me that his mother was dead, but he hadn't.

'What? When? How?'

'Died. Five years ago. Stroke,' he said matter-of-factly like he was recalling morbid things from *The Generation Game* conveyer belt.

'And you tell me now?' I held my hands out in frustration as I saw his dad open the front door and walk towards the car with a Theo-like smile on his face. 'Why didn't you say anything? I bitched about my own mother non-stop to you. I never would have done that if I'd known.'

The sound of a car door opening broke off Theo's response and the greying head of his father poked in, smiling a cheery welcome.

'What took you so long?' he asked, and I knew right then that his sing-song accent was going to be impossible not to imitate.

'Hi, Dad.' Theo stood and pulled his dad into a hug as I got out and smoothed down my clothes, like I always did when I was nervous. 'This is Effie.'

The man turned to me and I saw an older version of Theo looking back at me. He had the same high cheekbones and gentle blue eyes. His chin was partially covered in hair, like Theo's, but unlike his son his hair was dark, almost black, with streaks of grey running through it like seams of slate.

'Nice to meet you, Effie,' he said bypassing my outstretched hand and going straight in for an overly familiar hug. He was tall, with long strong arms, and what was a hug for him was a near-death experience for me.

'It's nice to meet you too, Mr Morgan,' I said once I had regained the use of my lungs.

'Rhys, call me Rhys.'

'You have a beautiful home,' I said, because I thought that was something normal people would say. It wasn't a lie though; it *was* beautiful, with ornate bargeboards that hung down over the eaves of the house and the twisted chimneys that rose from the roof.

'It's all courtesy of Great-Uncle Alwyn of course, but Theo will have told you all about him already,' Rhys began. I noticed Theo smile from behind his father before I shook my head. 'Alwyn was the creator of the Morgan spring; tiny device, smaller than the nail on your little finger, but no piece of machinery can run without it. Genius man.' Rhys continued his story as he placed his hand on my shoulder and led me into the house, under the stone porch draped with ivy, and into the entrance hall; leaving Theo to get the bags.

Staying at the Morgans' was like staying in a luxury guest house, complete with freshly laundered towels on the foot of the perfectly made bed and an unopened travel-sized toothpaste in the glass cup beside the sink in the en suite. It made me slightly nauseous to think that people did this in their own homes.

At my house, you were lucky if you got to the new tube before Elliot indulged his twisted fascination of standing on it and watching the contents splurge onto the basin. After that you'd have to use the sink like a palette and scrape off what you needed.

I tossed my bag onto the upholstered stool that sat before an antique vanity table but didn't bother unpacking my things. I was only staying for two nights so what would be the point?

I pulled off my shirt, lifted it to my nose and inhaled the smell of sweat and soil and just a tinge of the oranges that Theo had packed for lunch. I would probably need to shower soon, although I felt like I had earned that sweat and shouldn't give it up so easily. I pulled on a shirt that smelled a little less like the musk of my armpits and walked to the door.

I heard the sound of Theo unpacking in the next room and padded down the hall, my bare feet enjoying the soft pile of the wine-coloured carpet.

Everything I saw looked perfect: the burgundy-painted walls, the gothic sconces that illuminated the ceiling and cast a soft, eerie light down the hallway. Everything had been placed with purpose, not slung there for convenience.

I passed a wall of photographs and stopped to look when one caught my eye.

The Theo in the photograph was younger, doughier and around four or five years old. His white blond hair flopped over his eyes and his chubby cheeks showed nothing of the striking cheekbones that they would come to be. He grinned at the camera, his mouth a mishmash of white milk teeth and gaping expanses of gum where they had fallen out and made him money while he slept. I smiled to myself and turned my gaze to the photograph beside it. Theo was older in the next one, around twenty, maybe, each of his arms draped over the shoulders of the women beside him. The one on his right had to be his mother, Megan. She had the same crooked smile, the same shade of sandy blonde hair, bobbed at the nape of her neck, and the same glimmer of mischief about her. She was pretty and slender, with soft kind eyes that were brown, unlike Theo's, but held a look that matched her son's exactly.

The other woman could barely be seen, because someone had cropped the photo to exclude her. But that didn't matter; I still knew who it was. Her hand rested on his stomach, perfectly manicured and glistening with a sparkling engagement ring.

Had Theo folded her out or had one of the others done that for him?

Theo was standing beside the bed with his back to the door when I walked in. His room was large, with burnt-orange walls and so much paraphernalia that I almost laughed. The *Star Wars* figurines, still sealed in their packets, sat under a fine layer of dust on a shelf above his window and a *Labyrinth* poster sat framed on the wall. A punch bag hung from the ceiling in one corner and on the dresser were several awards and framed photographs of Theo in the ring, his fists raised, all expression of friendliness gone from his eyes.

I watched him as he unpacked, oblivious to my presence, and it was one of the rare moments I had seen Theo 'in the wild', as it were. Here, in his childhood room he wasn't trying to impress anyone with his witty banter or disarm anyone with that superhuman smile, he was just being Theo. He lifted a hand to his back and began rubbing up and down his spine. I felt his pain, literally, after climbing a mountain that I was unbelievably underqualified to climb.

I cleared my throat to announce my arrival, my eyes landing on a pile of old comic books that would probably be worth thousands, had they not been folded and thumbed to within an inch of their lives.

I picked up a Boba Fett Bobblehead and gave it a flick.

'Do not judge me, woman,' he said, still unpacking things onto his bed. 'This stuff could make me thousands.'

'Oh, so you're only keeping them for investment reasons?' I tilted my head and quirked my brow.

'Of course,' he lied.

I walked over to the giant *Labyrinth* poster and stared into the eyes of a life-size David Bowie. 'I guess it would be stupid of me to ask if this is your favourite film?'

'If you ask me that again,' he began in a terrible Bowie-esque voice, 'I'll have to suspend you head first in the Bog of Eternal Stench.'

'I'm guessing that that's a line from the film. I've never seen it.'

'Well, that is an absolute crime against cinema and will be rectified before you set foot back in England,' he said in a jovial yet highly serious voice. I wandered over to him as he pulled a toothbrush out and flung it onto the bed, perching myself on the nightstand and watching him as he ferreted around further into the depths of the bag that was seemingly bottomless.

'Do all the girls you bring here get to see your room or am I a special exception?' I asked, joking but at the same time wondering if this was something he had done before.

'Oh yes, I bring all my women here to join the harem. You will meet the rest of them later.'

He looked up at me and grinned, but it didn't quite reach his eyes; I wondered if the reason for this was the headache that had started on the mountain.

As he looked at me, something in his eyes changed and a moment later he abandoned his bag and stepped towards me, his eyes looking at me with an intensity that made me feel like I needed to turn away. I looked down at his arms, corded with muscle as they reached for me. He stepped between my knees and brushed the hair from my eyes before leaning down to kiss me.

I should have been used to it by now, but it still knocked the wind out of me like a kick to the stomach. It felt strange to have someone like him pressing his lips to mine, as if I was daydreaming and at any second would be woken from it by the sound and subsequent panic of Elliot relieving himself in my boots. A bloom of heat erupted in my chest as he curled his fingers around the back of my neck and ran his thumb along my jaw.

I kissed him back, timidly at first before taking his face in my hands and pulling him to me hungrily. Once I'd tasted him, I never wanted him to stop, never wanted him to stop wanting me like he did right now. He slid his hand under the hem of my shirt, his fingers warm on my stomach. In turn I slid my hands over his back, feeling his muscles tense beneath his shirt as he moved. My heart hammered like bass sounding from a passing car as I savoured every touch, every burst of electricity that fizzed and crackled in my chest.

'Theo?' a feminine voice called from downstairs and the spell was broken. He pulled away, his lips swollen from their efforts, the skin around them pink and a dead giveaway.

'That'll be Tessa,' he said with reluctance in his eyes and he stepped away.

I smoothed down my clothes and bit my bottom lip with embarrassment. I'd let my desire run away with me. I wished I'd let it run further.

He readjusted his rumpled clothing and shot me a grin before he took my hand and led me down into the living room.

Tessa waited for him in the archway of the room, her eyes lighting when she saw him. She was tall and thin, with billowy blonde hair that sat in a cloud of unruly frizz around her elfin face. Her skin was palest white and that, coupled with the light shade of her hair, made her look ethereal; like some sort of faerie.

Theo kissed her on the temple before lifting her from the ground and swinging her around like a little girl. Tessa squealed. He placed her down and then looked over at me, something very much like apprehension in his eyes.

'Tessa, this is Effie.' He held out a hand, which I took hold of and walked to his side.

'Hi.' I braced myself for another hug like I'd received from Rhys, but it seemed the Welsh friendliness ended with him. Tessa stepped back, her lips pouting, one eyebrow rising as she sized me up. I held out my hand and waited for her to shake it, but she just left it hanging there. And I'd thought that Tessa would be the least of my problems.

'It's nice to meet you,' I said, thrusting my hand towards her a little more and smiling as sweetly as I could with the tension between us rising by the millisecond.

'Tessa!' Theo whisper-shouted.

She reached out and took my hand, shaking it once before dropping it like hot iron.

'Hello, Effie.' She somehow managed to make it sound like a threat.

Rhys appeared around the archway and called us to the kitchen where a bottle of wine with an ancient-looking label and three glasses were set out next to a tumbler of orange juice.

'I thought we'd toast the return of our traveller and the arrival of his lady friend.' He uncorked the wine, even the *pop* sounded expensive. It made me salivate.

The kitchen was old, with exposed brick and a red Aga. In the window sat a small bed of herbs that glowed in the last rays of the evening sunlight. Rhys poured three glasses of the deep red liquid and handed the OJ to Theo.

'Actually, I'll have wine,' he said, walking over to a cupboard and taking out a glass that sparkled like new.

I bet they had a dishwasher, that'd be why all their stuff was so shiny. I wish we had a dishwasher.

Tessa and Rhys eyed Theo with trepidation as he poured himself a glass and retook his position beside me.

Was he a recovering alcoholic? Could that be the secret?

Rhys lifted his glass and said, 'Theo and Effie.'

Tessa lifted her glass, said Theo's name loudly and then drank without uttering mine.

The wine passing over my tongue felt like arriving home after a long day. I closed my eyes and savoured it. I bet this cost more than the usual £5.99 special from Bobby's.

Theo and Tessa made dinner while Rhys and I sat at the table in the room next door, sharing easy conversation. The table was long enough to seat twenty and made from oak that was stained a light colour that accentuated the knots and grains of the wood. The chairs were high-backed and heavy, but seriously comfortable. Every word seemed to reverberate through the air, all the way up to the high ceilings, as Rhys talked with ease.

'What is it that you do, Effie?' he asked, leaning forward on his elbows.

'I work in a bookshop and I . . .' I said before I stopped myself, wondering why I'd thought of telling him about my book. I knew I'd drunk the wine a bit too quickly but surely it hadn't affected me that much. '. . . I write.'

'Ah, a writer. Loving a writer is hard; our Theo has chosen himself a challenge,' he said, a far-off look coming into his eye. 'You can love a writer with every cell in your body, but you will always know that your beloved's affection is shared between you and every character they create.'

I smiled. It was poetic and sad and completely true. 'Do you speak from experience?'

'Megan was a writer, never published, but she loved

nothing more than to create the worlds that came into her head.'

Shit! I'd had one job and that was not to mention his dead wife and here I was, forcing him to bring her up in our second conversation.

I waited for him to clam up or break down and leave the room, but all he did was smile.

'I was sorry to hear about what happened to her. Theo only told me today.' I took another sip of wine, not sure if I was saying the right thing so I sated my worry with alcohol.

'It was a shock for all of us, especially Theo, seeing as how it happened,' he began, taking the stem of the glass in his hand and oscillating the wine. 'Tessa and I live in the house that *she* lived in. We use the pans *she* bought and we repaint the walls with the colours that *she* chose. We are used to her not being here anymore, even if we wish it wasn't so. Theo isn't as far along as we are, but then he had three times the loss we did.'

'Are you talking about Jenny?' I asked.

Rhys nodded. 'He lost his mother in February and his fiancée in May, his career somewhere in-between and then we almost lost him. Half of the people in his life and his vocation, lost to him in four months.'

'What do you mean you almost lost him?' I asked leaning in. He looked at me with something resembling pity and was about to open his mouth to reply but as he did, the others walked into the room and the conversation died on the terracotta floor tiles.

'Dinner is served,' Tessa said, placing a casserole dish down on a placemat and lifting the lid with a flourish. Steam billowed out and the smell of something incredible wafted into my nostrils. 'Coq au vin, almost. You know Theo never uses a recipe and we didn't have about four hours to stand around making it.'

'You made this?' I asked, looking up into Theo's smug face and wondering why he'd let me cook that swill for him when he could make stuff like this. He nodded and took a seat opposite me, nursing the same glass of wine he'd been drinking since we arrived, and we ate the meal to the sound of easy conversation. I thought back to all the times he'd drank with me. Had I been unknowingly fuelling his decline back into alcoholism?

His mum died, his boxing ended for some reason, Jenny left him, it all pushed him over the edge and he got a drinking problem. I bet that's what it was.

I felt something brush my ankle and almost yelped, but one look at Theo's grin and I realised that it was his foot, his naked toes tracing circles on my skin.

I looked at him over the steaming casserole dish and watched as he took another swig. I wanted to reach over and smash the glass so that he wouldn't fall deeper. Had that been what had attracted him to me? A kindred, pickled spirit?

After dinner Rhys showed me an album of baby photos, I laughed at the two-year-old Theo who stood beside his sister's cot and sneered at the new arrival, before Theo snatched the album away and hid it out of sight.

It was full dark when Theo made us all sit down to watch *Labyrinth*. Tessa groaned and Rhys settled down for a snooze. I noticed that Tessa had placed herself as far away from me as possible at the other end of the sofa. I was used to people not liking me, but I usually gave them a reason to do so before they decided to hate me.

Theo slid the Blu-ray into the machine and rubbed his hands together.

'Oh, for the love of God.' Tessa sighed. 'You do know other films exist, right?'

'Shut up or I'll call the Goblin King to come and take you away,' Theo said as he pressed play and the opening credits rolled to the sound of Bowie's voice.

I watched him as he bobbed his head to the Eighties music and mouthed every line of dialogue along with the characters.

By the time the credits rolled Rhys was snoring loudly into a velvet throw pillow.

'Well?' Theo turned to me excitedly.

'I liked it, except for the obvious green screen and the wires that you can clearly see holding up the set,' I replied.

He shook his head in disappointment. 'Effie, this is an Eighties classic. The flaws only help add to its charm.'

I agreed rather than ruin his evening and excused myself to the bathroom.

I sat on the lid of the sparkling dual flush toilet and prodded my finger into a bowl of potpourri on the windowsill. I withdrew my finger, sniffed it, winced.

It stank of vanilla; I hated vanilla.

I stood and washed my hands, the lights surrounding the mirror illuminating my face as I stared into it. I'd been so nervous about meeting Theo's family that I looked drained from all the worry, and the mountaineering probably hadn't helped the bags beneath my eyes. I needn't have worried when it came to Rhys. He couldn't have been nicer to me. Tessa, however, had disliked me on sight, if not before. I had seen that in the almost invisible curl of her top lip and the slant of her eyelids when she'd first turned to acknowledge me. I didn't know what Tessa had decided I lacked, but it was clear that I wasn't welcome to have her brother.

I turned off the bathroom light and walked out onto the landing, hearing hushed voices arguing in the hallway below. I moved closer, my feet padding gently over the burgundy carpet as Theo and Tessa came into view. I sat down on the top step and pressed my face through the spindles.

'. . . you just need to be careful is all I'm saying. You can't just do whatever you want, whenever you want to do it,' Tessa half whispered half shouted, her brows drawn up in frustration.

'It was half a glass of wine, Tessa. I didn't exactly go on a bender.' His hands became fists at his sides, his jaw set.

'And that's all you've had recently is it, just that half glass? That girl clearly drinks like a fish – Dad and her drank that whole bottle like it was Ribena.'

I frowned and gritted my teeth.

'Hey! Don't talk about Eff like that. She's been really nervous about coming here and I assured her that you and Dad would be nice, but I didn't get the round robin about you going in for surgery and having that stick implanted up your arse.' I clenched my fist in solidarity with him. 'I like her, Tessa. You know I wouldn't bring her here if she was just some girl, not after . . .'

'After Jenny?' Tessa finished his sentence for him. 'Jenny is the exact reason that you *should* be careful with this Effie. You haven't told her yet, have you?'

Theo went quiet, his nostrils flaring, relaxing, flaring, relaxing. I waited for one of them to mention it. The secret I wasn't allowed to know, but neither of them did.

'Have you?' Tessa almost shouted. Theo shushed her and stepped forward, his voice quieter than before.

'No . . . I haven't told her.'

'Then you had better tell her soon and find out if she's anything like Jenny was. If she's different, then that's fine, I'll drop the attitude and be happy for you, but until then I'm not going to welcome someone into our lives, love her and trust her like we all did before, if she's going to turn out to be like *Her*.' She stepped closer and took his face in her hands. 'I love you. You are my big brother, the only one I'll ever have, and it is my job to protect you from evil people.'

'Effie isn't evil,' Theo said, his voice softening, his fists now only hands.

'Then tell her and prove it.'

I walked back into the living room as if I'd heard nothing. Tessa glanced my way before throwing a blanket over Rhys and scurrying off to her studio by the lake to finish what she was working on. When she was gone, Theo took my hand and led me back upstairs.

Was he finally going to let me in on whatever it was that seemed so important?

He pulled me into his room, shut the door and turned around, hitting me with that smile that excused him of anything before he'd even been accused.

'I have a confession.' He took something from the top of the dresser and hid it behind his back.

'Should I be worried?' I stepped closer, my hands clasped and fidgeting in front of me. I prepared myself for the truth.

Would it change anything? Would it change how I saw him? I hoped not.

'I had an ulterior motive in bringing you here this weekend.'

'Is this when you reveal that you're actually a prolific serial killer and lock me in your kill room?' I said, trying to keep the mood light so he would feel at ease to tell me. I noticed his gaze flicker to my lips and then back up to my eyes.

'Almost, but not quite.' He pulled his hand from behind him, his fingers holding two tickets to see The Rosehipsters the following day.

'How? I didn't even know they were touring.' I looked at him, wide-eyed.

'I have my sources.' He tapped the side of his nose. 'They were sold out but an old friend from college works there and he got us in.' He stepped forward and held them out to me. 'We still need to tick off mission two after all.'

My lips fell apart as I looked from him to the tickets and back again. I'd wanted to see them for a decade and now I actually had tickets. This time tomorrow night I'd be there, watching them.

Something quite like, but more pleasant than indigestion burned in my chest and all I wanted to do was kiss him.

'So, do you want to go?' he asked, after words had failed me.

His hand trembled slightly as he held the tickets out to me, a beaming smile on his face.

Blood whooshed in my ears as I swallowed my worries and knocked the tickets from his hand.

I suddenly resented everything that came between us: the air, our clothes, the self-consciousness I felt at the thought of being liberated from those clothes. All thoughts of unveiling his secrets had vanished and were now only thoughts of my skin touching his, of his warmth seeping into me. I wanted to know what he felt like, what the expanse of his chest smelled like and with that in mind I moved closer still.

I rose to my tiptoes and pressed my mouth to his with a desperation that I hadn't felt quite so keenly the last time. His lips were soft and were flavoured with the rich wine that I had drunk earlier; it tasted better from his mouth than it had from the glass. At first, he seemed to go rigid, startled by my sudden step into action, but after a moment I felt him give way; his hands rising to the back of my head and pulling me close.

Lip slid over lip. Tongue over tongue. Tooth nicked lip and then slid away, the mild pain of it forgotten instantly. Hands fumbled, touching familiar places and places that had yet to be touched. I urged him back, the mattress knocking his knees out from under him. The springs twanged as he landed, his eyes stricken with a look of intoxication as he stared up at me. I gritted my teeth, not knowing where this sudden burst of confidence was coming from. I almost let the embarrassment stop me as I pulled my top over my head and discarded it, but I wanted him to see me, all of me. I reached behind and unhooked my new bra, flinging it to the ground and standing there, half naked in front of him. His eyes moved over me as he sat up, his hands reaching out and moving over the arch of my waist, the curve of my breasts. I reached down and unbuttoned his shirt, pushing it back over his wide, solid shoulders.

His skin gleamed with the subtle light of the bedside lamp as my eyes devoured every inch of him: the rapid rise and fall of his chest, the strong arms that reached for me as he pressed his lips to my stomach, the dappling of sandy hair that covered his chest. I could wait no longer and, as a small sigh escaped my lips, I pushed him back and climbed on top, my hair falling over his cheek as I looked down at him, his hot breath on my face.

He pulled my lips to his once more and he made a small noise in his throat when they touched, as if their being apart had been a terrible agony. He rolled over, his arms tensing as they held his weight above me, although his body still knocked what little breath I did have out of my lungs.

I tugged at the shirt that still hung from him and tossed it to the floor, my hands wasting no time in returning to his back and feeling the muscles tense and relax beneath his skin.

Every nerve within me tingled with excitement; every breath felt like the first. He had a tiny scar on his shoulder, a thin white line that barely stood out at the end of his collarbone. I leaned up and kissed it, the taste of his skin filling my mouth as his lips marked a path in kisses down my neck.

He pulled away, his face a blur of proximity, and the breath caught in my throat. I waited for him to speak, to tell me that he couldn't do this. But all he did was lift a hand to my cheek and kiss me, softly, tenderly. It was a kiss that spoke louder than any words when given in the midst of such careless passion.

Nevertheless, I felt the words rise up in my throat and sit on my tongue, ready to be said. My lips parted, the words demanded to be spoken and yet I found myself mute.

It had never been a question of *if* I would fall in love with Theo; I knew that now. The only question had been *when* and as I looked at him, his lips pulled into that smile I had known would be trouble from the very start, I knew that *when* was now.

He fell asleep before I did. His head lolling to face me, his eyes closed in peaceful slumber. His arm was outstretched and hung on my hip as I lay watching him from a few inches away. It was as if he didn't want to let me go, even in sleep.

It seemed that the fourth time had been the charm. There had been no sign of any vomit, no allergic reactions and no passionate declarations about seahorses. It had been exactly how it should.

I felt oddly still, maybe even a little serene.

I noticed him move and thought that he'd woken, but his eyes remained closed. His shoulders trembled slightly, the movement audible in his breaths. I wondered if he was cold. He wasn't wearing anything and the blankets that covered us weren't all that thick, but the room wasn't cold.

I scooted towards him, pulling the blanket up and over his exposed shoulder, my arm wrapping around him, my nose pressing into the warmth of his chest as our breaths fell into a unified rhythm.

I vowed then to remember this moment, the feeling, the smell, the happiness of it. I wanted this to be the memory that came back when my life flashed before me. This memory was my happy place.

# Chapter Seventeen

It took me a second or two to remember where I was when my eyes finally fell open, but the wall poster and the smell of Theo that lingered on my lips brought the memories back with a smile. I turned my head to the side and saw him, sprawled on his front, his mouth ajar and his hair jutting out at every angle.

I grinned and lay on my side, facing him and watching as his back rose and fell.

I wanted to wake him and recreate the night before, but he was such a picture, snoring gently into the plaid pillowcase, that I felt like waking him would be a crime.

I clambered out of bed, my muscles feeling like they'd turned to rock from yesterday's hike, and made for the pile of clothes that lay crumpled on the floor. I looked at the lacy purple knickers/mild torture device and decided to forgo those for a pair of well-worn cotton briefs. I'd be sure to find the ones I'd hidden at the bottom of my bag when I got back to the room I should've spent the night in. I scrunched the knickers into a ball and pushed them into my pocket. I donned the rest of my clothes and tiptoed towards the door. As I made to leave, I noticed a collection of silver packets lying on the top of the dresser. I glanced behind me, checking that he was still asleep before beginning my first official snoop on a lover.

I picked one of them up and turned it over. There were five of the blister packs; all were half empty and contained different drugs. I glanced at the names, recognising one as an antihistamine, but I didn't know about the rest.

Maybe they were for his nut allergy, or for hay fever. I knew Joy always had a pack of them ready for those first few weeks after the seasons began to change when she'd start annoying me by sneezing hysterically, but it was November and so that seemed unlikely.

I was about to leave when I spotted another packet, hidden between the wall and a book named *100 Films to See Before You Die*. I pulled the pack out and turned it over. Diazepam.

I'd heard of it before but I had no idea what it did; there was only one pill missing.

Back in my room I ruffled up the bed sheets for effect and then pulled the long, draping curtains back from the window. It was only just light and yet Tessa was already outside, sitting in the grass that jutted out a little way into the lake like a pier.

I found my phone and typed diazepam into the search.

The results came up slowly, the remote location causing a sluggish internet connection, but when they had finally loaded, I saw that the drug was used to treat several anxiety disorders.

Theo, anxious? I couldn't think of anyone less likely to display anxious behaviour.

Was this what he was hiding – some sort of mental health problem?

Before heading to the bathroom, I took the list from my

jean pocket and found mission four – *Fall in love.* I took my eyeliner and crossed out the words, feeling something stronger than accomplishment when they disappeared behind the line of heavy black liner.

I showered and dressed in an oversized green jumper and leggings before tiptoeing down the stairs, letting my damp hair hang over my shoulder and soak into the fabric.

At the bottom of the stairs I found my old brown boots sitting neatly by the wall and slipped them on before stepping out into the chilled morning and making my way to Tessa. After last night and what I'd found this morning, I wanted to know everything.

He had seen me, my body exposed to him in a way that made me feel vulnerable. He had seen into my soul and yet he wouldn't let me peek at his.

Tessa sat with her back to the house as I tentatively approached. She had her legs crossed, her feet pulled up onto her knees and a glass cup of what looked like old dried leaves crammed into boiling water sat beside her in the grass.

'Good morning,' I said, my voice coming out quiet and small.

Tessa didn't open her eyes or turn to face me, she just exhaled and patted the ground beside her. I sat down; the grass was damp. When she didn't speak, I decided to just bite the bullet and say it.

'I heard you two arguing last night in the hallway.'

'Good to know. Next time I'll pick a more private place to talk about you,' she replied, her eyes closed, the tips of her middle fingers pressed to the tips of her thumbs.

'What is it that you're all keeping from me?' I didn't mean it to come out as accusatory as it did.

'What has *he* told you?'

'I know that something happened around the same time that your mum passed away and I think that it might be the reason Jenny left, but that's purely speculation at this point.'

'Is that all?'

'Your dad told me that something happened and you almost lost him, but Theo's told me nothing other than what I know about Jenny and that he stopped boxing, but he didn't tell me why.' My curls were now on the verge of freezing into a solid mass across my shoulder. The chill made me shiver.

'Was he . . . *is* he an alcoholic?'

'Why do you ask that?' She raised an eyebrow.

'Because of how weirdly you all acted when he had wine last night.'

Tessa turned her head, her eyes opening; they sparkled cornflower blue in the morning sunlight. 'You're observant,' she said, sounding almost impressed.

'Not really – it was hard to miss,' I replied. I could almost feel her softening towards me . . . almost.

Tessa took a breath and waited a while before speaking. 'No, he's never been an alcoholic.'

I thought for a moment or two before speaking again.

'What about the pills in his room? I saw them this morning.' I picked at a blade of grass with my jagged thumbnail, bitten to oblivion by nervous teeth.

Tessa cocked an eyebrow and smiled. 'You were in Theo's room this morning?'

I flushed the colour of beetroot and occupied my eyes with looking at anything other than her. 'That doesn't matter. Please, just tell me what happened.'

'What exactly did he say when you asked him?' she said, exhaling loudly through her nose.

'He said that he would tell me, but when the time was

right.' I remembered back to yesterday when he'd said that. The look that had clouded his eyes showed he wasn't ready to relive it.

Tessa sighed; she looked as frustrated as I felt. 'Look, if it was down to me it would have been the first thing I'd told you. But it's not my story to tell. What you need to know about Theo is that he can't let anything go. People, places, things that happened.' She glanced back at the house and sighed again. 'Dad and I, we lost so much five years ago. But Theo, he lost more than both of us. When he's ready to tell you how his life fell apart, he will, and when he does, you'll have to ask yourself if you are the kind of person who will stay and watch him fall apart or the kind who'll leave the pieces. God knows, most people are the latter.' She fixed me with a look, its meaning I wasn't sure of, and closed her eyes, retaking her meditative pose. I took that as my cue to leave. I stood, my ass wet from the moist grass, and began walking back towards the house.

'Effie!' Tessa called. I stopped and turned back; she looked like a water nymph ready to lure me to the water and drown me in its depths. 'I know it doesn't seem like it, but I like you. In some ways you're good for him – I can see it. But hurt him like Jenny did and I'll hunt you down like an animal.' She smiled sweetly before returning to her meditation.

In the bathroom, I towel-dried my thawing hair and applied some make-up to my eyes, before returning to Theo's room where I sat down on the bed cross-legged and waited for him to wake. He breathed heavily, loudly, as he dawdled in slumber. His face was half buried in the pillow, the sheets pulled down to reveal his back. I slid onto my side and lay down next to him, my fingers moving to his shoulder and gently tracing patterns onto his skin. His breathing changed as he fell upwards through the levels of consciousness, his eyes flickering as he slowly woke.

When he eventually stirred, he seemed shocked to have company, but once the confusion of slumber faded, he put an arm around me and pulled me close. I was overly conscious of the fact that he was still naked, separated from me only by my clothes and the thin sheet that had remained after all others had fallen to the floor.

'Good morning,' he said, shuffling closer.

Despite his grin he looked unusually tired, his eyes ringed in dark shadows. He pressed his lips to my cheek; the fogginess of sleep still clinging to his eyes. I tried to keep the thought of why I was there in the forefront of my mind, but as his lips moved from my cheek to my lips all thoughts of confronting him slipped away. The layers of clothing and bed sheet that separated us were quickly disposed of and thirty minutes later I lay back, my attempt at staying on track utterly abandoned.

He looked at me with contentment in his eyes, a contentment that I was about to shatter.

'I need to ask you something.' I sat up, pulling the sheet around my chest.

'I know what you're going to ask.' He turned to me with serious eyes. My stomach flipped. 'Did I always know that I had such skill in the bedroom or was it just a happy surprise? I hope I didn't startle you too much, but then I did warn you that I was a screamer.' He grinned, and it was everything I didn't need right now.

I looked over at him, his smiling face and the look of satisfaction in his eyes. He was perfect. Everything that just happened had been perfect.

I didn't want to push him. He'd promised me that he would tell me everything and I had to trust that he would.

'You know you can tell me anything, don't you?' I asked, leaning over and kissing his shoulder. 'Anything, even if you think it will change how I feel about you. You can tell me.' I felt his hot breath dancing on my neck and a moment later a kiss was planted where that breath had danced.

'Of course I do,' he replied as his face came parallel and his lips fell back to mine.

I tore the end from my croissant and bit into it with hungry teeth. My stomach groaned as the first bit of flaky pastry landed inside it.

Theo sat beside me with his head bowed over a tall mug of coffee – decaf, black. The steam curled from the dark liquid and rose up towards his face. His eyes stared down into the depths of his drink like it was a Magic 8-Ball.

'You all right?' I asked, placing my hand on his knee beneath the table.

He inhaled sharply through his nose and turned to me as if I'd woken him from a particularly deep daydream. 'Fine. Just tired after our mountaineering and . . . other exertions.' He twisted a smile and I felt the smile catch onto my own lips.

'Why are you drinking decaf then?' I asked topping up my own mug from the cafetière that buzzed with caffeine.

'Normal coffee makes me jittery,' he replied.

Rhys wandered in from the kitchen, his hair standing at all angles and a bowl of Shreddies in his hand. He slumped down opposite and nodded us both a hello before tipping the cafetière and swigging at his mug as if it held some sort of antidote. A minute or two later he was his usual self, the caffeine rebooting him to full working order.

223

'What's the plan for today then?' Rhys asked as Tessa came in from the garden wearing a pair of colourful patchwork dungarees. There was terracotta clay smeared along her cheek and in the pale blonde hair just beside it. She sneered at what her father was eating, wandered into the kitchen and returned with a bowl of fruit, which she swapped for his bowl of cereal.

He grimaced and begrudgingly ate his new meal.

'We have a gig later on today, in Chester,' Theo said, sipping his coffee slowly. 'But I thought I might show Effie around before we go.'

It didn't seem like there was much to do around here, but maybe there was a hidden treasure that would surprise me.

'Oh yeah,' Tessa said with sarcastic enthusiasm, 'you could show her the world-famous bench outside the Nisa or if you're lucky there might be a craft exhibition on at the church hall.'

Theo feigned a laugh and sipped his coffee again. He winced and pushed the mug away.

We walked out of the gates at the end of the driveway and Theo took me on a whistle-stop tour of his history. I saw the nursery he'd attended for a few months before he moved to England, the tree where he'd kissed Carys Evans in the summer of 2005 and the shop where he'd stolen a Mars bar when he was twelve. He then went on to tell me how, crippled with guilt, he had returned the Mars bar twenty-four hours later, melted and misshapen from the pocket it had sat in on his bike ride there.

My legs were beginning to work properly again as we reached the final stop on our tour, the muscles regaining their movement after yesterday's climb.

Theo turned right through a metal gate and I stopped walking. I felt my chest tighten as I saw the curve-topped stones scattered around the field. A graveyard.

'Don't say I never take you anywhere,' he said holding out his hand, I took it in mine and let him lead me through the gate. The graves sat in varying stages of disrepair, some tended beautifully with fresh, unwilted flowers, whereas the majority were nothing but overgrown forgotten plots.

We passed a squat little church where a woman pottered around in the flower beds by the doors. She glanced over at us, greeted us in Welsh and then returned to tending the beds. On the outer wall of the building was a small war memorial showing the fewer than twenty names of the men from this tiny town who had left it to fight for their country and never come home. My eyes lingered on the name that sat four from the bottom, carved into the stone and burnished in gold, *Bryn Morgan*.

'A relation of yours?' I asked, running my fingers over the letters.

Theo nodded, but said nothing as we continued to the back right-hand corner.

We stopped before a dark marble stone that sat beneath a tall oak tree, its branches all but bare. Her name was carved in silver. Her life reduced to five lines of text.

Sitting beside the stone was a sculpture, one of Tessa's I presumed, a bird perched on a branch that had been pushed into the ground to make it look as if it had grown there. The bird and the branch were white and the bird held its wings up as if about to take off. It was one of the most beautifully sad things I'd ever seen. At the base of the stone sat several shards of what looked like an old vinyl record, marked and dulled by years under rain and wind.

'Hey, Ma.' He crouched down and brushed the rotting leaves from the grave before sitting down and placing his hand on the grass.

I felt like I was intruding. I hadn't known her. This was a private moment between mother and son. I wasn't meant to be here.

'This is Effie.' He pointed a thumb at me over his shoulder. 'I'm pretty sure you would have got on. She's a writer too and she's clumsy. Trust me to pick someone who's just like my mother. Didn't Freud have a theory about that? I'm sure you would have known it.'

I knelt down beside him and lay my head on his shoulder. His heart was beating so loudly, so quickly. 'I think you would have liked Mum too,' he said, looking back at me with reddening eyes. He wore the sadness on his face in the form of half-mast eyelids and tightened lips.

'If she was anything like you, then I'd have had no choice,' I said, kissing the side of his face and trying not to cry.

I'd asked him to share something, to open up and let me in, and if taking me to his mother's grave wasn't doing that then I didn't know what was. He surreptitiously ran his thumb over his eyes and wiped them dry. I don't know why he tried to hide it – I'd cried in front of him more times than I could count. We were quiet for a long while, the sadness weighing in the air around us as we both looked at the marker of his mother's life. I curled myself around him, my chin nestling into the curve of his neck, my arms around his shoulders.

'What are those shards?' I asked, nodding my head in the direction of the unplayable vinyl.

He took a deep breath. I could almost feel the pain of a memory ripple through him.

'We were sorting through her old record collection one Sunday. She was going to throw them out but I said that I'd have a few and so the whole living room was covered in them. She must have had hundreds, maybe more. There was barely room to sit down,' he said through a sad laugh. 'Tessa and Dad went out to get us an Indian takeaway while Mum and I carried on listening. She put on a Kim Carnes album and "Bette Davis Eyes" came on. It was her favourite song and so she took my hand and danced with me, knocking piles of records over as we twirled around the room. She realised that she'd left her glass of wine in the kitchen and so I went to get it for her. I was gone less than a minute, but when I came back, I found her lying on the floor.'

I felt his jaw clench against mine, his shoulders tensing as he relived it.

'She was lying so awkwardly, her body arching over the piles of records like she'd broken her back. I dropped the wine and ran to her but no matter how I tried to wake her, she just kept on staring at the ceiling. I shouted her name until my throat was hoarse, but . . . nothing. I remember that one of her eyes was slightly off-centre, like they were both looking in different directions.'

I felt my stomach churn at that small, vivid detail.

'The song carried on playing, the same song that we had been dancing to while the blood clot travelled around her body, before we knew that anything was wrong. I called an ambulance and then I called Dad, but there was never any phone signal in town and so I waited, alone.' His voice hitched as he spoke, dangerously close to tears. 'I held her hand while I waited for someone to arrive, but by the time the ambulance got there her hand was cold.'

I pressed my cheek to the shoulder of his shirt and let my tears sink into the fabric. I remembered back to when that very song had come on in the treehouse and how he had quickly skipped it. It had annoyed me back then, when I had thought his mother alive and well, but now I knew that the song would never be the same. Not for me, not for him.

'The next morning, I took the record from the player and smashed it to pieces, but it was her favourite song, so I brought the pieces here.'

I opened my mouth to tell him that I was sorry. Sorry that she'd died, sorry that he'd had to go through that, alone. But no words could express what I wanted them to. No words would bring her back or heal that broken record. And so, I just held him, tighter than before, as he shed a few silent tears, the muscles of his back tightening and slackening when the pain grew and then subsided.

In the distance a bird sang a high-pitched, mournful song and it sounded like a requiem. We listened to the birdsong until the church bells tolled and Theo stood. The tears were wiped away, the memories put back into their boxes and set aside for another time.

We didn't speak much as we walked back to the house. Time was getting on and we'd soon have to head out if we wanted to make it to the gig on time, but there was nothing rushed about the way we meandered back along the winding roads.

I didn't know whether it was the fact that I'd seen Theo vulnerable back there or if it was because I'd found those blister packs this morning, but something about him was worrying me.

I worried every time he raised his hand to his head and then swigged down a painkiller. I worried when I caught him

228

staring off into the distance, his eyes looking straight through the view, and I worried when I noticed the circles that darkened around his eyes.

Was this what life was when you loved someone: endless worrying?

# Chapter Eighteen

I had thought that I'd been one of very few British fans of the obscure American band, but as Theo and I joined the queue outside the tatty-looking venue, I realised that I had underestimated their popularity. There was only an hour to go and yet we were miles away from the front of the queue. It was okay for someone like Theo, six foot tall and with shoulders that could barge through a crowd like a charging bull, but for me – all five foot, five inches of me – I tended to get lost in the crowd, surrounded by views of nothing but shoulder blades and chests. Theo was dressed in a denim shirt that put me in mind of the Wild West, beige chinos and a zip-up hoodie that did nothing to stop the cold from creeping in. He juddered and hopped from foot to foot as he tried to generate some warmth.

I hadn't packed for a night out, so Theo had talked Tessa into letting me borrow something of hers, much to her chagrin. I wore a trendy asymmetric grey jumper that hung down exposing one of my shoulders under a black coat and the jeans that I'd arrived in. My clunky Dr Marten boots had seen better days, with their scuffed brown leather and frayed laces, but all Tessa had to offer were tiny size fours and so there was no hope of me squeezing my giant hobbit feet into a pair of her shoes.

'How many missions will be left on the list after tonight?' Theo asked, his voice trembling as dragon's breath danced from his lips.

'We've done seven, so that means six are left, I think,' I replied, feeling a sense of accomplishment at what we had achieved together.

'Six?' he asked, reeling off the missions in order of completion. 'Did you do one without me?'

I pressed my lips together and shrugged. 'Maybe I miscounted.' I hadn't. I smiled and all was forgotten. I loved him, of that I was certain, but he didn't need to know that I'd crossed that one off just yet. 'Thank you for this.' I reached out and took his hand. His palm was slick with sweat despite the way his lips were turning blue.

'There'll be a lot more gifts coming your way if you react to them like you did last night.' He pushed his arm around my waist and pulled me against him.

I still wasn't used to being touched. The most touching I'd had for a long time was from the brief contact of a customer's palm when giving them their change. It made me feel like everyone was staring and thinking, *What is she doing with him?*

I'd been the same when seeing a happy couple, instant venom building inside me as I thought the words that my mother had always mumbled when she saw lovers: *'Put him down, you don't know where he's been.'*

The inside of the venue was as poorly maintained as the outside. I looked around with mild disgust at the paint-chipped walls and debris of past music enthusiasts that smattered the floor and the faint smell of urinal cakes and stale urea that exuded from the men's toilets.

I was here to see the band, not to move in. I'd just be sure not to touch anything I didn't have to.

Theo led me to the bar and bought me red wine without even checking. I might have been annoyed at that if it wasn't what I'd have ordered anyway. He got himself a pint of foaming beer and we made our way to an area where we had a good view of the stage, but were out of the general crush of the main crowd.

I watched him sip tentatively at his drink as the room grew louder and louder, slowly filling to capacity.

There were so many different types of people here. Young, middle-aged, old. Women, men, even a couple of kids. There were goth types and hipsters and one group who looked like they'd come for a work night out from the office. One of the party – a man sporting a bright red turtleneck and a comb-over – looked as if he might burst into tears at any moment; whether that was due to excitement or purely wanting to be elsewhere so much that the only option was to cry, I could only guess.

After a while the lights went down and the crowd cheered. My heart leapt with excitement and I looked around to place my empty plastic wine glass somewhere. I found that I was hemmed in by bodies on all sides and so just let it drop to the floor; everyone else was doing that anyway.

The band entered the stage to a crescendo of flashing lights and dramatic intro music and then the set began. I tapped my foot and sang along to song after song. It was about all I could do in the space I had. I'd loved this band for ten years, never getting tickets in time or missing a tour completely by being out of the loop, but now I was finally seeing them. It didn't feel real.

The vibration of the music rattled through the floor, zinging up through my legs and making me feel alive. I sang so loudly that my throat began to feel sore but I didn't care.

No one could see me, hemmed in and hidden, so I danced and sang like no one else was there. I felt totally free.

I looked up at Theo and smiled, my heart hammering in every part of me, but something wasn't right.

He looked pained, his eyes made hollow by the lights and his cheeks and forehead beaded with sweat. He stood completely still and stared at the stage with blind eyes looking through the music, his lips slightly parted, his jaw clenched tight.

I squeezed his hand and he turned to me. I saw him in slow motion, his vacant expression transitioning as he turned, so that by the time he looked at me his smiling composure was back in place, a mask of lies.

'You're not okay, are you?' I said, the sound lost in the musical chaos. 'Are you sick?'

He frowned and shook his head. 'I'm fine.' I read his lips as he turned back to the stage, his half-finished pint of beer still clenched in his hand. I stared at the amber liquid swilling around in the thin plastic cup, my body still, every sense on edge. As I watched him, I noticed his hands were shaking; it was the same trembling I'd seen last night as he lay in bed.

'You're lying,' I said, with that same feeling of doom. Then everything seemed to switch to half speed. His hand slackened and the beer fell to the ground, soaking the legs of the man in front of him. The man spun around in anger, his arms raised in confrontation, but I wasn't concerned with his shouts of ruined jeans. I was too busy watching how the colour drained from Theo's face and how his eyes rolled back inside their sockets. I lunged forward as he fell, my arms wrapping around his torso and stretching to link behind him. I pushed my weight onto my right leg, hoping that it would be enough to keep him upright, but he was too heavy and the momentum of him made me lose my footing. He fell with the dead weight of someone who was completely unconscious as I desperately tried to slow his descent and stop him from injuring himself. The crowd parted, making room for us to fall, our bodies hitting the tacky floor with a *thump*, rendered inaudible by the music. I cried out as he landed hard on my wrist, a jolt of pain prickling up my arm as I felt something twang.

I called his name and tapped his cheek, but his head just rolled to the side, unresponsive.

My mind jumped back to the conversation Tessa and I had had this morning and the pills I'd found in his room. Was Theo ill? Had he missed a pill or taken something he shouldn't have? Had a few more to drink without me looking? Or was this all a terribly unfunny practical joke?

The band played on and I recognised the song as one of my favourites, but at that moment I would have given both my eardrums to make it stop. The loud aggression of the guitar scratched at my ears; the bright lights scalded my vision in colourful lines. Claustrophobia began to swell like a dark cloud above me as the knees drew closer. Theo's fingers crunched beneath the rubber sole of a Converse All Star and a drunk girl stood on my calf, unaware of what had been happening behind her. Theo's spilt beer was all that I could smell and it made me want to be sick.

I looked up and called for help but no one was looking at us, lying there on the dirty, dark floor. The lights from the stage couldn't reach us here. I called out again but I couldn't even hear my own voice as the people around us closed in.

I placed my hand on the ground and hovered above him, trying to ignore the stickiness that glued my skin to the floor.

The circle around us was growing smaller by the second, a sea of knees that I couldn't see past. Soon they would be on top of me, on top of Theo. Standing on us both like we were uneven sections of flooring.

And still the music played. I felt my chest go tight, my lungs refusing to expand and take in the sweat-soaked air. I couldn't breathe.

Why was no one helping? Why did no one care?

It was as if I was trapped behind glass, looking desperately up at the people around me for help but they couldn't hear a word I said.

Just then two employees appeared, one taking Theo by the shoulders and the other pushing me aside to get to his legs. They picked him up with difficulty, his large, cumbersome frame proving hard to manoeuvre through a crowd of people who were unwilling to move and lose their space. I scrambled up, my palms stinging once I'd ripped them from the floor like waxing strips, and followed them out of the room, the music quietening as the doors shut behind us.

I felt as if I wasn't really there, but seeing it from afar. Not ten minutes ago I was thinking of how tonight felt like a dream, but that dream now felt nightmarish.

I followed the men to a small room where a woman with

pink hair declared herself as the first aider and rolled Theo into the recovery position, ordering one of the men who'd carried him to call an ambulance.

I stood in the doorway cradling my aching wrist against my chest and watching helplessly as the woman tried to rouse him. She asked me questions that I didn't know the answers to. *Does he have any existing medical conditions? Does he take any medication?* I told her that I'd found some pills in his room but I didn't know what they were or if he'd even taken any.

*Has he taken any recreational drugs or been drinking?* I told the woman that he'd had half a pint of beer and thrown the rest on a man when he'd fallen.

I felt utterly useless.

If only Tessa were here – she'd know what to do.

Panic immediately turned to purpose as I knelt down and pulled Theo's phone from his pocket. I clicked the power button and the lock screen illuminated, with a keypad ready to receive his password.

SHIT!

I didn't know it.

How would I let Tessa and Rhys know?

I was alone and dealing with something I was completely incapable of handling.

Just as I gritted my teeth in fury, I heard the pink-haired woman say that he was coming around. My heart jolted as I stepped over his legs and knelt down beside him.

His eyes lolled inside his skull for a moment or two before they remembered where they were supposed to be and opened wide.

He tried to sit up and look around but was abruptly ordered to stay put by the woman who took his wrist in her hand and measured his pulse.

'What's your password? I need to call your family,' I said. My voice was stripped down to the bare bones of efficiency. He didn't speak, just lifted his thumb to the fingerprint reader and unlocked it. Of course, if I didn't have a phone from the reign of Richard III, I might have thought of that. I quickly dialled Tessa and on the third ring she picked up.

As she did, two paramedics filtered into the room, replacing the two men who had carried Theo in.

'Tessa, it's Effie. Something's happened.'

'Effie? What's wrong?' she asked, her voice panicked. I didn't answer her just handed the phone to one of the paramedics – a bald, middle-aged man with lots of studs running up the curve of his ear. He listened to what Tessa had to say, tapping information into his tablet with lightning-fast fingers. All he said was *'Uh-huh'* and *'Yep'* and *'Okay'* giving me absolutely nothing to go on.

The female paramedic said the word *tachycardia* but I didn't know what that meant.

I felt Theo take my hand and I looked over. His face looked like it had been sapped of all youth, all wellness, everything that made Theo, Theo.

'I'm sorry I ruined your night.' His throat was hoarse, his voice coming out as a high-pitched croak. The female paramedic frowned and looked down his throat before shouting, 'Potential tracheal angioedema' at the man with the tablet. I didn't know what that meant either.

I should have paid more attention when I'd watched *House*, then I might have some fucking idea of what was happening.

The male paramedic nodded and handed the phone back to me.

'Tessa?' I said into the phone.

'Effie! What happened?' Tessa did her best to sound composed, but a telltale skip of panic could be heard in her voice. I told her everything that I could remember and then followed the paramedics as they loaded Theo onto a stretcher and wheeled him to the ambulance that was parked out front. I could hear the band playing another song from inside, the music muffled through the walls.

'Listen, Effie. Just make sure he gets to the hospital safely. We'll be there as soon as we can to take over.'

I hung up and climbed into the back of the ambulance, sitting down in the wall-mounted seat beside the stretcher.

I looked over to Theo, the man who had always seemed so strong, and saw his eyes were pulled wide, staring at the ceiling as his skin turned the slightest tinge of yellow under the harsh fluorescent lights.

'Is he going to be okay?' I asked the man who was attaching a blood pressure cuff to Theo's arm. 'I didn't understand what she was saying before, when she looked in his throat.'

'Tracheal angioedema – it means his throat is swelling up. Like an allergic reaction,' he replied. 'It's not a typical anaphylactic shock, but we're going to treat it as one anyway and hopefully that will sort him out.'

'He's allergic to nuts,' I blurted, in case that would help and then turned back to Theo; his denim shirt was now soaked through and sticking to his skin. I watched his chest as it shuddered up and down, drawing in rapid, ragged breaths.

'Hon,' the paramedic said, pulling a seatbelt from the wall, 'I'm gonna need you to strap in. His blood pressure is very low so we're going to have to blue light him to the hospital.'

I did as he said and then reached for Theo's hand. He

238

looked over and I could see by the glazed look in his eyes that he wasn't behind the wheel right now.

He parted his pale lips and said, 'Sorry I ruined your night, Jen.'

I held my hand to my head and tried not to cry.

# Chapter Nineteen

The tuneless humming of a clerk sat at the A&E desk.

The faint buzz of the fluorescent lights overhead.

The faraway bleeping of a machine that had been sounding for at least thirty minutes.

The torn patch of lino flooring that sat in a ragged triangle as it stuck up and caused a shadow to fall behind it.

The smell of sterile cleaning fluids and stale coffee lingering in the air.

I looked down at the royal blue splint that sat around my hand and lower arm. I'd been taken to get my arm x-rayed and strapped when they found that I had a bad sprain in my wrist after it had broken Theo's fall. I'd been waiting for so long that I could barely remember a time before I was waiting, as if all I'd ever known was this one depressing room.

Opposite sat a pregnant woman and her partner. The partner, a young woman with a round, friendly face looked stricken with anxiety as the pregnant woman smiled and told her that everything would be fine.

Don't believe her. She'll lie to you just like Theo lied to me. He said everything was fine. He said he was well.

A drunk man who could barely form a comprehensible sentence had come in some time ago and sat in one of the highly uncomfortable metal chairs. I was pretty certain that there was nothing wrong with him, other than the one too many Jägerbombs he'd drunk, and he'd just wandered in for somewhere warm to sleep it off before he went home.

I'd been taken to the waiting room after they'd scanned my wrist and I had no idea if anyone even knew that I'd come in with Theo. I'd asked the clerk twice for information but all I'd received in response was a sneer and a curt comment about waiting my turn. In the time since I'd been 'waiting my turn' I had shifted position about eight times a minute, the stress making my muscles fuse into positions that they'd never been in before. I'd drunk so much water from the cooler that I'd peed six times. The added difficulty of having a useless left hand and giant splint made it impossible to go to the bathroom without fear of getting pee on the asymmetric hem of Tessa's jumper. I'd raced back so quickly each time, in case I missed anything, that I was fairly sure I had half a roll of toilet paper trapped down the leg of my jeans. But that didn't matter – nothing mattered except Theo and what was wrong with him.

I hated hospitals. That's a stupid, cliché thing to say, I know. Who really likes hospitals? No one, that's who. They are terrible places, where terrible things happen, but then I suppose terrible things happen everywhere. At the supermarket. At home when you're clearing out your record collection. In the crowd at a gig.

I'd watched my grandad die in a place like this. I'd been there when it happened and it was nothing like I had expected. His breath had stopped; his eyes stared blankly at the ceiling, the life instantly drained from them. There is no confusing live eyes with dead ones.

In the films, people die gracefully with a quiet puff of air trailing from their lips, their eyes gently falling closed as they utter a meaningful goodbye and fall into the abyss. You think this will prepare you for the situation, should you ever find yourself in it. I'm telling you now, it doesn't.

There was no gentle puff of air, no grace or sentimentality. He was simply there one minute and gone the next. I barely even noticed him leave. His eyes didn't fall closed. They stayed fixed on the same bit of ceiling tile that he'd been watching for hours and they stayed that way until someone closed his eyelids for him. I don't remember who had done that. It hadn't been me.

One thing they don't show you in the films is the post-death spasms that cause dead hands to flinch and life-less legs to twitch. That's a sure-fire way to give yourself nightmares.

I looked over at the desk to where the clerk was typing notes into a computer. I couldn't see her hands but I knew that she had acrylic nails from the sound as they hit the keys. I looked down at my own nails. Bitten, jagged, long on one finger, short on the next. The three coats of 'Barbados Blue' nail lacquer that I'd painted on two days ago had already chipped. I picked at the paint on the thumb of my left hand and peeled it off in three pieces. I collected them and put them into the empty polystyrene cup from the water cooler that sat between my knees.

How long had it been since we'd arrived? Two hours? Two days? Two decades?

'Effie?' a nurse in a pale blue uniform called and I shot

up so quickly that my knees clicked audibly. 'You can come through now. He's asking for you.'

She was smiling; surely that meant he was all right.

I followed her to cubicle nine and found Theo lying on a trolley with a thin pale blue waffle blanket covering his legs, his head tilted to the side, his eyes closed. His shirt hung open at the chest and I could see the stickers that they'd used to hook him up and read his heart rhythm.

'The doctor should be back to see him again shortly,' the nurse said with a smile, before pulling the curtain shut behind me.

His sleeve had been rolled up and a taped cotton wool ball showed where they'd taken his blood.

I picked up the plastic chair from by the wall and placed it beside the bed, the noise rousing him.

'Effie?' He lifted his head, realised that it was too much effort and lowered it down to the pillow again. He reached up with one hand and I placed my good hand inside it. His fingers were cold against my skin.

I looked up into his red-ringed eyes; how hollow they looked now, how vacant of expression.

I felt the tears gathering behind my eyes before they began to fall and I did nothing to stop them. They scattered down my cheeks like raindrops, tinged grey by my mascara.

'What happened to your arm?' he asked, his eyebrows knitting in the centre.

I looked down at the blue splint. 'I tried to catch you when you fell. You landed on my wrist.'

'I'm sorry,' he said, his voice still scratchy but at least it sounded like him this time.

I shook my head, causing more tears to fall. 'Stop apologising.' I leaned forward and pressed my lips to his knuckles.

He sighed heavily, as if he barely had enough energy to exist.

'Tessa and Rhys are on their way,' I said.

He nodded and closed his eyes. His fingers remained entwined with mine and he swallowed hard, as if it was a struggle to do so. I noticed an empty paper pill pot lying on the blanket and wished that I knew what they'd given him.

I watched as his chin began to judder, his face creasing until veins bulged in his temples and deep lines lay etched into his brow. He opened his eyes and they shone with tears that sparkled with the glow of the sodium lights overhead. A tear or two rolled free and pooled in the hollows of his eyes.

I reached over and wiped them away, wishing that I could do something to help, anything.

I reached down and pulled his shirt closed. I remembered the feeling as I'd laid my head on that chest; now all it did was shudder as he struggled to take a breath.

It was typical really.

I'd found myself the perfect man, or rather, he'd found me. He was practically flawless in every way, then he'd spent a little under two weeks with Effie 'Meh' Heaton and I'd drained him of everything until all that was left was what I saw lying in the bed in front of me.

I retook his hand and laid my mouth against his knuckles; the smell of stale beer clung to his fingers. I would always think of tonight whenever I smelled beer in future. More tears quietly fell as I watched him, hunched over in the thin hospital sheets with tears pooling around his eyes. He looked frail, not in stature but in the way he held himself.

Thirteen days ago, I hadn't known that Theo even existed, but now I knew that I didn't want to let another thirteen go by without him being part of my life.

'Theo?' I spoke softly. His eyes flickered over to mine and struggled to stay there. He grunted and I looked into his pupils; they were the size of pennies. 'I love you.'

He didn't smile. He didn't say it back, just looked at me as if he couldn't comprehend what I'd said.

His eyes left mine and retreated to look down at his hands, which were fidgeting on his lap. He sucked his lips into his mouth and lines deepened in his brow as he squinted.

The floor fell out of my stomach. I shouldn't have said it. I'd been a fool, a love-struck fool. He didn't love me yet, maybe he never would. I looked down at the bed, mortified, my eyes falling onto the open screen of his phone.

A text chat sat open and ready for my snooping eyes to devour. Four or five messages sat in coloured bubbles. I looked up at the top of the screen and saw who they were from. My mouth turned dry.

**You don't need to come. I'll be fine.** Theo's last message read.

**Of course I'm coming. I'll be there as soon as I can. X** Jenny had replied.

I looked back up at his face as he fumbled for words.

I was here with him, me, and still he wanted Jenny, after all she'd done to him.

I wasn't good enough.

I wasn't her.

I simply wouldn't do.

'Effie, I . . . erm, I don't . . .'

At that moment the curtain flew back and Tessa stepped in, followed quickly by Rhys. She threw herself onto Theo and instantly bombarded him with questions. Rhys saw my moistening eyes and placed a reassuring hand on my shoulder. He seemed overly worried about my wrist, but I kept telling him that I was fine. I lied through my teeth; I was far from fine.

The curtain moved again and in stepped a doctor, a smiling man with glasses and an armful of notes.

'Theodore Morgan is it?' He nodded us all a greeting and then splayed the notes out on the end of the bed. Theo seemed uncomfortably squashed into the bed, the length of his legs and his slouched position making him look far too big for it. 'Does the family want to stay while we talk or would you rather they wait outside?'

Theo looked around at the others, but didn't meet my eye.

'Effie,' Theo said quietly, 'would you mind giving us a minute?'

I blushed, embarrassed, and reluctantly went back to the waiting room. There I was again, being pushed out. And he'd had the cheek to tell me that *I* kept pushing *him* away.

The waiting room was less packed when I returned, wiping the grey tears from my cheeks and slumping down into the cold metal chair. The drunken man was gone, so were the pregnant couple. New ones had arrived to take their place but I wasn't looking at them, I was trying to hide the fact that I was crying. How could he have dismissed me like that? What could the doctor possibly be telling him that I didn't have a right to know? I was the one who damn near broke my arm trying to save him from falling. I was the one who had helped bundle him into an ambulance and yet I was the one who was asked to leave. My whole body seemed to be splitting down the middle, the one half of me terrified and concerned for Theo and the other half wanting to storm back in there and scream the place down.

I leaned forward and cupped my face in my hands and tried with all my mental power to erase the memory of me saying 'I love you'.

I'd been certain he would say it back. Hadn't that been love in his eyes this morning when he woke up to find me next to him? Hadn't it been there in his eyes from the very start, growing stronger every day, like it had for me? Theo was my first love, the one everyone always talks about, the one who either makes or ruins your life. But I hadn't been Theo's first love, no, Jenny held that title and it looked like she was coming back to defend it. How could I ever compete?

I leaned back, my head resting against the mauve wall, and looked up at the ceiling. It was one of those panelled ones with the metal grid between the squares. Each panel was white flecked with dark grey and before long I'd counted every fleck in the square directly above me. I multiplied it with the number of tiles, came to a total and looked for a new way to kill time.

Why had he gone to Jenny for comfort? Why wasn't I enough?

The incessant bleeping of machinery ceased to be an annoying soundtrack after a while and instead became a sort of lullaby. I closed my stinging eyes and felt the heaviness of sleep fill my head.

I woke, startled, when a heavy hand shook my shoulder. I jolted up, my head spinning as I quickly worked out where I was and regained my balance.

'Rhys!' I said, poised on the edge of the seat and ready to go.

Rhys sat down beside me in the now empty waiting room and sighed. I glanced out the window. It was getting light outside; I'd been asleep for hours.

'He's been moved to another hospital,' he said with a loud exhalation.

'What? Why? Where have they taken him?' I asked, confused.

'They've transferred him closer to home.'

'Birmingham home or here home?' I asked.

'He'll be near Tessa and I.'

'Are we going to him now?' I asked, but Rhys didn't answer.

'Effie, I need to take you home.' His tone was apologetic.

'Home?' What did he mean? I needed to be with Theo. 'No, I need to see him.'

'Tessa went home and got him some things before they moved him and she brought your bag with her. It's in my car. Come on, if we leave now you can be home before the streets are warm.' He stood and started walking towards the exit.

I stood, blind rage turning my face puce. 'No, Rhys. I need to be with him.' I didn't care if he didn't love me yet; I would wait until he did. I'd fight for him. I'd battle Jenny to the death if that's what needed to happen.

Rhys turned around and walked back, his eyes remorseful and his voice quiet. 'Effie. The best thing is for you to go home and we will call you when we know what's happening.'

'No. I'm going to see him.'

'Effie—' he stepped towards me with exasperation '—Theo doesn't want you to come.'

It felt like he'd punched me in the gut.

I recalled Theo's response, or lack thereof, when I'd told him I loved him. Maybe it was then that he'd realised his mistake. Maybe he'd always known that Jenny was the only one.

'Come on. Let me take you home.' Rhys turned on his heel and walked out of the door, leaving me standing breathless on the torn lino floor.

# Chapter Twenty

We drove into the sunrise, watching it crest over the horizon and ignite the sky with the colour of autumn leaves. The roads were quiet and Rhys was a fast driver. I began to recognise my surroundings sooner than I'd thought.

Neither of us spoke on the journey. I didn't know about Rhys but I'd forgotten how to. My brain felt like it was running on power-saving mode, only computing the bare minimum. My forehead pressed against the passenger-side window, leaving a greasy smear on the glass as I stared at the landscape rushing by.

Rhys had tapped my postcode into his satnav before we left the hospital so not even directions were required.

I would have thought that I'd be feeling too much, that I would barely be able to contain my emotions. But it was almost as if I was so sad that I wasn't sad anymore. I'd delved so far into the ugly pit of devastation and now I had found myself unable to feel it around me.

He didn't want me there. He didn't want me. Full stop.

I swallowed, my throat bobbing as I let that fact sink in.

Rhys pulled up a few doors down from mine and turned off the engine. He sighed quietly and looked over; I watched his reflection survey me in the side mirror.

'Not even ten yet. We made better time than I thought we would.' He attempted to be cheery, but his tone was nothing but strained and unconvincing. I didn't respond.

I turned to him, my eyes feeling like they were coated with a layer of sand.

Was it true, what Rhys had said? I was only taking his word for it that Theo had said that he didn't want me there. Maybe it was all a misunderstanding and he'd wake, furious that I wasn't at his side.

'Do they know what's wrong with him?' I asked, my voice crackling from my dry throat.

'No, not yet,' Rhys replied.

'When will you call me and tell me how he is?'

'I don't know, but we will, Effie.'

I blinked for the first time in an age. 'And can I come and see him when he's out of hospital?'

Rhys looked down at his hands and sighed. 'Let's wait and see how he fares first.'

'Okay, but you promise you'll keep me informed?' He nodded. I grabbed my bag from the back seat and popped the door, pausing on the edge of the seat. 'Is Jenny with him?'

Rhys looked down at his hand again, as if he was struggling to look me in the eye. 'No, she left when they moved him.'

I felt my tear ducts kick back into action. She'd been there as I slept in the waiting room, blissfully unaware that she was sitting beside his bed, taking the place that I should have held.

'Does he still love her?'

He looked up into my eyes and I could tell that he pitied me. 'I don't know.'

'Thank you for not lying to me, Rhys.'

He smiled sadly. 'Take care of that wrist,' he said, pointing to my splint. 'It was a pleasure meeting you, Effie.'

I couldn't help but feel that he sounded kind of final.

'You too.' I meant it. I liked Rhys, I just didn't like what he was saying to me.

I got out of the car, lingering by the door, unable to close it. It was as if by closing this shining black car door I would be closing it on the part of my life that contained Theo, that contained the best version of myself. 'Goodbye, Mr Morgan.'

'Goodbye, Effie.'

I pushed the door; the sound of it closing was a gunshot in the quiet street. He sent me one last glance before driving away and leaving me on the pavement wondering what the hell I was supposed to do now.

I walked inside and pressed my back to the door, the latch clicking shut in my left ear.

I let my bag fall from my shoulder and it landed with a *thud* on the laminate flooring. I stared at the spot on the floor where the laminate hadn't been cut with enough skill to manoeuvre the radiator cover, leaving a gap that had filled with dust and detritus blown in on the breeze. A dry leaf . . . a small red button with a tendril of snapped thread still attached.

The toilet flushed and a pair of feet drummed on the stairs as Joy descended.

'Effie, is that you? We weren't expecting you back until . . .' She stopped at the bottom, her eyes falling to my wrist. 'What happened?' She stepped nearer, my eyes moving to hers. I must have looked distraught because she raised her hand to her mouth and creased her eyes. 'Oh, honey, what is it?'

A sob burst from my throat as I stepped forward into my mother's arms and cried into the shoulder of her canary yellow angora sweater. I bawled the story, my voice hitching and catching as I lost my breath and then caught it again. This was to be my second 'mama hug meltdown' in under a month, which was quite possibly a record, even for me. I was almost certain that she understood less than fifty per cent of what I said, but that didn't stop her from leading me to the kitchen, where I sat against the closed patio doors and was force-fed a cup of scalding, too-sweet tea.

My wrist ached and the splint was starting to itch but the pain in my chest was the worst of all, dull and sharp at the same time and tearing through me like a bullet in quarter speed.

I lay in bed, exhausted after my meltdown, with a damp flannel on my forehead; it had been cool when Mum had brought it to soothe my headache but the raging heat of my skin had caused it to turn tepid.

Dad had lingered at the threshold of my room for a time, peering in and listening to me sob. He'd never been what some would call a 'hands-on' dad and he'd shuffled back to his computer room when I'd started bawling again. I didn't mind though – I didn't want anyone to touch me or talk to me or do anything at all to me. I wanted to either be alone or be with Theo and only one of those options was possible.

I held my phone in front of my face, the screen blazing into life and blinding me in the dark room. I turned down the brightness and texted him:

Hey, how are you feeling? Do they know what's going on yet? Please keep me in the loop. Xxx

I almost signed off by telling him that I loved him, then remembered how he hadn't said it back and deleted the letters.

I left the chat and went to my camera roll. I found the photo I was looking for and brought it up full screen. I looked at myself, happy and smiling as Theo kissed me atop the mountain we'd climbed together. How had everything turned from bliss to shit in just over twenty-four hours?

I hated this, the not knowing, the waiting for the call.

But what else could I do?

What were my other options?

The next day I decided to honour the shift I'd agreed to, even though Mum begged me to stay home and take a 'mental health day'. I walked to work in a daze, my feet leading where my brain could not, and when I arrived the shop was bustling. I eventually managed to get inside the door after battling past two of those *I've-had-a-baby-therefore-I-have-the-right-to inconvenience-everyone-with-my-double-buggy* parents and I quickly busied myself straight away. I threw myself into mindless tasks that occupied the methodical part of me, locking the crying little girl inside my brain until I got home.

Arthur was so busy that he barely had chance to yell a hello to me as he disappeared behind the bookcases to find something for a customer. He didn't notice my splinted wrist until I'd already been there for an hour and only because I managed to drop a man's copy of *The Count of Monte Cristo* on his toe after forgetting that I could no longer grip with my left hand. He'd made a fuss about it, saying how I'd damaged his purchase. I ignored him and served the next customer while he sucked lemons on the way out the door. As the man walked away with his own copy of Theo's favourite book, I found myself wondering what Theo was doing, and why that was more important than texting me back.

When the queue had finally gone Arthur came straight over and demanded that I tell him what had happened. I stared at him, my face an emotionless mask until I began uttering my first sentence and couldn't stop – before I'd reached the end Arthur had a tissue pressed to my cheek and an arm around my shoulder.

'I'm sure it's just because he doesn't want you to see him like that. You've only been seeing each other for a couple of weeks and he probably doesn't want to drop the veil just yet.'

'Drop the veil?' I snivelled as I withdrew my face from near his armpit.

'Yeah, like when you start out and everything is new and exciting and you don't let them see the bad parts. Then you drop the veil and before too long you're having a piss while they're in the shower and the veil is torn to tatters.'

I wiped my nose on my sleeve – the tissue had long since been soiled – and tried to ignore the snail-like residue that I left on the fabric.

'I called Rhys twice this morning, and Theo, but they're both ignoring me. I even looked up their number online and called the house but no one was home.'

'If I were you, I'd wait another few days and if they're still ignoring you, I'd drive on down there and see him with my own eyes.'

'You really think so?' I asked, ready to drive there right now.

'Do you love him?'

'Yes.'

'Then it's worth it.'

\* \* \*

Two days had passed since Rhys had dropped me at the kerb like the cowgirl doll in the movie and I'd still had no reply. I think it was fair to say that I was going a little mad.

I was standing at the counter when a stout woman with cropped grey hair came in and placed her myriad shopping bags down on the sofa, the rain from the torrential downpour dripping from the plastic and darkening the leather. I sighed inwardly and stood up a little straighter.

'All right, Bab. I was wondering if you could help me. I'm looking for a book,' she said in a thick Brummie accent.

No shit, Sherlock, you're in a bookshop.

'Of course,' I said with feigned politeness, 'what book are you looking for?'

'That's the thing, I don't know the title.'

'What's the author's name?'

'I don't know.'

I heard my teeth grinding over each other.

'What about the genre: thriller, romance, horror?'

'Don't know that either.'

'Do you know the general plot?' I asked, barely managing to keep my voice in check.

'No. I just know that the cover is red,' she replied, unapologetically.

There really is no job like customer service to make you realise your potential for psychopathy.

'You just know it's red?'

She nodded.

'Well, that doesn't give me much to go on does it?'

'It's red and there's a spider's web on the spine.'

I literally had no idea what book she was referring to. 'I'm sorry, but I don't think I can help you. Feel free to have a look around though and see if you can spot it.'

I looked back down at the cat that I'd been mindlessly doodling for over an hour.

'Well, I don't have time to search every single red book. You might not even have it.'

'They do say that the thrill is in the chase.'

The woman let out a disgusted sigh and placed her hands on her hips.

'Well really, I feel I need to speak to your manager about this.' I looked back up; she'd turned red in the face. I had half a mind to ask her if she was trying to change her facial colour to match the hue of the book she was seeking.

'What do you want to complain about, the fact that you want me to magically know what book you're thinking of without a title, author or plot? Who do you think I am, Derren Brown?'

She puckered her lips and sniffed loudly. 'Call the manager, please.'

'Why? He's not Derren Brown either.' We stared each other down, her cheeks turning puce and my resting bitch face unwavering. I didn't break my gaze as I shouted upstairs. 'Arthur! Customer wants to speak with you.'

He arrived a few moments later, the tension making him recoil as he entered the scene.

'I want to make a complaint about this girl.' She dived right in.

'Okay, complain away,' Arthur said.

I was told to go upstairs into Arthur's flat and wait until the woman had been appeased. I sat on his comfortable sofa and checked my phone for the thousandth time that morning, but it was still devoid of contact.

I dialled Theo's number and raised the phone to my ear. It went straight to voicemail.

After ten minutes or so Arthur called me back down to where he sat with his hands clasped in front of him on the rain-spotted sofa. The red-faced woman was nowhere in sight.

'How did you get rid of her?' I asked.

'I wrote her a gift voucher,' he replied.

I sat beside him, waiting to receive my first official telling-off. He exhaled loudly before speaking.

'Do you want a promotion?' he asked.

I frowned and turned to face him. 'What?'

'A promotion to manager – do you want it?'

'Are you being serious? I was just a complete bitch to that woman,' I replied, confused.

'You were, and while your behaviour was thoroughly understandable, I must ask you not to do that again, no matter how much of an idiot the customer is.'

I nodded my agreement. 'Why make me manager?' I asked.

'This is what I wanted to talk to you about: Toby and I have decided to go travelling.'

'Travelling?' I repeated. 'Where?'

'We haven't decided yet. We just thought that we're both middle-aged and we need to see as many places as we can with the time we have. So, we're starting in Prague and staying at his cousin's over Christmas and then going on from there. But while I'm away I'm going to need someone to run this place. So, do you think that you're up to it?'

I shook my head and held it in my hands, my temples pulsing. I wasn't fit to put on jeans by myself with this bloody splint on my wrist and now he was handing me his business, his baby.

'Did I mention it comes with a pay rise?' he said, sweetening the deal. 'But I'm going to need you clear-headed, so the offer comes with one condition.'

'And that is . . .'

'Go to Wales and sort this situation out. You've been a zombie ever since you came back and I can't have you biting the head off any more customers, no matter how annoying they are.'

I leaned back and closed my eyes before Arthur could see the moisture that was collecting there. 'I feel like I'm intruding on family matters that don't concern me.'

'You're not going to rest until you know he's okay. So, go and see him, then come back and take the job offer.'

I wanted to go now and drive to Theo, but the rain was heavy and I was a nervous driver at the best of times.

'I'll go first thing tomorrow,' I said, suddenly feeling quite apprehensive.

I barely slept a wink as I waited for the sun to rise and when it finally did, I called all three of the phone numbers I had, to tell them I was coming. All went straight to voice-mail. I left before Mum and Dad woke and tried to talk me out of driving with an injured wrist. I set up the satnav on my phone and found the perfect album to drive to. I couldn't listen to The Rosehipsters, not after what had happened the last time I'd been listening to them. I don't know if it was enough to put me off them forever, but for now it was plenty.

I chose Bowie's greatest hits, because almost every song reminded me of a moment I'd shared with Theo, and I started the engine. Before I left the driveway, I spotted Elliot sitting in the grass of next door's front garden. He stared me down with unadulterated judgement.

*He sent you away for a reason, my dear. He didn't want you there before; what makes you think he'll want you there now?*

'I don't know,' I answered, pulling out of the driveway before he could talk any more sense into me.

I'd never driven this far on my own before and around an hour into the journey I began to wish that I had someone to talk to. There was no one for me to bounce my anxiety off, to talk me down from the state of panic I was slowly rising to. The Bowie playlist had finished once and was on its second loop by the time I neared the Morgans' and when I recognised the churchyard where Megan Morgan lay, I began to feel sick.

Two more minutes of driving and the gates came into view. I could easily have pulled over and spewed all over the side of the road, but I held it in and took a breath. This was Theo I was talking about, the man who had struggled to win me over, who had fought to make me open up and let him in. Why would he have done that just to toss me aside?

I looked at the gates at the end of the Morgans' driveway and saw that they were opening and the nose of a pearlescent purple Volvo began poking through.

Whose car was that?

I drove closer as the car pulled out and headed in my direction. The driver slid on a pair of shades, even though the day was not particularly bright, and flicked her black curls from her face. I felt the nausea return when I recognised her.

Jenny.

The car zoomed past as I turned into the driveway, too late to make it through the already closing gates. I thought that Tessa vehemently hated Jenny and Theo had told me himself that he had felt nothing but betrayal at her hands. But maybe something had changed. Maybe he'd seen his life flash before him when he'd passed out and he'd known that something was lacking and whatever that something had been, it hadn't been me.

I rolled down my window and pressed the small silver buzzer.

Nothing.

I buzzed again.

The same.

There must have been someone inside, otherwise how would Jenny have got in?

I buzzed three times in quick succession and spoke into the speaker.

'I know that you're in there. I'm not going away until I see one of you, so someone is going to have to talk to me.'

I buzzed three more times and waited for a response.

Nothing.

I felt dangerously close to crying. Why were they ignoring me? What had I done to deserve this shunning?

I gripped the steering wheel with my one good hand and shook it, something very much like a growl rolling from between my gritted teeth. I leaned forward and laid my head on the wheel, my breaths sounding like whines as I tried to calm myself. I tried to remind myself how to breathe. In, out. In, out.

I thrust myself back into the seat and looked ahead, only now noticing that someone was standing on the other side of the wrought-iron gate. My heart somersaulted as I scrambled from the car, leaving the engine running in the driveway as I went to face him.

'What are you doing here, Effie?' Rhys asked.

I lifted my hands to my head and shrugged, at a loss for words.

'It's not a good idea, you being here.' He didn't look at me as he spoke.

'No one would talk to me,' I said, fully aware of how desperate I looked. 'You promised me you'd let me know how he was. He could be dead for all I know.'

Rhys squeezed the bridge of his nose and sighed. 'I know, I'm sorry we ignored you. That wasn't fair. He's not dead but he is still ill.'

'What's wrong with him?' I moved closer, my right hand closing around the cold metal that lay between us.

'No one knows yet, but they are trying to find out.'

'Is he here?'

'Yes.'

'Can I see him, please?'

'He said he doesn't want to see you.' Rhys still wouldn't look at me.

'I don't believe you,' I said as a tear rolled down into the crease of my nose. 'Why would he change so suddenly?'

He stepped forward, his eyes finally rising to meet mine. 'He doesn't want to see anyone.'

'You let Jenny in,' I said accusingly. 'I never did anything to hurt Theo, not like she did, but you let her in. Tessa hates her, so does Theo.'

Rhys nodded. 'She only wanted to help, Effie.'

'*I* could have helped. Me!' I shouted, my voice echoing around us. I raised my hands to my head and wondered if this was all some deeply psychological dream that I couldn't wake from. 'Please, just let me speak to him. I need to hear it from him.'

'Effie!' He sighed in exasperation and his voice took on an authoritative tone. 'Effie, go home and I'll get Theo to call you in the next couple of days.'

'You can't just send me away. I drove all the way here,' I begged. I didn't care how I looked; I needed to see him. 'Please, Rhys. You can't cut me off like this.'

'I promise you that he'll get in contact soon.'

'You've broken promises to me before, Rhys,' I said as more tears fell.

'I'm sorry, Effie. I really am.' He turned and began walking away.

'Rhys, no. Please.' I reached my outstretched arm through the gate, as if it could somehow reach him and pull him back. The bushes were almost bare, stripped of their summertime beauty by the ravages of autumn, and I could just about make out a silhouette in the upstairs window. It was male, of that I was certain, and who else could those shoulders belong to but Theo? I called his name, my voice so loud in the morning quiet that it seemed to echo through all of Wales. 'Theo, talk to me!' The figure took a step back, reached up an arm and pulled the curtains shut.

# Chapter Twenty-One

I didn't bother calling Arthur and telling him that I wouldn't be coming in to accept my promotion. I just drove all the way home with grey, mascara-tinged tear tracks drying onto my cheeks, the radio silent. How could he have just turned away from me like that? How could he have invited Jenny back to take my place? Had their meeting at the service station reopened old affections? Had Jenny suddenly realised what she'd thrown away with Theo and gone running back to him and had he then forgotten the pain she'd caused him and welcomed her back into the arms that had been holding me only days earlier?

When I got home there was no one in and I wasted no time in running to my bed, throwing myself onto it and screaming into my pillow.

I couldn't comprehend it.

What had I done? Was it when I'd told him that I loved him? Had that been too much?

Had his affections for me been sated when we'd slept together and now that he'd got what he wanted I was nothing but a used-up husk to throw aside? Maybe it was all about the chase with Theo.

I cried into my pillow until it got dark, falling asleep somewhere between angry and despondent.


'Effie, hon?' I woke to the sound of my mother's voice. My eyes peeled back to see her hovering over me with a brown block clutched in her hands. 'A package came for you. The postmark says Wales.'

I sat up and snatched the package from her hands. It was thick and heavy; it felt like a book.

'Thank you,' I said sharply. 'Please leave.'

Joy turned up her nose and marched from the room with a haughty gait.

I tore the brown paper away with my nails and a heavy book dropped into my lap. I turned it over and recognised it as the *100 Films to See Before You Die* book from Theo's room. I pushed it aside and found a letter below it.

I ripped the envelope so impatiently that I almost tore the letter in half, unfolding it and reading it with manic eyes.

*Effie,*

*I'm sorry I ruined the gig for you. I guess I could have waited until they'd finished playing your favourite song before I passed out. Thanks for coming with me in the ambulance, by the way. I know that you waited for a long time.*

*We never did find your favourite film so I thought I'd send you a book of all the best ones and you could work your way through. Maybe you'll find it that way.*

264

*I know you must be confused by me asking you to leave, but I heard what you said to me in the cubicle just before my family came in and I realised that I'd let you believe that what we had was a lot more than it actually was. It's not fair for me to continue seeing you, now that I know this.*

*I wrote you this letter because I wanted to tell you to finish that list. We made a good dent in it, didn't we? But there are still more to check off and you can do that without my help. You never really needed me anyway. You could have done this all by yourself. You just needed a push in the right direction.*

*We had a lot of fun and I'll never forget it, but the list is almost done and that's all we really set out to do, isn't it? Maybe I'll give you a call sometime and see how that novel is coming along, but in the meantime try and be happy, Effie.*

*Theo*

I lowered the letter to my lap and frowned at my feet. Had I read that correctly?

I raised it once again and reread his words, scrawled in his atrocious handwriting.

I found the words exactly as I had before.

I heard the sound of a dying animal, the sound of pained whining, and then I realised that the sounds were coming from me.

The ink slowly blurred behind the tears that collected in my eyes, so thick that I could do nothing but let them fall.

I heard thudding footsteps approaching and a moment later Joy pushed her way into the room. 'Effie! What is it?' When I responded in only whimpers and whines, she pushed further. 'Effie, tell me what's happened. Is it Theo?' The sound of his name caused a wave of furious devastation to flood my chest.

'Leave me alone!' I shouted, grabbing the giant film book and throwing it across the room. It hit the wall beside the door with a resounding *thud* and toppled to the floor. She sighed heavily and left the room without a word, but not without sending a scowl my way first. It was a scowl that may well have made me cry in fear, had I not already been crying. I felt the structure of me break down inside myself, the walls crumbling, the foundations sinking, everything returning to the chaos of how it had been before he came along and built me up.

I cast the letter aside, letting it sweep to the floor like a discarded feather, the paper weighing so little when the words felt like anvils.

I lay on my side, curling myself into the small, insignificant creature that I was and I closed my eyes, thinking that that might make the tears stop, but it didn't.

An hour or so later, after I'd resoaked my pillow in salty tears, I decided that I couldn't stay in that dusty room filled with too much stuff. I made the decision to go up to the treehouse, the place that reminded me of him.

I don't know why but the thought of sitting there on the floor where we had spent so many hours kept the pain keen. It felt just like when you have a toothache and the only thing that makes it even slightly better is prodding the gum and awakening the pain.

I went to the old shed, the one painted the shade of mint

green that made my eyes pulse with a migraine aura, and went inside. I pulled out two large sheets of cardboard that my dad used to box up the things he sold online and I carried them with difficulty up to the treehouse. I threw them on the floor before going back down, taking the staple gun from the bottom drawer of the kitchen cabinet, the sleeping bag from just inside the attic door, a torch, my chipped favourite mug and a bottle of bourbon from my dad's stash.

I retrieved Theo's letter and the book from my bed and took them with me before climbing back up the ladder and making myself a misery nest. I stapled the cardboard over the open gaps, leaving only a sliver open as a door, and rolled out the sleeping bag, crawled inside and poured half a mug of bourbon. I watched the letter as if it would at some point start moving, scrawled with Theo's words and sitting in the corner where I'd thrown it. I was almost frightened to touch it, as if touching it made it real.

I lifted the mug to my lips and took a swig, gulping it and feeling the burn in my throat. I lay back and stared at the ceiling, the light of day peeping in through the cracks.

I woke hours later to the sound of my mother's shouts from below. I poked my head out of the door, and looked down to see both of my parents and Elliot staring up at me with concern.

'What?' I called, my voice still slurred from the whisky I'd drunk too much of.

'What are you doing up there?' she asked, her hand cupped around her mouth, as if that made any difference to the volume of her voice.

I took a breath before answering. 'I believe it's called having an emotional breakdown.'

'What was in that letter? Come down, I'll make you some dinner and we can talk it through.' She beckoned.

'Okay,' I lied, walking inside and climbing back into the sleeping bag.

I wasn't going for the *Romeo and Juliet* tragedy ending. I'd always thought that those two were complete idiots: meeting, falling in love and getting engaged in the space of ten minutes and then dying because they couldn't be without each other. Ridiculous. But right now, I understood them better than I ever had before. Of course, Theo would not be dying for me, no, he had to love me for that to work and, as he had made very clear, he did not.

It wasn't that I wanted to die or that I couldn't live without him – I'm sure that it would be more than possible if I tried hard enough. It simply hurt too much and I didn't want to feel it anymore.

When the whisky hadn't numbed me, I'd moved on to the wine, which I'd found in the forgotten rack in the basement, and waited for the anaesthesia of sleep to come.

There was a knife in the drawer below the kitchen sink, razor sharp and unused from when Joy had gone through a sushi phase, buying all the stuff and then not doing anything with it.

It wouldn't take much with that, just one quick flash of courage and it would be over.

It had all come back at once – the darkness, the loneliness, the pain, the betrayal, the hopelessness – except this time they had heartbreak to keep them company.

I'd always thought that films overplayed the whole broken heart thing, but now that I was feeling it for real, I knew that the films never did it justice. I had done nothing of importance with the time I'd had. I had done no great things. I had changed no one's life in any great way.

If I were to slip away from this mortal coil, then the biggest impact I would make would be on the people who had to clear up the blood afterwards.

Theo wouldn't notice, I wasn't part of his life anymore, and my parents would finally have the house to themselves. Maybe Arthur would notice, maybe Arthur would care. But then I had been nothing but a nuisance to him from the moment I'd met him, and what person wasn't happier once a nuisance was got rid of?

I'd tried to see the light at the end of the tunnel, but the tunnel had been bricked up, plastered over and the inside filled with concrete. There was no light. There was no tunnel.

I'd gone down to fetch the knife at around 5 a.m. and taken it up into the treehouse. It was as good a place to die as any. It blurred in my hands, my eyes so abused with tears that I could barely see. I picked up the carved wooden handle and watched the blade shine with deadliness in the light of the camping lantern sitting in the corner. Every thought that hurt me fell into my brain. The friends I didn't have, the passion for writing that I *had* never, *would* never satisfy. I thought of the love that Theo had flung back in my face and of the heart that he had crumbled in his fist like a dry digestive biscuit and as those thoughts came, the courage began to swell. I took off my splint, let the blade fall to my palm and dragged it across with little effort to test its sharpness. It cut through me like warm butter.

I hissed through my teeth and dropped it onto the floor with a *clang*. Little beads of blood rose to the surface one by one until the whole line was slick with blood that began to pool in my palm.

For a second, the sharp pain in my hand obliterated the pain that was everywhere else, but all too soon everything fell back into place and ached all the more. I upturned what was left of the wine into my mouth, gulping down the final quarter and letting the bottle roll away.

I had been foolish, reckless, rash.

I didn't want to die. I just didn't want to feel.

I wanted things to get better. I wanted to be happy. Was that too much to ask?

I woke on Tuesday and went down into the house for supplies (a bottle of wine, freshly purchased and still in its canvas shopping bag, and a big bag of cheesy Doritos) and to put my phone on charge, all the time deflecting questions from my mother. I let my battery get to twenty-five per cent and then I headed back to the treehouse before she asked anything else. I saw that I had twelve missed calls from Arthur and several messages from him, asking where I was and if I was dead. I lied and told him that I was ill before turning the phone off.

For the rest of the day I drank the wine, I ate the tortilla chips and I cried some more. There isn't much more to tell.

Just as the sky was turning dark, I found myself down on the ground, vomiting into the flowerbeds and wondering if wine stained your insides if you drank enough of it. I had drunk more than my fair share, so was my stomach a delightful shade of magenta?

The vomit-speckled leaves of the bay tree gave off a fragrant scent that did little to mask the smell of wine, bile and Nacho Cheese Doritos that sat in a pile in the soil. My stomach convulsed and another stream of burgundy sick splattered to the ground. I wiped my mouth and groaned. Why was wine such a fickle mistress? There for you whenever you needed her, until she decided that enough was enough and hurt you beyond compare.

It was the next morning by the time I eventually came down from my treehouse of despair, for the simple reason that my mother wouldn't leave me alone until I did.

I still hadn't told her about what had happened in Wales. It was like I feared that talking about it gave it life.

I was pretty sure she'd already guessed that Theo wouldn't be coming back around like he had before, bagels in hand, a smile on his lips.

Oh God, how I missed that smile. How I hated that smile. How I hated that I missed that smile.

I closed my eyes and lifted my mug of too sweet, too cold tea to my lips.

Joy faffed at the stove, preparing some sort of beef-based casserole to eat that evening, while I sat at the table. I glanced up at the clock: 11.45 a.m. Too early. I lived for the night now, like a fox or a vigilante, I had become nocturnal.

I closed my eyes again and drank more tea. It tasted like metal.

I heard her sigh and slam the oven door with more ferocity than was necessary and I knew what was coming next.

'Effie, it's almost midday. Go and get changed – you've been wearing those PJs for days. They'll stand up all by themselves if you don't wash them soon.'

I opened my eyes and looked at her as she walked over and sat in the chair opposite, her best mum face on.

'What's the point? I'm not going anywhere and no one is coming here to see me.' I could see that my melancholia was starting to annoy her; it was starting to annoy me too.

'Because! You're not a hobo, you're my daughter.'

271

'The only difference between me and a hobo is that you haven't kicked me out yet. If you did, I'd be one in seconds.'

She sighed loudly and tilted her head. 'Effie, this has to stop. I know something happened with Lovely Theo, even though you won't tell me what. But whatever it is, you just need to pick yourself up and get on with it.'

I looked up into her eyes, my face a mask of indifference. 'What if I can't get on with it?'

'You just have to.'

'Why can't I just be miserable?'

'Because that's not what people do.'

'That's exactly what people do, all the time!' I was shouting – I didn't know why. 'Other people are just better at hiding it than I am.'

'Jesus Christ!' She flung up her hands in frustration. 'You're almost twenty-nine years old. Nearly thirty and you're living like a student.' Her pupils had reduced to pinpricks, her cheeks turning red. 'People are married with children at your age, Effie!'

I scowled, my blood beginning to bubble beneath my skin. 'Well, I don't want to get married. It's an archaic trap to ensnare people into forced monogamy and I have plenty of time to have children before my ovaries shrivel up and die.'

'Effie,' she breathed my name like it pained her. I knew the tone well. 'What are you doing with your life?'

I suddenly felt like my throat was blocked, blocked with anger, blocked with fear.

'I don't know! I don't have a fucking clue what I'm doing!' I could feel the control slipping.

'Language!' Joy slammed her hands down on the table, almost screaming the word.

I stood slowly, my eyes pinned to hers. 'You know what, Mother? I am almost thirty years old, as you have so diligently reminded me, and my life is literally non-existent. I have no friends, I've just had my heart broken for the first time, I'm no longer on the verge of becoming an alcoholic, I am one, and now you're shouting at me. So, if I want to fucking swear, I will fucking swear!'

Joy stood too, leaning forward over the table, our noses only inches apart. 'Not under my roof you won't.'

My breaths were ragged and fast. 'Then fuck your roof.' I moved, knocking my tea over by accident as I nudged the table with my hip.

'Fine, then leave!' she shouted after me.

'I will!' I cried when I reached the bottom of the stairs. 'Guess now I'm the hobo you always feared I would be.' I ran up the stairs and into my room.

It didn't feel like mine anymore. This room belonged to all the past versions of me, but not *this* Effie.

I grabbed a bag and stuffed in things I thought I might need. I changed into the first outfit I could find – jeans, boots and a grey jumper that didn't seem to fit me well – and threw the bag over my shoulder. I pushed my now fully charged phone into my pocket and stormed down the stairs.

I walked straight through the kitchen and up into the treehouse without pause, grabbing my booze and my sleeping bag and turning to look at Theo's letter, still lying where I'd flung it.

I snatched it up and stuffed it into my pocket before pushing the hefty movie book into my bag.

I was down and back in the house, storming my way

273

through to the front door when she re-emerged, red-faced and arms crossed over her chest.

'Where are you going?' she asked.

'As if you fucking care?' I pulled on my coat and then I was gone, my teeth gritted against the scream sitting in my throat as I marched down the street.

My feet fell violently into step and soon began to ache with the ferocity with which my boots hit the pavement. I no longer had blood in my veins; it was simply fury that fuelled me.

As I entered town, I walked past the park where Theo and I had gone on our first date, where he'd made me buy him coffee when I clearly hadn't wanted to go with him. Dick!

Not far from there was the diner, which I glimpsed down a crowded street lit by the festive glow of premature Christmas lights that for some reason were turned on all day.

I hated that diner. I'd hated it before I'd met Daz and before I'd run into Theo, but now I hated it with such vehemence that I wanted to storm in and burn the place to the ground. Shithole!

Why had he done this to me? I hadn't asked for this, for him. All I'd wanted was to be left in the shitty life that I'd grown accustomed to, believing that nothing would get any better than what I knew. But then he'd come in and shown me that life could be better, could be good. Why had he done that if all he was going to do was abandon me? Wanker!

Hadn't it all happened how it was supposed to? Hadn't it all been perfect? We'd had the nondescript meet-cute and the perfect first kiss (after the drunken, violent one I'd planted on him at Kate's party, of course). If we were in a romcom, then this would be the moment when he'd show up, his car screeching to the kerb as he desperately tried to apologise. But this was not a romcom, this was a tragedy of Shakespearean proportions and I had never been a fan of Shakespeare.

I let my feet lead the way and they took me to work. I pushed the door open, the door hit the sofa, the sofa hit the shelves and several books scattered across the floor. The bell, which the door had hit with some velocity, dislodged itself and skittered across the ground before coming to rest against the counter. Thankfully there were no customers as I marched to the concealed stairway and climbed to the mezzanine balcony. I walked to a corner that I knew was the best place to hide and sat down with my back against the shelves filled with antique books.

I took Theo's letter from my pocket and read it, reread it and then read it once more for good measure.

*More than it actually was . . . We had a lot of fun . . . Maybe I'll give you a call . . .*

Hatred blossomed inside me so brightly that I thought I might explode.

Fun! Had that been all I was? Someone to while away the hours with. A girl to screw and then screw over?

I had been wrong before; *this* had been my most disastrous sexual encounter to date.

I thought of him and his stupid floppy blond hair and the way he flicked it out of his eyes with that stupid tilt of his head. I thought of those eyes and how they were so blue, too blue. Of that ridiculous smile and how much power it had. I hated all of it, every single thing.

Had it all been a show from the minute he saw the pathetic girl in her pathetic outfit, on a pathetic date with a pathetic boy?

I sniffed and smelled something familiar. Had I finally cracked or could I smell beer?

I looked down at the grey jumper I was wearing and realised that, in my haste, I'd put on the jumper that Tessa had lent me. I looked down at the asymmetric hem and the brown stain on the fabric from the spilled beer that we'd both lain in when Theo had fallen.

I closed my eyes and breathed deeply, steadying the raging breaths that were making me feel lightheaded. It was only then that I became aware of someone below in the shop. I opened my eyes to see Arthur retrieving the bell from the floor and looking around with confusion at the wake of devastation. He looked up and saw me, his face set in a grimace.

He thundered up the stairs and brandished the bell. 'What the hell do you think you're doing, barging in here like a bull and breaking my bell?'

I looked from the bell to Arthur's disappointed face and back again before my own face crumpled and tears began to flow again. Next thing I knew, he was sitting down beside me and telling me that it was fine and that he could get a new bell. He asked me what was wrong and I told him, my tears soaking into his red and white flannel shirt as I recited the tale in wails and sobs, snorts and coughs. He read Theo's letter and held me until I was all out of tears. At one point a customer came into the shop and Arthur called out for Toby, who emerged from the apartment above and served her. When the customer left, looking back at me over her shoulder with concern, Toby came up and sat on my other side, his arms joining the embrace. They were bookends holding me together as I cried. Lo and behold, there were still some tears left to fall.

They let me get it all out without saying anything or trying to make me stop; they both knew that I needed to let the tears roll. When my tear ducts dried up, I wiped the snot from my philtrum and sat back, their arms unwinding from around me. Toby took me by the shoulders and led me up into the flat above, placing me down on the sofa and making me some soup that was both scalding hot and delicious. I drank it down and then promptly fell asleep.

I dreamt of mountains and white clay birds.

I dreamt that I saw Theo and tried to slap him hard across the face, but my hands wouldn't move – they were both in casts, casts that he'd put there when I'd tried to save him from falling.

I wished now that I'd just let him fall.

# Chapter Twenty-Two

It was four thirty in the morning when I found myself staring up at the ceiling above Arthur's fold-out futon, the blue light of the muted nature documentary illuminating the IKEA light fitting. I wished that the wine had done its job of putting me to sleep. I'd woken at half eleven. The others were asleep and so I rummaged in the cupboard for something to take the edge off. I'd found a cheap bottle of Cabernet Sauvignon and I'd drunk the whole thing, but it hadn't been enough. One bottle was never enough.

I'd never been a fan of futons. To me you might as well chuck a load of broken glass and spanners into a pillowcase and sleep on that for all the comfort they brought. But beggars can't be choosers; never had I found that saying to be more apt.

I lifted my phone to my face and let the too bright light sting my eyes. I lowered the brightness and opened the photograph again. I'd looked at it so often that I knew every detail. I could recall from memory the way a strand of my hair had been lifted by the breeze and lay across the frame like a russet crack in the lens. I could see without looking that the collar of Theo's coat was folded under and trapped beneath the strap of his bag. I knew everything by heart and yet I kept going back, because I was searching for something. I was searching for the lie. Was it hidden in the tautness of his neck muscles as he leaned in? Was it in the arm that wrapped around me? Was it everywhere, subtly seeping out of him and polluting the whole image?

I opened a new text and let my thumbs fly across the screen, every word coming out with an extra *f* or a random *q* thrown in. I told him what a dick he was. How he'd broken my heart. How I hated every fibre of his being and wished more than I'd ever wished before that I could go back and remember to pick up my purse from that diner table, because then all he would be was a stranger who had been eating in the same diner I got dumped in. I let everything out, the message barely comprehensible when I'd finished, then I placed my thumb on the backspace key and let it all fall away.

The next weeks passed in a blur of slow motion, one minute seeming to speed by like a freight train and the next grinding to a halt. Arthur and Toby booked their tickets for their adventure and Arthur began packing his things into boxes for storage. I ran on autopilot for a while, serving customers, keeping myself busy with tidying the shop. I begrudgingly accepted the managerial position, purely because it would give me more to do to keep my mind away from beautiful blond betrayers. I even cooked Arthur a meal or two. I didn't eat any of them but he assured me they were edible.

I hadn't brought any make-up with me when I'd left home and so I'd been going au naturel. Usually the thought of baring my corpse-coloured face to the world would have made me shudder, but right now I didn't give a shit.

On Monday I interviewed a few people for the job I would be trading for manager. I spoke to several people who I felt had the appropriate level of passive aggression to take over from me, but Arthur didn't like any of them and so I was left without.

On Thursday Amy came in to get the new issue of *Writer's Inspiration* and during a five-minute conversation at the till, Arthur offered Amy the job. I shrugged when he told me that she'd be starting on Monday and that I'd be the one who had to train her.

Amy arrived on Monday morning twenty minutes early and with an excited optimism that irked me from the moment she walked in and jingled the brand-new bell.

She lapped up my tutelage like I was some Grand Master of bookselling and, despite my overwhelming ennui, she stated that she thought we were going to be 'great friends'.

On Tuesday morning I went home when I knew that everyone would be out and boxed up all of my things. I hadn't spoken to Joy since our raging argument and I'd only spoken to Dad to tell him where I was staying. It was strange to see my entire life and everything that I had collected during my twenty-eight and a bit, years on this earth reduced to six large cardboard boxes sitting in the hall.

I took down the fairy lights hanging from the ceiling and stuffed them into a black bag, along with several photographs of me and Kate that I'd found in the bottom of a drawer. I took the stuffed green bear from the windowsill and pushed it into the box I was taking with me; I was not yet ready to relinquish all aspects of my childhood. I found the umbrella that Theo had bought for me at the juice bar and, without thinking, threw it into the bin bag.

I packed and disposed of things until the room was almost empty. The only thing left was the boxed manuscript under my bed. I pulled it out, my fingers touching it for the first time in an age, and I flipped off the lid, the words staring up at me with judgement.

I quickly replaced the lid and stood between the bin bag and the box. I leaned towards the bin bag, the novel almost falling inside before I pulled it out and placed it in the box instead.

When I was ready to leave, I called Arthur who brought his car and helped me load everything into the back. As I was getting the final box, I turned to find Elliot sitting on the bottom step, his accusing yellow eyes staring up at me. I leaned down and kissed his soft forehead.

I tried to think of something to say to him, something fitting and filled with sentimentality, not just to him but to the house I'd known my whole life. But I couldn't think of anything and so, with a feeling of anxious sadness blooming in my chest, I picked up the final box, left my key beside the kettle and walked away.

I don't remember the exact moment when my life began to suck.

Was it when I suddenly discovered that I was sitting alone in the school playground, eating a Babybel and chatting with whichever teacher was on playground duty? Or had it been when I'd thrown up on Marcus Roe, mid-coitus? I never was too sure.

However, I *can* pin down the moment when I *realised* my life sucked, but it had taken me a good long while to notice, arrogantly blundering through life without stopping to see how much of a loser I was.

It was around the time I finished uni and moved back home. Mum had a friend over, Julie Croft-Billstow.

Julie is one of those people who laugh at their own jokes while they're still telling them and has that creped, Ronseal skin on her chest from years of neglecting sun lotion on her frequent holidays to her timeshare villa in Spain. Her hands are the parts that freak me out the most. They reminded me of the Crypt Keeper from *Tales from the Crypt*, wrinkled and bony beyond their years.

Mum had made them both tea and they were sitting in the garden with the sun beating down on them; shades on, heads lolling back to catch the rays, Julie's chest crisping like the skin of a roast chicken.

The back door was open and so I quietly went to the fridge and tried to find something edible, but as I fumbled around trying to get a yoghurt out of a cardboard sleeve, I heard my name drift in from outside. I thought I'd blown it and would have to go out and make polite conversation while my pale redhead's skin turned to ashes in the sunlight.

I stepped closer to the door, keeping myself hidden behind the curtain as I listened.

'. . . at the job centre, but no one seems to want her,' Mum said.

Julie sighed and adjusted her sunglasses. 'She's a little adrift these days, isn't she? Shame. She could do so much if she just put her mind to it.'

'Sometimes I wonder where her life is headed. She only went to uni to stall real life for three years and now that there's no more stalling to be done she's just stopped. And she's so obsessed with this idea of being a writer. I want to be supportive but she has to realise at some point that it's probably only ever going to be a pipe dream. It's like she's refusing to grow up and become part of the world.' I heard the disappointment in my mother's voice and I suddenly didn't want the yoghurt anymore.

'She'll have to grow up soon. She can't expect you to keep paying out for her.' Julie sat up and placed her thousand-year-old hand on Joy's arm. 'You and William need your own space in your later years. You can't let Effie hold you back.'

With that I walked away, leaving the yoghurt to turn to cheese on the counter in the June heat. I'd gone straight out to the job centre and asked the snotty little man on the front desk if there were any classes I could take, anything that could help me in any way. I had a reasonable number of qualifications from school and a degree in Sociology that was almost as useless as I was. After what I'd heard Joy say I was willing to take anything. I would happily scrub floors with my bare hands if it meant that I felt like less of a loser than I already did.

The horrid little man sniffed loudly. It was that product-ive sort of sniff where you can hear a bogey dislodging and it makes you shudder. 'There's a class on Wednesday,' he groaned, leaning his head on his hand like he would liter-ally rather be cleaning the toilets with his tongue than talking to me.

'Great! What is it?' I'd replied enthusiastically.

He sighed so heavily that his breath almost blew the papers from his desk. 'Some guy who owns a bookshop is coming in to talk about business ownership.'

'Excellent. Sign me up.'

I guess I had to be grateful to Julie for that. If she hadn't said what she had, then I never would have met Arthur.

I hadn't given Arthur enough credit for the amount of goodness he'd brought to my life.

Theo was not the best thing to happen to me, Arthur was.

'Now, the book club comes by on Monday nights at eight and they stay for an hour or so. All they really do is bitch about everyone else at church and drink tea, so it's not too much to handle. Amy can cover it if you can't be bothered.' Arthur reeled off some final instructions as we approached the airport. He'd given me use of his car while he was away and it would be a lie to say that that hadn't brought an almost-smile to my face. Toby sat in the back seat, his accountant's suit swapped for jeans and a busy jumper, his bags clasped in white-knuckled hands.

'You okay back there?' I asked, seeing his face turn slightly green.

He turned to my reflection in the rear-view mirror and attempted a smile. 'I don't really like flying.'

I didn't have chance to respond before Arthur started up again. 'And the boiler is on the blink but all you need to do is smack it hard on the side when it makes that clunking sound.'

'I know, you already showed me what to do,' I said as I pulled in and parked in the drop-off zone.

I unbuckled my seatbelt and slipped out of the car, helping Toby with his bags as he uttered little 'Oh God's the whole time. I pulled him into a hug and spoke into his ear.

'You'll be fine. Just take care of him – you know how enthusiastic he gets and I need him back here in one piece.' I pulled back and looked into the eyes behind the glasses. 'And don't worry, aren't you more likely to die in the car on the way to the airport than in the plane?'

'With your driving, Effie, I would say so, yes,' he replied with a smile. He pulled me in for another embrace before letting me go.

I tried not to cry when I said goodbye to Arthur, but I knew it was going to be a losing battle. What was I going to do without him? He was one of the few people left who could stand to be in the same room with me and now he was leaving the country with the new love of his life. It was difficult for me not to be jealous. I'd been so close to the same level of blissful happiness, but I guess life couldn't work out perfectly for everyone.

'Take care of yourself, Effie,' he said as he squeezed me to within an inch of my life. 'By the time I get back I want to see you turned into a career bitch, you got that?'

He pulled back, holding me firmly by the shoulders and looking at me with rapidly pinking eyes.

'Be safe,' I said, only just managing to get the words out before a tear fell. He wiped it away with his thumb.

'You too,' he replied, and just like that the last person I had walked away.

When I arrived back at the flat, I sat down on the sofa and stared at the TV without turning it on. The silence pressed in on me like iron weights in my ears.

I decided to skip dinner and clicked on the TV to watch Sky for four hours instead, barely moving enough to adjust my position as I stared, hypnotised. At 11.41 p.m., after I'd finished off the dregs that were left at the back of Arthur's alcohol cupboard, I walked to the off-licence and bought a bottle of wine, warming the bottle beneath my good arm as I made my way back up to the flat. The bottle was empty by 1 a.m.

I did the same the next night and the night after that like an ultra-depressing version of *Groundhog Day*. I tried my best not to think of Theo, but then I would hear Bowie on the radio or drink wine that reminded me of the taste of it on his lips or I'd notice the stain on the ceiling in the bathroom that vaguely resembled his face in profile and he was right back in the forefront of my mind again.

On Saturday they were showing an Eighties film marathon on channel four and so, after I closed the shop for the day and sent Amy home, I made my way to the off-licence and bought myself a tub of ice cream, along with my usual wine, and a microwave dinner for one (a sad little watery lasagne that looked as pathetic as I did). I was quite used to cooking and generally keeping myself alive – it was one of the few things I'd learned at uni – but it was one of those nights when even pushing the buttons on the microwave seemed like a gargantuan task.

*The Breakfast Club* was first. I ate my ugly microwave mush while I watched that one and then I turned my attention to the ice cream while *Pretty in Pink* started.

I watched as the heroine fawned over the boy she liked, cutting up her dress and making a new one for the prom and walking in on the arm of Jon Cryer to impress the boy who'd screwed her over.

'Don't go back to him, Molly,' I said through my mouthful of chocolate brownie ice cream. 'Don't trust him, you fool. He doesn't love you. Sure, he says that now, but he doesn't mean it.'

I looked away as she returned to the arms of the boy she loved, who loved her too.

I could reimagine as many dresses as I wanted and show Theo how great I looked, how well I was doing. But there would be no telling me that he loved me, no reconciliatory kiss beside his car as Eighties music played in the background. Theo didn't want me and I had to try and accept that.

I shook myself as the credits began to roll and ate another spoonful of liquid ice cream.

I didn't need Theodore 'Fucking' Morgan anyway. Why would I when I had Ben, Jerry and Molly Ringwald?

It had been three and a half days since Arthur and Toby had flown away and as of yet I hadn't managed to do anything seriously wrong. I'd fallen asleep whilst making dinner, ruining one of his pans in the process and setting off the smoke alarm, but apart from that life had been pretty uneventful.

It was well into the run-up to Christmas now and the shop was busy, so much so that I barely had time to do anything else other than work. I went down to the shop, spilling my drink slightly as I went, and arriving at the counter with the smell of coffee and moroseness in the fabric of my black hoodie. I was feeling especially sorry for myself after a full two days of having absolutely zero calls, texts or emails. I mean, I didn't miss my parents that much, but they could at least have the decency to wonder if I was still alive or not and check in.

Amy sat behind the counter, refilling the bowl of mint imperials with that ever-present smile on her face.

'Effie!' she squealed when I arrived, bleary-eyed from a night of uneasy sleep. Amy took the mug from me, placed it down and took my hands in hers. 'Guess what?'

'What?' I replied; her excitement wasn't catching.

'I just had an agent request the rest of my manuscript.' She almost screamed and brought her hands up to her mouth as she giggled madly behind them.

'You're being published?' I asked, jealousy flaring in my gut.

'Not yet. They need to read the rest and see if they like it, but if they do, then . . .'

She came in for a hug before I knew what was happening and I had no choice but to hug her back. I tried to be happy for her, to not be jealous, but as you probably know by now, I'd never been too good at that.

That night I locked up the shop, turned out the lights and made my way up into the place I called home, for now. I sat down on the sofa, flicked on the TV and looked around at the boxes that I had yet to unpack. I'd just been grabbing the things I needed without unpacking, but now I realised that I would never settle until everything was in its place.

I spent four hours unloading and trying to make the flat a little homelier. It wasn't large but it wasn't small either. The front door was at the top of a staircase that led up from the back room of the shop and opened directly into the living room. The walls were painted an attractive shade of burnt orange (which annoyingly reminded me of Theo again) and a kitchenette sat in the left-hand corner. There was one modestly sized bathroom, Arthur's bedroom and a room I couldn't even get into for the sheer amount of books that blocked the doorway. I'd been sleeping on the sofa, abandoning the godforsaken futon after the first night, but tonight I vowed to sleep in an actual bed.

I emptied the box, avoiding my novel until last. I set it down on the table, sat on the sofa and took a swig of wine. With acid rising in my throat I picked up the wad of papers and turned to the first page. As soon as I started reading, I began to feel the burning in my chest, the passion for the story, the love for the characters. But as I read on, I began to notice things. Spelling mistakes, grammatical errors, even sentences that didn't make sense, and by the time I lowered the papers to my lap I realised that I had been a deluded fool.

I'd vainly sent it off without checking anything, so excited to get it gone that I'd rushed it and ruined my chances of it getting anywhere. I'd spent year upon year thinking that I'd done the most I could to ensure the future I thought I deserved, but now I saw that I hadn't done enough. I felt like such an idiot when I thought of all the time I'd wasted, moping around when I should have been rewriting and fixing it.

That night I crawled into my PJs and readied my clothes for the next day, laying out a pair of jeans and a billowy chiffon blouse that was burgundy and covered in lots of tiny green birds. As I laid the jeans down, I heard a rustling in the pocket and reached in to pull out a piece of crumpled paper. I unfolded it and my heart began to ache a little.

The list sat in my hand, half-finished and torn down the centre.

There were six tasks left unchecked:

5. *Move out*

9. *Do something that matters*

10. *Stop holding grudges*

11. *Achieve a dream*

12. *Learn to love myself*

13. *Earn more money*

I crossed off *Move out* and *Earn more money*. My new managerial position had proved to be more profitable than my previous role had been, and I had moved out, although not permanently. I looked at the list and felt the hatred swell. But for all the hurt and despair that man had caused me, at least he'd made me feel something, made me do something with my life, even if it was only for a while.

I took the list into the kitchen and pinned it to the cork noticeboard next to the door, beside a photograph of Arthur and Toby at the bowling alley, and I looked at the four remaining missions.

Theo might have sent me away like a disgraced nineteenth-century housewife, but he had been right about one thing. I didn't need him, not to complete this list.

Even though I missed him, hated him and loved him in equal measure, I knew that my life was my own charge and if I didn't like how it was going then I was the only one with the power to change it.

# Chapter Twenty-Three

I stood outside the ugly 1970s building that sat hidden away like the eyesore it was in a side street, away from the tourists. The charity logo blazed red from the centre of a desolate concrete façade and graffiti tags decorated the door. The building was terribly ugly, but what happened within its walls was not.

I'd always wondered if the choices we make in life change the path that we started out on, or if we just end up at the same predetermined destination.

A man could choose a red pair of socks over grey because his wife complained that he was boring. But then one of those red socks might end up getting thrown in with the whites, turning his wife's favourite blouse a shade of baby pink and that might start the row that makes her think about filing for divorce, like she planned to do in the first place. Is life a series of meaningless decisions that fool us into thinking that the choices we make matter or do we really have control over where we end up?

When I had found that list, I had chosen to try and change

my life. Whether that would result in it actually changing was another matter entirely, but simply making the choice felt like progress and so what did it matter if that choice was a little meaningless?

'Have you had any experience with the homeless before?' Cassandra Hamilton asked me over the pine-effect veneer of her desk.

Apart from my mother comparing me to one?

'No,' I replied as I completed my sign-up form and handed it back to her. She was a stout woman with an ill-advised pixie cut, dyed a shade of platinum blonde. She was wearing a shirt that didn't quite fit her across the bust, the fabric gaping open to reveal the white bra she was wearing beneath. I tried not to keep glancing at it, but most times it couldn't be helped.

'Well, we have several teams that take a different section of the city centre. They tend to start at 8 p.m. and work through until they've run out of aid. You'll be part of Caleb's team working along New Street.' She looked down at the form and grinned, her cheeks bulging out all round and pink. 'All seems to be in order here and your background check is all clear. I'll go and get Caleb so that the two of you can meet and we'll see you tomorrow at eight.' She pushed her rounded body up from the spinning lumbar support chair and disappeared around the corner.

I heard a *ping* come from my phone; it was an email from Arthur.

I smiled as I read it and saw the attached photographs of them at Prague's St Vitus Cathedral. He told me that a postcard was on the way and that they'd arrange a Skype call soon.

Before I could finish reading, Cassandra came back with a skinny man in tow.

'Effie, this is Caleb. He'll be your team leader starting tomorrow. I'll leave you two to have a chat and then you're free to go.' She shook my hand, limply, and trotted off again.

Caleb wasn't what I'd expected. He wasn't much older than me, with curly black hair that reminded me of Arthur and green eyes that smiled with friendliness.

'Effie, that's an interesting name. Is it short for anything?' he asked, wheeling the chair around the desk and sitting next to me.

'I think it's usually short for Euphemia, but mine's just Effie, thankfully.'

'What happened to your hand?' He pointed to the once blue splint that was now turning black with dirt.

'I fell down a few weeks ago,' I said simply. 'I tend to make a habit out of injuring myself.'

'Did it hurt?' he asked.

'Like a bitch.' I clapped my hand to my mouth in worry about my flippant use of the word *bitch* in a formal situation, but he just smiled and I relaxed. 'It's not so bad now. I think it can come off pretty soon.'

'Well, try your best not to injure yourself on my watch. The paperwork is a literal nightmare.'

He smiled and ran his hand through his hair, the curls bouncing back to their original positions like springs when his hand had moved through.

'Well, I'm Caleb, short for Caleb,' he said and I found myself almost smiling. 'What made you want to join us?'

I couldn't say, *'Because a man I love made me promise to do a list of missions before he kicked me to the kerb like one of those sad single shoes at the side of a motorway.*' So, instead I replied with, 'I just wanted to do something that matters.'

'Well, we need all the help we can get,' he said, wheeling the chair he was sitting on over to a cupboard. He sized me up with his eyes and took out a red sweatshirt and an armband with reflective patches. 'Around Christmas is when we need the most help. People have their turkey dinners and their gifts and they watch their *Morecambe and Wise* box sets and it's easy to forget that there are homeless people still out there, spending the day in a cold doorway.' He handed me the sweatshirt with the official charity logo and the armband, telling me that he'd get an ID made up and would give it to me when I started tomorrow night.

'Welcome aboard, Effie,' he said, shaking my hand.

I couldn't wait for Tuesday evening to come around and give my life some purpose and when it did, I arrived half an hour early. The only other person there was Caleb, who greeted me with a grin and handed me my ID. It was raining outside and so cold that dragon's breath fell from my lips, so Caleb got me a coat in the same red as my sweatshirt and handed me two bags full of food, energy bars and tokens for the shelter's soup kitchen.

'You ready to save the world?' he asked as we headed out into the night.

'Is it too cliché if I tell you I was born ready?' I said, with an unnatural spring in my step. I was excited to be doing something, anything, other than sitting alone at home and talking to myself or the people on the TV.

'Probably, but I'll forgive it just this once. The others will be waiting for us at the meet point. Let's go before they freeze to death,' he said with a smile.

We walked along the entire route of the main high street to the meeting point, Caleb chattering away the whole time. There were four others in our team: Janet, a middle-aged woman with warm brown skin and box-braided hair; Liz, a teenager with exceptionally large drawn-on eyebrows, who informed me that she was also part of Teens Against Animal Cruelty and the Stop the Badger Cull Campaign; and Ned and Cassie, a married couple who talked to me non-stop about their recent trip to visit family in Ireland.

Ned carried a tank of hot water on his back and Cassie made hot drinks for the people we found huddled in doorways, their hands shivering as they took the polystyrene cups.

'How are you finding it?' Caleb asked, rubbing his hands together to generate a little heat.

'I'm enjoying myself. It's nice to do something good for a change,' I replied.

'Well, there's another one for you over there.' He pointed across the street to where a young woman, around thirty, was sitting in a tattered sleeping bag in the doorway of a Boots. I headed over and crouched down beside her.

'Hi, I'm Effie.' I held out my hand. She looked down at it as if she didn't know what to do with it.

'Ali,' she replied in a far-off accent. She shook my hand. It was so cold that it felt like the hand of a dead person, her nails dirty and bitten.

I handed her some tokens for the soup kitchen and some food, which she took with a chorus of 'Thank you' and 'Great, cheers'. I looked at Ali, her brown hair sticking out beneath her black woollen hat, cut inexpertly at the nape, and the dark circles that sat around her eyes. I heard a rustling from by her legs and it was only then that I noticed movement beneath the sleeping bag. She pulled it back and the large head of a grey Staffordshire bull terrier poked out. He pushed his cold, wet nose into my palm and licked my wrist.

'That's Otis,' she said with a smile. 'He's my heart.'

I looked up at her, the smile on her face widening as he licked her chin.

The smile lit up her face and I saw, for a split second, the person beyond the circumstances. Had things worked out differently for Ali she might have been a dental assistant or a doctor – anything in fact. She could have lived in a flat, a house or a mansion and chosen her path through life, but the doorway of Boots was all she'd been given and that wasn't even hers.

'Where are you from, Ali?' I asked. 'That isn't a Birmingham accent I hear.'

'I'm from Boston, Massachusetts.'

'What brought you over here?' I asked. She looked at me, our eyes connecting as she spoke.

'My mom's American, Dad's from here. They broke up when I was twelve and Dad brought me here with him. Mom never hid the fact that she preferred my brother, so I was happy to come over here with him.' She took a breath and stroked Otis's head. 'Dad started gambling and drinking about a year after we moved here. Soon enough all our money was gone. I dropped out of college to try and help him but any money I brought in went straight out again on booze and slot machines.'

'Did you get through to him in the end?'

She shook her head. 'He died before I had the chance to. That was when I was seventeen and three years later, here I am.'

My eyes widened in shock. I had thought her around thirty years old, not eight years my junior.

'I'm sorry,' I said, knowing that it wasn't enough.

'Gotta take the good with the bad. If that hadn't happened, then I wouldn't have met Otis.' She smiled down at him again, her eyes igniting while they lingered on him.

'What do you do when you're not here?' I asked, looking around at the dingy doorway. It smelled of human dirtiness and the faintest smell of acrid urine drifted in from the corner.

'I spend most nights here and a few at the shelter, if I can get in. In the day I go where I can; every day is different.' She smiled at me, but it didn't quite reach her eyes. She was missing a tooth right at the front. 'What about you?'

'Me? Oh, I work in a bookshop,' I said, surprised by her interest.

Her smile widened for a moment and she raised a hand into the air. 'What is that book called, the one about the lion and the wicked ice queen?'

'*The Lion, the Witch and the Wardrobe*?'

'Yes! I used to love reading those books.' She regarded me for a few seconds before saying, 'Dad got me the set one year for Christmas, but that one was always my favourite.' She leaned back and looked at me, as if trying to fit my whole body into the frame of her eyes.

I heard Ned's voice behind me as he and Cassie arrived to pour Ali a cup of coffee. I said goodbye to her, promising to come back and see her on my next shift and when I stood, I found Caleb standing behind me, a satisfied smile on his face.

'What?' I asked as we walked on.

'You were incredible back there,' he gushed.

I suddenly felt embarrassed; praise was not something I took with grace.

'Was I? I didn't do anything except talk to her.'

'Yes,' he replied, 'but you talked to her like she was a human being.'

'That's what she is.'

'A lot of people don't see it that way.'

Ali stuck in my mind that night, the sadness that surrounded her and the happiness that I'd seen when she'd looked down at Otis, burning the image of Theo from my mind. It was incredible that she could still find it within herself to smile.

On Wednesday morning I woke with a feeling that was almost enthusiasm. It was strange to feel something positive for once. My body wasn't used to it, not after such heavy and prolonged doses of wallowing. Apart from the short but scarring portion of my life that Theo had been a part of, I couldn't remember the last time I'd felt enthusiastic about anything that wasn't writing-related. I couldn't wait to go back and help someone else, to revisit Ali and Otis and see the others in the team who I had quickly grown to like.

The shop didn't need opening for another hour so I decided to make myself some breakfast, frying some bacon and brewing some coffee. The weight had slid from me in the twenty-eight days since Theo had made me leave Wales and cut contact. So, I made enough bacon for two. I'd just put the bacon into a floury bread roll and sat down to watch some crappy breakfast television when my phone rang.

'Dad? You're where?' I asked with astonishment.

I went down to the front door and let him in through the shop.

He came up and sat down on the sofa. I handed him a cup of coffee – black, no sugar – and then sacrificed half of the bacon to make him a sandwich. He looked around the

298

flat as if he'd never set foot outside his own house before, which wasn't too far from the truth. I couldn't tell if he liked it or hated it, but that was one of the quirks of my father: you could never tell what he was thinking.

We ate without conversation – this wasn't unusual for us but it still felt pretty weird – and watched as a weather man told us that this Christmas was unlikely to be a white one, but he'd inform us again nearer the time.

'I don't know why anyone bothers hoping anymore,' Dad said, his voice startling me. 'We haven't had a proper white Christmas in almost fifteen years.'

I slid my empty plate onto the table and turned my body round to face him.

'Why are you here, Dad?'

He swigged his coffee and looked at his knees. 'I wanted to see if you were okay. You're still my daughter even if you live elsewhere.'

'I'm fine,' I said, and realised for the first time in a while I meant it. I filled him in on Arthur and Toby's travels and my volunteering at the shelter and Ali and Otis and Caleb.

'It sounds like you've picked yourself up.' He smiled and looked me in the eye for a split second before looking back at his knees.

'Does Mum still hate me?' I asked. I couldn't say I regretted anything I'd said. I'd meant it all, in the moment at least.

'She doesn't hate you, Effie. She's just angry, is all.' He sighed and stood abruptly. 'I wanted you to know that you're welcome at home for Christmas Day.'

'Does Mum know about this?' I asked.

'She's the one who made me come here and tell you.' He smiled. 'I think she's calming down about it all.' We chatted some more about what had been happening since I'd left home, and when it was time to open the shop, I hugged him and he left. I felt ever so slightly like things were finally going well for me.

That evening I sat talking with Ali as she ate an energy bar and sipped at her tea, the night air biting at our faces. Caleb gave Ali a blanket and she wrapped it around Otis who shivered with his big head on my lap.

As we walked back to the shelter, the quietness of the street somewhat calming, Caleb turned to me and asked how I was getting home. I'd told him that I'd walk but he insisted that I let him drive me home. I didn't do much in the way of refusing; my feet were killing me. I sat down in the seat of his car, letting out a long old-person groan as I did, and directed him to the shop.

'You live in a bookshop?' he asked as he pulled up onto the kerb. 'That's awesome.'

'It's not really mine. I'm looking after it for a friend while he's off gallivanting around the world,' I replied, popping the door and feeling tiredness weighing down my eyelids.

'You staying here alone?' he asked.

'Why? You gonna try and attack me if I say yes?' I answered, the tiredness evaporating.

'Yeah, that did sound kinda creepy didn't it?' He smiled and rubbed the back of his neck. 'I only ask because . . . well, would you, perchance . . . want to . . . go on a date . . . with me?'

I choked on nothing, the surprise lodging in my throat and making me splutter.

'All right,' he said, patting me on the back, 'no need to try and kill yourself, a simple no will suffice.'

I laughed and composed myself. 'I'm sorry. You just took me by surprise.'

I looked over at him as he waited patiently for me to reply. The feeling in my chest, the one that felt like my skin was tearing, like my heart was falling loose, began to flare. I thought of Theo, as I did every day, and wondered if I could do it again. If it was possible for me to let someone else in to plaster over the cracks he'd made inside me. I wasn't as well versed in love as other people were, but I was sure that what I'd felt for Theo wasn't the run-of-the-mill love affair that happens all the time. I looked at Caleb's dark hair, his green eyes, his quirky style, his smile that was nice but didn't have the hypnotic powers that Theo's had. He was the opposite to Theo in every aspect of appearance and maybe that's what I needed: someone different, someone new.

'Yes,' I said with a wavering voice. 'I'll go on a date with you.'

As I said the words, I tried not to wonder what I was getting myself into and I tried not to think of how I wished it was Theo who had asked.

Caleb arrived at the shop at six thirty the next evening. He was wearing black jeans, oxblood winkle-pickers and a Seventies-era shirt beneath a sheepskin-lined denim jacket, on the lapel of which sat several enamel pins.

I wore a dark green dress over black leggings with calf-high boots, a green beanie hat on top of my freshly tamed curls and a long purple coat that I'd had since I was seventeen. I'd taken off my splint. The inside had looked like the bottom of a used Petri dish. I'd worn it for long enough now and it barely hurt at all, so I called time and said goodbye to the splint.

He greeted me with a smile and a gift.

'What's this for?' I asked as he placed it in my palm. It

was a small pin in the shape of a dog's face. I couldn't help but notice the resemblance to Otis.

'I didn't know where you stood on flowers. I don't have a problem with feminism, but it has confused me somewhat on the flower front.'

'This is much better than flowers,' I said, pinning it to the lapel of my coat before we set off.

We walked into town and it was only ten minutes or so before we got there. The streets were filled with people doing late-night shopping in the manic rush of Christmas.

'Where are you taking me then?' I asked, my hands pushed into my pockets for warmth.

'Do you like art?' he asked.

'Depends on the art,' I replied as he turned in the direction of the Museum and Art Gallery. I followed on.

'There's an opening and I'm going to try and impress you with how very cultured I am.' He shot me a smile – it didn't quite leave me cold but it didn't make my knees buckle either.

'Very smooth,' I said as we climbed the sandstone steps and met the buzz of people gathered on the mosaic floor on the other side of the heavy oak doors. I'd been here before, once with school and then once again with Kate when we'd had an art project to research. I found myself wondering what Kate was doing now after the long radio silence following our fight. She was probably at some fancy cocktail party with business big shots, wearing a sexy dress and heels that never seemed to make her feet hurt.

Stop it!

Don't think about Kate. She's gone. Just like everyone else.

I turned around to talk to Caleb but we'd been separated by the crowd. I looked around for his dark curls but all I saw were comb-overs and quaffed white blonde bobs fixed with hairspray. The sound of chit-chat and kitten heels clomping against the floor echoed around the room, amplified by the large domed ceiling. I felt someone take my hand and when I turned, I saw him through the crowd. I let him pull me from the throng, up the ornate marble staircase and into the gallery where a woman sat at a desk awaiting payment.

I reached into my bag to take out some money but Caleb placed a hand on mine and told me he had this one covered. He sauntered over to the woman and gave his name. She checked her list and then nodded him through, telling him to enjoy his evening.

'I know the artist,' he said with a slightly embarrassed smile.

'Show-off,' I said, quietly but loud enough for him to hear, as we followed the crowd.

Five minutes later I found myself staring, confused, at a piece of art on the wall.

What the hell was it supposed to be about? The swirling purples and blues looked like waves, but the piece was called *Galaxy of Sinners*. At one point, Caleb asked me what I thought, I'd just nodded and said words like *interesting* and *juxtaposition* – I'd remembered that one from my Fine Art theory paper.

He introduced me to the artist, a girl with caramel-coloured skin, lips painted black and a buzz cut that she'd dyed turquoise. She seemed to be wearing every colour in existence as she glided around, her chiffon jacket billowing out behind her like rainbow smoke.

'Effie, this is Molly. We went to school together,' Caleb said, leaning in and kissing her cheek. Molly's girlfriend, Luna, joined us as conversations and reminiscences of their school days began. I tried not to zone out, but there's only so much interest you can have when hearing stories about people you don't know, doing things you don't care about.

The air in the room was stifling and it began catching in my throat.

'Do you mind if I steal him away for a moment? My mum wants to say hi,' Molly asked, already taking Caleb's arm and leading him away.

Before I could answer she'd pulled him halfway across the room. He shrugged his eyebrows and smiled at me before disappearing from view. Luna nodded me a farewell and followed them.

I wandered through a pair of glass doors into a room that didn't have anywhere to sit. Through the next set of doors, I saw a curved wooden bench and set my feet on their path towards it. My legs ached from standing all day and when I slumped onto the seat, I let out a long sigh that echoed around the empty room.

It was nice in here, quiet, calm. In here I could breathe again. I took my phone from my bag and, for the millionth time, I tried to write to Theo. I had so much to say to him, so much weight that I needed to get out of me and place on him. He'd had his say in his letter. His closure was complete while mine was still wide open. I watched the empty space and waited for the words to come, but as they had so many times before, the words failed me.

I pushed my phone back into my bag and looked up at the room around me. It was almost silent, apart from my quiet breaths and a mechanical whirring sound that made me feel like dozing. The light was diffused and sleepy as it emanated from the sconces up near the domed glass ceiling. I looked back down the gallery at the two sets of glass doors that sat between me and all the people I'd just left. They smiled and enthused and drank Prosecco from plastic flutes. Why hadn't I been offered any Prosecco?

I couldn't hear them from here. It was like watching a very dull silent movie with no storyline. I closed my eyes and took a deep inhalation of the culture-infused air. I didn't know if I could do this. I had never been good at social chit-chat or just participating in life in general. I wasn't wired like the rest of them. I didn't know how. I held on to the bench with both hands, as if it was keeping me grounded, and looked up at the painting on the wall opposite.

In the picture sat a woman, her eyes closed, her head tilted back and bathed in a light that sparked at her fiery hair. On either side of her stood a figure: one shrouded in shadow, the other lit from above by a heavenly light. Her open hands lay in her lap holding a flower that had been delivered by the bird perching on her arm.

I stood and took a step closer. There was something forthright about it, in the combination of anguish and relief on her face, in the way I almost heard the sorrowful breath leave her lips. I looked at the small plaque of information beside it and read.

*Beata Beatrix* by Dante Gabriel Rossetti 1870
Rossetti made this a memorial to his wife, Elizabeth Siddal, after her death. They shared a tumultuous relationship during her time sitting for her husband's work and the work of the other members of the Pre-Raphaelite brotherhood. She died of what is believed to be suicide, by overdose of laudanum, in 1862.

I suddenly hated the picture, yet I loved it too. We were the same, she and I. Ruined by the men we had loved, driven to contemplate the worst, and only one of us had seen the light before we'd gone a step too far. A tear rolled down my nose but I didn't wipe it away. I didn't care; there was no one to see it. I caught my reflection in the glass that separated us both and stared into my misty eyes. I wasn't crying for Theo or for Rossetti or for anyone else, except me and her. I wanted to reach out and take her hand, to tell her that everything would be okay, that he wasn't worth her life; he wasn't worth her tears. I took a step closer and lifted my hand to the glass, my fingers resting an inch away from hers. At that moment, I heard a voice in my ear and my thoughts were broken.

'You can get kicked out for doing that,' he said, nodding to my hand against the glass. 'Here, take this instead.' Caleb handed me a glass of Prosecco. I took it and drank down the bubbles. 'Nice, isn't it? I meant the painting, although the drink is also pretty good . . . and free. That's always a bonus when it comes to art openings,' Caleb said as he sat down. I wiped away my tears, drank down the rest and moved to join him. His arm was touching mine as we both stared forward at the woman on the wall. 'Molly tells me off for using that word when it comes to art. She says that "nice" is just a way of getting out of an answer.' He shifted closer. My initial instinct was to move away and open up the gap between us, but I forced myself to stay put.

'Do you know the painting?' he asked.

'I do now,' I replied. 'I love it.'

'That's Elizabeth Siddal in that painting too—' Caleb abruptly turned and pointed to another image '—only this time the painter is Millais.' The painting showed the same woman, younger and less pained, lying back in a lake surrounded by flowers, her dress dragging her under to her death. He pointed to another and another and I began to notice something about them.

I stood and looked behind me to a painting of a woman with smouldering orange hair that she combed as she looked wistfully into a mirror in her hand. She was stunning, in a white smock dress that fell gracefully from her shoulder. In the frame beside her was a woman playing the harp, her red hair falling down into the strings as angels perched above her head. Each work was bordered in an ornate frame that only added to the majesty of the paintings; each one special and in pride of place and redheads, almost all of them. Something about them made me feel empowered, like I'd finally found my people, except my people happened to be nothing but century-old paint and canvas.

I looked at image after image and all the women looked the same: red hair, round hips.

'You know, the Pre-Raphaelites painted women like you because they thought that that was what true beauty looked like.' I slowly turned around to face him. 'I'm inclined to agree.'

I hated flattery; it made me feel uncomfortable, but not as uncomfortable as the way he was looking at me did. We looked at each other for far too long and at one point it seemed as if he was about to move in to kiss me, but thought better of it.

'Sorry.' He looked away, embarrassed, and ran his hand through his dark curls.

Breathe.

You can do this.

I took his hand and waited for him to look back up.

'So,' I said, 'where are we going next?'

# Chapter Twenty-Four

What is it called when you grieve for someone who isn't dead, just gone away or nothing like you thought they were?

I suppose the name doesn't matter, the feeling is still the same no matter what you call it.

My grief for the Theo I had made myself believe existed had softened over the month of his absence, the razor-sharp edges had ground themselves down over the weeks since I'd seen him last. The corners still prodded me every few hours or so, but they were blunt now and hurt much less.

That portion of my life seemed like a dream to me now, so far removed from what my life had been before and what it was now, that it seemed impossible that any of it had happened, like it had all been a story.

It was helpful to look at it like that, like a hurt I'd felt whilst reading a book or watching a beloved character die on screen; that way it wasn't as real and it made seeing Caleb a whole lot easier.

Caleb took me to a restaurant where they served food on wooden boards and drinks in old jars. The place was beautiful, with vines made from repurposed plastic bottles running over the walls and tables with mosaic pictures on the surfaces.

He ordered a butternut squash and goat's cheese pie – at which point I learned that he was a vegetarian – and I had the chicken. It felt slightly insensitive to eat a piece of dead bird in front of him, but I'd be damned if I was going to pay that much to eat butternut squash.

The atmosphere was pleasant, the food tasted amazing, Caleb looked handsome and we were sharing easy conversation, but the only thing I could think about was the candle that sat on the table between us.

Even though he wasn't here, Theo still managed to ruin the evening, or rather the memories of him did. Why couldn't I stop remembering the time we'd had our non-date and I'd lost my shit over the candle? Why couldn't I focus on what Caleb was saying and enjoy the way he looked at me without feeling like I was in some way being unfaithful? Why wouldn't Theodore 'Fucking' Morgan just leave me alone?

I abruptly excused myself and went to the bathroom, locking the cubicle door and standing with my back against it as I looked down at my phone. I pulled up the image of us on the mountain again and felt the tears come to my eyes once more. I couldn't believe how happy I had been in that moment and I still felt the remnants of that happiness trying to bloom in my chest. But the happiness of that picture was cracked now, just like the screen that it sat behind.

More than anything I just wanted to stop missing him, to reroute the love I'd been left with to Caleb and let him fill the void that Theo hadn't wanted to. But he was still with me, haunting me like a ghost. Would this be my life now? Would I spend my life looking for another Theo, never finding him and letting guys like Caleb slip away because they weren't him?

I brushed a tear from my cheek as I pressed delete. The question coming up in bold over the image: *Are you sure you want to delete this?* Was I sure? Did I want to be rid of the only photographic evidence of the time we'd spent together? I pressed *No*. I couldn't let it go just yet, I couldn't let *him* go.

The bathroom door opened and the sound of words being sobbed into a phone filled the otherwise empty room.

'I told you this would happen, Soph. I told you that this date was a bad idea,' the girl cried. Muffled sounds came from the earpiece and then the crying girl replied. 'He didn't even bother to turn up.'

The muffled voice came again for a minute before she said, 'I'll be home soon.' She hung up and at that moment I opened my cubicle door. The girl stood directly outside, her face streaked with tears, her red lipstick smeared down onto her chin. She looked from the phone in my hand, the image of Theo still emblazoned on the screen, to the tears that I hadn't bothered to wipe from my cheeks. Her face crumpled and, before I knew what was happening, she walked into the cubicle and hugged me, continuing to sob into my shoulder.

We stayed like that until another woman walked in, looked at us with distress and then moved on to the next cubicle. The girl pulled away, sniffed loudly, gave me a sad smile and then walked out of the door.

The next day I went back to the Art Gallery on my lunch break and bought a poster of the Rossetti painting before taking it back and Blu-tacking it to the wall beside my/Arthur's bed. I sat on the edge of the mattress and looked up into the closed eyes of the painted woman. Caleb was right: she did look like me a little, and she was beautiful. So, why did I think so little of myself?

I turned my head to the mirror on the opposite wall and looked at my reflection. The weight I'd lost over the past month had returned to me like an old friend, but somehow, I didn't seem to care as much as I had before. And something in my face had changed. I seemed to look slightly older, not in the sense of wrinkles and lines but in the darkening of my green eyes and the way I held myself as if without me noticing, a button had been pushed and I now found myself in the midst of an adulthood that I'd been hiding from for years.

I stood up and looked at my whole self in the reflection. I peeled off my baggy jumper and looked at the shape of me that sat beneath a thin vest. I looked at the wideness and the curvature of my hips and the lack of tautness of my stomach. I looked at the slight dimple in the centre of my chin that I'd always disliked and the pale skin dappled with freckles that shone, almost luminescent, in the late morning light. My hair was longer than it had ever been and sat over my shoulder in a river of russet.

I looked up at the painted woman on the wall, the one I considered beautiful, and then back at myself, the one I'd always found wanting, and I saw little difference. Did I hate how I looked simply because the body I saw belonged to me? Or did I hate my body because, deep down, I knew that I hated the angry, jealous person I had become inside?

It was hard to remember a time when I didn't feel inadequate in some way to the people around me. I never felt funny enough, witty enough. I never felt like I looked as good as them and I never fitted in as neatly. I never liked what everyone else liked and I didn't know how they did it, mingling without feeling like they were Martians trying to learn about humanity by forced interaction.

I considered my reflection and, in that instant, I had a sort of epiphany. I'd been hiding myself beneath baggy jumpers and shirts for years because I was embarrassed about what other people would see when they looked at me. But who cared what anyone else saw? If someone wanted to find flaws in me, then they would find them anyway, but I didn't need to search for flaws within myself. I walked over to the wardrobe and pulled out a top that I'd been afraid to wear because of the way it clung to my body and showed the shape of me, but this time as I slid it on and smoothed it down over my skin, it felt like nothing had ever fitted me so well.

Footsteps approached and a moment later someone knocked on the front door.

Amy was standing there when I reached the door, her forehead beaded with sweat but her smile still intact.

'Effie, there's someone waiting for you down in the shop.'

'Who is it?' I asked, suddenly becoming unsteady.

'They didn't say,' she replied. 'You look really nice.' I followed her down into the shop, which was busy, no wonder Amy was sweating.

'Over there by the window.' She pointed and I followed her finger.

I don't know why I had expected it to be Theo. Blind hope, I guess. But the person I saw was not the blond I was looking for.

'Kate?' I walked over to her, my brow furrowed. 'What are you doing here? Aren't you meant to be in Toronto?'

Some dark and vicious part of me slightly enjoyed the way that her hair lay in an inartistically messy braid over her shoulder and the way that dark circles ringed her eyes. She was wearing a faux-fur jacket that was slightly matted in places where she'd leaned on things. Her make-up had been applied sparingly and with little skill, her foundation sitting in messy blobs and there were patches that she'd missed altogether.

'Things didn't work out so well for me in Canada,' she replied, her voice quiet. She stepped forward and sniffed; she'd been crying. 'Can we go somewhere and talk?'

I looked around at the queue of customers, ten people deep and growing. 'We're pretty busy here. I don't know if I'll have time,' I said bluntly.

Kate's face fell, her eyes growing wetter as she looked down at the floor. I sighed at the annoying twist of guilt in my stomach. I clenched my jaw to stop myself from saying anything, but the words came out all the same. 'I'll work through the last half of my lunch break now and take the rest when the shop is quieter. If you want to wait, then we can go somewhere and talk.'

She looked up and nodded. 'I'll wait here,' she said, sitting down on the sofa next to the sleeping husband of a shopper. She looked so lost sitting there with both hands clasping the bag in her lap and I hated myself for feeling sorry for her.

Once the queue was cleared and the shop emptied, I apologised to Amy and left with Kate. I'd make it up to her by giving her an extra fifteen-minute break and letting her take a power nap upstairs.

Kate and I walked in silence to the nearest café where I ordered a latte for myself and Kate ordered a cappuccino. I crossed my legs and rested my hands on my knee, looking over at her with unyielding eyes that waited for her to speak. She shifted uncomfortably in the chair and slipped off her jacket before turning to me. She seemed to be finding it difficult to meet my eye.

'You look good, Eff, have you lost weight?' she asked.

I rolled my eyes. She couldn't win me over with flattery.

'Why did you come, Kate?' I asked in a calm voice. 'I haven't heard a peep from you in over a month.'

'I wanted to apologise.' She sat forward and placed her hands on the table. I noticed that something was missing from her hand. 'I've been a shitty friend to you and not just recently either. I've treated you like crap and tossed you aside for people I thought were better than you, but they *weren't* better than you and I wanted to tell you that I'm sorry.'

'Where's your wedding ring, Kate?' I asked, my voice still cold.

She looked down at her hands and clasped them together, hiding her bare-naked ring finger. The waitress brought our drinks and I nodded a thank you her way before turning back to Kate.

'You're the one who brought me here to talk, so talk,' I said as I sipped at the warm foam.

She tore the tops from three tubes of demerara sugar and tipped them into her coffee before speaking. 'Toronto was a bust,' she said, finally. 'We didn't get the deal and it was partly my fault. I won't bore you with the details but it went *badly*.' She stressed the last word and shivered as if reliving it. 'I was asked to fly home and I was too ashamed to tell anyone. My plan was to come home, forbid Callum from saying anything about me being back and to just live in hiding for a while. After that I could just reappear and pretend I'd only just got back and people wouldn't know that I'd failed.' She sipped frantically and sighed once the caffeine and sugar were safely inside her body. 'I got a taxi from the airport and got home at around lunchtime. I knew Callum would be out at work and so I decided to go to bed and cry it out for an hour or two, but when I got there, I found that the bed was already occupied.'

It didn't surprise me; Callum had always been a twat.

'Him and Eloise have been sleeping together for over a year behind my back.' Tears coated her eyes, making them shine like glass. 'They even did it at my party – that's why I couldn't find either of them for so long.'

'Eloise "Fucking" Kempshore?' I said, a little too loudly, causing a woman to frown and shield the ears of the young boy beside her. 'And Callum?' Kate nodded and wiped her eyes.

'I should have listened to you, Effie, back in year eleven when we had that huge argument and you told me that Eloise was the devil.'

'"Spawn of Satan" I believe were my actual words,' I replied, remembering the moment well.

'You told me that she was a user. You told me that Callum was no good and all I did was ditch you, for them! You were right about everything.'

I didn't tell her that I knew I'd been right. I'd known it when I said it and I'd continued to know it all the way up until now.

'Are you getting a divorce?' I asked.

'I filed this morning.'

'So, where are you living?'

'I moved back in with Mum and Dad. The apartment was never mine, nor was anything in it. Callum was the one with the money to afford a place like that, not me.'

Was this really happening? Had I wished this into existence?

I'd been so jealous of her, of her apartment, of her wedding, of her life, and now she was telling me that what she'd had was never hers in the first place. She had not been the perfect wife that everyone had believed her to be; she *had* been a very good actress though.

'I'm sorry, that must have been awful for you,' I said with little emotion. 'And while we're in the habit of apologising, I think it only right that I say that I'm sorry too. I shouldn't have gone off on one like I did at your party.' It almost killed me to say it, but this was a new leaf, the start of a new Effie. A new Effie who apologised for things, even if it gave her acid reflux to do so.

'Effie.' She leaned forward and took my hand. 'It's already forgiven. I didn't invite you, my oldest friend, to my wedding because I was playing at being someone I wasn't. I didn't want you there because you are nothing like those people; you know exactly who you are and don't care what anyone else thinks.'

I looked a question her way. Was that really how she saw me?

'I *do* care about what people think of me, more than anything. Or at least I used to,' I said.

We sat, looking at each other over the table, her hand in mine, and for the first time in over a decade, we saw each other as we truly were.

'I'm sorry, Effie. Will you forgive me?' she asked, her brow rumpled as she waited for my answer.

I looked at Kate and remembered all the years I'd spent quietly hating her, of the betrayal I had felt at her hands and my first thought was, no, I can't forgive you. But then I thought back to the list and the last remaining missions. I remembered the time Kate had left me waiting at the cinema for an hour before I'd called and found out she'd ditched me for Eloise or when I'd caught glandular fever and she hadn't even texted to see how I was. I felt the anger swell in my stomach and felt it dissipate as I opened my mouth and said, 'Yes, I forgive you.'

*10. Stop holding grudges.*

Why had I felt the need to hang on to them for so long? My grudges with Kate, my mother and now Theo. I was terrible at letting things go, but as I finally let go of my grudge with Kate, I felt a weight lift. We had a new understanding of each other and even though I would never forget the betrayal she'd made me feel, I didn't hate her anymore.

She smiled widely, her dead eyes coming alive for a moment or two.

We drank our coffees and talked, the anger slipping away with every word. For once we weren't trying to one-up each other or throw in a spiteful dig. We just talked, like regular people. Dare I say it? We spoke like adults.

'Are you still with that guy you brought to the party?' she asked, and I almost broke our new détente and threw my coffee at her. He hadn't crossed my mind in almost twenty straight minutes.

'No,' I replied, looking down into the small pool of coffee sitting in the bottom of my cup. 'Not anymore.'

'What happened?'

'He didn't give me much of an explanation, but I'm pretty sure something is going on with him and his ex.' I looked down at my nails. My cuticles looked dry and ragged.

'Do you want to talk about it?' she asked, sensing me holding back.

'Not really. He's gone, what more is there to say?'

Tons, there was tons left to say.


Kate and I stood on the pavement as the last few minutes of my lunch hour ticked away.

'I know that apologising doesn't make up for years of me being a bitch and I know that we aren't magically going to become the best of friends again, but if you ever fancy talking, I'd love to see you.'

I smiled a small smile. 'You weren't the only one who was a bitch, and it would be nice to see you again too.'

She took a step back, knowing that a hug was too familiar; the relationship was delicate now, more delicate than it had ever been. 'Have a nice Christmas, Effie.'

'You too,' I said. She turned and walked away.

I couldn't help but feel a blossoming warmth in my chest, one that seemed to melt a corner of heart I'd put on ice after Theo damaged it beyond repair.

Life was surprising sometimes.

That night I sat down at my laptop. It almost squealed as I pulled it open for the first time in an age to begin rewriting my novel. The release of pent-up anger from my reconciliation with Kate had cleared my head and given me the kick up the arse that I needed to get back to it. At first my fingers only hovered above the keys, afraid to get back to what they loved in case they found out that they weren't any good at it. But I had realised my error with the novel I had been so heartbroken over and although editing it was not a guarantee that someone would want it, I needed to give myself the best shot at the dream I'd dreamt for so long. So, with a deep breath and a bottle of wine at my side, I began writing.

# Chapter Twenty-Five

I'd forgotten the feeling, the warm glow and the burst of excitement that came with writing and creating the world that I wanted, from references of a world that had disappointed me. I worked out all the kinks. I changed the parts that irked me. The parts that were wrong and didn't make sense were altered, the characters fleshed out. I took instances from my own life, warmed them in my hands and moulded them into something new, like plasticine.

My protagonist became stronger, her love interest became less of a focal point and by the end of an epic rewrite, I had something that I could be proud of. I worked through the night, spending every waking hour tweaking and changing, until it was finally done and I could flop back onto the sofa with a satisfied sigh.

I ummed and ahhed about showing my work to anyone for the first time, but, in the end, I came to the decision that if I wanted to be a writer, I had to let people read what I'd written. I gave the first three chapters to Amy to read, her face lighting up with excitement when she learned that I was back at it. She read them while I stared at her the whole time, gauging her reaction and forgetting to breathe.

'This is good, Effie,' she said with a shake of her head. 'It's really good. Have you sent it off yet?'

'No,' I replied, 'I'm too scared.'

She handed the papers back to me with an encouraging grin. 'I'll come with you after work. You're posting this today.'

That night Caleb and I went on our second date, to see a film at The Electric Cinema. I didn't ask what film we were seeing, I was just happy to be out. It turned out to be some artsy film with subtitles, which had been shot with a sepia filter. I didn't really know what was going on and halfway through my mind began to wander. I looked over at Caleb. He was enthralled. His eyes drew wide as one of the characters drank down a vial of poison and died to the sound of a cash register. *Cha-ching!* I'm sure it was all meant to mean something, but what that something was I had absolutely no idea.

I looked at Caleb's lips, parted and with a popcorn shell stuck to the lower lip. I almost reached over and brushed it away. He turned and caught me staring. I felt a jolt of panic, but then he smiled and looked down at my hand, lacing his fingers through mine. They felt alien, new, exciting. I felt a flicker in my chest and, stupidly, I felt a little guilty. I *was not* Theo's. I was no one's but my own, and if I wanted Caleb then I would have him. I settled back into the seat and tried to enjoy the feeling of someone showing me affection, but somehow, I couldn't let myself relax.

Caleb walked me home and I invited him up into the flat. Maybe it would lead somewhere. Maybe I would look into his eyes and we would let whatever happened, happen. Or maybe I'd throw up on him, who knew? My luck had been so up and down when it came to men.

He sat on the sofa as I poured us some wine. I took a large swig from my glass before topping it back up to match the other.

I sat down beside him and put on some music to make the silence a little less deafening.

'Did you enjoy the film?' he asked, taking a sip of his wine. He grimaced.

'It was okay,' I replied, before sipping at my own wine to see why he'd sneered. It tasted fine. 'What's wrong?'

'Nothing.' He placed the wine down and turned to me with a smile in his eyes. 'I have a confession to make: I don't like wine.'

I gasped. Blasphemy!

'I know, I know,' he apologised. 'I'm a grown-up and I'm into art, so you would think that wine was something I'd be heavily into, but I just hate it.'

I picked up his glass and poured his into mine. 'This may cause a rift in our friendship,' I joked. 'Can I get you something else? I think I've got some gin somewhere.'

I went to stand but Caleb's hand on mine stopped me. 'Actually, I think I'd rather . . .' He stopped speaking and instead pressed his lips to mine. His lips were chapped; I guess that was from so many nights out in the cold.

I tasted the wine on his tongue and I remembered the last time I had tasted wine on a kiss. I kissed Caleb harder as I tried to push Theo from my mind. Caleb seemed to take this as an invitation to push his fingers through my hair. Before I really knew what was happening, we were standing up and stumbling to Arthur's bedroom. I cringed at the idea of having sex in Arthur's bed, but still I let myself tumble to the mattress with him. His lips moved over mine, but I felt no electricity where they landed. I felt no love blooming in my chest, just a sort of bewildered excitement.

I opened my eyes and saw that his were closed. I shut my eyelids again and that's when I saw it, what I wished was happening instead of what *was* happening. My hands moved through his hair and I imagined that it was blond. I let my hands run over his shoulders and I wished that they were wider, firmer, Theo-er. His hands moved over my dress and I suddenly began to wish I'd never invited him here. I should have turned him away at the door. This was wrong. I couldn't sleep with Caleb and be imagining that it was Theo the whole time. It wasn't fair on him; it wasn't fair on me.

His lips fell out of rhythm and his eyelashes fluttered against my cheeks. I opened my eyes and found that we were staring at each other. My lips grew stationary, my hands fell to the mattress and after a few moments Caleb drew back.

He stared down at me, an almost unbearable silence lying between us.

'There's something not quite right here isn't there?' he said, breaking the silence and the building tension.

'Oh, thank God,' I said, putting my hand to my forehead and sighing. 'I thought it was just me.'

'It's definitely not just you.' He breathed out heavily from his nose. 'I didn't want to stop because I didn't want you to think that I didn't find you attractive. I do.' He sighed and climbed off, sitting on the edge of the bed. 'I don't know what's wrong. I like you, you're nice and funny and really pretty. This should be working.' He rubbed the back of his neck with his hand.

'I feel exactly the same!' I sat up and drew my knees to my chest. 'It kind of felt like . . .'

'Snogging a family member?'

'Exactly!' We stared at each other for a moment and then, for some unknown reason, we both began laughing. We laughed until our eyes clouded with tears and our stomachs ached.

'Look,' he said, placing his hand on my knee, his face pink from laughing, 'I like you, Effie, and I don't want this to ruin anything, so let's start again, shall we?'

'Please,' I said.

'Effie—' he held out his hand '—will you be my friend?'

I took his hand and shook it firmly, three times. 'Yes,' I replied. 'I think I will.'

I'd never really been a dog person.

I found that the aloof and generally passive-aggressive nature of cats was more befitting my personality, but as I sat in the Boots doorway with Ali, Otis's heavy head lounging on my knee, I finally became one.

'Where will you go on Christmas Day?' I asked Ali as she tucked into the burger I'd bought for her, mustard running down her chin.

'Here I suppose,' she replied, smearing the sauce over her skin with the sleeve of her grubby hoodie and picking up the cup of steaming tea from beside her, 'unless a better offer comes along.'

I'd quickly grown to like Ali, spending a little longer with her than I should as the group made our rounds of the street. Otis had to be held back most nights from following me home and sometimes it was all I could do not to take him with me.

Otis looked up as a glob of ketchup fell onto his nose. As he moved, he caught Ali's elbow and her tea went flying. She managed to save half of it, but the rest seeped into her hoodie. She tutted and called Otis a 'silly boy', but there was no trace of anger in her voice. She rooted around in her meagre bag and pulled out a cleaner hoodie before quickly pulling the sodden one over her head. She shivered in the cold and reached for the new one. As she did, I noticed the track marks in the crook of her elbow that bled down onto her forearm, purple and angry.

I quickly looked away, but she'd already seen me.

'Not pretty, are they?' She held up her arm and my eyes moved back to the river of indigo that travelled from her wrist to her elbow. Along the river were four red scabs, three semi-healed, and a speckling of white scars that looked like stars against her olive skin.

'Do you use often?' I asked, looking down at Otis and running my hand over his wide forehead. My hand came away waxy. I wondered how long it had been since he'd had a bath.

'Not as much as I used to.'

'Why do you do it? If you saved all the money that you spend on drugs, you could have enough to get yourself out of here.'

She pulled the hoodie on and smoothed it over her slight frame. 'Do you drink, Effie?'

I took a breath and nodded. 'I do, sometimes a little too much.'

'Then tell me how that's different from what I do.' She looked at me and I let my eyes rise to meet hers. She didn't look angry or accusatory, she just looked deeply sad.

'Well, drinking isn't illegal for one thing,' I replied.

'Why do you drink?' she asked before sipping her tea. 'Honestly.'

324

'I drink because I'm unhappy and alcohol helps numb that unhappiness.' I rubbed my face and sighed into my palm. 'I'm sorry. I feel like such a dick saying that to you.'

'Don't apologise, Eff. We all have our own problems. Just 'cause I'm here on the street and you aren't doesn't mean that your problems don't matter.' I felt her hand on mine. Her palm felt like the surface of a pineapple. 'I use because it helps me to forget where I am, what I am.'

Otis looked up and licked Ali's hand.

'What do you do with Otis while you're . . . well, while you're out of it?' I asked.

'I make sure he's safe. I wouldn't ever leave him in harm's way.' She smiled the genuine smile that she kept only for him and kissed his nose. 'He's my heart. I wouldn't let him get hurt.'

I turned to her and squeezed her hand tightly. 'Promise me you'll be careful.'

She laid her head down on my shoulder; her beanie hat sat against my cheek.

'Thank you, Effie. It's been a long time since someone cared.'

I wanted to tell her that she was being stupid. That the drugs wouldn't help her, but then, if I was in Ali's dirty second-hand shoes, maybe I'd want something to take the edge off too.

'He's pretty that one,' she said, nodding her head in Caleb's direction. He stood laughing with an elderly homeless man called Norman.

'We went on a couple of dates,' I said. She squeezed my arm and drew her eyes wide. 'We decided to stay friends; it was like kissing my cousin.' I shuddered at the memory.

'That's a shame, but then I guess there's still a chance for me, eh.' She cocked her head and observed him from a distance. 'I like his hair.'

'It is good hair,' I agreed.

When I'd arrived at the shelter that evening, I'd thought that things between Caleb and I might be awkward, but he'd greeted me with a smile and gave me a Santa's hat to complete my uniform and everything had been as it should. I hoped that it would last; Caleb and I had the makings of a great friendship, just so long as we didn't have to go on another date.

'Hey, Eff!' Caleb called as I packed up for the night and grabbed my bag. I saw him jogging towards me, his cheeks red from the cold. 'We're all going to the German Christmas Market tomorrow evening before our shift if you want to come?'

'I'd love to,' I replied. I looked at my ragtag group of heroes. Ned and Cassie jostled each other beneath a sprig of plastic mistletoe, and Janet and Liz shared a cupcake that one of them had bought for the other as a Christmas gift. A few months ago, I would never have dreamed that I would be here in the centre of town in the freezing cold, thirteen days before Christmas and verging on being happy. But here I was.

That morning I got back to the flat at around half one. I felt elated, too buzzed to sleep and too tired to do anything. I wandered to the kettle and clicked it on. It was too late for coffee, but I wanted one and it was better than going into the bedroom and finishing the quarter bottle of Shiraz that was left on the bedside table. As I waited, the sound of bubbling water filling the air, I walked over to the corkboard and looked at the list.

9. *Do something that matters* . . . CHECK

10. *Stop holding grudges* . . . CHECK (in Kate's case anyway)

11. *Achieve a dream* . . . In the process of Checking

12. *Learn to love myself* . . .

. . . I wouldn't say that I was vain now. That I woke up in the morning and saw my pillow-creased, puffy face looking back at me and thought . . . I would.

But I'd learned to love myself in a different way. I no longer gave a rat's ass about what anyone else thought of me. When I left the shop, I didn't instantly begin looking around like I used to, watching people's eyes and wondering what they were thinking about me, about what I was wearing, about if I was good enough. I was not some grotesque gargoyle from the top of a cathedral, I was a young woman with red hair, pale skin and sturdy thighs and I was happy with that. And if I was happy and comfortable then what did it matter if other people occasionally mistook my thighs for honey-roasted ham hocks, or if they took offence at the orange-ness of my hair. I was who I was and I would never be anyone different, so I thought it about time that I started appreciating what I had. So, I guess, in short, CHECK!

I woke to a tinkling sound coming from my laptop. I didn't remember falling asleep or even going to bed, but, lo and behold, here I was waking to a pool of drying saliva across the pillow beneath me. I pressed a button without really knowing what I was doing, knocking my wrist on the edge of the screen and uttering a stream of obscenities as Arthur and Toby's faces appeared on the screen.

'Good morning to you too,' Arthur said with a beaming smile.

'Arthur!' I pulled the laptop onto my chest and lay back down, my chin doubling in the unflattering webcam. I didn't bother adjusting myself.

'How's the trip?' I asked.

Toby leaned forward and rolled his eyes. 'This one went and got himself a tattoo, didn't he?'

'A *holiday* tattoo,' Arthur corrected him. 'I wanted to remember the trip.'

'And you couldn't just use your brain for that?' Toby chided, his Scottish accent thickening as he raised his voice.

'I see that you two are already acting like an old married couple,' I said through a laugh.

I told them about how the shop was doing and about Amy and my date with Caleb.

'Two boys in one year!' Arthur remarked. 'You'll be getting a name for yourself, missy.'

'And you'd know all about that wouldn't you,' I replied. Toby pretended not to hear and then went on to tell me about their trips to Charles Bridge and Karlštejn Castle and The Dancing House and the Lennon Wall. Arthur looked happier than I'd ever seen him before and that made me happy too.

I was just about to sign off when Arthur stopped me.

'Just in case you thought I'd forgotten, there's a Christmas gift for you in the airing cupboard. I'll be expecting mine when I get back.'

'I miss you, both of you,' I said without really knowing why. Arthur and I had never been sappy with each other; we were barely even polite.

328

'Ah, we'll be back before you know it and then you'll wish we'd stayed away forever.' Arthur beamed a smile and Toby blew a kiss my way. The screen went blank and they were gone. My heart feeling a little bit fuller than it had before.

Once I'd wiped the drool from my cheek, I went to the airing cupboard and took out a rectangular parcel. I ripped off the wrapping – I was never one to wait until the actual day until I unwrapped everything – and found inside a note-book, bound in mahogany leather. In a strap on the side was a silver fountain pen. I flipped it open and saw that he'd written something inside:

> *For your next masterpiece.*
> *Remember me in the dedication.*
> Arthur X

Eleven days till Christmas and the shop was so packed that I considered putting an ad out for an emergency member of staff. I stood behind the counter with my eyes closed and too many sounds in my ears.

Christmas was always a manic time, but this was the first year that I was beginning to feel like I couldn't handle it. It was probably because this time I was in charge and all the failings fell onto me.

The sound of a hundred voices, all talking at once, filled the air and the shuffling of feet against floor seemed to drum out a staggered rhythm. The *ching* of the till was both music and torture to my ears, on the one hand we were making money (yay); on the other hand it was yet more noise. The *thump* of books being pushed back onto shelves added a bassline and the tinkle of the bell was the soprano. *That bloody bell!* I'd tear it down with my bare hands if I had the energy.

I took a deep breath and tried to push it all out and think of something calming, wind maybe.

I heard the *whoosh* of the wind and the image of a bird, red and swooping, came into my head. I heard the sound of the breeze whipping through my hair and I saw the approaching figure of my companion. I was on the mountain, Cadair Idris.

It was odd to think that, right now, even though this chaos was happening here, that mountain was still right where I'd left it, as peaceful and calm as ever.

The image of the happy couple celebrating with a kiss at the summit stone made me wince. The girl who was enjoying that kiss did not feel like me – she was too happy, too naïve.

'Effie,' Amy called, her voice taut with stress, 'I really need some help over here.'

Time's up, get back to work. You're not on that mountain anymore.

That night I found it. My favourite film.

I hadn't used Theo's stupid book or even searched for it, it had found me. Thank you Film4. I'd flicked on to it three minutes late, only missing the opening titles.

*Moulin Rouge.*

It was insanity and opulence and music and romance and tragedy, all the good things.

It was an assault on my ears, eyes and emotions and I loved every second of it. When it finished, I found myself sitting back with a sigh of satisfaction, my face well and truly tear-stained.

I sent Caleb a gushing text about the film and it transpired that he had never seen it. I told him that I would grab the DVD when I next went into town and we could have a movie night. I was pretty sure he'd like it as much as I did, with his taste in weird, artsy films. It would be nice to have someone else at the flat with me. Caleb didn't make me nervous; I didn't feel like I had to look pretty or be normal in his presence. He seemed to accept me for who I was and that was really all I wanted.

'Shitting hell!' I exclaimed as the scalding glühwein scorched my tongue. 'You didn't tell me that we'd come here to drink lava.'

Caleb chuckled at my pain and took a sip of his overly spiced wine, burning his own tongue, at which I laughed with cruel spite.

The German Market is an annual, detestable tradition that is a festive thrill for all who visit Birmingham, but a pain in the ass for anyone who lives here. The smell of sickly-sweet nuts and bratwurst filled the air and made me feel a little nauseous and the wine wasn't helping. I never quite understood the appeal, but I guess if queueing beside a line of garden sheds that sell generic shite at ridiculous prices is your idea of a good time then who am I to question it? Wizzard blared from the speakers beside the carousel and annoyingly got stuck in my head as we chatted beside a giant fibreglass Santa.

Liz hadn't shown up and Janet had had to stay home to look after her son, so it ended up being only me, Caleb, Ned and Cassie who arrived to drink the cup of blistering spiced wine.

Ned was in the midst of telling us about his stepdaughter, who was coming for Christmas with her fiancé, when I saw *Her*.

She was standing next to one of those faux log cabins that they insist on erecting every year in the pursuit of festiveness, with a young girl in her arms and another at her hip. The child in her arms stared at a glistening bauble, her eyes wide and sparkling with the reflection.

The last time I'd seen her she'd been driving away from the Morgans' after seeing Theo, but this time I saw her standing right in front of me. A tall, broad-shouldered man came up behind her and wrapped his arms around her stomach. I felt a jolt in my chest. Theo. She leaned back and kissed him, the child giggling in her arms. I wasn't sure if my heart was still beating. He turned and the blue lights of the carousel illuminated his face. It lit up his wide smile, his dark blue eyes, his straight nose. I felt the air release from my lungs as I realised it wasn't Theo, but her husband, Matt.

Did Matt know that she'd been to see Theo? Did he know what his wife was up to?

'You okay, Eff?' Caleb asked, drawing me back into the conversation where Ned was telling an anecdote that had something to do with zombies. Cassie hung on his every word, grinning up at him and cradling her glühwein in both hands for warmth.

'Yeah.' I handed him my mug and stepped away. 'I'll be right back.'

I jogged towards her, losing her for a moment in the crowd before I found her again, standing alone beside a stall selling painted candle jars.

'Jenny?'

She turned and cocked her head as she tried to place me.

'Hi,' she said unsurely. 'I know you, don't I?'

Of course, she didn't remember me – who was I to her? Nothing. Nothing but the girl she'd beaten to the prize.

'I met you at a service station not long ago. I was with Theo.'

Her eyes widened with understanding. She reached out and placed her hand on my arm. 'That's right. Ellie, isn't it?'

'Effie,' I corrected her. I wished she'd take her hand off me.

'That's right. Effie. Sorry, I didn't recognise you, you look different.' She grinned and let her hand fall. Thank God. 'How is Theo doing?'

'I have no idea. I haven't seen him in a while.' I didn't know how many days it had been exactly. I'd stopped counting at some point.

'Oh.' She didn't seem displeased.

'I was hoping you could tell me how he is. You've seen him more recently than me anyway,' I said with a raised eyebrow.

She looked me a question and stepped closer. 'The last time I saw him was at the service station, with you.'

She was lying and I was about to catch her out on it.

'I drove to the house to see how he was. They wouldn't let me in. I don't know what I did to make them do that but they wouldn't,' I said, and I was pleased to notice that I didn't feel myself breaking as I recalled crying at the gates. 'Theo wouldn't see me, but *I* saw *you*. You left through the gates as I arrived, and I know that you went to the hospital too.'

Her smile fell and she stepped closer again. 'Look, Matt doesn't know that I went. He'd flip if he knew – he gets very jealous.' She looked almost fearful.

'Are you having an affair with Theo? Is that it?' I asked.

She laughed an abrupt single laugh and threw back her head. 'Of course not. Theo and I ended years ago and I have a family now.'

'If having a family stopped people from having affairs, then there would be no such thing,' I replied.

'I'm not seeing Theo.'

'Then why were you at his house? Why did you go to the hospital?'

'Theo hadn't updated his medical notes and I was still down as his emergency contact. They said he couldn't remember if anyone had gone with him to the hospital, so they called and told me he'd been taken in by ambulance. I didn't know what had happened to him, or if Tessa and Rhys knew. So, I texted him to let him know I was coming.' She kept her voice low as her eyes darted about, checking that her family wasn't nearby. 'When I arrived at the hospital, I sat with him while he slept. Tessa left the second she saw me and went to get his things from home and Rhys wouldn't sit in the same room as me. So, I didn't bother staying long. Not if they were going to treat me like that.'

She rolled her eyes and looked down at the ground. 'I still had a key fob to get through the gates so I went to the house a few days later and let myself in to try and find out what was happening with him and learned that Theo had been sent home. Tessa found me in the driveway and blew her nut. She screamed the place down and kicked the side of my car. I didn't know she hated me so much.'

'Oh, she really does,' I corroborated. 'So, you didn't actually see Theo?'

'No, and we are certainly not having a bit on the side.' She softened slightly and reached up to tuck a piece of her hair behind her ear. 'Look, Effie, you're lucky that it didn't work out between you two. I left him for a reason. You're better off, trust me.' She took a step back and a moment later one of her daughters ran into her legs. She smiled down at the little girl who had a skewer of chocolate-coated marsh-mallows in her hand and chocolate smeared over her face. 'I have to go now, but Merry Christmas, Effie.'

I slowly walked back to Caleb and the others, my mind boggling. I'd been sure that Jenny was the reason why Theo had sent me away. I'd been certain that Jenny was the problem. But as usual, I'd been wrong. The problem had clearly been me.

# Chapter Twenty-Six

'You're back.' The trainer's South African accent cut across the room of Brummies and made me smile. It was such a strange, jumbled accent – so difficult to get your mouth around. I had tried to imitate it before but I'd just ended up sounding like a skipping record.

I remembered him from the last time. He'd been Theo's trainer back when he was still boxing. What had his name been . . .? Mason. That was it.

'Hi, Mason,' I said, hoping that I'd remembered it right.

'You back for some training?' he asked with hopefully raised brows.

I nodded. 'Yeah, well I seemed to be pretty good at it before and I need something to get me out the house.'

He looked down at my arms and reached out a hand to squeeze the one on the right. 'Your arms are skinny, we'll have to work on that, but you've got form – we saw that when you lamped Theo, didn't we?' I remembered the moment well. I wished I could do it again, what I wouldn't give to punch the smile off that man's face. 'How is Theo? He still interested in coming back?'

I kept my composure, even though I felt a twinge in my chest. 'I wouldn't know; we broke up.'

Mason frowned. 'I'm sorry to hear that, you looked like you made a good pair.'

'We did, for a while,' I said, trying to keep the sadness from my voice. 'But it didn't work out and now I'm ready to hit things, so show me to the nearest thing I can punch.'

'I tell you what—' he crossed his arms and nodded, as if concocting a plan '—I'll put you through your paces today, free of charge, and when we're done you can tell me if you want to carry on or not. Sound like a plan?'

'An excellent one,' I replied.

Mason grinned, his hazel eyes gleaming under the sodium lights.

I informed him of my recent wrist injury and he said that we'd take it easy with the left hand and focus mainly on the right hand and the legs. He said I had 'good, strong legs' – it was the first compliment I think I'd ever had about them – and he suggested trying out some kickboxing and seeing how I felt about it. I agreed and he led me to a corner.

He told me we'd be starting with stretches and I copied what he did. This was easy. I was going to be just fine at this.

Then we went on to cardio, he handed me a skipping rope – I think I'd been about five the last time I'd held one – and he made me skip until I literally dropped to the floor like a very unfit sack of potatoes.

'Thinking about bailing yet?' he asked, his sculpted arms folded across his chest.

'This? This is nothing.' I panted. My heartbeat was so loud that I could barely hear him when he told me to get up.

He taught me how to stand and block, holding a pad for me to hit. I only used my right hand and my legs, giving my left one a little more time to heal.

The hour came to an end as I slouched down onto a windowsill and let my head hang between my knees.

'So,' Mason said, sitting down beside me, 'still want to sign up?'

I looked up at him with my red face and my limp limbs and said, between pants, 'Where do I sign?'

'I'll get the papers.' He grinned and disappeared into an office before coming back with a clipboard and a pen that had been chewed at the end.

I filled in the form. It was long and detailed and too much effort after the military drill he'd just put me through.

'We'll have another couple of sessions like this one and then we'll move you on to a sparring partner.'

'Will that be you?' I asked, not really sure how I'd fare against him.

'No,' he said through a laugh, 'I'll pick one of the other beginners, someone who's in your weight and height range, and we'll see if you can't drop them like you did Theo.'

I left the gym and fell down into the seat of Arthur's car like a rag doll. Every part of me ached, but despite that, I felt energised. Who would have thought it, hey? Effie 'Meh' Heaton signing up to a gym and even more surprising, enjoying it. But this was the new and improved Effie. Effie 2.0. The Effie who was going to learn how to knock out a fully-grown man and not even break a sweat.

After three sessions with Mason I was beginning to ache less in the days that followed. I could already feel myself getting stronger, firmer, and I was beginning to have more energy too.

I reached into the microwave and pulled out the bulging bag of popcorn, before tearing it open and decanting it into a large red bowl. Caleb sat on the sofa with a blanket over his legs and a hot chocolate in his hands. He absentmindedly played with one of his curls while he listened to Amy, who was sat at the opposite end, talking about her book and how she hadn't heard anything back from the agent who requested it. She didn't annoy me as much anymore; in fact I quite liked her. We'd gone to the post office and she'd given me the encouragement I needed to send my manuscript out into the world for its second try. That sort of thing bonds people. I hadn't heard anything back from any of the agents I'd sent mine to either, but then it was far too early to feel disheartened. Sometimes it could take up to a year to hear back and it *was* Christmas, so there was no chance of them responding just yet.

I walked over and placed the popcorn on the table before sitting between them. Caleb opened up the blanket and draped it over my knees. I did the same for Amy and we huddled together for warmth. The boiler had made that freaky clunking sound this morning and since then the heating had been a little unreliable.

It transpired that neither Amy nor Caleb had seen *Moulin Rouge* before and so with excitement, I put on the film.

The orchestra swelled, the curtains drew back and the show began.

As we watched, I couldn't help but think how far I'd come from the morose person I had been not too long ago. I still felt terribly sad from time to time. I missed Arthur, much more than I thought I would. I missed my parents (I know! How did that happen?). I longed to feel Elliot's soft fur on my face, and I didn't even want to go into the complicated feelings I had towards Theo. But even so, here I was, smiling and sitting between two people I was proud to call my friends. I didn't for one moment worry about what they were thinking of me or if they actually wanted to be sat here with me. I just enjoyed the company and I felt – wait for it – happy.

I met Caleb for lunch on Friday at a café in the centre of town. He wanted to meet there because, apparently, they had good veggie food and not the 'same shite' that they had in most other places. I sat upstairs beside the window and looked out at the sea of heads rushing below in a stream of bobble hats and bald patches. Caleb arrived with a tray that held a coffee – cappuccino, extra foam, no chocolate – an avocado and sundried tomato baguette, a small pot of soup, a still lemonade and a white chocolate muffin. I had no idea how anyone could possibly eat so much and remain so skinny. I took a sip of my lunch, i.e. my latte, and watched as he tucked into his mountain of food.

'So,' he said with a mouthful of rocket garnish, 'have you spoken to your mum yet?'

I slouched back in the unyielding chair and shrugged.

'I'll apologise if she does,' I replied like an angst-ridden teen.

Caleb rolled his eyes and took another bite before pulling the lid from his pot of soup and delving into it before he'd even swallowed. 'Christmas is gonna be mighty awkward if you don't sort this out before then.'

'I'm not going to just let it slide if she's not going to admit fault.' I took another swig and felt the liquid scald my tongue.

'Eff, mothers are never wrong.' He stared me down over the steaming soup. 'They show up at hospital, have their baby and then the nurse wheels them to the door and says,

340

"Congrats, here's your baby and as a gift from the hospital, here's a selection of ridiculous phrases to use and an inoculation against ever being wrong". Did they not teach you that in sex ed?'

I unknotted the frown that I had only just noticed I was sporting and tried to quell the tension in my chest. 'I just don't think that I'm the only one who needs to apologise.'

'Irregardless, you should still apologise.'

'Oh! What do you know?' I said, balling up a napkin and throwing it at his head. It bounced from his forehead into his soup. 'And irregardless isn't even a word. You've been watching too much American TV.'

He shook his head and bowed it over his soup before slurping it like someone who was seconds from starvation. Annoyingly, I knew that he was right. I did need to broach the subject at some point.

'What are you doing tomorrow night?' he asked when he was done. 'I wondered if you wanted to go and see that new Marvel film?'

I sucked in the air through my teeth. 'Sorry, bud. I'm not really into the whole superhero hype and I'll be at training anyway. I get to meet my sparring partner tomorrow.'

Caleb blew a puff of air between his lips. 'Good luck to them. I wouldn't want to fight you.'

On Saturday I showed up at the gym early and changed in the dressing room. I DID NOT strip down to my nothings and parade around like the others. I may have grown to like myself a lot more but I was far from going bare-breasted and flashing my fanny around for all to see. I caught more than an eyeful of several pairs of jiggling breasts – one pair in particular caught me off guard as they rippled in the hot air

341

that spewed from the wall-mounted hairdryer and almost hypnotised me.

Mason was ready and waiting for me on the mats. I strapped on my gloves and made my way over. He'd given me a few exercises to strengthen my wrist and they'd helped a lot. I felt like I was ready to punch with that hand and give my new partner a good wallop.

'Afternoon,' I said with a cheerful lilt to my voice.

'Hey, Eff. You ready to kick some arse?' he said with a grin.

'Just show me my partner and I'll make sure I make her cry.'

'Actually, your partner is a he.'

'Really? I just assumed you'd put me with a girl.'

'I'm all about equality.' He grinned. His teeth were the whitest I'd ever seen.

Mason and I did some warm-ups, while we waited for my sparring partner to arrive. I'd only had a few sessions with Mason, but even so, I could feel myself getting quicker, fitter, better.

Finally, he turned up, fifteen minutes late. I didn't see him at first. His body was blocked by Mason as I landed a hard kick to the pad strapped to Mason's arm.

'I know, bruv, I'm late,' he said. I frowned in recognition. I knew that voice. Mason stopped and turned around, revealing my partner.

'Great, you're here. This is Effie.' Mason began to introduce us; he needn't have bothered. 'Effie, this is . . .'

'Daz.' I sent him a smile and waited for the recognition to kick in. 'We've met before.'

Daz frowned for a moment or two, I could practically see the underused cogs whirring inside his brain, then the penny dropped and his brows raised in a look of panic.

\* \* \*

I showered and washed my hair in the changing rooms, the hot water soothing the bruise that would soon develop on my shoulder from where I'd dodged a little too slowly and Daz had caught me. I hadn't quite beaten the shit out of him, but I hadn't held back either. All it had taken was a quick replay of our diner date in my mind and I was ready to go. At least I could rest easy that my bruise would be hidden, but Daz would have a hard time covering the entire left-hand side of his face.

I let the hot water douse my skin and exhaled with contentment. Today had been a good day.

On Christmas Eve I said goodbye to Amy at midday, giving her enough time to delve into the panic of last-minute Christmas Eve gift shopping. I closed the shop and went up into the apartment to wrap what few gifts I had bought. For Dad, I had got a desk organiser, something to clear the clutter that he was getting buried under. For Mum, I bought a spa day voucher; maybe they could loosen that stick up her arse and send her home smiling. For Caleb, I got an enamel pin to add to his collection. It was a pair of hands high fiving with the word *friends* behind it in a colourful comic book-like burst. I'd bought a rawhide bone for Otis. I'd be taking that to him tomorrow when I did my Christmas Day shift before heading home to endure the awkward tension of my first encounter with my mother since our fight a month and a half ago. I placed Ali's gift in the centre of the penguin print wrapping paper: a copy of *The Lion, the Witch and the Wardrobe*. It had stuck in my mind since she'd told me that she used to love it and, with the festive spirit filling me like a virus, I wrapped it up and shoved it into my bag with the other presents.

That night I drank half a bottle of wine before bed and when I eventually lay down I couldn't sleep. I stared up at the ceiling and thought of him.

Would he be spending tomorrow at home with his family? Was he still ill? Fully healed? Dead?

I'd given up hope a long time ago that he might be coming back for me. That one day I might find him standing at my door telling me how he'd made an awful mistake and he would do anything to have me back. In some versions of that fantasy I kicked him so hard that he fell backwards down the stairs; in others I pulled him close and kissed him, but both scenarios were improbable. Theo was over me and I was attempting to get over him. That didn't stop my heart from skipping every time someone knocked on the door or my phone *pinged* with a new message.

Believe it or not, my phone had been *pinging* more often than not since I'd pulled my head out of my arse and started living. Caleb messaged me hourly about anything and everything and he'd added me to a WhatsApp group that contained everyone from our volunteering team. Ned would often chime in with the odd Dad joke, most of which I found embarrassingly hilarious, and Liz would post links to other charitable causes that she wanted us to get involved in. Arthur and Toby sent me pictures and emails telling me how they'd moved on from Prague to Vienna. The last had been a photograph of Toby, silhouetted against the setting sun, his glass of beer glowing amber in the light.

But still, every time that sound *pinged*, I hoped that it would be *Him*. There was no word from Kate, but then I hadn't expected any. She probably had enough going on, reorganising her life to fit the new order of things, to have time for a drink.

I rolled onto my side and looked at the empty space beside me, cold and untouched by anyone except me when I spread myself out like a starfish as I slept. I wished there was someone to complain about my stretching out, someone to keep me awake with their snoring or their spasms and kicks during the night.

I closed my eyes as the heavy feeling of sleep filled my head and when I was finally sleeping, I dreamt of mountains and Staffordshire bull terriers and Daz's bruised face.

# Chapter Twenty-Seven

Christmas had always been a strange one for me. I'd always loved the build-up and hated the actual day. The build-up was filled with music and traditions and carols, all happening while the thrill and excitement of the 'big day' hung in the air. But when the actual day came around it was nothing but twenty-four hours of gently stewing yourself in various forms of alcohol until one of you has one port too many and starts World War Three over the pigs in blankets. Someone would inevitably end up crying or injuring themselves by trying to de-segment a Terry's Chocolate Orange with their fist and the day would wrap up with everyone sitting in separate rooms, drunk, and telling themselves that next year's Christmas will be 'the one'.

I woke up early and dressed in my shelter uniform. I folded a green velvet top that I'd bought a week ago, when I'd gone out and bought clothes to replace the baggy jumpers that I'd decided to forgo, and placed it in the bag with my gifts. I'd change into that before I made my way to what could quite possibly become the world's most awkward Christmas. I put my bag by the door – I was bound to forget it otherwise – and went to make myself some coffee.

As I stood by the kettle, watching the blue light illuminate the bubbles inside, my eyes drifted to the bottle of wine sitting on the counter. I smacked my tongue against the roof of my mouth. It suddenly felt as if I had no saliva left. I clicked off the kettle and unscrewed the wine, pouring an inch or two into the bottom of the mug. I lifted it to my lips and inhaled the rich smell. Before the liquid touched my lips, I lowered the mug and stared down into the dark reflective surface.

What was I doing?

I knew that Christmas gave everyone an unofficial excuse to drink from the moment your eyes popped open in the morning, but this wasn't a one-off for me and my head was still heavy with the wine from the night before.

I tipped the mug over the sink, then grabbed the bottle and poured the rest of the blood-coloured liquid down the drain. Maybe an early New Year's resolution was in order. I grabbed my bags and headed out.

Caleb's gift twinkled in the morning light as it glinted from his lapel. He'd laughed when I'd given it to him and then he'd presented me with my gift. It was exactly the same. I pinned mine to my bag strap and gave him a high five, both of us shouting the word *friends* when our palms touched, then laughing at how dumb that must have looked to the rest of the office.

Ned, Caleb, Janet and I were the only ones who could make it from our group that morning. We'd met in the foyer and Caleb and I split a mince pie before we headed out onto the street.

347

Since I'd been doing this, I'd learned a lot about the people who I'd walked past and ignored only months earlier.

Carl and Denny slept in an alleyway between New Street and the train station and even though Carl had recently had to have his leg amputated at the knee, he always had time for a chat and a laugh. Today they had another member of the group, Maggie, a Polish woman who'd come here looking for a better life and found this instead.

Down at the Square, George and Nina sat on the edge of the city's famous fountain, a nude woman reclining in a tub of water, affectionately known as the Floozie in the Jacuzzi. They were whispering about something that seemed intense, but the second they saw us all gossip fell away and they turned to us with expectant smiles.

We handed them some food and a hot drink and shared a chat before heading down towards the bottom of the street. I reached into my bag and took out the two gifts, the book for Ali and the bone for Otis.

'What you got there?' Caleb asked as we waited for Janet to hand out a cup of tea.

'It's for Ali – not the bone obviously, that's for Otis,' I replied. 'It's the Narnia book that she told me about when I first met her.'

'That's really nice, Eff. But don't let the others see; we're not meant to have favourites.' He winked my way as we approached Ali's doorway, but when we got there it was empty.

'Where is she?' I asked Caleb, who frowned.

'Maybe she's staying at a friend's, or she could just have moved on. People don't tend to stay in one place for too long,' he explained. I sighed with disappointment and pushed the gifts back into my bag. We carried on down the street, handing out hot drinks and chatting with the people who would find Christmas Day to be very like any other, only quieter.

When we got back to the office there was a crowd of people in the break room, a solemn atmosphere tainting the festive vibe. Janet and I returned the equipment while Caleb went to find out what was going on. He returned a few minutes later with a grave look on his face.

'What's wrong?' I asked. I think I knew before he told me.

'One of the volunteers has just quit,' Caleb began. 'He found Ali's body this morning. She'd OD'd.'

Otis had been brought in by the volunteer who found them and they'd shut him in one of the office cubicles. He'd been sitting beside Ali's body waiting for her to wake when they arrived. The moment I walked in he ran to me and licked my hands, and he laid his head down on my knee the second I'd sat down on the floor.

I unwrapped his gift and he tucked in ravenously. I sat red-eyed and watched him with tears wetting my cheeks.

I thought back to all those years I'd spent feeling sorry for myself, when I'd had so much more than Ali ever had.

After a while Caleb came in and sat beside me, his arm linking through mine. 'Will you be wanting to leave us now?' he asked as we watched Otis's saliva drip from the gnawed remnants of his bone and seep into the carpet tiles.

'No,' I replied. 'If anything, it's made me realise how important this is.'

He looked over at me and sighed. 'We'll have to get someone from the Dogs Home to come and collect him,' he said, nodding towards Otis.

'Caleb,' I said, 'can I take Otis home for a few days? I hate the idea of him spending Christmas in a kennel.'

He smiled and squeezed my arm.

'Sure thing. The mutt's all yours.'

It was midday when Otis and I showed up like the ragtag band of outcasts that we were. Dad didn't even mention the dog as I stepped into the hallway for the first time since I'd left with my things.

'Merry Christmas, Dad,' I said as he pulled me into a hug. It was the strongest he'd ever squeezed me. A garland of fir branches and poinsettias twirled up the banister, the flowers looking slightly dishevelled from Elliot's attack on it the previous year.

My aunt, uncle and cousin Felicity lounged in the living room, already half a bottle of scotch and a tub of Celebrations down. I left Otis with them while I prepared myself for the only person I had left to see.

Mum was in the kitchen stirring the gravy when I walked in. The smell that filled the air made my mouth water instantly.

'Hello,' I said meekly.

'Hello, Effie,' she replied without turning around.

Silence.

I closed my hand around my wrist – it still ached from time to time – and pressed my lips together into a line.

'Dinner smells good.' My voice sounded little in the quiet room. She didn't reply. 'I didn't know that Aunt Rita was coming. Has she drunk you out of wine already?' That was rich coming from me, I know. When she didn't answer I knew that I had to call her on it or we'd be like this all day. 'Are you going to speak to me?'

She began savagely whisking the gravy and I saw her tense her jaw through the curtain of her bob, which was now beginning to grow out and looked much nicer.

'What would you like me to speak to you about?' Her voice was taut, ready for a row.

'I'll apologise for what I said if you will too.' As soon as I'd finished speaking, she whipped around, the gravy pan slamming down hard on the counter and drops of molten gravy spraying out like a geyser.

'What do I have to apologise for, Effie?' She crossed her arms and set her jaw. There it was again, that steadfast ability to hold a grudge until the last. I guess that's where I'd inherited it from.

I sighed. I didn't think I could handle an argument after the morning I'd had.

'I was in a terrible place. I was the lowest I'd ever been and instead of trying to help me out of it you kicked me and kept on kicking me until I snapped.' I kept my voice in check, although I wanted to shout. 'I know I've not been the best of daughters. I didn't turn out how you wanted me to and I've come to accept that, but there are two people in this relationship and neither of us has been perfect.'

She let her hands fall limply to her sides, her eyes drawing back with a look of despondency. She flapped her hands as if struggling against what she wanted to say and what she felt like she should say. 'You wouldn't tell me what happened. You turned up with a splint on your arm and decided you were going to live in the treehouse. You cried non-stop and wouldn't eat a thing and I had no idea why. I'm your mother; why wouldn't you talk to me?'

I swallowed the rapidly rising lump in my throat and tried not to cry. 'Because I couldn't. I could barely even think about it without wanting to go and throw myself off a building and I knew exactly what you'd think when I told you. You'd think that I'd done it *again*, I'd chased away another man because I didn't know how to make one happy and I'm always so moody and how can I expect someone to love me when I'm always so cross?' I looked up at her; she'd started crying already. 'Your disappointment in me is something that I've become used to, but after what happened I couldn't bear to hear it.'

She walked over and took my hands. The contact made me want to cry too. 'I'm not disappointed in you, Effie.' She leaned in and kissed my forehead, her tears smearing over my face as she did. There was no point holding back now, so I let myself cry.

'But I've failed at everything. I'm a failure.' I sobbed into her festive apron.

'No, you're not,' she said over my shoulder as she rubbed my back and held me firmly. 'You're not a failure.'

I told Mum everything, about Theo's letter and how I'd been convinced that Jenny was the cause of him dumping me and how those ideas had been dashed when I'd met her at the market.

I told her about Caleb and Ali and Otis. I talked for over an hour, the dinner slowly growing crisper as we both forgot the hungry people waiting in the other room. I talked and she listened and when I'd spoken my last, I felt like we saw each other clearly. The cloud of judgement had gone from our eyes and for the first time in years I smiled at her and meant it.

When we walked back in and told them that dinner was ready, they all looked at us sheepishly, saw that our arms were linked and applauded. I guess they must have heard the whole thing.

Mum was smiling. She'd finally found joy in something. That was until she saw Otis lying on the sofa, his legs up in

352

the air and his tongue hanging out to the side, and almost had a mental breakdown.

I watched my cousin Felicity staring aimlessly through the kitchen window as I sat in the treehouse with Elliot beside me. When he'd finally come in to welcome me home, he'd seen Otis and hadn't stayed long.

I turned to him, his unimpressed yellow eyes already fixed on mine.

*Don't for a moment think that he's staying,* he seemed to say.

There was something strange about the smile that had found its way onto my lips and lingered for at least two consecutive hours. For the first day in the almost two months since I'd last seen him, I hadn't thought about Theo much at all.

When I did find myself thinking about him, I still felt the ache, like when I sat with my legs dangling over the drop from the treehouse or whenever I saw the lighter, still stuffed into the plant pot where I'd hidden it that first night he'd come around for our non-date. But it wasn't as sharp as it had been and nowhere near as unbearable. Even so, I knew that this new ache was here to stay. It would remain like the residual pain of a broken bone, going unnoticed until something reawakened the pain for a moment.

I still had so much to say to him, so many words that needed saying, and for the first time since he'd said goodbye to me I felt like I was ready to say them.

I found his number in my contacts and stared at it for a minute or two before I called and hoped for voicemail. I needed to *say* the words, typing them would not help me purge myself of the things I needed to get out of me.

It rang six times, each ring making my heart flutter. When I heard the woman's voice asking me to leave a message I sighed in relief and cleared my throat.

The beep sounded.

'Hey, it's Effie. I know that you didn't want me to get in touch and that you probably let this ring out because you didn't want to speak to me and lead me on any more than you did.' I paused, swallowed, carried on. 'I'd be lying if I said that I didn't hate you a little, but I guess that's only because I loved you so much.' I paused again, my voice wavering. 'I finished the list, or I finished it as much as it's possible to anyway. I moved out, I did something that really matters and I love doing it, I even went on a date with someone I like a lot, and I would have done none of those things if you hadn't stalked me that day.'

I laughed a sad little laugh, a single tear falling to my cheek. 'I found my favourite film. I made a friend and I lost a friend. I even went back to the gym and Mason's training me, and you'll never guess who my sparring partner is.' I stopped, realising that I was babbling and brought myself back into the present. 'What I'm saying, or trying to say at least, is that I would never have done all of those things without you pushing me to do them. So, I guess that, as well as a goodbye, this is thank you. Thank you for pulling me out of myself and forcing me back into life. Thank you for convincing me to do things that I would never have done and, I guess, thank you for breaking my heart when you did, although a little sooner wouldn't have been a bad idea. That way you could have broken it off before I fell for you.'

I took a breath and readied myself for goodbye, the last goodbye. '"Ashes to Ashes" came on the radio the other day at work and one of the lines stuck with me because it made me think of you and what I wanted to say. So, in the words of the man himself, "I'm happy, hope you're happy too". Merry Christmas, Theodore Alwyn Morgan. Thanks for the memories.'

I hung up the phone and gasped for air. For a moment I thought that I would suffocate and die, right there in the treehouse beside the cat who wouldn't even care if I did. My eyes blurred and my hands shook so much that I dropped the phone to my lap. But then I felt my lungs expand, the air filling them up and calming my trembling hands. The words were gone now, the clog of unsaid things no longer blocking my throat. I breathed. In. Out. In. Out. And after a while it wasn't torture anymore.

Felicity took my old bed and so I slept on the sofa in my parents' living room, with Otis lying on his back in the crook of my arm. He was smelling sweeter after Dad and I had given him a bath and I was beginning to suspect that Dad was falling in love with him already. The light from the TV turned the room a pale shade of blue as I watched an old black and white movie that I'd never seen before. I wondered if Theo had listened to my voicemail yet. Maybe he had and it had made him cry or maybe it had made him feel nothing. Maybe he had just deleted it and never listened to a word. It didn't matter really. I had said the words that had been slowly choking me and now I was free.

I heard a quiet knock on the door and a second later it opened and Mum's nose poked in.

'Do you mind if I come in?' she asked. I beckoned her in and she joined me on the sofa, placing a bottle of port and two glasses down on the table. She pulled out the cork and filled the glasses. Otis roused and moved to see what she was doing, laying his heavy head on her lap. She stiffened and held up her hands. She'd always been wary of any dog that wasn't a Labrador. He knew how to work it though, turning onto his back and looking up at her with those huge buffoon's eyes. She tentatively stroked his belly and was soon smiling and as enamoured with him as I was.

She handed me one of the glasses and held hers up in the air. 'What shall we toast to?'

I pondered the question for a moment then raised my glass. 'To forgiveness and to Ali.'

She smiled and we touched our glasses together with a *chink!*

We swigged it down and she topped them up again.

'What are we watching?' she asked.

'*Some Like It Hot*,' I replied.

'Oh, I haven't seen this in years.' She settled down, her hand resting on Otis's chest as she sipped at her port. I couldn't remember the last time we'd sat together in a room and felt something other than resentment for each other. It was nice. So much nicer than holding grudges.

# Chapter Twenty-Eight

Life as a mostly sober person was absolute purgatory, for a while.

I threw out the bottles of wine that had accumulated over the dark period of my life and replaced them with soft drinks and those chewy butter mints, which I quickly became addicted to instead. Alcohol had always been like a Zorb that kept me at a distance from the world. It hid me away, dampened the noise and protected me from the sharp edges of life. But I was now learning to live with the sharpness and the noise.

I lay in bed in the flat with Otis splayed out beside me in a pose that reminded me of that line from *Titanic:*

*Draw me like one of your French girls.*

I'd grown so attached to Otis that I'd asked if I could adopt him and I'd paid for another dog to be given to one of the homeless people that I still went out and helped three times a week. It was strange to think that he'd lived most of his life on the street and now, because of something terrible, he had a soft bed to hog and heating to keep him warm.

I looked at the clock; I had twenty minutes before I had

to open the shop. I got up and dressed in a flash, smearing on a little make-up and letting Amy in to set up. I was halfway up a ladder changing a light bulb when my phone started to ring. I had almost got the bulb in and Amy was off in the back, so I let it ring out. I climbed down the ladder and went to price up the post-Christmas bargains, forgetting entirely about the call I'd missed.

As I pushed the books onto the shelves, I wondered where my novel was now. I had been so angry the last time it had been returned to me, so hurt and appalled that they couldn't see my genius. Now I knew that it wasn't genius at all – just a jumbled, garbled idea that I hadn't explained well. This time I knew that what I'd sent was good. It was really good. I was nervous about what they would respond with. I'd put everything into this book and if this wasn't enough, then I didn't know what would be.

The shop was quiet, the lull between Christmas and New Year had hit particularly hard this year, so Amy and I cleaned the whole shop. By the time we'd finished it was almost three and I told Amy that she could go.

'What are you doing for New Year's?' she asked as she pulled on her parka.

'Caleb's invited me to his parents' place. His family do this annual New Year's extravaganza, but Mum's invited me home as well,' I replied.

'You're cutting it close, aren't you? New Year's Eve is tomorrow.'

'I know.' I sighed. I didn't want to bail on Caleb but I had actually enjoyed spending time with my parents since we'd made up. 'I guess I'll have to flip a coin.'

It wasn't until I closed up the shop that I looked at my phone and saw the missed call. It was a number I didn't recognise, but they'd left a message. I dialled voicemail and played it.

'*Effie, it's Tessa.*' Something jolted in my chest.

No! I'm over this. I'm getting over him. Don't drag me back in.

'*Rhys told me not to call but you asked us to let you know about Theo and I don't think it's fair to not tell you.*' She sounded exhausted, her voice cracking as she spoke. '*There's so much to tell you that I think it's best if you come down to the house, so I can tell you in person. That's if you want to, of course.*' She hung up abruptly and left me holding the phone to my ear and staring off into nothing.

I *will not* go.

I'd spent months trying to forget that bloody family and I would not be drawn back in now.

What could she want to tell me?

I'd been warring with myself for over three hours, staring at the phone and then trying to ignore it, then staring at it again.

Why did she have to call?

I'd accepted what had happened. I'd left him the voicemail that had said all I needed to say. I was on my way to going a full day without thinking of the blond-haired, blue-eyed bastard and now she'd wrenched me out of my new life and back into theirs like I was some patchwork doll that two children were fighting over and tearing apart.

'I'm not going. It's too far and how dare she think that I have so little going on in my life that I can just drop everything on New Year's Eve and drive to Wales,' I said, turning to Otis, who stared up at me like he was waiting for something. 'I'll call back and ask her to tell me now.'

I called the number and waited for her to answer but it went straight to voicemail. 'Shit!' I threw the phone across the room, Otis looking from the discarded phone to me and back again, his brows drawn up in confusion. 'I am not going, Otis. I'm not – stop looking at me like that – I'm *not* going.'

At 4 a.m. I found myself driving to Wales in Arthur's car, the sounds of Noughties emo rock – which matched my mood – playing from the speakers and Otis sitting up in the passenger's seat.

'This doesn't mean I'm going to their house,' I said. He turned as if listening. 'I might just veer off course and go to the beach for the day. The fact that I'm driving to Wales does not mean that I am going to that house.'

I began to feel sleepy as I entered Wales and when I was a few miles away from the Morgans' I pulled over into a lay-by and slept with Otis curled up beside me to keep warm. He slept better than I did. I suppose he was more used to sleeping rough than I was. When I eventually woke, groggy and aching, it was almost eight. The sky was a pale pink that kissed the tops of the trees as the sun made its way up and birds sang their loud little songs into the morning.

I dialled Tessa's number and called again. It went straight to voicemail . . . again.

'Tessa, I'm in Wales. I'll be at yours in ten minutes, but I can't stay long.' I hung up and felt Otis's eyes on me. 'I'll only be as long as it takes her to tell me what she needs to. Then we can go home and I'll never have to see any of them ever again.'

I turned the key in the ignition. The radio kicked into action and the sound of My Chemical Romance made us both jump. Otis growled at the disembodied voice (he was more of a Fall Out Boy fan) before I turned the radio off and pulled onto the road.

The gates were open when I arrived and it took all the willpower I had to stop myself from driving past and heading home. I saw Theo's car in the driveway and the bottom fell out of my stomach.

Was he here? Would I have to see him, be in the same room as him?

I parked up beside it, the tyres hemmed in by moss and grass that was sprouting from between the gravel.

It hadn't been moved in a while.

I cracked the window for Otis. The weather was neither warm nor cold so I left him snoozing on the front seat.

As I turned towards the house, I saw that the door was open and Tessa was standing in the doorway, thin and pale as a ghost.

I wanted to turn and run. Why was I here? Why was I torturing myself and prising open old wounds that hadn't fully healed yet?

I cursed under my breath and walked towards her; she stepped back as I neared her and I passed through the door. The moment I walked in I knew that it was a mistake. The smell that lingered in the air was his smell; the one I'd inhaled as I'd lain on his chest.

Stop it! Don't think about his smell or his chest or anything else about him for that matter. You are here to talk to Tessa and leave. You'll have no more thoughts of how solid he felt as he slept beside you or how he'd kissed you in the room just upstairs. STOP IT!

'Hi.' I spoke only to stop myself from thinking.

She shut the door and walked over to me, her hands clasped in front of her. She looked older. Her skin was pallid, her red-lined eyes glistening. An air of exhaustion hung around her. 'I'm glad you came.'

She walked through into the kitchen and I made to follow her, but as I did, I caught a glimpse of something that made me feel sick.

There was something about the abandoned wheelchair at the bottom of the stairs that made me terrified. The way that the wheels weren't in line, the seat that was fraying in places and had clearly been used a great deal but now sat unused in the hallway.

I swallowed the fear in my throat and wondered if I could take it. I thought I was only being dramatic when I feared that he might be dead, but was that actually the case? From the look of Tessa, it was a possibility.

She sat on a stool at the counter and waited for me to join her. A pot of tea steamed between us as I ungracefully hoisted myself up onto the too-tall stool.

I couldn't ask her outright. I couldn't even put the word *dead* in the same sentence as his name, so instead I just asked, 'Is he here?'

She looked down at her hands and cleared the emotion from her throat. 'No.'

I felt the crude stitching in my heart *ping* away. Her shaking hands took the teapot and poured two china cups full of the yellow-brown liquid. She handed one to me. I added milk and two sugars before sipping; the sugar calming my nerves as I drank.

'Rhys didn't want me to call you,' she began. 'He said that we'd already caused you enough pain and it wasn't fair to drag you back in, but if I were you, I'd want to know. I couldn't leave you not knowing what happened to him.' When I didn't speak, she carried on. 'Theo got a lot worse after he was moved. His illness came back harder than it had before.'

'Illness? You mean his anxiety?'

She shook her head. 'That was never what it was. The doctors got it wrong.'

I wished I hadn't drunk the tea. It swilled around in my gut and made me want to sick it back up into the cup.

'Jenny said they sent him home a few days after he fell ill.' My voice was a whisper.

'You spoke to Jenny?' Her face turned red; her pupils grew small. 'She had some nerve coming back here and letting herself in like she was still part of this family. It was all I could do not to drag her out back and drown her in the lake.' She composed herself and carried on. 'They sent him away because they were convinced that it was all in his head. We told them it wasn't, but they wouldn't believe us and, in the end, he had to go back in to hospital.'

I couldn't help but wince at her choice of words: *in the end*. My breaths came faster, my chest aching and stinging all at once.

'When did he . . .?' I asked, my voice quavering as a tear found its way to my cheek. I couldn't say the word *die*; my tongue had forgotten it. I waited for her to say something to contradict me, to tell me that he was alive and upstairs watching that ridiculous film he loved.

'Three weeks ago.' She looked down at her hands. 'It was such a relief after seeing him in that place for so long, with people poking him and puncturing him and taking every bit of him that they wanted.' She was crying now. It was strange to see her, strong, fearless Tessa, being anything but strong and fearless. 'He grew so thin and became severely anaemic. Then his joints began to seize up and . . .' her tears dislodged my own '. . . his skin turned grey. His throat kept swelling and we had to sit there, Dad and I, watching as he gasped for air while the doctors told us that there was nothing wrong with him.'

All the stitching fell loose, my heart tearing open again as everything I'd tried to lock away came back to me.

I thought of the first moment I'd met him, how angry I'd been that he'd been listening, and the time he'd pulled me towards him, taking a photograph at the top of that mountain, the photograph that had haunted me ever since. All of the hatred I'd felt towards him fell away and I'd have given anything to feel him in my arms again.

She handed me a tissue and looked up as a car pulled into the driveway. 'Crap! That man is a quick driver. Rhys is going to be angry that I asked you here.' She looked towards the door as we heard it open.

I wiped the mascara stains from my eyes and caught my breath. 'Did I miss the funeral?'

'Funeral?' Tessa looked confused as the sound of slowly approaching footsteps and a quiet clicking sound travelled down the hallway. I turned to the archway and saw Rhys come into view, a paper prescription bag in his hand. 'Whose is that car in the driveway?' he asked, his eyes landing on mine and his body tensing.

The clicking noise came again and then I saw someone else arrive beside him, leaning heavily on a crutch.

I stopped breathing. The man in the doorway looked like Theo, only thinner, greyer, younger and older all at the same time. I saw that his skin was the colour of ash as he came into the light, his clothes hanging off him like they were two sizes too big. He looked up when he realised that his father had stopped walking and his eyes found me. *He was alive.* Theo was alive and here in the same room as me.

'Effie?' His voice was gravelly and thin as he shuffled forward into the kitchen. Rhys helped him along, waiting to catch him if he fell. He stopped a couple of metres away and attempted a smile. 'You look so different.'

*I* looked so different?

Tessa stood and walked to my side. 'I'm so sorry, Effie, I didn't mean to make you think that . . . that he was . . . He came home three weeks ago – that's what I meant.' She squeezed my shoulder as I caught my breath and she told Rhys to give us some space. He smiled apologetically at me before they left us.

I would have stood but I didn't trust my legs to hold me, so I just sat and stared at the ghost of the man I used to love . . . still loved.

A second ago, when I'd thought he was dead, I'd thrown all of my anger away and all I'd wanted was to hold him one more time. But now that I saw him, the pain of the betrayal was back.

'How . . . how are you?' he asked, his body swaying as he leaned against the wall.

'I'm okay,' I lied. 'You look like shit.'

His lips drew up into what I presume was meant to be a smile, but it was not the smile it had once been, stripped of its magic. 'There's the Effie we all know and love.'

I stood now, the anger suddenly powering me. 'But you don't love me. You made that very clear in your letter.'

'Effie, I . . .' He took a step forward, his weight leaving the wall as he tumbled forward and fell towards me. I lunged, out of instinct, and grabbed him, my wrist prickling as he landed on me. He leaned on the crutch and stabilised himself while I tried not to think about how good it felt to touch him again, to feel the familiar weight of him against me.

We both looked up at the same time, his breath on my face. I frowned and let my hands fall away.

'Come with me,' he said, turning and slowly making his way out of the kitchen and to a room I hadn't been in before. Just off the hall was a pair of large wooden doors. He slid one open and stepped inside what had once been a study, but was now a makeshift hospital ward. A single bed sat below the window, a puzzle book with a half-finished crossword sat on the table beside it. The desk was now a pharmacy, covered in ten, fifteen different types of medication. I stepped inside and he slid the door closed behind me.

It felt too intimate being in a room alone with him.

'What is it that you have?' I asked, turning over one of the drug boxes with my finger.

'That doesn't matter.' He waved my question aside and sat down on the edge of the bed, his face creasing as his knees bent. He tried his best to hide the whimper of pain as he landed but I heard it all the same.

'Theo.' His name felt familiar and alien in my mouth. I kept my voice as stern and emotionless as I could. 'I watched you collapse and saw you dragged into an ambulance. Then you abandoned me in the waiting room and told me that I wasn't wanted anymore. Now your bloody sister has dragged me back into this saga and I still don't know what's going on. So, you're going to tell me, in explicit detail, what is wrong with you and when I know the same as everybody else, *then* we can talk about whatever you want.'

'I see your temper hasn't changed.' He sighed and looked down at his hands as he spoke.

I moved a book from a chair and, as I turned it over, I saw the cover. *Jane Eyre.* I sat down, my eyes hard, my jaw clenched.

'You read it then?' I said, holding up the book before I placed it on the floor.

'I'm almost finished. I really like it. It reminds me of you quite a bit.'

'I don't think I'm anything like Jane.'

'Neither do I. Mr Rochester is the one you're like.'

I rolled my eyes. 'So, you think I'm like a cantankerous, hot-headed older man.'

'In some ways, yes.' He tried to smile but I was having none of it.

'Thank you, that's so flattering. Now, tell me everything, from the very beginning. If I have questions, I will ask them. Go.'

He took a breath and looked down at his hands; the skin was dry. When he eventually spoke, his tone was reluctant.

'When Mum died, I became ill,' he began.

'How ill?'

'Let's just say that I didn't see myself turning twenty-six. I wrote letters to everyone I loved and left them somewhere they would find them, just in case. I had to take time away from boxing. I hated it. I'd worked so hard and got so far and every day away from it was a step in the wrong direction. I couldn't do anything for myself except lie in bed and wait to get either better or worse. I became weak, my muscles faded, my fitness all but vanished.'

He paused, swallowed, carried on. 'For a good few months, we were all pretty certain that I was going to die and even if Tessa and Dad hadn't accepted it yet, I had. I remember thinking that nothing could be worse than waking up every morning and counting the seconds until I could go back to bed and be unconscious again, not even dying.' I heard the telltale wobble in his voice as his eyes became slick with tears.

His chin began to judder and all I wanted to do was to rush forward and steady it.

But I couldn't let myself fall back into the trap. Since he'd been gone, I'd built myself up into the person that I had always wanted to be. I was happy and I couldn't let that slip for anyone and especially not for the man who'd sent me away.

'No one knew what was wrong with me and, in the end, they all thought that I was a hypochondriac. They tested me for everything: cancer, infectious diseases, TB, AIDS, lupus, everything that I could be tested for, I *was* tested for. But they all came back clear and so I was diagnosed with depression and anxiety. They gave me drugs for it, but they didn't help; if anything they made things worse, so I stopped taking them.'

I remembered the diazepam and how I'd found it discarded away from the others.

'I tried to box again, but my body wouldn't let me. I just couldn't do it anymore.' He laughed a cold, joyless single laugh and looked down at his hands, which were clasped tightly on his lap. 'All my life I'd worked to get to Team GB and just when I'd finally got there, I couldn't do it anymore. Jenny had loved the lifestyle of going to the fights and parties and mingling with the future gold medallists. Then I became ill, I lost my looks, my sport, my everything. It became clear that I wasn't getting any better and she realised that, if this was going to last forever, she didn't want to spend the rest of her life looking after me. So, she packed her things and left her engagement ring on the bedside table while I slept. She didn't even say goodbye.'

I remembered her words to me at the market, '*I left him for a reason. You're better off, trust me.*' Had that been her only reasoning, because she saw Theo as a burden and nothing else?

'After four or five months I began to get better.' His eyes slowly filled with tears that had yet to fall. 'It took a long time, but I got back to normal, or as normal as I would ever be again. I took it easy and within a year I could go about my life as if it had never happened. It all but went away for four years; then I met you.' He looked up and met my eye. I looked away. I couldn't make eye contact with him. If I did, then I would be putty in his hands. 'I knew that doing certain things made me worse but I did them anyway because I didn't want you to miss out on anything; I didn't want *me* to miss out on anything.'

'What happened this time?' I kept my voice cold, calm.

'The same, only worse. I couldn't walk for a while, still can't, not properly anyway.'

'Do they know what it is?'

He nodded. 'Most doctors don't know much about it, it's a relatively newly discovered illness, but luckily I found someone who did. I got diagnosed a month ago by a specialist. It's a rare cell condition called mast cell activation syndrome.'

'I've never heard of it,' I said.

'Not many people have. It's where the cells that are meant to protect me from infection and injury work too hard and leak harmful chemicals into my body. I have allergic reactions for no reason, triggered by my body and nothing else. I'd always thought that I was allergic to nuts – turns out I'm not, I'm allergic to myself. The nuts just don't help matters.' He smiled as if it was funny; it wasn't funny at all.

'Sometimes my throat and mouth swell up and I wake in the night, gasping while my tongue blocks the air and makes it so I can't even swallow the drugs that could help me. I have inflammatory arthritis in my knees, elbows and hips; that's why I needed the wheelchair, but I'm getting stronger now and I'm doing well. I'm already down to just the one crutch.'

'Why did it come back?' I asked.

'I was trying to fight how I felt by pretending I was fine and by doing so I let the illness win. I stopped taking my medication, simply because I didn't see why everyone else should go about their day without having to keep stopping to take six different types of medicine. I'm meant to have a strict diet and I can't drink alcohol and basically, I have to live like a hermit. Everything is a trigger for an attack. I get worse if I'm too hot or too cold, if I'm nervous or excited, if I smell a strong perfume or if I exercise. Even having sex sets it off.'

I sat back in the chair realising just how much risk he'd put himself in while I'd been around. We'd eaten anything and everything, we'd drunk (me much more than him), we'd had sex, we'd climbed a bloody mountain together, and all the time it was harming him.

I leaned forward, his eyes meeting mine again. A shiver ran through me.

'Why did you try so hard to hide it? Why didn't you just tell me?' I asked.

'Because once you're ill, like properly ill, that's all people see. After the first time, all people did was ask me how I was feeling and about the treatments and tests I'd had done, like the illness had taken over me and that's all I was now. I wasn't a boxer, I wasn't engaged, I wasn't anything but my illness and it infuriated me.'

I took a breath and kept myself composed. The next question was going to hurt.

'Why did you send me away?' I felt myself on the verge of breaking. I gritted my teeth and waited for his reply.

'Because—' he rubbed his face with his hands and sighed '—because who wants this?' He held out his arms, wincing, and gestured to the room around us. 'This is why Jenny left me, because I went from being the person I want to be to the person I am.'

I looked down at the floor then back to him, gathering my thoughts and trying to quell the anger.

'Have I got this right? You were scared I'd leave you because this wasn't what I wanted, so you sent me away, for my own good?' I asked with a furrowed brow.

'I didn't think I could cope with having another person I loved leave me, so I beat you to it. Why else would I have told you to go?'

I stood up angrily, the chair legs clattering against the ground. 'Because you didn't love me like I loved you! Because you didn't want to see me! You were bored of me!'

'Bored of you? No, I wasn't!' He pushed himself, shakily, to standing. I watched him struggle, sighed dramatically and then handed him his crutch. 'When this gets bad, and believe me, it gets bad, I move like a pensioner. I need help doing the simplest of tasks, my skin gets covered in red wheals and all I do is lie in bed all day wondering when this will all be over and I'll have another reprieve.'

'You didn't give me a choice!' I spat.

He scrunched his face in frustration, his eyes moistening as his voice rose to a shout. 'This is for life, Effie! I am stuck with this until the day I die and if you'd have stayed then you'd have been stuck too.'

'I wanted to be stuck with you.'

He ignored my words and carried on. 'This thing it works

in cycles. I can be fine, stable and eating and drinking and doing what I want for months, years even, and then everything will turn. I'm stuck like this forever, but that doesn't mean you have to be too.'

He wiped at his eyes, getting rid of the tears before they could fall, like they angered him.

I stepped back. 'You told me that you didn't love me.'

'I lied. I loved you; I still do.'

'What about everything your dad said?'

'I begged him to say it. I convinced him that it was for the best,' he replied, reaching out for my hand. I moved it away. 'After what happened with Jenny, he didn't need much convincing. I loved Jenny more than anything and she broke me when she left.' His eyes pleaded with me to listen, to understand why he'd done what he had. 'I love you so much – more than I ever loved her. I don't know what it is about you, but I think I knew I'd fall in love with you from the moment I saw you in that diner. If you'd have left me, then it would have been so much worse.'

'But you lost me anyway!'

'Knowing that you still loved me was better than sticking it out and seeing you grow to resent me.'

'Resent you? It's like you don't know me at all. How could you do that? How could you do that to me when you knew I had no one else.' I felt the tears on my cheeks before I even knew that I was crying.

'I was only thinking of you.'

I turned to him and almost screamed the words he'd once said to me. 'No, you were thinking of *you*! How dare you think you could make a decision like that on my behalf! It wasn't your choice, it was mine and I would have chosen to stay.'

I sat down and sobbed into my hands as Theo stood

and watched me, not knowing if it was all right for him to touch me.

'You don't understand what you did, Theo.' I bawled into my hands, my palms becoming slick with tears and saliva. 'I had absolutely no one. I thought that I'd done something wrong or that I was unlovable and it was all because you thought you knew better than me.' I let my hands fall after I wiped the tears from my cheeks. 'Jesus Christ, Theo, I even thought about killing myself.'

He recoiled slightly and his own tears fell.

'I'm so sorry, Eff. I almost called you so many times,' he said, his hand reaching out to mine. This time I let it sit there, his thumb moving over my skin. After we had both calmed, he sat down defeatedly. 'I had the phone in my hand on Christmas Day when you rang. I almost picked up but I didn't know what I could say. Then, I got your voicemail and it sounded like everything was going so well for you. You finished the list, you moved out, you . . . you met someone new.'

I wiped my face again and turned to him.

'What's he like?' He tried to smile. It was the fakest smile I'd ever seen. 'In fact, don't tell me. I don't want to know.' He shook the thought from his head.

'His name is Caleb. He looks nothing like you. He's vegetarian, he collects enamel pins and he works for the homeless charity that I volunteer for.' Theo looked up into my eyes and nodded, his chin puckering. 'And I don't love him. Not in that way anyway. We're just friends.'

'Oh.' He didn't even try to hide his relief. 'I'm so sorry, Effie. I truly thought that it was for the best.'

'You broke my heart when you sent that letter. You undid all the good you'd done since I'd met you.'

He shook his head and wiped his cheeks. 'Maybe I did ruin all the good I'd done, but I didn't ruin what *you'd* done.' He held out his hands and smiled. 'Look at you. You're happy, you're strong, you're confident. You're exactly where you wanted to be and I had nothing to do with that. That was all you.'

I shook my head and looked away from him; looking at him for too long made my heart hurt too much. 'No, I'm not exactly where I wanted to be, Theo. I wanted to be with you.'

'And what about now?' he asked, his shoulders sagging. 'Do you still want to be with me now that I can't walk without help or go more than three hours without swallowing some kind of drug?'

I thought about telling him that I didn't and what that would mean for me. I'd get back in the car and drive Otis home to the empty flat. I'd probably order myself a pizza, drink a bottle of wine and put on some soppy film that would have me bawling into the stuffed crust within ten minutes. I could leave and never turn back. But I knew that if I did do that, I would forever be glancing over my shoulder, looking for him and feeling his absence in everything I did, every memory I made, every moment I lived. He reached out his hand, his wan fingers brandishing a tissue. I took it, my fingers brushing his, and wiped my cheeks dry. I looked into his eyes, filled with pain, both physical and otherwise, and held his gaze as I knelt down between his knees.

I lifted a hand to his cheek and it felt like drinking a glass of chilled water when dying of thirst. He closed his eyes and leaned in to my skin, his hand pressing my palm closer to his cheek. That would have been the perfect time for me to say something romantic, to tell him that I loved him and that I didn't want to spend the rest of my life missing him, but what I said instead was, 'Theodore Alwyn Morgan, you're a fucking idiot.'

His face drew into a smile, which caused a tear to fall down onto my thumb; he wiped it away with his hand and looked into my eyes. I leaned forward and kissed him and it felt like coming home.

I had thought that I'd be spending New Year's pressed into the armchair in my parents' house, watching the fireworks on BBC and toasting in the next 365 days with a glass of Prosecco, or at Caleb's, awkwardly mingling with his family and friends and watching middle-aged couples getting smashed. Instead the New Year passed me by without the usual pageantry as I lay in bed with Theo in my arms and Otis at my feet, looking out through the window and watching the moon travel across the sky; the faint sound of fireworks echoing in the distance.

It was taking me a long time to fall asleep, my head was too full of noise to find a quiet moment. The anger at all those wasted days, those months spent in misery, all for nothing.

'Happy New Year, Effie,' he said, the tip of his nose against mine.

I looked into his eyes, blurred and distorted by our proximity. But no matter how blurred they became, I would always know that they were his. They were the only eyes I wanted to look into, to be this close to.

'Happy New Year,' I replied.

When I woke the next morning, I felt the weight of Theo against me and I breathed the smell of his hair. For a second I thought I was dreaming or dead and on my way to some sort of heaven.

I lay there for a while, watching him sleep and fretting about the way his breaths rasped in his throat. It must have taken a lot for him to send me away when he loved me like he did, but I guess he loved me enough to want a happy life for me, a life without the troubles he would face. But what he didn't know was that the happy life he wanted for me wasn't possible without him. I had been close and I *was* happy, but there would have forever been something missing.

I saw Tessa pass the window with a steaming mug in her hand on her way down to the lake and I slid out of bed. I pulled one of Theo's jumpers over my sleep-crinkled clothes, slipped on my boots and left the room as quietly as I could, Otis trotting along at my side.

I walked to the kitchen and made my way to the back door.

'Good morning.' I jumped and turned to see Rhys sitting at the table with a coffee in his hands, his lack of sleep clearly etched around his eyes.

'You scared me.' I held my hand to my chest and took a few steps towards the table.

He sighed heavily and looked down into his half-empty mug. 'Do you want some?' He pointed to the cafetière that steamed beside him. I nodded and moved to get a mug from the kitchen.

'I'll get it.' He stopped me and went himself. When he returned, he poured in some coffee and handed it to me, standing beside me with unsaid words making him dither. 'I'm sorry for what I did to you, Effie. It was on Theo's orders. I didn't want to do any of it.'

I was about to say that it was okay, but I wasn't quite there yet.

'Theo explained everything to me. I understand why you

thought it was best that I wasn't in the picture,' I replied. 'I mean, it was a stupid idea and none of you knew me well enough to make that decision on my behalf, but I understand.'

'It won't happen again.'

'It better not.' I smiled and stepped forward. I pulled him close and gave him a quick squeeze. 'I didn't enjoy trying to hate you.'

The air was cold, crisp, silent, as Otis and I made our way out to Tessa. It was the first day of a brand-new year, one that I would begin in a completely different state of mind than the last. It felt, in all senses, like a new start.

I sat down beside her in the dewy grass, took a sip of my coffee and placed it down. I crossed my legs, letting my hands rest on my knees and my eyes fall closed. Otis sat between us, his eyes glued to a moorhen that glided across the water.

It was a while before she spoke and when she did it was quiet. 'Are you going to stay with him?' she asked bluntly.

'Yes,' I replied without opening my eyes.

Tessa breathed deeply. 'It's hard, you know, seeing him like this and being able to do absolutely nothing about it.'

'I know. But I'm still staying.'

I opened my eyes and turned to her. She was looking straight at me. She took the steaming cup of herbal tea from the grass and raised it into the air, much like she had when I'd first met her and she'd refused to toast to my name. She looked at me with tired yet glad eyes and said with a smile, 'Welcome to the family, Effie.'

# Chapter Twenty-Nine

**Eight Months Later**

I stood in front of the mirror with my palms sweating into the skirt of my dress. I couldn't ever remember being so nervous. I stared at my reflection and quietly congratulated myself on drawing matching eyeliner flicks. There would be no lopsided eyes today.

I wore a dark green dress, cinched in at the waist, the skirt falling down to my knee. My hair was braided across my forehead and down into a long plait that fell over my shoulder. Tiny purple flowers had been pushed into it by the flower girl, Toby's niece, who now sat in the corner tearing the remaining flowers in her basket to pieces and laughing maniacally.

My bouquet of peonies and thistles sat on the table next to me, an undrunk flute of champagne beside it.

I closed my eyes and breathed deeply. Weddings were always stressful; everyone knew that. But I had never attended a wedding before and so I hadn't known just *how* stressful, until right now.

I heard deep breathing behind me and wondered if a woman in labour had wandered in. I looked in the mirror and saw that it was only Arthur. He appeared beside me with a sweating brow and hands that fumbled with his tie.

'Why do *you* look so nervous? *I'm* the one getting married,' he said.

'I've never walked someone down the aisle before,' I replied. I turned around and took the tie from him, knotting it with the little skill that remained from my school days. 'You know me, it's highly likely that I'll trip and pull you down with me.'

'You'd better not – this suit cost more than all the clothes I own put together.'

Arthur didn't have much in the way of family. He was an only child whose mother disapproved of his sexuality and refused to come and see her son marry the man he loved. His dad hadn't had a problem with his son being gay, but he'd died four years ago. The only other person was his Aunt Muriel, but she was ninety-seven and lived in Geneva, so that left just me.

Arthur and Toby had returned after five and a half months of their trip. They'd spent two days in Amsterdam and that's when Toby suggested that they get married. He hadn't thought that Arthur would agree, but he did and they'd flown back earlier than expected to start planning. They'd shown up unannounced and the first thing Arthur had said to me was, 'Is that a dog on my sofa?'

I'd thought that he'd want me to move back to Mum and Dad's, but they'd decided to live at Toby's house. It was bigger and nicer and they both knew I wanted to stay. The flat might not have been huge or impressive, but I loved it and so did Otis.

Theo had stayed in Wales until the end of March and by then he was able to walk properly again and his symptoms were under control. His apartment in the city was let out to a young entrepreneur and I spent a few days taking his things up to Wales, bit by bit. I split my time between home and Wales, helping as much as I could when I was there and missing them all terribly when I wasn't – even Tessa, who had finally begun to stop eyeing me with suspicion whenever she saw me.

Theo had moved in with me after that. At first, we thought that the stairs would be a problem for him, but once he was better, he had little trouble.

Rhys had offered to buy Arthur's flat for us as a joint birthday gift. Of course, I'd done the polite thing and told him that we couldn't possibly accept, all the while silently praying that he wouldn't rescind his offer – which he thankfully didn't. Rhys was forever grateful to me for sticking around, as if he thought that being with Theo was holding me back in some way. But there are many ways that a person can be held back, I of all people know that, and being with Theo was most definitely not one of them.

'We'd better get going,' I said, glancing at the time and watching as the colour drained from Arthur's face. I took his arm and walked him to the door, waiting behind it as the people inside quietened down and the music began playing.

'I'm really glad you stalked me and stuck around,' he blurted, his face pulled into a look of pure panic.

'Me too.' I smiled as the doors opened and we began our walk.

The wedding was being held in a small but beautiful room in a gothic hotel just outside the city. It had cost a small fortune but, as I had later discovered, Toby was minted.

At the end of the aisle stood Toby, dressed head to toe in cobalt blue with a lime green tie. I smiled to myself; he was far from the uptight accountant that he'd been a year ago. As we reached him, I kissed them both and stepped aside, giving his hand to Toby and standing behind Arthur with my bouquet held in front of me.

The celebrant began her reading and my eyes started to mist over. Arthur was my family and now, so was Toby. A year ago, I had thought myself completely alone, a lonesome failure, floundering in an ocean that was too big and too frightening. But I wasn't floundering anymore; I'd finally learned to swim.

I looked into the crowd and saw Theo.

He smiled and my stomach twisted in response; the magic of his smile had returned.

He was almost back to the Theo I had known when I'd first met him: strong, solid, charming. But this time there was something different. We were no longer separated by the secrets that he kept or the issues that I had. I knew him now, all of him, and he knew all of me.

We both knew that any period of good would be followed by a spiral of bad, but the next time he fell I would be there to catch him, and hopefully I'd do a lot less damage to my wrist.

Caleb sat between Theo and Amy, the lapel of his suit jacket covered in enamel pins, including the one I'd got him. He leaned over and whispered something in Amy's ear; she smiled and playfully pushed him away.

Theo and Caleb had become pretty good friends. Theo even came out with us one night to help with the handouts. I'd spent the whole time watching him and worrying that the cold was getting to him, but it had all been fine in the end. He was learning his new limitations and although it was hard for him to stop eating what he liked and doing whatever he wanted, it was better than the alternative.

Ali's funeral had been in early January and it had been a solemn affair.

There had been no coffin, only a cardboard box, and no flowers except for the three yellow roses I'd placed on the lid before the service, along with the Christmas gift that she never got to unwrap.

There had been eight mourners in total: Caleb, Ned, Cassie, Liz, Janet, me and the volunteer who'd found her, who cried soundlessly into a cotton handkerchief throughout. The eighth mourner, Otis, had been snuck in under the guise of a medical assistance dog. Caleb had bought him a reflective jacket online because he thought that, of all of us, Otis was the one who should have been there to say goodbye the most. He *had* been her heart after all.

He'd sat quietly beside me, looking up at me when the curtains closed around the plain little box. He'd looked terribly confused. If I was him, I think I'd have been too.

In two months, it would be a year since I met Theo in that diner. I guess the metal sign on the wall with the grinning woman on it had been right after all; that had been the day that had changed my life.

I'm not going to lie to you, I haven't changed entirely.

I still lose my temper over things, like when Otis ate his way through a second edition *Jane Eyre* in the store room, I still drink occasionally and I still get jealous of other people from time to time. But life was good and I could honestly say that I was happy.

The wedding reception was held in a small function room with a bar, a dance floor and a DJ who'd gone over to and

382

requested 'Heroes' by David Bowie, just to take Theo's mind away from the fact that he couldn't drink. We'd danced to the euphoric music, his arms around my waist, his smile back in place.

'Do you want to do this?' he asked as we rocked from side to side under the colourful disco lights that shone from the DJ booth. 'Get married, I mean, not this highly sophisticated dance we're doing.'

I laughed and looked around. Toby and Arthur sat at a table eating cake, their ankles touching beneath the table, Arthur's holiday tattoo of Toby's glasses – the Czech flag reflected in the lenses – poking out over his sock.

'Why? Did Chad Michael Murray call back?' I asked, recalling my and Kate's teenage bucket list. He smiled. God, how I'd missed that smile when he'd been away. 'I don't mind either way. As long as I'm with you, then I don't care what letters go before my first name.'

Theo made a fake throwing-up gesture at my words and then kissed my forehead. 'That's a shame, Effie Morgan has a nice ring to it.'

I thought about it for a moment. No longer would I be MEH.

I shook my head. 'What about Theo Heaton? You could take my name.'

'What, and give up the name of the man who invented the Morgan spring? Never! My father would have a mental breakdown.' He moved his hand from my waist and held my face; my skin tingled where he touched. 'I suppose we can cross that bridge if we come to it.' He leaned in and kissed me as the music built to the final crescendo. The music swelled in my ears and the love swelled in my chest. If there was any such thing as perfection, then this moment was it.

The sound of a throat being forcefully cleared made us turn away from each other to find Toby and Arthur standing beside us.

'Wanna dance?' Arthur asked, a grin on his face. I'd never seen him so happy. 'Not because I like you or anything, just because you're the best I've got.'

'How could I refuse a heartfelt offer like that?' I took his hand and twirled him around, which is difficult, might I add, when your dancing partner is more than a foot taller than you.

The joyful introductory drumbeat of 'Never Gonna Give You Up' played out from the speakers and Arthur and I danced like no one was watching, while Theo, Toby and Amy did the same in a trio of people who had less than an ounce of rhythm between them, but a ton of enthusiasm.

Theo and I arrived home late and stone-cold sober.

I know, unbelievable, isn't it? Me, sober. Ha!

We'd picked up Otis from my parents and he'd wasted no time in running into the flat and diving onto the sofa, glad to be home.

Mum and Dad had been more than eager to have Otis for an entire day. Dad loved him, his face lighting up whenever he saw the dog's ever-present smile.

My mum was quietly ecstatic that I no longer drank as much and I'd seen her checking my eyes for fuzziness when we'd arrived to pick Otis up. Things between us had been good for a while now, probably for the longest time since I was around twelve.

Theo still found it hard not to drink or do the things that he felt he should be able to, and a month ago I had begun to see him growing despondent. He'd never before had to stop and think about what he could or couldn't do. Adjusting to his new limitations was always going to suck, but I was doing my best to try and ease him through it.

I'd known that he was slipping for a while, so I'd decided that it was time to make another list, but this time for Theo.

His missions were a lot less ambitious than mine, but to him each mission checked off was a step closer to normality. After three weeks we'd already completed four missions:

1. *Go for a thirty-minute walk* . . . CHECK

2. *Eat a tomato* . . . CHECK

3. *Throw out the crutch* . . . CHECK

4. *Have a cheeseburger* . . . CHECK

I'd fished the crutch back out of the skip that he'd ceremoniously tossed it into. I knew he hated it, but I also knew he'd need it again at some point. Each mission that we completed had come with some side effects, but we'd been ready for them, and now that he was officially diagnosed, he was on the right drugs and getting better.

In five weeks, it would be his thirty-first birthday and, on that day, he'd be having a drink, a proper one. He hadn't decided what yet, but he was looking forward to it immensely.

As I pushed open the door and walked into the shop, I felt something hit against my shoe. It skittered across the floor and stopped against the edge of the sofa. I turned the lights on and found Theo bending over to pick it up.

Theo read the stamped envelope and handed it to me with a grin.

'I think this is for you,' he said.

I took the envelope and recognised the name as the agency I'd sent the first part of my book off to before Christmas.

'Aren't you going to open it?' he asked, stepping closer.

I looked up at him and saw the anticipation in his eyes.

A year ago, I would have torn the envelope without a second thought. But holding it in my hand, I realised that even if the letter was another rejection, I wouldn't be crushed by it.

'I will,' I said, 'but not just yet.' I leaned in and kissed him once; I kissed him twice. I made up for every kiss that we'd missed while we were both too busy underestimating ourselves and I would keep making up for those missed kisses until my lips couldn't kiss anymore.

The bevy of weary people freshly released from the purgatory of the workday moved against me, but for once, I didn't mind swimming against the current. I watched as a man played Candy Crush Saga on his phone while his son reeled off an unheard story at his side and a woman knelt down and frantically fumbled in her bag for something she couldn't find. I turned the corner and made my way to the post office, the brown envelope containing my full manuscript clasped under my arm.

I'd always wanted to be a writer. I wanted to see someone reading my book on a train and feel pride swell in my chest as they read my words. I wanted one of those little recommendation cards that sit on the shelves in Waterstones. I'd wanted it so much and for so long and now someone wanted to read more; this was my chance. I handed the envelope to the cashier who slapped on a stamp and sent it on its way.

There was nothing more I could do now. It was out of my hands.

I had always been so worried about how I compared to everybody else, about how inadequate I was. But if this last year had taught me anything it was that I had a lot more than I gave myself credit for. I'd lived my life to other people's standards for too long. I only cared about my own standards these days.

As I arrived back at the shop, I stopped and looked in through the window, just out of sight of the people inside. Arthur hung from the ladder by one arm while Amy smiled and handed him a book. He was telling a dramatic story to Toby and Theo who sat on the sofa, listening intently with Otis wedged between their knees.

I'd come to realise that I didn't need a London apartment with a balcony; I had the little flat that I loved and had painted in shades of green. I didn't need the fiancé who posed with me in photographs and spent hour upon hour in the gym to get a torso like Khal Drogo; I had Theo and I didn't want anyone else.

I'd failed a great deal in life, but my biggest failure had been refusing to be happy.

I smiled at the reflection of myself in the window.

Maybe I had made a hash of a few years of my life, but now that was over and the only thing I was failing at these days, was failing.

# Acknowledgements

I have dreamt about writing one of these since I first picked up a pen and decided I wanted to write. In the ten years since I wrote those first few words of a novel that I pray will never see the light of day, I have had support from a few very special people.

Mom, thanks for letting me freeload on you for longer than either of us ever planned on, so that I could spend my time tapping away at my computer to make this dream a reality. You've been my biggest supporter and I hope that I'm doing you proud.

Dad, thank you for giving me the literary bug in the first place and for your verbal pearls of wisdom, some of which have made it into this book.

Matt Goode, thank you for being my real-life Theo and helping me cross a few things off my own list.

I also want to thank Steve Bartlett, for giving me the most important pep talk of my life and stopping me from putting down the pen for good when the rejections had knocked me down. And to Heddwen Roberts for coming to the rescue when I needed an English to Welsh translation. I'd also like to thank my real life Ali, Michael Michalak, who allowed me to use his experiences to inspire Ali's backstory.

Thank you to Sam Sargent, for spending endless hours reading through the first ever drafts of this and helping me straighten out the kinks when I had no idea where Effie's story would take her.

And a big thank you to Fraser Hewett, for helping me out of the same situation that Theo finds himself in. I wouldn't have been physically capable of writing this book without your help.

But I think the biggest thank yous have to be reserved for the people who saw something in Effie, when no one else did. Elena Langtry and everyone at CMM Agency, thank you for setting my dream in motion and supporting me every step of the confusing way. Helen Huthwaite and everyone at Avon, thank you for taking Effie that step further and making what a lot of people thought was a pipe dream a reality.

Some people go looking for love.
Others crash right into it.

Don't miss this gorgeous tale about taking risks
and living life to the full – perfect for fans of
Beth O'Leary and Josie Silver.

Out now!